A Twelfth Dan Master of Dimac and Magus to the Illuminated Order of the Celestial Sprout, Robert Rankin has also had a total of thirty-nine jobs, including illustrator, off-licence manager, market-stall trader, rock singer and garden gnome salesman. He is the author of five other novels published by Corgi Books: *The Antipope, The Brentford Triangle, East of Ealing, Armageddon: The Musical* and *They Came and Ate Us, Armageddon II: The B Movie. The Sprouts of Wrath* will be available soon in paperback and his new novel, *The Book of Ultimate Truths*, will be published by Doubleday in 1993. Robert Rankin lives in Brighton with his wife and family.

D0357773

Also by Robert Rankin

THE ANTIPOPE
THE BRENTFORD TRIANGLE
EAST OF EALING
ARMAGEDDON: THE MUSICAL
THEY CAME AND ATE US,
ARMAGEDDON II: THE B MOVIE

and published by Corgi Books

THE SUBURBAN BOOK OF THE DEAD

ARMAGEDDON III: THE REMAKE

Robert Rankin

CORGI BOOKS

THE SUBURBAN BOOK OF THE DEAD
ARMAGEDDON III: THE REMAKE
A CORGI BOOK 0 552 13923 8

Originally published in Great Britain by
Bloomsbury Publishing Ltd

PRINTING HISTORY
Bloomsbury edition published 1992
Corgi edition published 1993

Set in 10/11½pt Palatino by Kestrel Data, Exeter

Corgi Books are published by Transworld Publishers Ltd,
61–63 Uxbridge Road, London W5 5SA,
in Australia by Transworld Publishers (Australia) Pty Ltd,
15–25 Helles Avenue, Moorebank, NSW 2170,
and in New Zealand by Transworld Publishers (NZ) Ltd,
3 William Pickering Drive, Albany, Auckland.

Made and printed in Great Britain by
Cox & Wyman Ltd, Reading, Berks.

For
George Geoffrey Arthur Rankin

THE SUBURBAN BOOK OF THE DEAD

ARMAGEDDON III:
THE REMAKE

1

Along the crest of the hill a line of trees broke wind. And beneath them in the valley, paradise was looking just so. Well-tended gardens cloistered quaint dwellings of a rustic nature. Pine-scented smoke drifted gently from chimneys. Children played amongst the flowering scullion and scandaroons nestled in the dovecots. It was the 27 July 2061. It was the Garden of Eden. And it was a bad day for Rex Mundi.

Rex had dodged the bread rolls. Side-stepped the crockery and ducked beneath the salad bowl. But it was the wok that really did for him.

Had it been one of those aluminium wedding-present jobs you store dead insects in, he might have survived.

9

But this lad was in a class of its own. A real hand-beaten bronzer with a formidable fighting weight. It was no contest. Rex went down for the count.

He passed backwards through the open kitchen doorway and out into the pleasant summery sunlight. And here he came to rest in the sprout bed. Little transparent birds twittered in a circle around his head. The incidental music went WAB-WAAAAAH.

The furry face of a small terrier appeared through a hole in the hedge, an ear cocked to the sounds of breaking china and tumbling whatnots which issued from the family home. When at last these had ceased, the owner of the face, Fido, crept from his refuge and peered down at his fallen master.

'Hardly a fitting entrance for the hero,' was his considered opinion. Rex had no comment to make at this time.

Fido viewed him along the horizontal plane. Even in this undignified repose Rex was a handsome fellow. Tall, well muscled and still bearing the same uncanny resemblance to the young Harrison Ford he had since book one. Pity about the wok-hurling wife, though.

'It's my duty to care for this man in his time of need,' said Fido. 'And having no bucket of water to paw, I regret I must add insult to injury.' He lifted his rear offside leg and took careful aim.

'Don't even think about it,' Rex whispered through gritted teeth. 'If you want to help, then whimper a bit and look concerned.'

'Gotcha, man. Play for sympathy, eh? Shrewd thinking oooooooh—' The contents of the slop pail, issuing even as it did from the upstairs window, caught them both with unerring accuracy.

Fido took to his heels. Rex clambered to his feet.

'Now just you see here,' he began.

The spade missed him by inches.

'Dig it deep and dig it now,' were his wife's final

demands. The window slammed shut and Rex was left very much alone.

He gazed around at his wonderful garden. The toil of his hands and the sweat of his brow had brought all this into being. He had planted every plum and pulse, pepper and pimento, pomegranate and passion fruit. He had pampered each pear and peach and pomelo, particularly the pineapples, papayas, parsnips and potatoes. He'd even been patient with the peas. It was a theme garden. Although for the life of him he couldn't remember what the theme actually was. Nor why he'd planted the sprouts.

And the house itself. He'd designed that from the ground up. High gabled, daub and wattle. A veritable tour de force in Arts and Crafts revivalism. All for her. Christeen, his wife. Christeen, twin sister of Jesus.

But was it enough? Not a bit of it.

Was she contented? Not one smidgen.

Grateful? As if.

Beautiful garden, lovely setting, fabulous house. And what did she want? An indoor toilet! One trivial oversight on his part, and all this fuss. Perhaps if he'd stayed around to supervise the actual construction of the house, rather than carousing with his chums at the local grog shop, he might have noticed the omission. Perhaps if he had not employed the services of Bloodaxe and Death-blade, Builders to the Aristocracy. Perhaps, perhaps. But there it was.

Rex considered the ramshackled outside dunny he had thrown together. It niffed a bit, but was surely adequate to their daily needs. There was just no pleasing some people. Women were strange and exotic creatures and no man, even one as obviously thoughtful and sensitive as Rex, could be expected to understand them fully. The lady wanted an indoor flush toilet plumbed to an outside septic tank system and that was that. She would brook no compromise and there would be no peace in the marital home until the pit was dug and the tank was in. That was the specific order of the day, as it had been for more days than Rex cared to remember. There was nothing for it. The deed would have to be done.

Rex fingered his big red ear, plucked up the spade and made a very bad face indeed.

Now, as with most things, there is a fine art to the successful laying in of a septic tank. And its correct location plays a very large part in the thing. It must be placed just so. Too near to the house and it can become a serious hazard to the nostrils in the hot weather. Too far and the pipes may freeze in the cold. The composition of the soil is of supreme importance, as is that the site chosen is at a lower level than the toilet. Then of course there are the planetary aspects to be taken into consideration, the local ley system and a careful check to make sure you're not digging up a fairy's house. You can never be too careful. The correct location is *everything*.

'That will do nicely,' said Rex, spying out the nearest area of untilled land. 'Ideal.' He stalked over, dragging his spade behind him, and peered down at old mother earth. Old mother earth stared back in a hard, uncompromising sort of fashion. She said, 'Just you try it.'

'I'm not really a spade man,' Rex told the sod. 'More a trowel and dibber fellow me. I generally leave the actual digging side of things to that nice little man with the wellington boots and wheelbarrow who comes in twice a week. In fact, now that I come to think about it, I generally leave all the trowel and dibbering to him also. In fact,' Rex stroked his manly chin, 'I hardly ever come out in this garden at all. I hate gardening.

'You see,' he continued, 'I'm more your man of action. My forte is for heroic deeds. The saving of civilizations. Putting my life on the line in the cause of truth, justice and some way or another. I'm the stuff of legend. I'm *not* a digger of poo pits.' Rex took the offensive spade in both hands and prepared to fling it. The bedroom window shot up and the slop pail whistled past his unreddened ear. The hero lowered his head and began to dig.

And he dug. He dug and he dug. He got all sweaty in a macho lager commercial sort of a way. But he didn't make a lot of progress. Digging holes is a funny old kind of a business. You either have the way of it or you don't. A friend of mine who once ran the London marathon had the way of it; he had served an apprenticeship as a grave digger and he could dig a hole two feet wide, six feet long and six feet deep with a precision nothing less than awesome to behold. Mind you, he did employ the services of a mechanical digger, something which Rex didn't have immediately to hand. And the fellow I'm talking about got a stitch and never actually completed the London marathon. I expect there's a moral in there if you care to look for it.

Rex didn't care to look. He was thinking about lunch. He was thinking that 'well begun is best begun and best begun is nearly finished', and he was thinking that now would probably be as good a time as any to down tools and repair to the drinking house. He'd just level out the bottom and then slip away. No need to mention it to Christeen.

Clunk! went Rex's spade as it made contact with a very hard something. Rex up-ended his implement and eyed the blunted blade. 'There,' he said, 'that settles the matter.' It would be folly to continue work with a blunt tool. You couldn't expect a craftsman such as himself to make a decent job of the thing with a blunt tool. Unthinkable.

Rex put the useless article aside and stooped to root out the blessed blunter by hand. He probed about with his fingers and found something smooth and cool. 'Hmm.' Rex dug his fingers about it and strained to pull it up. It remained firm and Rex checked his spine for severe injury. His digging days were over, he told himself. Rex kicked petulantly at the object. Now he hopped about on the other foot wondering just why he had.

Rex picked up the spade, raised it above his head and prepared to administer the killing blow.

And then he stopped. He was gazing down at something rather unusual. The object was a head. A marble head. There was no mistake about it. He could make out the hairline and a bit of a noble brow. A marble head. How about that then?

Rex stooped and he scooped. He dug and he delved. He trenched and he tunnelled. He burrowed and bored. He scraped and he scrabbled and scratched. And when he was done he sat down on his bum and marvelled greatly, saying such things as 'blow me down' and 'well, I never did'.

For there at his feet lay a full-sized marble statue, which even in its mucky state was clearly a thing of no small wonder.

It was the statue of a young man, clad in a wide-shouldered suit, legs akimbo. He was frozen in mid strum upon a carven guitar. He had a serious quiff and killer sideburns.

'Elvis,' said Rex Mundi. 'Elvis, it's you.'

'It certainly looks like him,' said Fido, who had been observing the feverish activity. 'Curly lip and everything. Nice big hole, by the way.'

'Give me a hand then, we'll lift it out.'

The dog gave Rex what is called 'the old fashioned look'.

'Well, fetch a rope or something. I'll rig up a block and tackle.'

'To hear is to obey, oh master.'

Rex spat on to his palms and rubbed them together. 'Soon have you out,' he said.

* * *

It was somewhat late in the afternoon when the statue of Elvis came to stand upright. And the garden that it now stared down upon was no longer the pretty and picturesque thing it had earlier been. This was now a garden littered with broken timbers, snapped ropes and fractured pulleys. A garden tainted by words of profanity.

The owner of the garden sat exhausted, his feet dangling in the hole of his own making. 'There,' said he, when finally he could find breath. 'A piece of cake.'

Fido cocked his head on one side and gazed up at the statue.

'It's a killer,' he said. 'The lad himself.'

'Certainly is,' Rex gasped.

'Cosmic, man. Dead cosmic.'

'And to find it right here in my own back yard.'

'Like I said, cosmic.'

'I wonder how it came to be here.' Rex climbed to his feet and perused his find.

'Probably went under in the Nuclear Holocaust Event. Hey, man, do you know what this means?'

'What?'

'It means that you probably built your house on the very spot where Graceland once stood.'

'No kidding?' Rex was well impressed. 'Some co-incidence, eh?'

'Hmm.' Fido didn't have much truck with coincidence. 'Perhaps.'

'It's a beautiful thing, though. Nice centrepiece for the garden.'

'Shame you took a piece off his nose with your spade.'

'They never put noses on,' said Rex knowledgeably. 'The Greeks and the Romans and whatnot always made the statues without noses. It was a tradition or an old charter or something.'

'Doesn't look Greek to me, it's of the Italian school, though.'

'Go fetch a stick or something.'

'Mind if I take a leak first? All this excitement . . .'

'Not in my hole you don't.'

'OK man.' Fido lifted his leg and sprayed the statue.

'Get out of here, Fido.'

'Sorry, man.'

'No, wait, look. You've uncovered some letters. Do it again.' Fido did it again. 'What does it say?' Rex asked.

'It's a name and a date. Michelangelo Buonarroti. 1504.'

'1504?'

'That's what it says. Michelangelo. Man, that guy was famous. He was the number one. Michelangelo.'

'The name rings a bell.' Rex scratched at his head. 'Yes, of course. He was a Teenage Mutant Ninja Turtle, wasn't he?'

Fido looked up at his master. Rex looked down at his dog.

'Sorry,' said Rex. 'It just slipped out.'

'Jump in the hole, man.'

'Do what?'

'Jump in the hole. Quickly.'

'I will not.'

'Then, sorry man.' Fido leapt up at Rex, striking him in the chest and knocking him from his feet. One man and his dog vanished into the hole.

And not a moment too soon.

There was a sudden roaring of engine and squealing of brakes, and something large and metallic smashed through the hedge with explosive force. It ploughed up the plantain, demolished the dovecot, scattered the scanderoons and came to the traditional shuddering halt on the very spot where Rex had just been standing.

'What the—' Rex struggled in the pit.

'Keep it down, man. Let go of my ear.'

'I'll do for you, Fido.'

'I saved your life, man. My ear, let go.' Rex released the pooch's mangy tab.

'How did you know it was coming? I didn't hear anything.'

'I'm the seventh pup of a seventh pup. Keep your voice down, I smell big trouble.'

Rex peeped over the rim of the pit. Above him loomed a big shiny chromium bumper and a licence plate. The licence plate read DEE 1.

'It's Simon Dee,' Rex whispered. 'Returned at last to do another series. I always knew he would.'

'I don't think so, man.'

Rex heard an electric window swish down, then the oiled click as the driver's door opened. He glimpsed a pair of polished brogues, a flash of patterned sock and a tweedy turn-up or two.

'Anyone at home?' Rex didn't recognize the accent. 'Helloooee.'

I don't like this, Rex thought. As he watched, the passenger door opened and similarly attired lower extremities lowered.

'Gorn off, do you think?' said a second voice.

'Puffed if I know. You set the co-ordinates correctly, didn't you?'

'Of course I did.'

'Then he's bound to be here.'

Rex edged along his hole. He could see the driver's back. A Barbour jacket and a tweed cap. Rex gasped. 'Devianti!' This man wore the costume of the cannibal bands which had once prowled the ruined streets of the post-NHE world. But they had gone forever, surely? Rambo Bloodaxe and Deathblade Eric were the last of their line, and they were now reformed characters, if somewhat doubtful builders.

Rex sought a weapon. His spade lay beyond reach.

'Fido,' whispered Rex. 'Fido!' Fido was doing his best to dig himself in. 'See them off, boy.'

'Get real, man.'

'You will too see them off.' Rex grabbed up the

17

cowardly cur and hefted him out of the hole.

'And what have we here?' The driver turned.

Fido did his 'wolf call'. It wasn't a sound to inspire much in the way of terror.

'See them off, Fido.'

'No, please.' The driver caught sight of Rex. 'Please sir, we wish you no harm. Call off this fearsome beast.'

'Fearsome beast, eh?' Fido managed an unconvincing snarl. Rex struggled out of his hole with as much dignity as he could muster. 'Have a care for your throat,' he advised.

'Oh I shall, I shall. My sincere apologies to you. We seem to have clipped your hedge.'

Rex gazed bitterly at the large and ragged hole. Christeen wasn't going to like that. He gave the driver a careful once-over. A weaselly-looking blighter with a pointy nose, closely-set eyes and a mean little mouth. These dishonest features were currently fixed into an expression of impeccable honesty. Rex glanced at the car. Long, green and expensive looking.

'A Volvo.' Fido woofed appreciatively. 'XL 5. Fuel injection. Top of the range.'

'You certainly know your cars, young pup.' The driver stooped to pat pooch. Fido bared his fangs. Rex came forward to take a closer look at the car. A look of alarm appeared on the driver's face. It had nothing to do with Fido's dental work.

'I shouldn't touch the bonnet, sir. A bit hot, wouldn't want you to hurt your hand.'

'Get off my land,' said Rex.

'Of course, of course. No wish to make offence. We will naturally reimburse you for any damage done.'

'Naturally.' The driver's companion appeared from behind the car. He was somewhat stouter than his colleague. Rex gauged accurately that of the two he was the more dangerous. 'We haven't introduced ourselves

18

have we? I am Ed Kelley and this is Mr Johnny Dee. And you are, sir?'

'Angry,' said Rex. 'Get off my land.'

'I see. And hello, what do we have here then?' Mr Kelley pushed past Mr Dee and approached Rex's statue. 'What is this?'

'A family heirloom.' Rex folded his arms. 'Extremely valuable. Please don't touch.'

'Valuable, you say?'

'Extremely. Where did you get this car from?'

'The car?'

'The car. There are no cars here. This is the new Eden. Where are you from?'

'Who is the statue of?' Mr Kelley enquired.

'My grandfather. About this car . . .'

'A handsome chap, your granddaddy,' said Mr Dee. 'I see the strong family resemblance.'

'Pity about the nose though, John. Considerably reduces the value does that.'

'The value?' Rex looked bewildered.

'Sadly so,' Johnny agreed. 'And it's not a particularly good example. Strictly "school of". How much did you say you wanted for it?'

'I didn't.'

'I suppose we could go as high as five. What do you think, Ed?'

'We'd be cutting our own throats. But I suppose at a push.'

'What are you talking about? Five?'

'Million.' said Mr Dee. 'You didn't think thousand, did you?' He and Ed laughed mirthfully. 'Whatever do you think we are?'

'I don't know. What are you?'

'Men of the trade. Men of the trade.'

'The antique trade,' muttered Fido. 'By their Volvos so shall ye know them.' Mr Dee gave Fido such a vicious look that the dog became quite wobbly at the knees.

19

'All right, sir.' Mr Dee was all smiles again. 'You strike a hard bargain. We will call it six.'

'Get into your car and drive away while you are still able.'

'Oh dear, oh dear,' Mr Kelley sighed deeply. 'We really have got off on the wrong foot. Please let me explain. We purchase old broken statues like this one.'

'For charity,' Mr Dee put in. 'There's little enough in it for ourselves of course.'

'Exactly. This is a happy coincidence really. We being here. This being here and you being anxious to sell.'

'I'm not.'

'And we being in the position to make you so generous an offer.'

'I don't call *seven* million all that generous as it happens.'

'*Seven?* Oh I see. Quite so, sir. Seven and a half then. Shall we spit upon palms and close the deal?'

'No,' Rex said. 'We shall not. The statue isn't for sale. And even if I was prepared to part with it, which I'm not, no amount of money could purchase it. This is the new Eden and money has no meaning here. Now I don't know where you've come from, neither do I care. But I suggest you return there with great speed, before my rabid friend and I set about you with violent intent. Do I make myself absolutely clear?'

'I can dig it, man,' woofed Fido. 'What's the fuel consumption like on this model, by the way? I understand the triple carbs have a tendency to eat.'

'Moderate to good,' said Johnny. 'I closed off one of the carbs and put in a by-feeder. You get nearly forty to the gallon on a straight run.'

'Diesel?' Fido asked.

'Fido!' Rex made throttling motions.

'Sorry, man.'

'I think I'll need a hand with this.' Ed was becoming

20

overly intimate with the statue. 'This second-rate marble is a tad weighty.'

Rex knotted his fists. 'Didn't you hear what I said?'

'Of course we did, sir.' Johnny Dee smiled sweetly. 'You said that you wanted no money for the statue. Noble gesture. We appreciate it.'

'That's not what I said at all.'

'Then if it's goods in kind you want. No problem.' Johnny considered the garden. 'Perhaps an electric shovel, or we have a solar-powered trenching tool which might be right up your street. And fertiliser, do we have fertiliser. Your paw paws look a mite jaded.'

'Jaded, eh?' Rex now had a definite twitch on. Enough was enough. 'Just stay here,' he said. 'Don't move, and keep your hands *off* that statue. I won't be a moment.' He turned away and stalked across to the house. Entering his kitchen he selected a murderous-looking meat cleaver from the rack above the Aga, tested its weight and found it adequate for the potential task in hand. He then returned to confront his two uninvited guests, who were even now worrying at his statue.

'Do you see this?' he asked. Johnny Dee nodded gravely.

'Then hear this. Leave upon the instant or henceforth all will know you by the appellation "Headless" Johnny Dee.'

Johnny had one last smile left in him. He offered it to Rex.

'Just give us a hand to load up the statue and we'll be on our way then.'

Rex raised his cleaver. The red mist was coming on and the psychotic glitter in his eyes wasn't lost upon Mr Dee, who saw it at very close quarters. 'No sale then?'

'No sale!

'My dear sir, if only I might . . .'

'Kill!' ordered Rex.

Emboldened by his master's fearsome aspect, Fido

had a sudden adrenaline rush and set about Johnny's ankles.

'All right, all right. We're leaving . . .' Dee and Kelly were all at once back in their Volvo and the Volvo was all at once making a very swift departure. It tore back into the hedge with much grinding of metalwork. The open passenger door was ripped from its hinges and slapped down on to the dirt. Rex and his dog peered through the brand new hole in the hedge. The not-too-pristine top-of-the-range model diminished and very suddenly vanished into nothingness.

There was a bit of a silence in Rex Mundi's back garden.

Fido looked up at Rex and Rex looked down at Fido.

There was a bit more silence.

Presently the scanderoons returned to perch in a sombre row upon the roof-top. There was a little bit more silence, but not quite as much as there had been on the first two occasions.

Finally there was no more silence at all.

'Well,' said Fido, in his finest Jack Benny.

'Well, what?'

'Just, well. That's all.'

'Just *well*? Nothing more?'

'Nothing more, man.'

'What? No smart Alec rejoinders, no snappy chapter-closing one liners? Nothing but *well*?'

'Not after the kind of day you've had. No sireee.'

'Well,' said Rex. 'I appreciate that.'

'Least I can do, man.' Fido turned upon his grubby heels and trotted away. Rex heard the undisguised canine chuckle and the words 'Simon Dee'. He leapt forward to level his foot at the dog's rear end, tripped and vanished once more into his hole.

2

New Eden did boast some really spectacular sunsets. They were red and gold and glorious. Folk sat upon the hillsides and watched them and sighed deeply. Aaaaaaaaaaaaah, they went.

On this particular evening Rex Mundi didn't. Not that he often did anyway, preferring the pleasures of the pot room to the marvels of the firmament. On this particular night Rex prepared his own supper and made up a bed in the spare room.

Christeen's ears were deaf to tales of unearthed statues and mystery Volvos. Septic tanks were as ever the mainstay of her conversation. And as, for now, she had at least stopped throwing, Rex felt it prudent to avoid mention of the punctured privet.

Now he lay upon the uncomfortable single guest-bed he had been meaning to have finished and stared up at the ceiling he had been meaning to get plastered. His thoughts were his own and as they weren't particularly interesting they will remain unrecorded.

Rex smoked a long joint, made a mental note that he really should have the room's windows glazed sometime soon, and at long last fell into a troubled sleep and dreamed about holes.

* * *

23

It was an hour before sunrise when Fido returned home. He had spent the night at a canine carouse and was now somewhat unsteady about the paws. As he neared Mundi Towers he paused to consider the nature of the strange lights he saw moving ahead.

'Now,' said Fido, with more than a hint of a slur. 'Now, what have we here?' He crept forward and did his best to focus.

'Those,' he told himself, 'would be torches going to and fro.' And indeed they were, and as Fido slunk nearer he found that he could hear voices also. And these said things like 'keep your end up' and 'OK, I've got it, back to me a bit' and 'it weighs a ton'.

And as he slunk even closer still he could see dark figures moving in the murk. Two dark figures struggling to drag something not nearly so dark toward something which even in the uncertain light displayed the classic contours of . . . 'A Volvo estate,' whispered Fido. 'Bastards!'

'Raise the alarm, fur boy,' said Fido. 'Woof! Woof! Woof! Rex! Rex! Rex!'

'It's that bloody dog,' came the voice of Mr Johnny Dee. 'Shoot it.'

'Oh Shiva!' Fido took to his heels. He zipped between the legs of Ed Kelley and made for the family home. A beam of yellow light whisked over his head and melted Rex's parsley patch. 'Oh double Shiva.' Fido made haste towards the dog flap. He legged it up the stairs and into the guest bedroom, where he correctly surmised Rex would be bedding down. Rex was already on his feet, glavanized into action by the noises.

'What's going on?'

'The Volvo. Dee and Kelley. They've got guns.'

'Let's get them.'

'Not me, man.' Fido took cover beneath the bed.

'Me then.'

24

'That's the fellow. Better be quick, man, they're ripping off your statue.'

'Bastards!'

'That's what I said.'

Now Rex was angry. In fact he was very angry. He was seething, fuming, frantic and frenzied angry. He snatched up the spade, which Christeen, upon departing for bed, had flung into his room, and rushed down the stairs. He wasn't exactly clad for combat, wearing only his underpants. But he rippled though, in all the right places and shone well in the moonlight. Not quite Conan the Barbarian perhaps, but definitely your pocket Hercules.

Ed and Johnny were loading at the hurry-up, the alarm now having been raised.

'I can't shut the tailgate.'

'Leave it then. Let's go.'

Johnny leapt into the driver's seat and pressed buttons, Ed fell in beside him. The car started first time, the way those expensive lads always do. And they'd had the door replaced. It had been colour-matched. And you couldn't even see the difference. Bastards.

'Let's go.' Johnny jiggled the automatic shift-stick and as he did so a ferocious figure rose up before him, spade held high as the Hammer of Thor.

'It's Conan,' wailed the fatter felon.

'Don't be ridiculous.'

'Let's get out of here.'

Thor swung his hammer. The Volvo's windscreen became a million plexiglass fragments. Naturally the inner safety skin, which is standard issue on all the top-of-the-rangers, shielded the occupants from harm. And the insurance company were bound to pay up without a murmur. Bastards!

'I can't see.'

'Back up. Let's get.'

Johnny swung the wheel. The Volvo pulverized the

petits pois and slewed into another section of Rex's prize hedge. It reversed over the ornamental fishpond, discomforting the Koi carp and stunning the stone gnomes. Rex flung himself at it. His spade skimmed over the roof raising a fine shower of sparks, three layers of enamel paint, two of primer and one of a rust-resistant additive with a complicated chemical composition.

'The Hyperborean Hero,' shrieked Ed, who was really showing his true colours. 'Shoot him.'

'I can't shoot *him*. You know that.' Johnny stuck the automatic into 'drive like the Devil' mode. Rex threw his spade aside and himself at the open tailgate. His fingers caught hold and he left his feet.

The car surged forwards, the engine purring like a good 'n even though the revs were well into the red range, and then suddenly fell silent. And all manner of very strange things began to happen.

'You have now entered free space,' said a disembodied voice. 'Please observe the following safety procedures. Secure all doors.' Rex, realizing that he was now floating weightlessly, hauled himself into the Volvo and slammed down the tailgate.

'Make extra certain that your co-ordinates have been doubled-checked and are mapped, logged and correctly aligned. Do not leave the vehicle for any reason whatsoever. Do not litter the lanes and under no circumstances tamper with the particle flow of ionized beta photons.'

'Wouldn't dream of it,' said Rex.

'We thank you for travelling in the cause of Ultimate Truth. Have a nice tomorrow.'

A nice tomorrow? Gravity made a surprise return and Rex plunged heavily to the floor. He mouthed bitter words and climbed slowly to his feet.

Now you shouldn't be able to climb to your feet in the rear of a Volvo estate and this did cross Rex's mind when he found himself able to do so with no difficulty at all.

In fact, when he reached up he discovered that he couldn't touch the roof and when he looked around, a long strangled kind of a gasp escaped his lips.

Although he knew he hadn't left the Volvo Rex found himself standing in the entrance to some kind of gigantic cargo hold. It was monstrous, vast. The Volvo's rear quarters owed more than a little to the interior of a certain doctor's telephone box. And even though spacious, it was extremely crowded.

'Art,' whispered Rex. 'It's art.' And indeed it was. Art by the gallery load. Row upon row of titanic paintings, framed in gilt, hung upon steel racks. Rex wandered amongst them, awestruck. There were statues and busts, sections of wall frescos, tapestries and mosaics. Hundreds of them. No, thousands. Rex hooched up his Y-fronts. He was in a serious museum here and no mistake about it.

His own statue lay on its side in the cargo bay, for such the inner tailgate appeared, and it didn't look out of place one jot with the stored collection surrounding it. And for why? Well, I'll tell you for why. Because, wherever Rex wandered amidst these treasures of the ancient world, his eye was drawn to a single detail. On each and every one of the pictures, murals, icons or whatever, the self-same face grinned out at him. Here it was grinning over Caesar's shoulder as Brutus put the knife in. And here, lit to perfection amongst the Night Watch. And surely that was it third from the right in Georges de la Tour's 'Adoration of the Shepherds'. Yes indeedy.

It was a face Rex knew almost as well as he knew his own. A face like no other that had been before or would ever come again. The face of Elvis Aaron Presley. The man, the lip and the legend.

'Elvis,' said Rex Mundi in a small and troubled voice. 'What in God's name have you done now?'

My office isn't exactly what you'd call fancy.

There's a desk I sit at and a chair I sit on. There's a

27

watercooler that ain't too cool and a fan that don't write me no letters. A telephone that won't speak to me and a carpet I wouldn't pass the time of day with if it did.

I got a hat stand without a hat to stand on and a filing cabinet full of memories. Oh yeah, and I got a door.

And that's where I come in. The name's Woodbine. Lazlo Woodbine. Private Eye. And although this is page 28 and there's been a lot of coming and going that I ain't had a hand in, I happen to be the real hero of this little epic. *The Tempus Fugitives* it's called, *A Lazlo Woodbine thriller*.

Now I ain't enigmatic, so don't expect too much art for art's sake. I ain't cheap, but I'm thorough and I get the job done. With me you can expect a lot of gratuitous sex and violence, a trail of corpses and a final roof-top showdown. No loose ends, no spin-offs and all strictly 'first-person' only. That's the way it is and the way it always has been. And this is the way it always begins.

It was another long hot Manhattan night. Shirtsleeve and singlet weather in the big city. My office was like the back seat of Guy Stravino's Chevy, no place to be after six p.m. I wrung the top from another bottle of Bud and fanned myself with a copy of *Wet Girls in the Raw*. Summer had the city by the throat.

The small-time heisters and back-row pocket dukes had taken a powder, the cops ran to fat on the street corners and the cars crawled by like fluff on a gramophone needle. My watercooler steamed gently and the ceiling fan turned at three revolutions an hour. It was hot.

I took off my trenchcoat and mittens. 'Dammit,' I said to myself, 'if it gets any hotter I'm taking my pullover off.'

The beer splashed its icy way down my throat and sizzled in chicken madras that had been my tea. I sat back in my chair and listened to the sounds of the city.

Through my open window I could hear the newsboy

hawking his last late editions, the ball game echoing from a neighbour's wireless, the crackle of neon lights, the poot of poodles and the celestial harmonics of the cosmos. I figure that from where I was sitting you could hear anything you darn well pleased on a Saturday night.

One thing I didn't expect to hear was the ringing of my telephone. And sure as sure that's exactly what I didn't hear.

What I did hear was a rappety-rap-rap-rap on my partition door. I yawned, stretched, put aside all thoughts of learning esperanto. This could be the Big One. 'Come,' said I.

The door swung open like water off a duck's back and there, framed in the portal, stood the most beautiful woman I'd seen all day. She was nearly wearing a white angora evening number. Off the shoulder but not off the peg. She was the kind of blonde you don't get from a bottle and her lips looked more at home around a long Martini than a dwarf's dongler. This lady had class written through her like rock has Brighton.

'Hi toots,' I said, smiling from the waist down. 'You looking for a little action?'

She shot me a glance like she was putting out a bad cigar and came over with a lightning Veronica Lake. 'Is your name Woodbane?' she asked. 'Woodbane the dick?'

'The name's Wood*bine*, maam. Lazlo Woodbine. Some call me Laz.'

'I'll just call you Mr Shithead,' she responded in a manner I considered most winsome. 'I need your help.'

Well, I never played reggae in the Australian hinterlands so I don't know how to beat around the bush. And this lady looks as though she meant business and business is my business, if you catch my drift, and I'm sure that you do.

'I ain't cheap,' I told her. 'But I'm thorough and I get

29

the job done. With me you can expect a lot of gratuitous sex and violence, a trail of corpses and a final roof-top showdown.'

'No loose ends or spin-offs?' she asked.

'None. I charge five hundred thousand dollars a day, plus expenses and I only work in the "first-person".'

She twitched a languid dewlap and movied in my direction. 'I think I'll just call you Shithead for short,' she quipped. I was beginning to fall in love. 'Five hundred thousand dollars a day and no expenses.'

'You drive a hard bargain, maam.' I let the *hard* sink in. 'Who needs to die?'

She dipped into her purse, took out a small contrivance and tossed it on to my desk. I gave it some perusal. It was hard, black and buttoned and occupied the space of a Camel pack.

'A-ha,' said I, in a fashion which suggested an almost mystical insight into all things electronical. 'What you have there maam, is a watchmacallit.'

She ran her velvet tongue around her up-town dental work and smiled me a bitter-sweet. 'Press button A.'

I did as I was bid. Light locked up into a cube above my desk and showed me a range of 3D images that were beauteous to behold.

'A-ha,' said I, it being a favourite with me when lost for words.

'Artworks.' The lady manipulates a manicured mitt midst the mirage. 'Religious artworks.'

'I don't know what I like. But I know about art.'

'And do you know these men?' I was now looking into faces. Unsmiling. Unlovely.

'Do I know them?' I leaned back in my chair and narrowly avoid falling out of the window. 'Maam. These two cost me my wife, my job at the department, a dog named Blue and six months in intensive care. And you want I should go looking for them?'

She looked me up and down like a Times Square neon

and Devil take the hindmost. 'Think you're up to it, Shithead?'

I gave her the kind of smile I generally keep for Tuesday. 'Lady,' said I, with more panache than a muff diver in a Maltese meatball factory, 'do you realize that every law enforcement agency in the galaxy is looking for these two?'

She nodded.

'And that the future of civilization and probably the very fabric of universal existence hangs upon the apprehension of these men and the return of the artworks?'

She nodded again.

'And you come to me?'

She leaned into the hologram. The faces of the two hoods glared at me from her bosoms. 'What do you say, Woodbone?'

'I say, what took you so long, lady? I've been expecting you for a week.'

'Please extinguish all cigarettes, fasten your safety belts and prepare for touchdown.' Rex assumed the foetal position.

'Kindly observe all landing procedures and do not leave the vehicle until the green light flashes and the little hooter goes peep peep peep. We thank you for travelling in the cause of Ultimate Truth and hope you enjoyed the trip.'

There came a terrible shuddering and buffeting, and light soared in through the Volvo's rear window. The car came to a sudden halt depositing Rex at the front end of the art store where he lay seething.

'I think a bite to eat would be the thing.' It was the voice of Ed Kelley. Rex climbed once more to his feet. Above him a lozenge of light showed. Rex tested himself for broken bones.

'A snackerel before we conclude our business.' Rex craned his neck to the bright little lozenge. A glass hatch

31

to the cab. Beyond it he could make out the pair of talking heads.

'Okey doke,' went Ed Kelley.

'Peep peep peep,' went the little hooter.

'You'll get yours!' muttered Rex Mundi.

Rex heard the doors open and slam, and then nothing but for a dull humming. He made his way back through the artworks to the cargo bay and peered through the rear window.

'Shiva's Sheep!' gasped Mr Mundi.

There was a city out there. But what a city. Rex had seen New York in the nineteen-nineties and there was much of that here. Only a whole lot more. He was looking at a broad thoroughfare, along which mighty cars, all low sleek bodies, high trailing fins and bulging chromium, drifted like fantastic land yachts. On the sidewalks, beautiful people in stylish costumes strolled and sauntered. They looked young, tall and proud. Rex wasted no time in taking an instant dislike to them. Above and beyond. Most of all, above, rose buildings of preposterous proportions. They dwindled into the sky, but their design was unmistakable. They resembled nothing more nor less than titanic jukeboxes. Between them, decked with twinkling lights, great airships came and went.

'The future.' Rex sank on to his bottom. 'I'm in the future.' He hugged his knees and began to rock slowly back and forth. Had he not been half the hero I, for one, believe him to be, there seemed a strong chance that now would be an ideal time for a mental breakdown.

'Now would be an ideal time for a mental breakdown,' said Rex Mundi, beginning to burble.

Oh no you don't!

Rex considered his options. He was down but by no means out. Certainly he was shut in a time-travelling Volvo, wearing nothing but his underpants. But he'd been in worse situations than this and lived to save the day.

'I have to get out of here.' Rex sought the rear window of opportunity. Passers by were passing by. They all seemed pleasing to gaze upon and, Rex noted to his satisfaction, all were very well dressed indeed. He watched them as they went about their business. The moment had to be right.

A young man drew near to the Volvo. He was tall, nobly built and wore his hair in the order of the times. High combed and laquered, long sideburns. He was dressed in white shirt, pencil tie, wide-shouldered dark jacket, slim lapels, one button low. Grey peg pants and white brothel creepers. As he prepared to cross the street Rex rapped upon the window.

Seemingly deaf to Rex's rappings the young man took a step forward. Rex pounded the window with his fist. The young man paused and glanced down. Rex smiled up at him. The young man looked bemused. Rex made an encouraging face and finger pointings at the door handle. 'Locked in,' he mouthed.

'What?' came a silent reply.

'Locked in!'

The young man shook his head. Rex whacked the window anew. 'Help!'

The good Samaritan smiled and reached toward the handle. He turned it and swung up the tailgate. Rex grasped him by the shoulders and dragged him into the Volvo. It was all the work of a moment. A deft blow to the jaw, the tailgate pulled almost shut. The sounds of the brief struggle were swallowed up by the noise of the city. Rex stripped his unconscious victim and togged up. The jacket was a little tight beneath the armpits, but the shoes were comfortable enough.

Rex put his ear to the young man's chest. His breathing seemed measured. Rex hadn't hit him too hard. Rex felt bad about hitting him at all. Striking down the innocent did not lie well with him. But the situation was somewhat extreme and once he had found satisfaction from Dee and

Kelley, who were far from innocent, he would apologize to the young man and bung him a couple of old masters by way of compensation.

His conscience now thoroughly salved, a well-dressed Rex slid out of the Volvo and entered wonderland. He examined his reflection in the nearest store window. 'Damnably handsome,' was his considered opinion.

Rex rubbed his palms together. Options now lay open to him. The big question was which to take. 'Take the Volvo,' said Rex without further hesitation. He stepped around to the front of the car and tried the driver's door. It was locked. Rex peered into the car. No keys dangled in the dashboard. But then this was not the kind of dashboard that keys seemed likely to dangle in. This was one of those big spaceship jobs, all flashing lights and little television screens with expensive animated graphics.

Rex whistled. Trying to figure that lot out could take all day. Best to deal with the driver directly. 'A bite to eat,' he had said. Rex scanned the nearby likelys.

'Oh no,' groaned Rex. Ed and Johnny sat not twenty yards distant outside a café. It was another chrome and neon affair. They hovered comfortably upon legless chairs. Dead futuristic. But Rex's 'oh no' was not directed thataways. It was given vent due to the sign which flashed on and off above the café. It read 'The Tomorrow-man Tavern', and Rex really wished it didn't.

'Paper, bud?' It was the first voice he had heard and it had an American accent.

'Sorry?'

'You wanna paper?' The news vendor waggled said article beneath Rex's nose. 'I said d'ya wanna paper you dumb—'

'Yes I do. Yes.' Rex accepted the thing as it was thrust into his hand.

'Buck.'

'Nice to meet you, Buck.'

34

'Buck for the paper, you stupid . . .'

'Oh, I see.' Rex rooted in his new jacket. He turned up a billfold and unbillfolded it. Money notes. Rex took out a big bright one and offered it to the news vendor. 'Is this enough?'

'I'll say.' The news vendor snatched it from him and pocketed it away. 'Goddamn thick-assed son of a . . .' Rex let it slide by. Punching the news vendor's lights out in the middle of a busy street was probably not the wisest move in the world.

'Are you here all day?' he asked.

'Till the crowds go.'

'I'll catch up with you later then.'

'Huh?'

Rex took his newspaper and merged with the passers by. He found a vantage point before a store window which displayed a fetching line in bondage leisurewear, and raised his newspaper 'spy' fashion. And two things hit him right in the face. The first widened his eyes and the second lowered his jaw.

The first was the newspaper's title. The *Presley Enquirer*.

The second was the date. 27 July 2061.

'27 July 2061.' It didn't matter which way Rex read it, it still came out the same. It was his own time. The time he was living in. The very day he was living in. Or had been living in. But this wasn't his world. Where was he? Another planet? Couldn't be. Not with the American news vendor and the *Presley Enquirer*.

Rex studied the headlines in search of a clue.

SPACE ALIENS KIDNAPPED MY TWO-HEADED LOVE-CHILD

'Ah,' said Rex. 'One of *those* newspapers.' He leafed through it.

IRATE PUBLISHER FEEDS TRILOGY AUTHOR TO THE SHARKS

HUNDRED-YEAR-OLD WOMAN GIVES BIRTH TO SINCLAIR C5

'Hmmph.' Rex folded his newspaper and consigned it

to the nearest litter bin. He glanced across the street. Ed and Johnny seemed to be enjoying themselves. Rex watched the beautiful people as they came and went. The fabulous automobiles and drifting airships. The neon lights flashing, the news vendor vending.

And then he caught the flicker of movement in the Volvo. He looked on entranced as the half-naked figure of the good Samaritan squirmed through the little glass hatch and dropped into the driver's seat. He was even close enough to observe the deft finger motions on the space-age dashboard and to hear the peerless purr as the engine took life.

Making horror's open mouth, Rex watched the Volvo pull out into the street and lose itself in the stream of passing traffic.

The melodic tone of the highly-tuned engine brought Rex no joy whatever. Neither did the fact that the superb power steering responded to little more than a fingertip's application, whilst leaving the driver's other hand free to make an obscene gesture in his direction. And as to whatever subtle pleasures lay in the contemplation of rear indicators, these slipped by him completely.

A friend of mine who was once in the AA says that the indicators of all posh motorcars can be programmed to flash out messages in a secret code. Apparently the knowledge of which buttons to press and how the code works lie in the hands of the Freemasons, who commonly pass on information to one another in this fashion during motorway traffic jams.

I once broached the subject with Mad Tony Long who does the MOT on my Cortina. He neither confirmed nor denied it, although he did give me a very funny look. Whether this means he's a practising Freemason I couldn't say. And as I've never felt the desire to shake his hand, I'll probably never know for sure. But it certainly makes you think, doesn't it?

It didn't make Rex think. In fact, if there was ever

a moment when a burgeoning interest in automotive arcanum was less distant from his mind, this was most probably it.

'Damn!' went Rex Mundi. 'Damn damn damn!' He raised knotty fists and shook them at the sky. He made to run after the Volvo but stopped short in his tracks and threw up his hands again. He kicked at the air. He stamped his feet. He wasn't pleased.

His choice of options, slim as it was, had become positively anorexic. There was nothing for it. He would just have to go over and have the thing out directly with Dee and Kelley. Demand explanations and deal out blows whenever the need arose. With difficulty Rex composed his features into something approaching normality, flexed his shoulders and stared across the street towards the Tomorrowman Tavern. Here, two floating and now thoroughly vacant chairs met his thoroughly jaundiced eye.

'Gone!' Rex began to shake in a manner most unbecoming, and passing folk steered carefully around him. The news vendor, who had been enjoying the unsolicited performance since it first began, could contain himself no longer.

'Is this some kind of street theatre, buddy?' he asked. 'Or are you just a whacko?'

Rex turned slowly upon him. 'Does your mother know how to sew?' he asked in an even voice.

'My mother? Sew? Sure, I guess.'

'Then get her to stitch this up.'

3

1. *And when the ark was finished Noah said unto Elvis, 'What do you reckon?'*
2. *And Elvis checked out his own cabin and shook his head saying 'poky'.*
3. *And so did they knock several walls through and install a jacuzzi.*
4. *And when this was done Noah scratched his beard and said, 'We don't have room for all the animals now.'*
5. *And Elvis perused the livestock list and in his wisdom said, 'Lose the dinosaurs.'*

The Suburban Book of the Dead

Now, I know what you're thinking. You're thinking, how come this Lazlo Woodbine with the nineteen-fifties' office shows no surprise when confronted by sci-fi holographic gizmos and comes out with lines such as 'every law enforcement agency in the galaxy is looking for these two'. Ain't ya?

Well, I'll lay it on the line for you. Because, like I say, I ain't enigmatic.

Firstly, this novel is called *The Tempus Fugitives*, which is a pretty Goddamn clever title by anyone's reckoning, and I should know, as I thought of it myself. And secondly, although I might look like the guy in the trenchcoat and fedora, which I am, these are changing times. And the changing times that I happen to live in are those of the twenty-fifth century. And if you want to get by as a private eye in these changing times, certain things are expected of you.

A sense of propriety is one and impeccable credentials is another, and I got both. I got a bloodline in this business that goes back five hundred years. Class, see, born with it. Take my hat, for example. Snap-brimmed fedora. Classic. Same hat my ancient ancestor wore when he was a private eye back in the nineteen-fifties. Sure it's had thirty new brims, eighty new bands and more crowns than the House of Hapsburg since then. But it's the same hat. Same old hat, same old joke. Class never dates, see?

Take my office furniture. Priceless antiques. The water-cooler alone is worth more millions than I would care to shake a stick at. Not to mention the carpet, which I rarely do.

So, you are asking yourselves, and I can hear you. So how come if this Lazlo is such a class act does he let the dame insult him? Well, that's the way business is done in this business. Always has been done, always is done and always will be done. It's a tradition, see, or an old charter or something like that.

I'm the last of the greats, with a literary legacy that reaches back to Philip Marlowe and Mike Hammer. And that's why I get hired. I don't come cheap, but I'm thorough and I get the job done. And I only work four sets. My office, Fangio's Bar, an alleyway that could be anywhere and a roof-top. A really great detective rarely needs more than that. Some stretch a point and add a hotel room, a hospital ward, or a police cell, but not me. I keep it basic.

My first three sets speak pretty much for themselves. You gotta work somewhere, drink somewhere and get into sticky situations somewhere. And the roof-top's pretty obvious, too, if you think about it. Your super-villain always has to fall off a roof-top, or somewhere real high at the end. Doesn't matter who he is, Dick Jones,

Darth Vader, the Shredder or the Joker, they each got to take the big plunge in the final showdown. Probably started with King Kong, I guess, or when Quasimodo threw Dom Claude Frollo off the bell-tower of Notre Dame. But it's never been bettered yet when it comes to the spectacular ending. So when you see old Laz climbing over the slates at least you'll know the end's in sight. Which should offer some kind of comfort.

So, all this said, and pretty damn articulately said if you ask me, I tuck the lady's contrivance into one pocket of my trenchcoat, my trusty Smith and Wesson into another and go off in search of a lead. And if there is one place in this town where I'm likely to find it, that one place is Fangio's Bar.

Behind the counter of the Tomorrowman Tavern, the one-eyed barman straightened his spotted cravat and smoothed down the lapels of his quilted smoking jacket. He had built up quite a substantial cult following since his first appearance in *Armageddon: The Musical*, and he was looking well on it. One literary critic described his performance in *They Came And Ate Us* as 'quintessential . . . controlled and deeply felt . . . moving, poignant and about the only near decent thing in an otherwise turgid potboiler'. On the strength of this alone Bloomsbury had signed him up for *The Suburban Book of the Dead* and brought in a ghost writer to replace Rankin.

But making a really decent living as a professional fictitious character is a tricky business, as the barman knew well enough. You generally come up trumps if you can swing the lead in a Jackie Collins or a Julie Burchill, all baby oil, meat and two veg. But find yourself in a Clive Barker or a Stephen King and like as not you'll wind up with maggots coming out of your nostrils before you reach chapter five. The barman had previously done a Zane Grey where he got dry gulched on page one, and a Sven Hessel where he came to an even bloodier end as a German tank commander. Neither had won him any critical acclaim. This was his first time in a trilogy and he was warming to the challenge of giving his best performance yet.

And parts, no matter how small, are never easy to come by. Many fictitious characters turn out to be nothing of the sort. They are merely friends, relatives or enemies of the author dressed up a bit and given different names. And many heroes are actually played by the author himself. But although your genuine professional fictitious character knows this goes on, there is very little that he or she can do about it. 'Speak up in this game and you're Tipp-Ex', as they say.

Of course, the pay's a flat rate and you don't get a share of the royalties, but there are perks to the job. If you can work your way into a 'classic' then you've cracked the secret of immortality. The author may snuff it, but you will go on for ever and ever and ever. Nice work if you can get it, eh?

Rex looked up at the Tomorrowman's neon sign. It flashed on and off, the way some of them do and the way this one did all too often. The establishment beneath it appeared, at first sight, an extremely swank affair. A study in cold chrome, cool marble and warm leatherette. Rex examined the floating chairs, perhaps in search of clues. He noticed with no particular surprise that they hung upon cunningly concealed brackets. 'Hmmph,' went Rex.

He eyeballed the bar proper. It looked reasonably convincing. The tall glass street-doors were anchored back to reveal a spacious lounge. To the left, numerous, chrome pedestals offered their support to glass table-tops ringed with neon tubes. About these, fashionable folk arrayed themselves and conversed in merry tones. To the right, further chrome in the shape of the bar-counter which ran back the length of the room, although from what, was anyone's guess. The glass counter-top was lit from beneath and behind this the wall was the usual clutter of back-of-bar ephemera. Glittering optics, stacked glasses, cocktail shakers, drink dispensers, row upon row of exotic-looking bottles. And lodged between bar and backdrop stood a lone figure, his single eye fixed upon Rex Mundi.

'Ah,' said Rex. 'Ah indeed.'

'You want something?' the barman enquired in a deep Shakespearean tone.

Rex strode up to the counter and placed himself upon one of the raised barstools which had somehow failed to get a mention earlier. He faced the famous barman. 'Why are you wearing that?' he asked.

'Wearing what?' The barman made an extravagant gesture.

'That.' Rex pointed to the barman's head which, though bald in episodes past, was now lavishly furnished. 'That.'

'I ain't wearing nothing. What do you mean?'

'The syrup,' sighed Rex. 'The rug, the pompadour, the toup, the Blodwyn Pig.'

'It's all my own hair.'

Rex leant his elbow upon the bar-counter and his chin upon his palm. 'Shall I come in again?' he asked. 'When you have removed the wig, the smoking jacket and the silk cravat?'

'Eyeball the screen station, boy.' It was the line his fans always called out to him in the street.

Rex shook his head. 'Shall I come in again, or is it Tipp-Ex time?'

The barman now had a definite pout on to go with his wig. 'My public expect . . .' he began.

'No, they don't.'

The barman got a huff on to go with his pout. 'But I can keep the cigarette holder?'

'No.'

'What about the spats?'

'Oh, I hadn't seen the spats.' Rex leant across the counter and perused said spats. 'No spats,' said he.

'You're just jealous because I—'

'What did you say?'

'Nothing.'

Rex mimed the dread bottle and the little brush going back and forwards across an invisible page.

'I just have to pop out,' said the barman. 'Do you want a drink before I go?'

'Yes please. Tomorrowman Brew if you will.' The grumbling barkeep turned away to do the business.

'And a *ham* sandwich,' said Rex loudly.

'Oh cruel, cruel.'

'And an icebucket.'

'An icebucket, yes.'

'And barman.'

'Yes?'

'Don't return dressed as a pirate.'

Muttering bitterly, the literary legend slung food, drink and bucket before Rex and slouched away.

'Any chance of getting served here?' a young toff asked. Passing at close quarters, the barman offered him the use of two fingers. 'Well, really.'

Rex chuckled, placed the fist which had seen service upon both Samaritan and news vendor in the icebucket and began what surely was his breakfast.

'Cheek of the fellow,' said the young toff.

Rex shrugged and continued to feed.

'And that ghastly peruke. I ask you.'

Rex sipped his Tomorrowman Brew. It tasted as noxious as ever. The young toff was giving him a critical once-over; he didn't seem too sold on Rex's footwear. 'Something wrong?' Rex asked.

'No, no. Nice jacket.'

'Thank you.'

'A tad pinched beneath the armpits, though. No offence meant.'

'None taken, I assure you.'

'Jolly good.' The toff peered hard at Rex. 'Don't I know you? You look mightily familiar.'

Rex shook his head. 'I don't think so.'

The toff scratched a pampered chin. He wore a dove-grey triple-breasted suit of immaculate confection. Pale silk shirt, blue suede shoes. His blackly-dyed hair was tortured into a shark's-fin quiff. Moleskin sideburns showed off his cheekbone implants to good advantage. A wide kipper-tie flashed short-range holographics, all of which were keen to sell Rex something.

Rex wasn't in a buying kind of a mood.

'I *do* know you. Chap off the telly, isn't it? Now, what's your name? Don't tell me, I'll get it in a mo'. Laura.'

'It's not Laura.'

'No, Laura.' The toff called to a young woman seated nearby. 'Laura, it's that chap off the telly.'

'Oh.' Laura rose from her seat.

'Ah.' Rex rose in his, and beamed at the beauty now heading in his direction. She was tall and tanned and young and lovely. A bit like the girl from Ipecacuanha. Or is that the South American shrub used in the prep-aration of emetics? She wore the 'little black dress' that all men know and drool about.

'This is Laura,' said the toff. 'I'm Garth, by the way.' He dipped a manicured finger into his top pocket and drew out a calling card. Rex didn't bother with it. He just wiped the crumbs from his mouth, thrust the icebucket into Garth's arms and as an afterthought, dried his smiting hand upon the holographic tie.

'No offence meant,' he said.

The toff made a pained face. 'None taken, I assure you.'

'Pleased to meet you, Laura.' Rex vacated his stool and steered the young woman on to it. She was indeed a rare orchid. She took his hand in hers. She didn't release it.

'Hello,' said Laura.

'Chap off the telly,' Garth explained. 'Fancy that, eh?'

'Laura.' Rex maintained the eye contact. 'Can I buy you a drink?'

'Surely.' Laura crossed her long slim legs with slow erotic deliberation. Rex bit his lip. Even without the visuals, there are few sounds more delicious than those made by a woman's stockings when she crosses her legs.

'Shop!' Rex pounded his fist upon the bar-top.

Dominant, thought Laura, I like that in a man.

As if on cue, the barman reappeared. He was now the grim and scabious fellow that ever he was. Clad once more in the soiled leather apron and gloves, bald of head and wild of single eye.

'Watcha want?' he demanded.

Rex winked at him kindly. 'That's the stuff. One more for myself, and whatever the lady's drinking.'

The barman gave Rex his finest cyclopean and rubbed thumb and unspeakably-gloved forefinger beneath the hero's nose. 'I'll see your coin if I will. He that has money has what he wants.'

Rex dug into his purloined pockets and came up with a handful of small change. He dumped it on to the glass bar-top. 'There you go.'

Gauging accurately Rex's current lack of knowledge regarding matters monetary, the barman said 'good enough' and swept the entire amount into his apron pocket. 'Thanks for the tip,' he muttered as he set about the optics.

'So Laura,' Rex smiled upon the beautiful woman, 'exactly what do you do?'

'Chap off the telly,' called Garth, waving to his friends. 'His icebucket also.'

'Garth,' Laura's eyes never left Rex, 'Garth, go away and sit down.'

'But I . . .'

'Garth.' Garth went away and sat down. Dominant, thought Rex, I like that in a woman. Well, some women.

'What do I do?' Laura ran her tongue lightly about her

45

sensuous lips. Rex wondered if she might feel up to another leg cross. 'Actually I'm a prostitute.'

'A prostitute?' Rex swivelled back to the bar. 'Hurry up with my change, barman,' he called.

The barman pushed two drinks across the counter and short-changed Rex. Rex, for his part, thrust the coins into his pocket without a second glance. Which was a shame really, because he failed once more to take in the significant detail that each and every one of them bore the raised profile of Elvis Presley's head.

'So,' Rex passed Laura her drink. It wasn't Tomorrow-man Brew. 'A prostitute. Interesting work?'

'Hardly as interesting as yours. Have you just come from the studio?'

'The studio?' Rex went into lying bastard mode. 'Actually yes. I'm putting together a new show. Perhaps you might be interested.'

'Not if it's anything like . . .'

'Totally new. It's called *Amnesia*. The host pretends he's from another planet, or say, another time, and he asks the contestants questions to find out where he is.'

'Sounds pretty dull.'

'Big prizes,' said Rex.

'Tell me more.'

'All right. Pretend you're a contestant.'

'What, here?'

'Certainly. Call it an audition, if you like.'

'Do you want me to take all my clothes off then?'

Absolutely, thought Rex. 'Of course not,' he said. 'Just answer the questions.'

'Go on then.'

'Right, what is your name?'

'Laura Lynch.'

'And where do you live?'

'Right here.'

'Do try harder. Where is right here?'

'Sixth precinct.'

46

'Could you be a little more exact?'

'1010 Van Vliet Street.'

'And the city?'

'This one of course. This is some dumb show.'

'What country then?'

'Are you for real? This show will never sell.'

Not the way you play it, Rex thought. 'OK. One final question.'

'Go on . . .'

'How much do you charge for a blow-job?'

'Two hundred and fifty dollars. Do I win?'

'You certainly do.' Rex began to pat once more at his pockets.

'Er chap . . .' Garth ventured forth. 'Chap off the telly . . .'

'Not now, Garth. I'm very busy.' Rex found the billfold.

'Chap. The pals just wanted to ask. The contestants on your show. Do they really . . . that is . . . do you actually . . . ?'

'No,' said Rex. 'Whatever it is.'

'Thought not.' Garth made a dispirited face. 'Special effects, I suppose.'

'Something like that.' Rex flicked through the billfold. 'Do you take any of these, Laura?' He forked out what he took to be a credit card. It wasn't. Laura gaped at it in horror.

'Repo Man!' she squawked.

'No,' said Rex. 'Great movie, but I wasn't in it. Harry Dean Stanton. How about this one, then?'

'Repo Man.' Garth was impressed. 'Then you do actually . . . you know . . .'

'Garth, I'm a little strapped for cash, lend me two hundred and fifty dollars. I'll pay you back.'

'Two fifty? No problem. Can you change a five thousand?'

'Garth!' screamed Laura. 'He's a Repo Man for E's sake.' She slipped down from the stool and backed away.

47

Rex enjoyed the stockings as they crossed. But some sixth sense told him he'd probably heard them do it for the last time.

'I don't think I quite understand.' Rex looked around at the suddenly silent crowd. It seemed more than likely that he was all alone in this particular piece of ignorance.

'Chap off the telly,' said Garth lamely. 'You know. Does that *Nemesis* show . . . Rex Mundi, that's it. Knew I'd get it in the end.'

If there had been a big silence before, there was an even bigger one now. And much of it was coming from Rex himself.

Exactly how long the silence might have lasted is anyone's guess. There was a tension about it which verged upon the awesome. But it was over almost as swiftly as it had begun. Broken by the noisy arrival of a certain news vendor whose mother knew how to sew. And he was flanked by two very large policemen indeed. Rex took no pleasure at all in noticing that they were played by the henchman Cecil and his brother Sandy out of *They Came And Ate Us*.

'That's him,' cried the little man with the big lip. 'Socked me right in the kisser. The son-of-a-bitch off that crummy gameshow. The guy's a whacko, better shoot him right now.'

4

1. *And Elvis said unto Jacob, 'Where's
your coat of many colours, then?'*
2. *And Jacob replied saying, 'You mean
Joseph, he's the one with the coat. I'm
Jacob, the guy with the ladder.'*
3. *And Elvis shrugged and asked, 'Then
who's the guy over there in the denim?'*
4. *And Jacob answered, 'That's my son,
Levi.'*
5. *And Elvis did smite Jacob upon the
chin and go his way from him.*

The Suburban Book of the Dead

Fangio's Bar lay over on the East Side beneath
some old stock footage of night-time sky-
scrapers and the Jersey Bridge. In a changing world like
this is some things never change, and Fangio's maintained its old-world charm. It was still a haven of bad
breath, worse language, poor pool playing and cheap
cigar smoke. The fat boy considered himself a bit of a
psychologist and had always fancied writing a book
about his colourful career. Like I say, some things never
change.

I might have taken a cab over, or perhaps I had my
own car; I'm certain I never took the subway – but when
I walked in the door love walked out the window, or so
the old song says.

Fangio's Bar was cosmopolitan. Which is to say that
the fat boy didn't care which part of the cosmos his clients

blew in from. As long as they could speak the King's English, figure out which end of the bottle to drink from and pay in hard currency, it was fine by him.

On any given night, except possibly Tuesday, you could lean on Fangio's bar-counter and exchange small-talk with guys born under any one of a dozen different suns. Fange treated them all with equal grace, which must say something for him. Personally I would have heaved the lot of them out and put up a sign saying NO DOGS OR OFF-WORLDERS, which must say something for me. But nothing favourable. I've never been happy working with aliens – messes up the detective genre completely for me.

As I entered the bar the fat boy was at the counter parting pastrami with a cleaver. Possibly a father fixation; I didn't ask. What I did ask was for three fingers of Old Bedwetter. I found my regular stool, upended its squatter and parked my butt. The barman slid my drink across the polished bar-top.

'This on your slate?' he enquired.

I nodded, cool as a mountain stream. 'Have one yourself, Fange.'

The fat one swung his goitre. 'You wouldn't care to settle your tab?' he enquired further.

'Sure thing.' I did some pretty professional pocket patting. Such things are expected between old friends and I knew the score. 'Well, swipe me,' I declared in a voice of considerable surprise. 'I seem to have—'

'Left your wallet in your other trenchcoat again?'

I smiled bravely. 'What can I say?'

'You can say, Fange, my best buddy, please accept my watch as a small down-payment on my not incon-siderable bar-bill.'

'Sure thing.' I reached for my watch and I swear I almost had him going this time. 'Well, swipe me double.' I displayed the naked wrist. 'My landlord got there first,' I explained in a voice of deep regret.

'So what's the deal, Laz?' It's three drinks on and Fangio, who is now wearing my fedora, is also taking a lively interest in my necktie. 'You on a case?'

'It's the Big One,' says I, munching upon a hot pastrami on toast. 'The crime of the century. The Religious Artefacts Heist.'

'Religious artefacts, eh?' Fangio makes a knowing face, which I know and he knows I know, means he knows nothing. 'What are they, exactly?'

'Holy objects,' I expand, because it costs me nothing. 'Holy objects. Statues, pictures, icons, things of that nature. And all of the Big E himself.'

Fangio hums; he's never learned how to whistle. 'Are you buying or selling?' he asks. 'Because if you're selling, I'd prefer the necktie.'

'I'm tracing is all. Strictly off the record. They wanted the best and I'm the best.'

'You certainly are, Laz. What I always say is that although you don't come cheap, you are thorough and always get the job done.'

'Thanks.'

'With you one can expect a lot of gratuitous sex and violence, a trail of corpses and a final roof-top show-down.'

'True.'

'No loose ends, no spin-offs and all strictly in the "first person".'

'You noticed that?'

'I certainly did. So when will you be wanting to book the bar?'

'Come again?'

The fat boy winked me his old-fashioned wink. 'For the exchange.'

'You've lost me.'

'Come off it, Laz. You only work the four sets . . . the office, here, the alley and the roof-top. Now, if you'll take my advice, the best place to make the exchange, the girl for the artworks, or whatever, would be here. No-one will want to hump those heavy statues up to your office, the alleyway's too risky and the roof-top is strictly final showdowns. My bar is the obvious choice.'

'Yeah, I guess so.' I guessed so.

'So, when do you want to book the bar?' The fat boy takes out his appointments diary. 'Shall I pencil you in now? What's this book called by the way? Do I get a big part? Should I have my agent give your agent a call?'

'One thing at a time.' I put my hands up. Everyone always wants to get a piece of the action. 'Here,' says I, 'there's a guy down the end of the bar wants serving.' I gesture towards the lawnmower rep from Beta Reticuli who is rattling his wattles on the counter and miming death by thirst. Fangio, being the professional he is, goes off to do the business.

I loosen my necktie. I need another drink. Of course, if I book the bar I might get several on the house. Or I might get a request for a down-payment on the booking. It's a tricky business. But then ain't everything?

I take time out to think. But not too much. I need a lead on this thing and I need it now. Or possibly I needed it yesterday although I didn't know it at the time. But then perhaps yesterday was where I was going to find all the answers. Answers to questions I hadn't even asked. Or was likely to. Thinking's a tricky business. But then ain't everything?

I knew I had to make a phone call and I had to make a meet. I hail the fat boy who is now clubbing the lawnmower rep around the heads and saying things such as 'this isn't that kind of a bar you . . .'

'Phone,' says I.

'Necktie,' says he.

I dial out the number. It has twenty-seven digits. We've got a lot of telephones now but I've got a good memory.

Paid a small fortune for it. Something in the distance goes BRRR BRRR and this is followed by a voice which goes, 'Who's making this noise?'

'Is Vic there?' I ask, like sand in a salad dressing.

'Who's that?'

'The name's Woodbine,' I reply. 'Lazlo Woodbine. Some call me Laz.'

'Vic.' I hear the voice call. 'There's a Lazlo Woodbean on the line for you.'

'Wood*bine*!' But to no avail.

At length a voice from the past says, 'Laz, is that you?'

I concur that indeed it is and make some pretty specific enquiries. 'You still got that thingamejig that you keep in the bucket?'

'The bucket with the lid?'

'The very same.'

'I still got it. You want it for a while?'

'I'll have it back before you know.'

'You always do.'

'We got a deal, then?'

'Same price?'

'Twenty-five big ones. That OK?'

'Sure. Where do we meet?'

'You know Fangio's Bar?'

'Sure. You buying?'

'The alleyway outside?'

'Sure. You ain't then.'

'Five minutes?'

'Better make it six. I gotta book up to get a hernia.'

'Dodging the draft again?'

'What did you do in the war, Laz?'

'We had a war? No-one told me.' I replace the receiver. 'Thanks.' I tell Fange as I part with my necktie.

'You suit the open neck, Laz.'

'I got six minutes to kill,' says I. 'Why don't you give me a complete history of your sex life?'

53

'Sure,' says Fange. 'But what are you going to do with the other five?' A true professional, I kid you not.

Police Chief Sam Maggott was having a 'rough one'. He came from a long line of sweaty fat two-dimensional cops who are always having a 'rough one' and always push back their caps, mop their brows with over-sized red gingham hankies and say things like 'someone's gonna have to tell the commissioner we've got a psycho on the loose'.

I don't know why they say it. Probably tradition or an old charter or something. I think the hankies are some kind of running gag, although I've never found them particularly amusing.

Sam's office was of great interest, containing, as it did, many vital clues to exactly what was going on. But sadly not yet.

Sergeant Murphy peeped in at Sam's door. 'Any leads, chief?' he asked in that unconvincing Pseudo-Irish brogue you only find in books like this.

Sam shook his jowls. 'Someone's gonna have to tell the commissioner we've got a cycle on the loose,' he said.

'Shouldn't that be a psycho, sure and begorrah?'

'I said a *psychic*, didn't I?'

'Sure you did, chief.' Murphy closed the door behind him. The chief was having a rough one.

Rex wasn't having a particularly smooth one himself. He was sitting in a paddy wagon between two very large policemen.

It was a very large paddy wagon, although it looked quite small from the outside, and it was very crowded with the patrons from the Tomorrowman Tavern, none of whom seemed inclined to indulge in any merry converse. Most nursed bruises and all had been arrested upon offences not unconnected with the Riot Act.

Rex had tried the 'You've got the wrong man' angle,

but it hadn't got him anywhere. He rubbed his head. 'Just listen please, I got hijacked in this Volvo and the Volvo got stolen and . . .'

'Do you want me to read you your rights or simply go on beating Shiva's sheep out of you?' Officer Cecil asked. 'It's all the same to me.'

'Please let me explain . . .'

'I don't want you to explain. Take this.'

'Stop hitting me.' Rex came up for air. 'I'm innocent. Please stop.'

Officer Cecil wiped Rex's blood from his nightstick and applied himself to his official police notebook. 'You are Rex Mundi?'

'Yes, but . . .'

'Did you attempt to give this nancy boy the Vulcan Death Grip?'

'Chap off the telly.' The battered Garth fingered his neck.

'He hit me with an icebucket.' Rex protested. Officer Cecil bopped Rex on the head.

'Ouch,' said Rex.

'This your billfold?'

'No, but . . .'

'Did you punch out the news vendor?'

'Yes, but . . .'

'Did you proposition this hooker in a public drinking house?'

Rex turned towards Laura, who silently crossed her legs and looked away in disgust.

'I may have . . .'

'You want I should bop you again?'

'No. All right, yes, I did.'

'You wearing white shoes in a *blue suede shoe zone*?'

'I what?'

'This guy's going down,' Cecil told his brother. 'White shoes. We're talking "The Chair" here.'

'Hold on,' cried Rex. 'What is all this?'

'Best soften him up a bit more, Cec,' Sandy advised Cecil. 'The chief's having a rough one today.'

Cecil waggled his nightstick. 'These your genital organs?'

'Yes, but—'

There's some garbage cans and a wino from central casting who sings to them. There's a fire escape with one of those retractable bottom sections. There's some flashing coloured lights which give the effect of nearby mainstreet and some noises off like cars going by. It's wet underfoot and night sky overhead. Brick walls to either side.

I come down a couple of steps from a door with either NO ENTRY or EXIT painted on it. It doesn't make a lot of difference. It's an alleyway. It's very like the one Arnie materializes in in *Terminator*. But then an alleyway is an alleyway, and I ain't gonna give this one too many airs and graces. After all, I never described Fangio's at all.

I turn up my trenchcoat collar. The open neck doesn't suit me. Nor does the chill wind which is ruffling my kiss-curl. I'm strictly a hat man. Known for it. Admired for it. I was hat man of the year back in 'fifty-two. I merge enigmatically into the shadows and listen to the sound of a lonely saxophone being dubbed on afterwards.

'Laz?' calls a voice from the past. 'You there?'

'Who's that?'

'It's Vic here.'

I step from the shadows like a penny-whistle player in a cellar full of handbags.

'Ever the master of disguise and description,' says Vic, which I appreciate like you do when someone has stepped *on* the truth rather than *in* it. If you know what I mean, and I'm sure that you do.

'You got the thingamejig?'

'I got it.' Vic pats at his pocket. His pocket is in a safari suit of a type one rarely sees nowadays. But then that's

Vic. He's an original. I could spend hours telling you what this guy's done and what he's got in his wardrobe. But I figure, who gives a damn? Not me, for one. I just hope he doesn't notice I'm bare-headed.

'I notice you're bare-headed,' says Vic.

'So you say.'

'I gotcha.'

'The thingamejig.' I never studied verbal gastronomy so I don't know how to mince words.

Vic pats his pocket again in a way I find mildly irritating.

'I'm gonna want something big up front for this, Laz,' he says.

'Happy to oblige.' I knee Vic in the groin. Vic goes 'erg' the way one would and crumples on the ground the way one does. He's out of the army now, but I'm not looking for a big thank you. What I'm looking for is in his patted pocket. I stoop down and root it out.

It's a green and leafy spheroid about twice the size of something only half as big. A miniature golf ball, say. I hold it up to the light to assure myself that it's the real Sylvester McCoy, which it undoubtably is.

'Barry,' says I, for such is its name. 'Barry, you and I got business.'

'No sweat, chief,' the Time Sprout replies. 'Which one of your ears you want I should squeeze in?'

5

Rex sat in the police cell clutching his privy
parts and bitterly regarding his white shoes.
He knew well enough what was coming next. It always
came around this time in the plot. He would be dragged
from the cell. Manhandled along a corridor. Flung into
a room with a bright desk lamp and a gore-bespattered
floor. Whacked in the ear and interrogated about things
he knew nothing of. Then, when things were really
reaching a crisis point, he would come up with some
ingenious scheme and make good his escape.

As it was all so inevitable, Rex wondered if perhaps
he might simply scrub around the painful bit and make
his escape now.

A key turned in the lock and Rex rose to meet his fate.

'OK, Rex,' Officer Cecil grinned into the cell. 'You're
on.'

The journey up the corridor wasn't too bad. Cecil
truncheoned him about a bit and Sandy kicked him in
the ankle a couple of times. But it was no great shakes.
He was booted through a doorway, which hurt a little,
but not too much, and there was a carpet to break his
fall this time.

The door slammed shut upon the usual manic
chuckles.

'Take a seat,' said the voice of Sam Maggott. Rex looked up at the fat man. 'Have we met?' he asked.

Sam shook his head. 'But I know you, boy. Not often we get a big cheese like you in here.'

'Big cheese,' Rex made a wary face. 'Ah, yes.'

'Yes indeed. Here, let me help you up.' Sam did so. And while he was so doing Rex took in his surroundings. They could have been far worse.

The office had more than enough room for even amateur cat swinging. It was evenly lit, adequately furnished, pleasantly decorated, moderately well heated. Very adjectival. There was a desk, a chair, a watercooler, a ceiling fan, a filing cabinet, a previously-mentioned carpet, a window and a door, which was where Rex came in. Rex did notice two things of considerable interest.

The first was the 1947 *Rock-Ola* jukebox. It was clearly the 1426 model. Basically the same as the 1422, but with the metal grille which replaced the earlier wooden one and the now classic Mother of Plastic jewel effect. The side pilasters featured the new turning cylinders and the diamond-quilted gold fabric superseded the original Art Deco mural, which was, by then, looking somewhat dated.

The other was the large portrait of Elvis Presley that hung behind Maggott's desk.

Sam's plump paws manipulated Rex into the vertical plane. He dusted down Rex's jacket.

'Nice fabric, if a little tight under the armpits. You OK?'

'Not especially.'

'Take a seat.' Sam indicated a comfy-looking sofa.

Rex dropped on to it. 'Thanks.'

'You want a drink or something?'

'That would be nice.'

'Murphy.' Sam spoke to the ceiling. 'Get our guest a drink, will ya?'

'Ten-four, chief,' said a voice from above.

'I don't think I quite understand.' Rex studied the

ceiling and then he studied Sam. 'Will you not be wanting to beat me up then?'

'Beat you up?' Sam made mirth. Rex knew he'd be reaching for the red gingham hankie, and he did. Sam mopped his brow. 'Beat you up? Hell, no. How would that look for the department? Not good in the ratings, that's how. Nah, I just want to sort things out is all.'

'No electrodes?'

'Nah.'

'No nightsticks in the nether regions?'

'Nah.'

'No reading me my rights?'

'Nah.'

'I'll be off then,' said Rex, brightening not a little. 'Very nice to have met you.'

Sam showed Rex his 'piece'. It was a big chrome one with a long polished barrel.

'Hmm,' said Rex.

Knock knock, went the door.

'Come,' said Sam.

Murphy came. Drinks on a tray. And napkins.

Sam made the introductions all round. Murphy shook Rex warmly by the hand. 'I never miss your show. Tell me, those folks, do you really . . . ?'

'Every time.'

'Shiva's sheep!'

'Goodbye, Murphy.'

'Goodbye, chief. Nice to meet you, Mr Mundi.' Murphy took his leave whistling 'Danny Boy'. Sam passed Rex a drink and waddled back to his chair. 'You wanna tell me all about it?'

'About the show?'

'Nah. I don't give *that*—' Sam made an explicit gesture, '—about your show.'

'Ah.' Rex sipped his drink. Tomorrowman Brew. 'Then there's not much to tell. My car was stolen. I went into a bar to call a policeman. A mad news vendor arrived and two cops brutalized me. I shan't press charges. Will you call me a cab?'

'You're a cab.'

'I've never thought much of that gag. Am I being charged with anything or what?'

'Do you want to make your phone call?'

Rex finished his drink. 'Not yet.'

'OK. Then we'll keep this off the record. I don't want to hold you, you know that. I give you grief, your station gives me grief. That's showbiz, I guess. But listen to me. I don't like who you are and I don't like what you do. If it was up to me, then you and your station would be off the air. I can't touch you, but I can make your life difficult. Know what I mean?'

Rex had a reasonably good idea. He let Sam continue.

'I can harass your boyfriends, screw up your credit, bust you every time you take a tinkle. I don't need your kind of trouble and you don't need mine. Got me?'

'Got you.'

'So what are you going to do about it?'

'Bribe you?'

Sam shook his head.

'Get out of your sight and never darken your doorway again?'

Sam shook it once more.

'I'm sorry.' Rex was. 'What do you want me to do?'

Sam delved into a drawer and brought out a pair of blue suede shoes. He tossed them to Rex, who almost caught them.

'Put them on.' Sam gestured with supreme distaste towards Rex's footware. 'Take off those Goddamn blasphemous brogues and dump them in the bin. I'll say nothing this time, but you owe me a big one. Got it?'

'Got it.' Rex had got many things in his time but this however wasn't one of them. He took off the loathsome loafers and dropped them into the wastepaper bin, slipped on the blue suedes, and prepared to take his leave.

'Just one more thing, fella.'

Rex half turned. 'Yes?'

'Any chance of tickets for your show? The wife's a big fan.'

Barry and I walk these mean streets together. These streets have no name, there's blood on the tracks and a darkness on the edge of town. But that's the way we like it. We're on the road to Hell and it ain't paved with good intentions.

I take Barry back to my office. Outside my window the neon sign flashes on and off the way some of them do*, and inside the carpet looks no better for it.

'So what's the deal then, chief?'

I place Barry upon my desk. He's put on a bit of weight since last we met, so it's a top-pocket number rather than an in-your-ear job. I crack open a bottle of Bud, light up a Camel and in the cause of exposition (cos like I say I'm not enigmatic) explain what's to do. I display the dame's watchmacallit, run the holographics and talk through the moving pictures.

'There's two to finger,' says I. 'The big heist at the Museum of Mankind. The entire theological section gone in the twinkling of a fly's eye. No alarms thrown. No evidence of break in. Just gone.'

'Some big number, chief. But how do these two fit into it? Who put them in the frame?'

I explain further. 'These two busted out from a penal colony on Cygnus Major a day after the heist. Same set up. No alarms thrown. No evidence of break out.'

*In the film version of *Blood On My Trenchcoat*, directed by Ray Dennis Steckler and starring Cash Flagg as Laz, the neon sign flashed the words JAEHBULON BEER. P.P. Penrose states in his biography of Woodbine, *Some Called Him Laz*, that Jahbulon is the 'ineffable name of the Great Architect of the Universe'.

'A day *after* the heist, chief? I don't get it.'

'Do the names Johnny Dee and Ed Kelley mean anything to you?'

'Dee and Kelley? But chief, those two cost you your wife, your job at the department, a dog named Blue and six months in intensive care.'

'I know that.' I knew that. 'Two of the most dangerous men in the galaxy. Tempus Fugitives. Time-travelling criminals. None meaner and none smarter. See the beauty of their evil scheme. Using a time-travelling device they bust out of jail, go back and commit the robbery on the previous day. This gives them not only the perfect alibi but a chance to sell all the loot, and raise the cash to purchase the time-travelling device to break out of jail with.'

'Er, chief . . . I don't think that quite . . .'

'This is one we can't play by the book, Barry. It's going to need a lot of thought.'

'Certainly more than you've given it so far.'

'What's that, Barry?'

'Nothing, chief.'

'I got a big score to settle with these two. A *big* score.' I suck upon my cigarette, strike a manly pose against the flashing neon and muse upon the exact dimensions of the score I have to settle.

'You suit the open neck, Laz,' says Barry. 'Good strong profile, also.'

'Thanks.' I never court a compliment, but when one's offered I know how to take it. Only a frog wets its own bed when there's a rain hat in the closet.

'Sounds like it could be a tricky business, chief. These two could now be anywhere, at any time, disguised as anybody and travelling under any name and if I recall correctly, you only work the four sets.'

'Just the same four.'

'Does rather limit our field of operations, chief. You couldn't stretch a point and add, say, a marketplace

63

in ancient Rome or a bordello in nineteenth-century Paris?'

I raise the eyebrow of admonishment towards the Time Sprout. He knows the score. Me and him go back a long way. A *long* way.

'Remember that run in we had in Atlantis?' I ask.

'Sure, chief. Wasn't that in *Death Wears a Green Tuxedo*?'*

'You got it.'

'Where we tracked down Micky "Spangles" McMurdo, otherwise known as the Manhattan Mangler?'

'Go on.'

'Well, as I recall, Spangles had gone Tempus Fugitive and set himself up as the high priest in the temple of BAH-REAH the All Knowing.'

'Correct.'

'A temple of unimaginable splendour, twice the size of the Yankee Stadium. A temple whose golden adornments and jewel encrusted statuary made that of Solomon look like a five-and-dime.'

'That's the one. And do you also recall where I made the arrest?'

'In a darkened alleyway at the rear of the temple, wasn't it?'

I lower the eyebrow of admonishment, which is beginning to give me a headache, and make a knowing wink. 'You ever see a city without an alleyway?'

'No, chief. You got me on that one.'

I knew that I had. The run in with Spangles had cost me three children, a goldfish called Neville, life membership of the Groucho Club and two years in Detox. But that was all water under the knee as far as I was concerned.

'So, Barry. To work.' I flick my smouldering cigarette butt out through the open window and settle back into

*A Lazlo Woodbine thriller.

my chair. From the street below comes a sudden cry of pain, a squealing of motor-cycle tyres and a number of deafening crashes. I get up and close the window. I need interruptions now like a five-bar gate needs a continental breakfast. 'To work.'

'Right, chief.'

'The way I see it, Barry. I got a big score to settle with these two. A *big* score.' I light up another cigarette, strike a manly pose against the flashing neon and muse once more upon the exact dimensions of the score I have to settle.

But as that kind of stuff can get a little samey after a while, I decide to take a dive under my desk instead.

The bullet sang through the etched glass of my partition door, ate a hole out of the middle of my chair-back and buried its face in my wall. I don't wait for Goddo, I tear the trusty Smith and Wesley from my shoulder holster and come up firing. The barrel spits its *Cargo of Death*.* I pump five rounds through the door and hear the body fall, rise to my feet and dust down my trenchcoat.

'Nice shooting, chief. Who do you think you killed?'

'Couldn't say.' I check my cuffs. Sometimes when you take a dive for cover you lose a button. This time I was lucky.

'Think we should go over and check out the corpse?'

I shake my head. 'No can do.' I give the belt loops the once-over, an awkward dive can often put undue strain on the stitching. It looked OK, though.

'But chief, the identity of the assassin could be just what you need to bust the whole case wide open.'

I give my head another shake. I noticed a small grease stain on my left lapel, but it was nothing to worry about. Any leading brand of spot remover could handle that.

'But chief . . .'

*A Lazlo Woodbine thriller.

'What, Barry?' I straighten my collar.

'The body, chief.'

'Do you see any body, Barry?'

'No chief, but . . .'

'And why don't you see any body, Barry?'

'Because he fell outside in the corridor, chief.'

'And?'

'And you don't work corridors, chief. Sorry.'

'Don't mention it, Barry. You just got carried away in the heat of the moment. That's why I'm the hero of this novel and you ain't.'

'That's all you know, Shithead.'

'What's that, Barry?'

'Nothing, chief.'

The big front hall of the police station looked very much the way they always do. Cavernous, echoey. A lot of cops with sharp-looking uniforms and seen-it-all expressions berating all and sundry and reading people their rights. Super-Fly-style pimps, all broad-brimmed hats, long leather overcoats and stack-soled shoes, making free with the 'F' word and demanding the return of their 'old ladies'. Street punks with bandaged heads being comforted by girls in black bondage wear. A padré consoling the parents of a murder victim. A bag lady singing. Gang boys with headbands and oily teeshirts calling everybody 'homes'. Winos pleading the fifth amendment. Detectives in shirtsleeves punching the coffee machine. Prostitutes in short fur coats looking like Tina Turner. Recidivists doing whatever it is they do.

You've seen the movies, you know what I mean.

Rex collected his 'personal effects' from a desk sergeant who bore an uncanny resemblance to Spencer Tracy.

'Sign here.' The desk sergeant turned clipboard and pen toward Rex. Rex shook his head and signed. It didn't make a lot of sense. They were giving him back the stolen billfold and everything.

'Well, I'll be off then.' Rex turned to be just that.

Officer Cecil loomed large. 'This way out, Rex.' He took a firm grip upon the hero's right elbow and steered him towards a side corridor which Rex correctly surmised led to a nice quiet alley.

'Oh no.' Rex jerked back. 'No more hitting. The chief says you are to extend me every courtesy. I will leave by the front door, if you don't mind.'

'I do mind as it happens.'

'Cecil.' Rex stood his ground. 'Don't you ever get tired of all the mindless violence?'

Cecil scratched his shaven head with the business end of his truncheon. 'Well . . . now that you mention it. No. And it's *Officer* Cecil to you. Come on.'

'Officer Cecil. Don't you feel that there might be a little more to life than whacking people about with your nightstick?'

'I've never given the matter a lot of thought,' said Officer Cec. 'I personally subscribe to a somewhat syncretic world view. It is my inherent belief, founded I might add, upon observation and experience, rather than conjecture and theory, that society consists of two basic castes. Namely, in essence, those who get whacked and those who do the whacking. Now, you might consider this an overly-simplistic dichotomy, issued by an apologist as a disclaimer for the practice of brutalism. But there you would be misinterpreting the underlying pluralistic duality which subdivides the sociological framework and constitutes what Jung referred to as "an unfolded totality symbol, the self in its empirical aspect".'

'I would?'

'You would. You see, the metaphor is axiomatic. Which is to say that at an unconscious level the whacker and the whackee become one and the same. The master becomes the servant, the punisher the punished. Have you ever read Sir John Rimmer's *Differential Determinations of Psychophysical Judgements and their Significance in the Transposition of Relational Responses?'*

'I believe I might have skimmed through it.'

'Fascinating work,' Cecil continued. 'Suggests that we each hold within ourselves the germ of Godhood, but that we create our own limitations through an ingrained subconscious desire to merge with the whole, rather than draw apart and find our true selves. The text does at time become somewhat sesquipedalian but I can empathize with the syllogism behind it.'

'Yes,' said Rex. 'I'm sure that you can.'

'So if you'll kindly accompany me to the alleyway I'll give you a sound whacking and we'll say no more about it.'

'Fair enough,' said Rex. 'Down this way is it?'

6

*5. And later Elvis did play Memphis
which was then in Egypt. And greatly
did the gig go down.
6. But afterwards the cheque of Pharaoh
did bounce mightily.*

The Suburban Book of the Dead

Rex didn't receive a whacking in the alley.
Instead, he and Cecil discussed Wittgenstein's
Philosophical Investigations, logical positivism and the
Hegelian dialectic, in which the contradiction between a
proposition and its antithesis is resolved into a higher
truth. They touched upon Gestalt psychology and behaviour potentiality and finally, as it was growing late,
Cecil shook Rex by the hand, hailed a cab for him, tucked
a fifty-dollar bill into his top pocket and instructed the
cab driver to drop Rex off at an inexpensive rooming
house where he might be put up for the night.

Rex thanked Cecil very much, promised to return his
copy of *Human Reactions in a Maze of Fixed Orientations*
as soon as he'd read it, and was driven off into the night.

Rex sank back into his seat, praying for all he was
worth that the road ahead was not paved with running
gags about psychology.

Having driven Rex through streets of ever-increasing
ghastliness, the cab driver dropped him off on a wind-
blown corner. He waived the fare upon Rex's promise of
free tickets for the *Nemesis* show and mentioned in

passing that he had once had Sigmund Freud's great-granddaughter in the back of his cab.

Rex smiled his thanks and enquired exactly which of the sordid-looking buildings in the run-down neighbourhood the cabby recommended.

'Over there pal. It's down at the end of Lonely Street, it's called . . .'

'No. Don't tell me,' Rex replied. 'I think I know exactly what it's called.'

'OK then, pal. Have a nice day.'

Rex trudged down to the end of Lonely Street and gazed up at the gaunt hotel. Warm and welcoming it wasn't. Four storeys of grey concrete relieved by windows of blackened glass. Rex shook his head; this promised to be a bundle of laughs.

He slouched up the down-trodden steps, pushed open a creaking door and entered an ill-lit lobby. A single naked bulb managed to cast a wan grey light, which suited the all-grey decor just fine. Rex peered through the gloom towards two figures, hunched in attitudes of disconsolation at the reception desk.

'Good evening,' said Rex.

'Good?' The bell hop's tears kept flowing. The desk clerk remained in that hue which is forever night.

Rex smiled cheerfully upon them. 'I'd like a room for the night.'

'A room for the night?' The bell hop collapsed into further sobbings. The desk clerk fixed Rex with a bitter glare.

'Are you taking the piss, or what?'

'No. I'd like a room for the night. That's all.'

'I'd like a room for the night.' The sarcasm in the desk clerk's voice was not lost upon Rex. 'Well, you can't have one.'

'Why not?'

'Can you read?' The desk clerk thumbed over his shoulder. The sign on the wall said

70

BROKEN-HEARTED LOVERS ONLY.
BY ORDER OF THE MANAGEMENT.

'Hmm.' Rex maintained an even tone. 'Then, if that's the case, you can consider me as broken-hearted as they come. Single room, please, just for the one night.'

'You don't look very broken-hearted to me.'

'I'm putting on a brave face. Where do I sign?'

'You don't.' The desk clerk folded his arms. 'If you want my opinion, I'd say that you're down but by no means out. It's probably just the jacket. If you'll take my advice you'll trot back up the street. There's a hotel there, The Elton, which caters for travellers with ill-fitting suits.'

Rex could feel the red mist coming on. He'd had a 'rougher one' than Sam Maggott. 'Now just you see here. I was recommended to this establishment by a certain Officer Cecil. Perhaps you know him. Big chap, penchant for sadism.'

'Everyone knows Officer Cecil,' blubbered the bell hop.

'Well, he's a very close friend of mine and he's going to be mightily displeased if he learns that you refused me a room. In fact—' as Rex had given up on the truth he thought he might as well press right on '—in fact, I happen to work for the Police Department as an undercover agent.'

'Undercover agent, eh?' The desk clerk fingered his chin. 'Well listen to me, fella. I don't care if you're an estate agent, a travel agent, a literary agent or a bloody chemical re-agent. It's more than my job's worth to let you in here. This is a *broken-hearted lovers' zone* and that's that.'

'Undercover agent?' The bell hop sobbed deeply. 'Damned heretic, more like.'

'Heretic?' Rex recalled the Curious Case of the Blasphemous Brogues. 'Now just let me get this straight. This is Heartbreak Hotel. It's down at the end of Lonely Street. It has a bell hop whose tears keep flowing and a desk clerk who dresses as you do. And it only rents rooms to broken-hearted lovers, who no doubt spend their time here crying in the gloom. Am I right so far?'

'You certainly know your scripture.'

'Scripture . . .' Rex paused. 'Scripture, you say? Thus it would be heresy for anyone other than a broken-hearted lover to check-in here?'

The bell hop and the desk clerk exchanged glances. Rex sought to discern a number of unspoken words being passed to and fro.

Finally the desk clerk spoke once more. 'Don't I know you?' he asked.

'No,' said Rex. 'You don't.'

'Yes I do. You're that chap off the telly.'

'No!' screamed Rex. 'I'm not!'

'He is.' The bell hop blew his nose. 'He does that game show where all the contestants get—'

'I don't.'

'Well, listen to me fella, and listen well. I don't care who you are or what you are. But broken-hearted lover you ain't. And if you don't get out of this hotel I shall be forced to call a Repo Man. And neither of us want that, do we?'

'A Repo Man?' The words went click in Rex's head. 'Tell me what you think of this.' He fished out the billfold and displayed the card which had waved goodbye to Laura Lynch's legs.

'Oh.' Whatever colour there might have been drained at once from the desk clerk's face. 'Oh, I see, *sir*. Yes indeed . . . Well, I trust you are satisfied with my stoicism . . . I do my job well, sir. You'll find no deviants or heretics here. Oh no, indeed.'

'Good.' Rex nodded politely. 'I'm very pleased to hear it. Now I shall require a room for the night.'

'Oh yes, sir. Certainly.' With an unsteady hand the desk clerk took down a key from beneath the BROKEN-HEARTED LOVERS ONLY sign.

'Bell hop. Check that this room is suitable for our honoured guest.'

'Yes sir,' The bell hop left his damp patch of carpet and sped off at the treble.

'Never stops crying, that one, sir. Credit to his calling.'

'I see.' Rex didn't really. 'Why does he cry all the time, by the way? I've always wondered.'

'I've never given it a lot of thought, sir. In my opinion it probably stems from some childhood crisis. Possibly a mother fixation. A deep-seated Oedipus complex would result in a negative psycho-physical response to outer stimuli. A subject in such a state of inner tension could only find relief from his retroactive inhibitions via an emotional trigger. More a conditioned reflex than a conscious desire to cry. Have you ever read—'

Rex stepped forward and punched the desk clerk's lights out.

'Very amusing,' said he.

Presently the bell hop returned. He spied out the prone psychologist but didn't broach the matter. He led Rex up a flight of shabby stairs and opened a door before him.

'This is our best room, sir. I hope it meets with your approval. Should you require anything don't hesitate to ring down. Of course, normally we ignore all calls from our guests. Management policy, all in keeping with Holy Writ.'

'Admirable.'

'Thank you, sir. We aim to depress.' He closed the door upon Rex and shuffled away down the corridor weeping at the top of his voice.

Rex gave the room the once-over. To say that it was wretched would be to sing its praises. The tomb-like chamber contained a miserable bunk, a joyless chair, a dispirited chest of drawers, a real Job's comforter of a television and a carpet so woebegone as to bring a tear to a glass eye.

Rex shook his head. 'Very cosy.' He wandered over to the chest of drawers and gave the top one a pull. The grief-laden handle came off in his hand. Rex sighed and wormed his finger into the hole. He worked the drawer open. Several bottles of gin, a cut-throat razor and a dozen boxes of sleeping pills caught his jaundiced peeper.

'Hmm,' went Rex. 'Courtesy of the management no doubt.' He helped himself to a bottle of gin and slumped on to the bed. The mattress had evidently been stuffed with flints. There was no sign of a pillow.

Rex uncapped the bottle and sniffed it suspiciously. He took a small swig and tried to make some sense of it all. Here he was in Heartbreak Hotel. In a city called Presley which appeared to be somewhere in the USA. In a time which was his own but a world which wasn't. A world of curious laws, where his living double ran the dreaded *Nemesis* show and Repo Men were something to fear.

It was all a little confusing. Or was it? Rex took a larger swig of gin and turned around to confront the Job's comforter.

'Let's see what you have to say for yourself,' he said.

Of course there was no remote controller, so Rex dragged the set across to the bed, sat down before it and pressed the 'on'.

A picture wavered uncertainly on to the screen. A female talking head of some familiarity announced, 'MTWTV news on the hour every five minutes.'

'Oh yes?'

'And the big story this evening is still the alien kidnapping.'

'What?'

'Two-headed love-child Harpo/Chico, son of Oscar-winning star Debbie Nixon and international rock idol Mojo, was snatched in broad daylight from the Graceland Shopping Mall by invisible creatures.'

'What?'

'The devastated couple, still under heavy sedation and seen here leaving the Tom Parker Memorial Hospital, took time out to speak to our reporter Dick Adamski.'

Dick: 'Debbie, Mojo, any word yet of Harpo/Chico?'

Mojo: 'Nope.'

Dick: 'How are you and your fragrant wife bearing up?'

Mojo: 'Obviously it's a pretty traumatic time for us both. I'm just glad we're with the Tom Parker medi-care plan. A programme tailored to the personal needs of its clients. A caring service which offers a complete across-the-range facility, employing full state-of-the-art technology and the back-up of qualified medical practitioners. For just fifty dollars down and twenty a month we get—'

'What?' Rex changed channel.

'Don't mess with this guy, he knows karate.'

'Goes with the sickle,' the on-screen Presley replied.

'*Roustabout!*' Rex brought the sound up further and peered at Elvis. It wasn't Elvis.

'It's not Elvis,' said Rex.

'And this particular sickle,' the lookalike continued, 'is a Koshibo Commander 7500. Six valve, hyper-glide turbo. It gives me the kind of ride I'm looking for at a price I can afford.'

'Eh?' went Rex, who had tired of 'what?'. He tried another channel. It broadcast non-stop commercials, as did another and another and another. Rex gave his head another shake, pressed another channel and then took a very unpleasant turn.

His own face leered out at him. 'Welcome,' it cried. 'To . . . wait for it . . . NEMESIS . . .' The band struck up, the lights all flashed, the bells rang, the special star-buzzer buzzed and a very large studio audience threw itself about with orgiastic fervour.

Rex gazed in horrified fascination. It was him. There. True in each and every detail. His very *doppelgänger*.

Rex gazed on, dumbstruck. He heard his own voice as

it whipped up the audience. Watched the face as it grinned and winked.

And then something touched him. Something that chilled him to the marrow and overwhelmed him with revulsion.

An uncontrollable loathing entered his veins like poison and struck at his heart. That creature on the screen wasn't him. Nothing like. It was some dark mirror-image, a travesty, a hideous mockery. An evil opposite.

The swallowed gin was once more in his mouth. Rex croaked, gagged and vomited into the face of his other self.

The face of the ANTI-REX.

7

7. And Elvis was dead put out that
Pharaoh should have stitched him up.
And he did curl his lip and cry out to
his many fans saying, 'Forget the
pyramids, we're out of here!'

The Suburban Book of the Dead

Rex pushed back the sick-bespattered tele-vision and wiped his mouth on the bed sheet. His hands were shaking and his head swam. He needed a glass of something, and not gin. Water, perhaps?

The room didn't boast a wash basin amongst its other lacks of attraction and so Rex sought out the house phone. It lay beneath the bed. Disconnected.

There had to be a bathroom somewhere, surely. Rex took himself off to hunt for it. He padded softly down the corridor; he had no wish to disturb any of the broken-hearted lovers at such a late hour.

Rex paused at the head of the staircase. Hushed, yet urgent voices reached his ear. He crept down a few steps and peeped between the banisters. The bell hop and the desk clerk were jabbering in low tones to a pair of tall, dark and dangerous-looking types. Rex craned forward to overhear the conversation.

'That's why I called you,' whispered the fat-lipped desk clerk. 'He represented himself as a Repo Man, but he's no LCP . . .'

'And he's not the chap off the telly,' the bell hop put

in. 'The chap off the telly was just on the telly a few minutes ago.'

'And he punched my lights out,' the desk clerk complained. 'Not the chap off the telly, that is . . .'

'Heretic,' muttered the bell hop. 'Deviant and subversive. No doubt about it.'

One of the dark and dangerous-looking types spoke. The voice was deadpan, metallic. More a phonemic broadcast than real speech. It was the voice of a machine.

'You have acted promptly and with correctness, citizen. We will deal with the matter now. Please vacate the premises and take cover from the blast.'

'The blast?' The desk clerk flapped his hands. 'No. Wait . . .'

'We must explode the entire building. Eliminate any possible source of contamination.'

'But destroy the whole hotel? Isn't that being somewhat over-zealous?'

The second dangerous-looking type spoke with the first. 'Perhaps these two have already become contaminated. Better they remain here and die.'

The desk clerk now took to wringing his hands. 'No sirs, please. We're not contaminated. We called you, didn't we?'

'Then leave at once.'

'But our livelihoods?'

'You will be allocated new parts. There are always vacancies at street level. As you will be both homeless and unemployed you will be perfectly qualified. Present yourselves here tomorrow at ten. An official from the Department of Human Resources will be waiting.'

The desk clerk gnawed on his knuckles. 'The other guests, then? You can't kill them all. That goes against the prime directive of Management Services. Waste not, want not.'

'Remain where you are,' ordered dark and dangerous number one. 'We will cogitate upon this matter.'

A long minute passed. The bell hop chewed his handkerchief and the desk clerk hopped from one foot to the other. Rex hovered in anticipation. The two enigmatic visitors remained still as dummies. They weren't breathing.

Suddenly they both spoke at once, frightening the life out of the bell hop.

'We are instructed to observe a course of damage limitation. We will localize the area of devastation. Which room does the deviant inhabit?'

'Room number six. Up the stairs and first on the left.'

'Thank you, citizen. You may return to your duties.' The dark and dangerous pair turned as one and stalked towards the staircase.

The bell hop broke down in tears.

'Ah, shaddup!' said the desk clerk.

The dark and dangerous pair strode along the corridor.

Rex watched them from the second-floor landing, where he now lay in hiding.

The dark and dangerous pair halted before the door of room number six.

'Heat trace and organic residues registered within. Two metres, 33° SSW,' said one.

'Three-metre controlled pulse, contained exterior shock effect,' said the other.

They placed their palms gently against the door. Rex heard a dull humming sound which rose swiftly to a shrill whine. There came a muffled thump from within room number six. Then a shock wave which popped Rex's ears and loosened his bowels. Then silence.

Rex peeped over the banister rail. The dark assassins turned from the door and marched back along the corridor.

Rex listened to their heavy synchronized footsteps. They went down the stairs, along the hall. Rex heard the street door slam. And then silence once more. With dry mouth and pounding heart he crept down the stairs and approached room number six. He tried the handle. Then he stifled his own scream. The handle was red hot.

Rex blew on to his scorched mitt and cursed beneath his breath. He thrust his hand into his jacket pocket and quickly turned the handle.

The door fell open and Rex's mouth did likewise. The room wasn't exactly the way he had left it.

A crisp circle of destruction, three metres in diameter had cut the very heart out of the room. Within it nothing whatever remained.

At the boundary of the circle the bed slumped forward in an attitude of prayer. Its bottom end, sliced off in a sweeping arc, exposed the rocky innards of the mattress to quite striking effect. The front of the chest of drawers had undergone similar heroic surgery, cleanly razored away. Rex glimpsed a bottle sheared from top to bottom.

Of the sick-splattered television no trace remained but for a sparking wire which terminated at the edge of the terrible circle of nothingness.

I used to shoot a lot of pool back in the old days. Helped me to forget, I guess. In this business there are times when you need to forget. And others when you need to remember. Like now, for instance.

Like now I needed to remember a face. A face I used to know before I shot pool. A face I had now forgotten. It was a long face. A face with a cleft chin, a broad mouth, even teeth and a small scar on the upper lip. There was a nose to crack jokes on and a pair of dark eyebrows which shaded two of the greenest eyes I've ever seen. The ears were small, the left had a mole on the lobe, the right didn't. The whole sheebang was framed by a mop of soft amber hair. I knew that face almost as well as I knew my own. But I just couldn't call it to mind.

'The man's a complete buffoon.'

'What's that, Barry?'

'Nothing, chief.'

'Did I ever tell you about how I used to shoot pool, Barry?'

'Many times, chief. Can't say you had me riveted.'

'You got something against pool?'

'The concept of men with long sticks knocking innocent green spheroids into holes doesn't hold a lot of charm for me, as it happens. Will we be making a start on solving the case soon, or do you want to sit back in your chair again and consider the exact dimensions of the score you have to settle?'

I give Barry the cold, hard look I usually keep for Tuesdays.

'OK,' said I. 'What have we got so far?'

'Very little in the way of action.'

'I'm saving myself.'

'Sure you are, chief.'

'The way I see it, Barry, we have to look for the connection.'

'I'm listening, chief. Just.'

'There's always a Mr Big behind every operation.'

'The guy who takes the plunge off the roof at the end, right?'

'Right. And the only way to find Mr Big is to go looking.'

'Shrewd thinking, chief. So where do you propose to start?'

'Well . . .' I make that quite a long well. Then I say, 'We start on 28 July 2061.'

'Good grief!' Barry falls off my desk on to the carpet that dare not speak its name. He's rattled. I pick him up and give him a quick wipe over. 'Rattled?' I enquire.

'Er . . . um . . . how, exactly, did you come up with that particular date?'

I have him there and *he* knows that *I* knew that I do. 'I just reasoned it out,' I tell him, casual as a courgette in a crock of court-bouillon. 'Let me explain . . .'

'Woodboon?' The voice comes to me from the corridor.

It's a voice I know almost as well as I know my own. It belongs to Charlie Swinburn, my landlord, and it continues thus: 'Woodboon, there's another stiff outside your office bleeding on my carpet. That's the fifth this week. Come out and shift it or there's gonna be trouble. And this watch you foisted on me for the rent don't work.'

'July 28th 2061,' I tell Barry. 'And step on the gas.'

'Any specific location you favour, chief?'

'How about the alleyway behind Heartbreak Hotel on Lonely Street?'

'Why there, chief?'

I have him again and he knows it, but I don't want to shame the little guy.

'Just a hunch,' I tell him as we head *Backwards Into Peril*.*

Rex found the fire escape, an iron staircase which terminated in one of those retractable bottom sections. Rex swung down upon it into the alleyway. He was cold, tired and hungry, and he dearly needed the toilet. Rex made the furtive eye movements of the fugitive and merged into the shadows.

'I wish I was home in my bed,' said Rex.

At the end of the alleyway a long black car cruised into the night. Rex glimpsed the passing profiles of the dark and dangerous non-men. The car rose suddenly into the sky and streaked away.

Rex turned up the collar of his armpit-hugging jacket and blew into cupped hands. 'If only I had the faintest idea of what's going on here,' he said, between blowings. 'I'm certain I could make a really positive contribution to the plot. It just isn't fair.'

And how right he was. But then, if there was any fairness in the world, this book would probably never

*A Lazlo Woodbine thriller.

have been written in the first place. Rankin would have retired years ago on the Nobel Prize money and the numerous lucrative film deals on books past. He would no doubt be laid out in some exclusive Thailand brothel with one of those exotic eastern ladies being lowered on to his John Thomas in the now legendary revolving split-cane bucket seat even as we speak. But there you go. Or don't, as the case may be.

Rex sank down the wall, hugged his knees and fell into an uneasy sleep. What he really needed was one of those useful coincidences to help things along. But they're such a cliché, aren't they?

A rear door opened and a figure issued into the alleyway. The figure was the desk clerk. He was drunk and he fell directly over Rex Mundi.

Rex leapt from sleep and pinned the man in black against the wall. 'Speak to me,' he said.

The desk clerk covered his face. 'No. You're dead.'

'Not yet. I need answers.'

'I don't know any.'

'What is a Repo Man?'

'I don't know.'

Rex smote the desk clerk. 'Tell me if you wish to live.'

'A Repository Man. An LCP.'

'LCP?'

'Liquid Crystal Person. Leave me alone.'

'Those two who blew up my room. They were . . . LCPs?'

'Who are you?'

'Your best friend or your worst enemy. What do they do?'

'Repo Men maintain the status quo. Maintain balance. That's what we all do, isn't it?'

'Who do they work for? The man on the *Nemesis* show? Tell me.'

'Him? No.'

'Who then?'

'The department. The Department of Human Resources.'

'And what about Elvis?'

'Elvis? Leave me alone.'

'Not yet. Elvis. Who is he to you? What is he?'

'Are you mad?'

'Who is he?' Rex slapped the desk clerk's face. He didn't like doing it, but . . . 'Elvis. What is he?'

'He's God. For God's sake. Elvis is God!'

The desk clerk slipped from consciousness. Rex eased him carefully down the wall. 'God,' he whispered. 'Elvis is God.'

There came a sudden sparkling in the alleyway and a great rushing of wind. Crackles of electricity snapped to and fro highlighting the garbage cans, the fallen desk clerk and the frightened face of Rex Mundi.

Rex took to his heels and fled.

Barry the Time Sprout said, 'We're here, chief.'

8

9. *And for forty years the children of
Israel did wander in the desert.*
10. *And finally Elvis said unto Moses
'Stuff this for a game of soldiers,
let's follow those guys on the camels.'*

The Suburban Book of the Dead

The new sun rose over Presley City, stain-
ing the jukebox towers with delicate tones
of cyclamen, strawberry, plum, peach, poppy, peony,
geranium, vermilion and a colour which is actually called
rose du Barry. In a muddy brown dumpster in a bad part
of town Rex Mundi cowered with the lid pulled down.
So he missed it.

I turn up the collar of my trenchcoat and stick my
chiselled chin out at the new day. This being one in the
eye for all those smarty pants who figure you can't
put a first-person character into a third-person chapter.
Peasants.

'Chef?' I hear the voice of Barry, who is hunkered
down in my top pocket.

'Say on,' says I.

'Chief, why did you have to choose 28 July 2061 when
you have so many other much nicer dates to choose
from?'

'You have some personal problem with 28 July 2061?'
I give my hems the once-over. Time travel can sometimes
play havoc with your trenchcoat hems. I had a hem go

down on me back in sixty-six; cost me the love of a good woman, a year's subscription to *Time* magazine, both of my nipples and a partridge in a pear tree. But that's another story.*

'Chief, I can live with the twenty-eighth, just. The twenty-ninth if pushed really hard. But on no account do I intend to be here on the thirtieth. You dig?'

'I gotcha. Would you like that I reveal all?' The hems are hunky dory but I might have my tailor put some reinforcement into the shoulder pads when I get back.

'Reveal all, chief.'

'Guess what I've got here.' I pull from concealment a big red book.

'*This Is Your Life*. I'm deeply touched. What can I say?'

'Say nothing, Barry. What I have here is *Miller's Antiques Price Guide for 2461*.

'Well, silly old me.'

'Quite so.' I flick idly through the big red book. 'A-ha!' I exclaim of a sudden. 'And what have we here?'

'The page you marked back at the office, chief?'

'The very same.' I read from the very same. 'The Presley hoard. Artefacts and artworks of the Living God. Three hundred items in all, housed permanently at the Museum of Mankind. Items date from 10,000BP to 2061AD. They were gathered together and hidden at the time of the Third Holocaust. They remained buried for nearly three hundred years until their rediscovery by eminent archeologist Sir John Rimmer 23rd.' I close the book. 'See a little light at the end of the tunnel, Barry?'

'Probably a train coming, chief. Would you care to expound further?'

'Naturally. You asked why I should choose 28 July 2061, did you not? Simple deduction. This is the precise date when the entire Presley hoard was gathered together and stored away. Previous to this time the items were

Farewell My Window, a Lazlo Woodbine thriller.

spread far and wide across the globe. But at this one moment they were all together. This moment is now. We are here. The Presley hoard is here. We are going to locate it and return it to the museum. What do you think about that, eh?'

'I'm gobsmacked, chief. But might I just ask a couple of small yet pertinent questions?'

'If you must.'

'Well, firstly, why have we come all the way back here when it would have been far easier to simply skip back a few days and lie in wait for Dee and Kelley to break into the museum. Catch them *in flagrante delicto*, as it were?'

'Poor detective work, Barry?'

'And how so, chief?'

'Because, Barry. If I catch them before they have committed the crime, then the artworks don't get stolen. And if the artworks don't get stolen then I don't get called in on a big fat fee to locate them.'

'Neat thinking, chief.'

'Exactly. Now, like you said a couple of chapters ago, the chances of finding Dee and Kelley are pretty damn remote. But the chances of finding the stolen artworks, which we know for a fact are at this very moment somewhere in the neighbourhood, these chances are another thing entirely.'

'All well and good chief, but . . .'

'But, Barry?'

'But, chief, if we locate the artworks and take them forward in time to the museum, then Sir John Rimmer can't dig them up.'

'Tough on Sir John.'

'No, but chief, if he doesn't dig them up then he can't give them to the museum. And if he can't give them to the museum then they can't be in the museum for Dee and Kelley to steal. Am I making myself clear?'

The little guy was on to something, but I didn't want

87

him getting a swelly head. 'A mere backgammon,' I tell him.

'It's bagatelle, you dumb-assed . . .'

'What's that, Barry?'

'Nothing, chief.'

'OK. So let's make tracks.'

'Er, chief, just one other tiny little detail.'

'Details, always details.'

'Well, perhaps this is quite a large detail. I did mention my small concern regarding the date. You are aware of exactly what goes down here in two days time.'

'Of course, Barry. The Third Holocaust. Nuclear devastation on a scale hitherto undreamt of. Millions dead, two-thirds of the world laid to waste. Twenty-five years of nuclear night.'

'On 30 July 2061. Just two days from now.'

'So?' says I with more *savior-faire* than a spaniel in a sperm bank. 'What's the big deal?'

'Chief, I don't think you realize what a very dangerous business this is.'

'You mean that the future of civilization and probably the very fabric of universal existence hangs on this one?'

'More than you know, chief. For one thing, if . . .'

I stuff Barry down deep into my pocket. Sometimes you can take just so much from a talking sprout and no more.

Rex awoke amongst the garbage. It didn't smell too bad. It was that Hollywood garbage that actors with special clauses in their contracts deign to fall into. Cardboard, polystyrene, shredded paper, that sort of thing. How come Rex hadn't jumped into the dumpster next door that was full of pig manure and dead chickens was anyone's guess. Perhaps someone 'up there' liked him. Or perhaps not.

Rex climbed from his hidyhole and gave the new day a cursory glance. It didn't look too promising, but he was still prepared to give it his best shot. His jacket didn't fit too well, but at least his shoes were kosher. And he did have the fifty-dollar bill. And he also had a really sneaky idea.

Rex straightened his shoulders, dusted himself down and hailed a convenient cab.

'Morning pal,' said last night's cabby. 'Caught your show. Great stuff. What about those tickets, then?'

'I was just on my way to pick them up.' Rex climbed into the cab. 'A couple of calls on the way if you don't mind.'

'No sweat, matey. Where to then?'

Rex's stomach grumbled bitterly. 'Breakfast,' said his mouth.

My office was just as I remembered it. Or would. Or almost would. The key fits the nice new lock and I walk within.

I'm impressed with the nice new carpet. Very spruce. And the nice new chair, which as yet didn't have a bullet hole in it. But then I was still in 28 July 2061, in case you're getting confused.

I know what you're thinking. You're thinking, how come I have these very items in my twenty-fifth-century office, when they are about to get blown to buggery in the Third Holocaust a couple of days from now. Ain't ya?

Well, if you come up with the answer, be sure and let me know.

I breathe in the ambience. It's sweeter than a Swiss cheese in a sword swallower's back pocket. I step over to the window and draw up the venetian blind. Presley City. The whole town laid out like a lady wrestler at a biker's barbecue. What a dump. Blowing this God awful travesty off the face of the planet was the least anyone could do. I'd do it myself if I'd had the time. But I don't.

I dig out Barry and set him up on the nice new desk,

drop into my chair and check messages on the answer-phone. I know the first voice almost as well as I know my own. It says: 'Woodborn, this is Sam Maggott. You got just two days left to pay back that five thousand dollars you borrowed, or else. Got me?'

'Sounds like Sam's having a "rough one", chief.'

'He'll have a rougher one in a couple of days. What else do we have?'

'Mr Wideburn. This is the Acme Watercooler Company. If your account isn't cleared by the thirtieth then we shall be forced to repossess your appliance.'

'Up yours.'

'Mr Wodbine, that car you sold me is a turkey. I want my money back . . .'

I fast-forward and listen to the next message. And the next and the next and the next. After a while they get a little boring.

'Seems that your many times great-granddaddy skipped town in the nick of time, chief.'

'The luck of the Woodbines, Barry. He had to survive the Third Holocaust or I wouldn't be here.'

'That makes sense at least. Any more messages left?'

'Just the one. Shall I play it?'

'Why not. In for a penny, eh, chief?'

I give Barry the kind of look you could slice bacon with, but I play the message.

'Mr Woodbine. I have the information you want. The whereabouts of you-know-what. I'm at the gorgeously-appointed Love Me Tender Massage Parlor on East Fifty-third and Mainline. I'll meet you in the alleyway at the back at eleven o'clock sharp. Come alone.'

I tip Barry the wink. 'We're rolling,' says I.

'Well . . .' The sprout looks doubtful, which is something you really have to see to appreciate. 'I'm not certain. Something doesn't smell quite right to me.'

'You mean the way he . . .'

'Exactly.'

'I noticed that, too.'

'I thought you had.'

'I knew that you did.'

'You did?'

'Of course I did.'

'That's OK, then.'

'I knew that it would be.'

'You knew?'

'Of course I knew.'

'That's OK, then.'

'You said that.'

'I did?'

'Of course you did.'

'I thought that I had. Shouldn't it cut to the next scene now?'

'You mean like—'

Rex wiped the crumbs from his chin and finished up his coffee. The cabby had the meter running so he joined Rex in another cup. 'Nice day for the race,' he said conversationally.

'Spot on,' said Rex. 'Tell me, do you have anything specific planned for today.'

The cab driver grinned wolfishly. 'Nothing special. I thought I might take a couple of movie queens out on my yacht and screw them rigid for about nine hours.'

'I'll take another cab then.'

'No fella, wait.' The cabby put up his hands. 'It was a gag. Just a gag.'

Rex viewed him with suspicion. 'Not a *running* one?'

'What's that exactly?'

'Never mind. Then I shall engage your services for the entire day. If that's all right with you.'

'You're a toff, guvnor.' The driver made furtive twiddlings at his meter. Rex spied out the sudden acceleration of the little dollar digits and the cabby's grin reflected in the driving mirror. 'Where to then, Mac?'

'A shop that sells sunglasses.' Rex kept his own grin to himself. 'Nice big expensive ones.'

'Tally ho then, squire.'

'Tally ho, indeed.'

The whistling cabby drove Rex away from the bad part of town. As they passed the end of Lonely Street Rex peeped from the back window and wondered about the large number of long black sinister-looking cars parked before Heartbreak Hotel. He also wondered if he should broach the matter of the cabby's recommendation of the place, but thought better of it. He had far more pressing affairs on his mind.

The journey from the bad part of town to the good part was for the most part uneventful. The cabby hurled the occasional wad of invective towards fellow motorists, but this, he assured Rex, was all part of the service. It was a tradition or an old charter or something. Rex, for his part, lazed in his seat and schemed in silence.

At no great length, but at what seemed considerable expense, the cab halted before the House of Meek. It was a large and swanky affair. Liberally dosed with neon and sporting a window display which appeared to consist of lootings from a pharaoh's tomb.

'Just the ticket, bro,' grinned the cabby. 'Sunshades they have.'

'Keep the motor running,' Rex told him. 'I won't be a moment.'

The House of Meek was a family concern. Founded in the former century by the now legendary Russell Meek. Explorer, swordsman, Member of Parliament for Brentford North, best-dressed man of 1995, three-times world snooker champion and stunt double for Long John Holmes. (That all right for you, Russ?)

The present proprietor was one Theodore Meek, a stunted hunchback with a penchant for necrophilia. Nature had favoured him with bad breath and a baldy head. The former he battled to suppress with a range of hopelessly inadequate patent medicines and the latter he disguised beneath a high-crested wig of black lacquered swan's down. He wasn't going to be caught quiffless in a *Quiffs Only Zone*.

Rex had a bit of a quiff on himself this particular morning. Not that this was due to any innate yearnings to conform. More that he had slept face down in the dumpster. And you know how your hair gets when you've had a really rough night.

The lad with the lop-sided Fabian entered the House of Meek. Theodore viewed him with only the slightest misgivings, certainly no more nor less than he viewed any other customer. He worried about that jacket, though. A trifle pinched beneath the armpits perhaps.

Rex swaggered towards Theodore, who stood to attention behind the antique counter. Rex smiled sweetly and leaned an elbow upon the highly-polished marble counter-top. He gazed around at the shop's interior. It was very swanky, and no doubt about it.

Rows of richly-cut leather clothes hung upon gilded racks. Gentlemen's things, calf-skin wallets, white-seal toiletry bags, badger-hair shaving brushes, porcupine-quill combs, ivory tooth-picks, koala-bone gaming dice, all neatly displayed upon mahogany shelves. The heads of stuffed beasties stared down upon him. Their skins pelted the floor. Rex shuddered inwardly and turned his gaze upon Theodore.

'Morning humpty,' he said. 'Giving the bell ringing a miss today?'

'Excuse me, sir?' Theodore fell back in alarm.

'Oh excuse me,' Rex put his hands to his face. 'I do apologize. I've been taking a lot of illegal drugs recently.'

'Quite so, sir. I understand.' The customer is always right, he told himself.

'Good boy.' Rex leered horribly.

'How might I help you, sir?'

'Well,' said Rex. 'My name is Rex Mundi. I'm sure you've heard of me. Millionaire gameshow host. Does the *Nemesis* show. Chap off the telly. Mundi. Rex Mundi.'

'I do believe I've seen your show. Yes, of course, sir.'

Rex fanned his nose. 'What is that funky smell?' he asked.

'Sir, I'm sorry I . . .'

Rex took to examining the soles of his blue sueders. 'I must have trodden in some shit or something. No, hang about, it's you. Good God, man, what did you have for breakfast, stewed rat?'

'Sir, I'm sorry, I . . .'

'Never mind. I'll just try to stay up-wind of you. Mundi's the name. Rex Mundi.'

'So you said, sir.'

'Do I have an account here?'

'No sir, you don't.'

'Pity. Still, let's see what you have. Don't stand quite so close. You don't half pong.'

'Sir, I really must object.'

'You must? You should stand where I'm standing.'

'I think you'd better leave, sir.'

'I'd like a pair of sunglasses, please. Nice big ones. The best you have. The most costly.'

'The best we have?'

'The very best. Money no object.'

'In that case.' Theodore stooped beneath the counter to seek out the drawer. Rex watched the wig go down.

He watched the wig come up again. Theodore displayed the drawer-load of sunglasses. 'These are our most exclusive, sir.'

'None of that "sir" stuff now. Mundi's the name. Rex Mundi.'

'Courtesy costs nothing, *sir*.'

'I'll bet that fur hat you're wearing didn't cost you an arm and a leg either. What did you do, skin your breakfast?'

'That really is the limit, sir. Kindly leave the building.'

'Whoops.' Rex beat at his forehead. 'I'm so sorry. The illegal drugs. Please bear with me. Those look nice.' He pointed into the drawer.

'These?' Theodore was trying to speak without opening his mouth. 'These are particularly exclusive. Designed by Pierre Montag of Paris, France. See the little logo on the lens?'

Rex snatched them from his fingers and tried them on. 'How do I look?'

'Very chic, sir.'

'Mundi. Rex Mundi. Gameshow host and drug fiend.'

'Mr Mundi. They suit you very well.'

'Are they the biggest you have?'

Theodore perused the drawer. 'The very biggest.'

'They'll do then. Just one thing.'

Theodore flinched. 'Yes, sir?'

'Tell me this. Do you know of any situation where the wearing of such sunglasses as these would be considered an affront to accepted religious dogma?'

'Certainly not, sir. We wouldn't deal in such items.'

'Good. Just the job, then. How much are they?'

Theodore turned the label which covered Rex's nose. 'Five thousand dollars.'

'Five thousand dollars.' Rex beckoned Theodore closer. 'Does your mother know how to sew?' he asked.

'My mother is a skilled seamstress, as it happens. Why do you ask?'

'Well . . .'

Some cases are so full of knots that Alexander the Great with a Texas chainsaw couldn't eat into them. I remember a case back in ninety-three. Seemed like a straight-forward affair at the time, but in five short days it cost me the best friend I ever had, a tree sloth called Cosmo, my right kneecap and four months in a decompression chamber. Some cases, you just can't tell. And I hoped real bad that this wasn't going to be one of them.

The alleyway behind the Love Me Tender looks much the same as any other. In fact it bears a striking resemblance to the one behind Heartbreak Hotel. But that's alleyways for you, and I'm not going to stand on ceremony with this one and salute the first pumpkin that calls me bwana.

I merge into the shadows with such skill that even Hank Marvin wouldn't have known the difference.

'I'm not happy about this, chief.'

'The Hank Marvin gag? I thought it was OK.'

'This set-up. Something tells me we're on a wrong'n here.'

'Have a little faith, Barry. I know my trade.'

'Mr Woodbine.' I hear the voice but I can't tell where it comes from.

'The name's Woodbine,' I reply. 'Lazlo Woodbine. Some call me Laz.'

'I have what you're looking for, Mr Woodbine.'

'You don't sound too much like a dame with really huge tits and a thing about men in trenchcoats.' I figure a little humour might lighten the situation. 'Where are you, exactly?'

'Right here.' I hear the creak of what can only be the retractable bottom section of a cast-iron fire escape. And I felt the impact as it hit me right on the top of my head.

And that was about all I heard or felt. Because suddenly I was falling into that whirlpool of darkness that all private detectives fall into at about this point in the plot. I fall down and down and down towards an oblivion of nothing much in particular. And then things go very black indeed for your friend and mine.

'You got him good.' Ed Kelley appeared from the shadows. 'Shall we saw his head off here, or take him back to our secret hideout?'

'Back to the secret hideout.' Johnny Dee came down the cast-iron staircase. 'You can never tell who might be watching here.'

Barry the sprout, who had rolled away to cover, *was* watching.

But he said nothing.

Rex got down to a serious day's shopping.

After his swift getaway from the House of Meek, he carefully wormed from the cabby the names of all the posh shops where the media folk cast their fashionable shadows. And very soon he found all the ones where the other Rex Mundi had a personal account.

Rex spent lavishly. Right up to and, wherever possible, well beyond the limits of his credit. He freighted his purchases back to the cab and loaded them in, leaving the shopkeepers to dwell upon the enormity of his verbal abuse and gross behaviour.

Rex now sported the absolutely very best in up-market menswear. An eight-thousand-dollar watch clenched his wrist like a gold tattoo. His pockets jingled with a collection of pointless pricey trifles. The cabby was looking pretty swell also. Rex had got him fitted out with no expense spared. He wasn't completely sold on the rhinestone-covered jumpsuit with the big bell-bottoms the driver had chosen. But each to his own.

Rex bit the end from a long green cheroot, which the tobacconist had assured him was 'rolled upon the thigh of a dusky South Preslian maiden' and spat it out of the cab window.

'Ouch!' went a passerby.

'Mundi's the name,' said Rex Mundi. 'Drive on, please.'

The driver did that very thing. 'Where to now?' he grinned most broadly.

'Time for lunch I think. Where would you recommend?'

'How about the Tomorrowman Tavern?'

Rex lit his cheroot with a laser-operated Dunhill. 'Why not?' he said.

As Lazlo is still falling into the bottomless pit the action stays with Rex. Which is only fair as he's having such a good time for once.

Rex and the cabby, whose name was Bill, entered the Tomorrowman. The barman doffed his silken scarf and donned his repugnant leather apron. 'Fuck off,' he said.

Rex was all sweetness and light. 'I come in peace for all mankind,' he said. 'Charge all yesterday's damage costs to my station. Here, I've brought you a present.' He pulled a small golden device from his pocket and passed it to the barman.

'Thanks.' The barman passed his manic eye over it. 'What does it do?'

'I'm not quite sure. I lost the instructions. But it cost a packet, I can tell you.'

'Well, thanks a lot. You're not kidding about charging the damage to your station?'

'Am I or am I not the chap off the telly?' Rex winked and fished out something silver which might have been designed for clipping nasal hairs. The barman accepted it. 'I never miss your show,' he said.

'A real professional,' Rex told Bill.

'I liked him in *They Came And Ate Us*,' the driver replied. 'Really saved the day there. Did you read the review, "What a load of old horse's poo this book is. If it hadn't been for the barman I for one would have ripped the whole thing up and used it for bog paper," *The Times*.'

'Easy.' Rex gave him a stony glare. 'Never bite the hand that clothes you.'

'No offence meant.'

'None taken, I assure you. So let's get stuck into some eats. Barman, whatever you have that's really expensive and costs a lot more at this moment because it's out of season and almost impossible to get, please.'

'I'll see what I can do.'

'I had that galloping gourmet in the back of my cab once,' quoth Bill. 'What a pillock. He sure knew how to feed his face, though.'

'Has Laura Lynch been in?' Rex asked the barman, who was ruminating upon the current availability of Rocky Mountain oysters.

'I expect she'll drop in later. Bigfoot noses are almost impossible to get at this time of year. I could send out for some.'

'Send out for lots and give us a couple of pints of champagne before you do.'

'Reserve stock?'

'Would the chap off the telly be seen dead drinking anything else?'

'I should think not.' The barman hastened to oblige.

'This is MTWTV news on the hour every five minutes,' said the TV above the bar. 'And top of the news this lunchtime, allegations of verbal abuse, violent assault, wanton excess, personal credit violation and possible use of illegal drugs levelled against a prominent TV game show host. This very morning . . .'

'Could we have that thing off, please?' Rex asked. 'It interferes with my spending.'

'As you please.' The barman switched off the TV and uncorked the champagne. 'I'll get right on to those bigfoot noses. A jet will bring them down from Oregon.' He decanted two pints into as many glasses. 'Cheers.'

Rex put on his big expensive sunglasses. This was one place he had no wish to be recognized in. Not until he'd had his lunch and refused to pay, anyway.

Bill took up his glass and drained the better part of it away in a single gulp. 'It's good this, isn't it?' said he.

'Yes,' Rex agreed. 'And it's going to get a whole lot better.'

I just keep right on falling. There's no today for me and no yesterday. And tomorrow don't look like being a jacuzzi full of cheerleaders neither. I've had some rotten breaks in my time, but those you've got to take in this business. I'm philosophical. The way I see it, when you're hanging by your fingernails, you don't take time out to wind your wristwatch.

Laura Lynch entered the Tomorrowman Tavern. Now I don't know what makes the perfect woman. I don't pretend to know. Well, I do pretend to know, but who doesn't? Physically speaking I do like a lot of leg. Not too much knee, of course, and I can't abide a fat ankle. The way I see it is, if you're overstocked in the ankle department, wear boots. Even in the shower. A dame with fat ankles can still make it to the top of the charts if she knows how to powder her nose and keep her feet off the table.

Hang about! I'm not in this bit. I'm still falling into the bottomless pit.

Laura Lynch entered the Tomorrowman Tavern. Rex turned in mid swig, tucked away his sunglasses and smiled warmly. The beautiful woman wasn't smiling.

'Lordy, lordy,' croaked Bill. 'Look at the jugs on that.'

'Laura.' Rex extended his hand. Laura shrank back. 'Laura, please let me explain.'

'You're back.' Laura's voice was cold and dead. 'Does this mean I'm . . .'

'It doesn't mean anything. There's been a mistake. I'm not a Repo Man.'

'Repo Man?' Bill emptied another bottle into his glass. 'Had one of those bastards in the back of my cab once. Ate my cufflinks.'

'It wasn't my card.' Rex explained. 'I picked up the billfold by accident.'

'Officer Cecil raped me.'

'Oh God. I'm so sorry.'

Laura put a brave face on it. 'I didn't know I'd been raped until his cheque bounced.'

'That's a good'n.' Bill raised his glass. 'Heard it before, but still a killer.'

Rex took to his drink. He'd never lived in a world of one-liners and he had no intention of starting now.

'Sorry.' Laura clasped his elbow. 'It's just that women in Rankin's books never get any good lines.'

Rex shrugged. 'OK, so we can be friends again?'

'I hoped you'd say that.' Laura climbed on to the stool next to Rex and . . .

'Ah.' Rex sighed. 'Those stockings. Tell me, Laura, I only have forty dollars in cash right now. What would that get me exactly?'

Laura leaned towards him. 'For forty dollars, I slowly take off all my clothes, cover myself all over in mint-flavoured body-rub and take a nap while you read a newspaper in the next room. How does that sound?'

'Not too tempting.'

'I can go for it.' Bill downed further champagne. 'Do you supply the newspaper or do I have to bring my own?'

'Bill, please.'

'Sorry, guv. Are those bigfoot noses on their way, do you think?'

'I like the new get-up.' Laura stroked Rex's arm. 'Black leather always did a lot for me.'

'Thanks. The underpants have a tendency to ride up.' Rex plucked at his trouser seat. 'Listen, Laura. We're getting smashed out of our heads on the most expensive champagne in town. Perhaps you'd care to join us.'

'I'd like that very much.'

'Another glass over here, please, barman.'

'I'm not in the bar any more you klutz, I'm out getting the bigfoot noses.'

'All right, I'll get it myself. Whacky stuff this, isn't it?'

'I had that Patrick McGoohan in the back of my cab once. Did you ever see that series . . .'

9

9. And Moses came down from the
mount bearing the two tablets of stone.
10. And lo, there was a whole lot of
shaking going on.
11. And Moses was well peeved and
did lose his rag, saying, 'Thou shalt not
Rock 'n' Roll, for this is the eleventh
commandment . . .'
12. And Elvis said, 'Stroll on, thou art
a lying git.'

The Suburban Book of the Dead

Barry lay upsidedown in the alleyway.

'I did warn him,' sighed the inverted Time Sprout. 'It's not my fault if he gets his head sawn off. I've done my best for that guy.'

That's not really fair Barry.

'Who said that?'

It's me, Barry. Rankin's ghost writer.

'What, that bloke down the pub who's always fancied writing a novel?'

That's me.

'Well, howdy.'

I thought I'd better have a word with you about the incredibly clever trick-ending.

'It'll have to go some to beat the last two.'

Have I ever let you down?

'Can't say that you have, chief. So what can I do for you?'

It's more what I can do for you. Bounce over to the typewriter and have a look at this contract I've drawn up.

'Without my agent present? Are you kidding?'

Barry. I hold the little white bottle. Do you want to come out of this covered in glory or covered in Tipp-Ex?

'Covered in glory, please.'

That's the stuff. Now it's quite straightforward . . .

The last thing I expected was to be woken from unconsciousness by an air hostess with the face of an angel, gently patting on my shoulder and telling me that the plane had just landed in Miami.

So I guess the bucket of cold water that hit me in the face didn't come as much of a surprise. Normally I would have come up fighting. I learned Dimac from a lama in Tibet and my hands are so deadly that I have to keep them in a locked closet when they're not in use. It was a real drag to find them handcuffed behind my back just when I needed them most, I can tell you.

'Wake up Widebarn.' I knew that voice almost as well as I knew the theme from *Doctor Zhivago*. 'We wanna ask you some questions.'

I kept my eyes tight shut. I was chained into a chair, but it wasn't the one in my office. And this place didn't smell like Fangio's bar. I was definitely indoors, so the alleyway and the roof-top were out. Things didn't bode too well for the four-set clause in my contract.

'Open your eyes,' went the voice of Johnny Dee. 'Or I'll open them with a shovel.'

I took a little peep. Apart from the desklamp that was shining in my face, all I could see was darkness. I could live with that.

'OK,' says I with more composure than a Confucian in a comfort station. 'You want to come quietly, or do I have to get tough?'

Something hit me across the face and it wasn't the first kiss of springtime.

'Just tell us where it is and we'll let you off with a mercy-killing.'

'And if I don't?'

'Then it will be all the worse for your trenchcoat.'

'You fiends. What do you want from me anyway?'

'Your means of transportation, Mr Woodbune.'

'Wood*bine*,' says I. 'Lazlo Woodbine.' So they were after Barry. There was no way I was going to sell the little guy out. 'Some call me Laz,' I added.

'Quit stalling. Where's the Time Sprout? It's not in your pockets, so where is it, inside your head?'

I figured that Barry must have taken the duck for cover back in the alleyway. But there was no way they were going to drag that out of me. 'I'll never talk,' says I.

'Saw off his *head*, Ed.'

'I'll switch the chainsaw *on*, John.'

Now, I don't know poetry from a hole in the ground and I draw the line at having my head sawn off, even if it's to save my trenchcoat. So, before the rhymes get too painful and the chainsaw too piercing, I decided to state the obvious.

'Fellas. I don't have the Time Sprout. If I did, do you think I would be sitting here letting you rough me up? I'd be gone in a flash, wouldn't I?'

There was a bit of silence then. But only a bit, because Ed said, 'Not necessarily,' and spoiled it.

'Not necessarily?' I was flabbergasted, I kid you not.

'Sure. You might have masochistic tendencies.'

'What?'

'A deficient libido brought on by a set of socio-physical determinants manifesting in a psycho-sexual syndrome, whereby you can only achieve sensual gratification through the experience of pain.'

'Now just you see here . . .'

'John has a point there,' Ed added. 'Take all this obsession with your trenchcoat. Most unhealthy. Over-fastidiousness is a sure sign of mania.'

105

'Exactly,' said Johnny. 'The trenchcoat is a symbol, a metaphor. An overskin reflecting the wearer's inner self.'

'You leave my trenchcoat out of this.'

'Oh ho,' Johnny continued. 'Touched a raw nerve there. It's the same with all you private eyes. All obsessed with your peckers. It's all lingams and yonis, isn't it? Buttons and buttonholes. Belts and buckles. Guns and shoulder holsters . . .'

'Probing into people's affairs,' Ed put in. 'I bet you really get off poking those bullets into the chamber of your pistol.'

'How dare you!'

'Were you breast-fed?' Johnny asked.

'What's that got to do with anything?'

'Evasive. Unable to answer a direct question.'

'I can too answer a direct question.'

'Yeah? So where's the Time Sprout?'

'Back in the alleyway where you jumped me.'

'That's all we wanted to know. Saw off his head, Ed.'

'You're on, John.'

Rex decanted champagne and munched upon a sasquatch sarnie.

'I need your help, Laura,' he said.

Laura smiled that silly sort of champagne smile that all men (all right, *some* men) look for before they move in for the kill.

'Go on,' she said. 'Hic,' she added.

'It's about the billfold.' Rex chose his words with care. 'I don't want to get into any trouble. I just want to return it to its owner.'

'I'll bet you do.' Laura giggled foolishly.

'I've been right through it but there's no address or anything. What should I do?'

'Dump it down the John if you're smart.'

'I don't think that's a very good idea.'

'Listen.' Laura waggled her glass at Rex, liberally distributing champagne across the table. 'If you've got something of theirs you don't have to go looking for *them*. They'll find *you* soon enough.'

'I'd be willing to pay for your help.' Rex topped up Laura's glass.

'What, you with the forty dollars in cash?'

'I was just kidding about that. Here, take a look at this.' Rex detached his wristwatch and passed it to Laura. 'You can take it as a down-payment.'

Laura turned the watch upon her palm. 'But this must be worth—'

'A very great deal and there's lots more where that came from.'

'Let's go to my apartment,' said Laura Lynch.

Bill was snoring away at the bar.

'You gonna move this heap of dung?' the barman enquired.

'Not so loud.' Rex hushed him into silence. 'The station director always takes a nap at this time of the day.'

'Station director? This crud?'

Rex held up the crud's wrist. 'Behold the watch.'

'Ooh,' said Laura. 'He's got one just like mine.'

Rex was rooting through the slumbering cabby's pockets. He found the car keys and availed himself thereof. 'Give him an hour or so please, barman. Then awaken him gently and present him with the bill. He'll settle up with you.'

The barman fixed Rex with a real one-eyed blinder. 'What do you take me for?'

Rex turned up his hands in all innocence. 'You know who I am. The chap off the telly.'

'Yeah, I guess so.'

'And so, farewell.' Rex plucked out his sunglasses. Perched them on his nose. Took Laura by the arm and bade adieu to the Tomorrowman Tavern.

'Wake up, asshole,' said the barman clouting Bill from his stool.

Rex drove the cab with considerable skill. There were two good reasons for this. The first being that he had driven such motor cars before, and the second that he had consumed only the barest minimum of champagne. The woman in the back, who was wildly diving amongst Rex's purchases, was a different kettle of fish altogether.

'1010 Van Vliet Street, wasn't it?' Rex asked. A beautiful woman's address being something that was never likely to slip his mind.

'First on the left after the Graceland Shopping Mall. Rexy, can I keep this scarf?'

'Of course you can. The Graceland Mall, wasn't that the one on the newscast?'

'That's the one. Wasn't that terrible about Mojo and Debbie's baby being kidnapped by aliens and everything?'

'Terrible.' Rex shook his head. There was an awful lot he didn't understand about this strange world. But little by little he would piece it all together. Time was on his side, after all. Because, after all, no-one had, as yet, told him that Presley City was going to be little more than blackened rubble in just two days time.

Perhaps if they had he would have been trying just a little harder and not preparing himself, as he was, for a long night of fornication.

Rex hung a left and cruised into Van Vliet Street.

'Do you have any mint-flavoured body-rub in?' he asked. 'Or should I stop off and buy some?'

'Now just you see here,' said I. 'You can't saw my head off, and you know it.'

'Oh yeah? And for why?'

I thought faster than a fly-half in a fire storm. 'Well for

108

one thing at least an hour's past since you said you would and you haven't yet.'

'That don't mean nothing,' said Ed Kelley. 'This could be a flashback.'

Johnny Dee nodded in agreement. 'Or you could be dead already. Or we could have left you for dead. There's loads of possibilities.'

I guessed there was. This wasn't your everyday kind of detective novel after all.

'Is this a flashback?' I asked.

'No. It's just bad continuity.' Ed revved up the chain-saw.

'Say goodbye, sucker.'

'No. I hang about.'

'Say goodbye.'

'Say goodbye, chief.'

'Goodbye.'

'Nice place you have here.' Rex was favourably impressed. He had expected some sordid den with a big wardrobe, a lot of shoes and a bed laid for business. But this was much much more. The apartment was sumptuous. And it was extremely elegant.

A Bakhtiari carpet of Qashqai design, interwoven with ivory cabochons, smothered the floor with a profusion of golden palmettes. Beside the long window stood a George III satinwood side-table, edged with rosewood and fashioned in the distinguished style of Hargraves of Hull. On this a large collection of frosted Lalique glassware captured the light to perfection.

In one corner a mahogany sofa rose upon cabriole legs, its Aubusson tapestry upholsterings augmented with hassocks of antique paisley. In another, a chair by Carlos Bugatti, all walnut, tooled vellum and burnished pewter, glowed a dusty bronze.

Against the far wall a cocktail cabinet, fashioned to resemble a Louis XV secrétaire, twinkled grandly. Upon its 'rouge royale' marble top stood a row of baluster wine goblets.

Rex was particularly taken with the Wurlitzer 600 Model jukebox, noting the elaborate grille of nickel-plated Art-Deco-type scrolls and the way the Lucite rods of the Model 24 had been reduced to straight green verticals in a manner he considered most pleasing.

'Can you manage all right there?' Laura was scarcely visible beneath the better part of Rex's purchases. 'Sure you didn't forget anything?'

'Rexy, you're such a nice man.'

'Laura. This is a most exceptional collection. How did you come by all this?'

'Clients.' Laura unloaded her cargo on to the sofa. 'Little gifts from satisfied customers.'

Rex ran his finger along the ormolu-mounted record rack. It contained a collector's dream. LPs. The Cray Cherubs, the Lost Teeshirts of Atlantis, Astro Laser and the Flying Starfish from Uranus, the Turbulent Priests, Sonic Energy Authority, Barisal Guns, Mike Petty sings Hank Wangford.

'Laura.' Rex drew himself to the business in hand. 'Is there much you wouldn't do for the $87,000 worth of merchandise you have there?'

'Not much. Would you like to see the bedroom?'

'Yes please,' said Rex.

It would, of course, be unthinkable to actually put down in print what Rex and Laura got up to during the next hour. But then again, to fudge around it and simply cut to Rex lying on a bed wearing a big smile would be a severe cop-out.

'Where do you keep your gerbils?' Rex asked.

'Goddammit, Barry, you cut that a tad fine.' I rubbed at my wrists. There was a bit of chafing there, but nothing I couldn't handle.

'Sorry, chief. Got held up on a bit of business.'

'A bit of business?' We were back in my office. It was once more about five minutes before we set out for the alleyway behind the Love Me Tender massage parlor. And this time I wasn't going to show up. You have to know how to keep ahead of this game if you don't want to wind up in a wooden trenchcoat.

'Better late than never, I guess.' I really wanted to thank the little guy for saving my life, but I have a hard-bitten image to keep up. 'Just try to stay on the ball in future,' I told him.

'Gotcha, chief.' I knew that he had, and he knew that I knew, etc, etc, etc. Or thought that he did.

'Thanks, chief.'

'Don't mention it, Barry.'

'So what are we going to do this time? Hit the alleyway in a hard hat?'

'Nope. We are going to hit the bar.'

'I don't think Fangio's has actually been built yet, chief.'

'And who said anything about Fangio's?' I asked, like snow on a Russian's boot. 'Did you ever hear me describe Fangio's?'

'Can't say that I did, chief. I wondered about that.'

I tapped my nose like solitaire was the only game in town. 'It's called keeping your options open. I never describe the bar, so I can use any bar any time without screwing up my contract. Pretty neat thinking, eh?'

'Pretty neat, you ungrateful two-dollar bum!'

'What's that, Barry?'

'Nothing, chief.'

Rex removed the crocodile clips and disconnected the car battery. He slipped out of the pony harness, withdrew the slim plastic tube and emptied the sticky gerbils back into their cage. The veal in the clingfilm had now thawed out so he consigned it to the wastebasket.

111

* * *

I walked into the bar with more finagle than a ferret in a tinker's trouser. A guy in a bell-bottomed jumpsuit flew by me at some speed and struck the sidewalk.

'And stay out, ya turkey!' The barman looked like he'd had a long day's journey into night, although the monocle and the silk smoking-jacket were as natty as ninepence. He spied me out with his lone ogler. 'Hi, Laz,' he said. 'Long time no see.'

I couldn't argue with that. I strolled over to a bar stool, mounted up and set Barry down in an ashtray. The barman reinstalled himself behind the jump and enquired after my pleasure.

'A hot pastrami on rye and a bottle of Bud,' I told him.

'Coming right up.'

I took in the surroundings and kept them to myself. In less time than it takes to master the rules of Kabaddi, a steaming sandwich and a matching beer were pushed before me.

'Twenty-five dollars.' The Barman's voice was lower than an ankle bracelet on a flat-footed pygmy.

'Put it on my slate,' I suggested.

'Ho, ho, ho.' The barman put his hands to his belly and made mirth. 'You jest, surely? But no matter, the joke is well taken. See how I turn up the corners of my mouth as I tell you again, twenty-five dollars.'

'Coming right up.' I began to pat at my pockets as if I really meant it but the barman shook his head. 'Sorry?' I said.

'Laz,' he said. 'I notice that you are hatless and currently sporting the open-necked look. I have reason to believe that if I were to ask you the time you wouldn't be able to accommodate me. Am I correct?'

I hung my head, which I also nodded sombrely as I hung it.

'I spy some chafing upon your wrists, suggestive of handcuffery. Bruising to the cheek and, I believe, cranial

112

damage caused, I would guess, by the retractable section of one of those cast-iron fire escapes. How am I doing so far?'

'You are the Brahma of Baker Street reborn.'

'My thanks. And so it is my conclusion that you are at present a man without funds, clearly ignorant of the axiom that "there is no such thing as a free lunch".'

I rose to take my leave. 'You got me fair and square,' I told him.

'Sit down!' ordered the barman. 'I haven't done yet.'

I sat back down. The barman fixed me with the kind of stare you could roast weenies on. 'I'm not a hard man,' he continued. 'It's just that I get real fed up with bozos like you trying to rip me off all the time. I have a business to run here and I ain't no charity. But I'll tell you what I'll do. You have obviously suffered considerable ill treatment and you are stony broke. Just this once I am going to break the habits of a lifetime and take your IOU.'

I hung my head even further. Sometimes you meet a guy with just so much plain humanity that it makes you feel humble. I choked back a heartfelt tear. 'I'll date it for the day after tomorrow, if that's OK?' I said.

Rex switched off the suction pump, hung up the miner's helmet, divested himself of the fisherman's waders and laid his snorkel aside. He was just scooping the lard out of the trout mask when there came a violent knocking at the bedroom door.

'Let me in,' Laura demanded. 'I'm fed up with sitting out here reading the newspaper.'

I finished my fifteenth bottle of Bud and pushed my plate away. 'Those bigfoot noses really blow you out,' I observed.

'You wouldn't care for a wafer-thin mint?' the barman enquired.

'No, I wouldn't. I'll take a large Jim Beam.'

'Coming right up.'

I chivvied Barry round the ashtray with a hot cigar butt and pondered fleetingly. Things weren't looking too good for me. I had come up real short on the gratuitous sex and violence so far. And there wasn't even a sniff of the now legendary trail of corpses that I'm known and loved for. What I needed now was a really violent interlude to liven up the otherwise turgid plot.

The barman passed me my Jim Beam. 'Keep your head down, Laz,' he advised. 'I smell big trouble.'

The front doors swung open like a piper at the gates of dawn and two of the biggest guys I'd ever seen swaggered in wearing more black than a Valentine Dyall fan-club dinner.

Now I don't know much about running gags from books previous that I ain't been in, but it seemed to me that one of them was toting a 7.62 M134 General Electric Minigun, which in my books generally spells *schadenfreude*. I saw the barrels begin to spin and that's when I snatched up Barry and whipped out the trusty Smith and West Wittering.

The big guy with the big gun strafed the place. I'd never seen so many shots go in so many directions all at the one time. Dudes started falling, dames started screaming. Bullets riddled the bar-top. Glasses shattered, bottles exploded. I came up firing. I let off three straight into the gunman's chest but he didn't look like he felt death coming on. He just kept pumping away.

The barman took the dive for cover as half the bar-counter went the way of all flesh, only faster. There was a hell of a lot of smoke about and a great deal of noise. At a time like this a man's gotta do what a man's gotta do. And if you think that's take a powder, then you don't know old Laz too well.

As *The Maniacs Came Killing** I rolled three more into

*A Lazlo Woodbine thriller.

the trusty Smith and West Point and took up a manly pose.

'Ease up on the populace, creeps,' said I with more heroism than an entire Audi Murphy season.

A whole bunch of muzzles turned in my direction. But like Elvis Costello, my aim was true. I hit the gunman right between the windows of his soul and he went down with a lot of sparks and technoflash that I for one wasn't expecting.

His buddy didn't seem too concerned about that and reached down for the big gun. I let him have two rounds in the top of the head, just to be social.

I could see the holes. But they didn't appear to be causing him much in the way of alarm. He came forward at me through the smoke and he wasn't smiling. I emptied my piece into his chest.

'Barry,' said I. 'Get us the Hell out of here.'

'I'm trying, chief.'

'Try harder, dammit.'

'No can do, chief. I'm all used up. Sorry.'

'Sorry? What are you saying?'

The guy in black came forward through the smoke. He was torn up real bad from all my gunfire. All sorts of bits were falling off, exposing lots of snazzy metalwork and futuristic circuitry the likes of which I had never seen the likes of.

'Dead or alive, you're coming with me,' he said, which seemed to ring a bell somewhere.

'Do something, Barry.'

'I'm trying, chief. Oh damn.'

It's a funny thing the way podoeroticism has never really caught on in the West, what with sex being so popular and all. We spend half our lives searching each other's bottoms for erogenous zones, while all the time there are two dirty great big ones lurking inside our socks.

Of course, the Chinese cottoned on to it centuries ago.

But then, as Hugo Rune said, 'not much slips past the damn Chinese when it comes to jigger jig'. Rune once took tea with a mandarin in Peking and he comments in his diary:

> The meal itself was a pretty lightweight affair consisting of a meagre forty courses, but made tolerable by the court concubines who, whilst the great lord and I took sup, lifted our robes at intervals and fanned our privvy members with their hair.

Sadly he neglects to mention whether they also gave his feet a bit of a squeeze.

Rex had always been something of a 'leg man' and very much of a 'foot man'. And so, at this particular moment, when Laz was finding himself somewhat up against it, Rex was indulging in a little foot fellatio and thinking instep.

The big guy hit me just the one time. But that was enough for me. I joined the feathered legions and took to the air. I only wish that someone had opened the exit door before I passed through it.

Rex took time-out. If you want the earth to move for you, it's best that it starts with small tremors and works its way slowly up the Richter. As Rex was currently at about five on the scale of ten he left Laura to steam gently and made for the cocktail cabinet. His naked feet left perfumed imprints upon the Bakhtiari carpet and his upraised wanger bobbed before him.

He reached the cocktail cabinet and leaned over it to scoop up a couple of two-hundred-year-old goblets. As he did so a jolt of static electricity hit him right in the tip of his unrestrained bobber.

'Oooooooooooh!' howled Rex, collapsing into an untidy heap.

* * *

'Oh' and 'ouch' I howled as I hit the alleyway. I landed in a heap of cardboard boxes, shredded paper and polystyrene which had evidently been laid out for the purpose and prepared to come up fighting.

Rex made with the crossed eyes and suitably pained expression. Clutching himself he crawled back to the cabinet and ran a tentative hand over the woodwork. Nothing. It had been well and truly earthed.

Rex fiddled with the raised carvings. There had to be something in there. And of course there was. A click, a swish and a panel slid away to reveal a . . .

'TV terminal.' Rex made a puzzled face. 'Now what do we have here, then?' He rose to his feet, padded silently back across the room and gently closed the bedroom door. Returning, he examined the terminal. Beneath the small screen was an intricate keyboard system, although nothing Rex hadn't seen before. He jacked it up and watched as a station logo which meant nothing to him appeared on the screen.

Rex tapped at the keyboard and requested access to the menu. Access was politely denied. 'INSERT CARD' flashed upon the screen.

'Hmm,' went Rex. 'Insert card.' He glanced about the room. If it was 'insert card' then it was probably 'insert Laura's card'. Laura's card was no doubt in her handbag. Her handbag was in the bedroom.

'Bother,' whispered Rex. 'But hold on there.' He reached over to his jacket, which had been thrown down with no particular care for its value, and pulled out the captured billfold.

'There is a card in here, unless I am very much mistaken,' he said.

'Unless I am very much mistaken, Barry,' said I, 'We are in serious difficulty here.'

117

'No more bullets for the trusty Smith and Welshman, chief?'

'You got it, little guy. And the way he did what he just did I find most discouraging.'

'You mean the way he walked out right through the wall rather than bothering with the doorway, chief?'

'That and the big gun he's carrying, yes.'

'I think I'll just kind of duck down in your pocket if that's OK, chief. Let me know later how it works out.'

'Brilliant.'

'Brilliant.' Rex dropped the dreaded Repo Man card into the slot in the keyboard and the screen lit up with all sorts of possibilities. Rex called up the menu once again.

The screen said:

LOGGING INPUT	AUDIO/VISUAL
STATISTICAL ANALYSIS	LOCATION
PROFIT MARGINS	INSTRUCT
MAINTENANCE	VOID
STATUS	FASHION TIPS

It all looked moderately intriguing. And somewhat too good to be true. Rex fingered the keyboard and called up LOCATION.

An area of Presley City appeared in map form on the screen. Enlarged and zoomed in. A little blip went blip blip blip in the alleyway behind the Tomorrowman Tavern. Rex called up AUDIO/VISUAL and then jumped back. A fist flew towards him on the screen, filled it as it made apparent impact and then vanished away. The fist's owner became visible, staggering backwards, clutching the wounded article and uttering cuss words. A voice which didn't come from this body, said, 'Return the stolen billfold.'

Rex glanced down at the billfold and then back to the

screen. The voice clearly wasn't addressing him. It continued.

'You were carrying a concealed weapon contrary to social format and I note that you sport the open-necked look in a *zany tie zone*. You are evidently a revolutionary. Therefore you must know the location of the stolen billfold. Hand it over or I will kill you.'

Rex whistled beneath his breath. These Repo Men certainly went about their work with zeal. But there was something dangerously lacking when it came to the matter of how they applied their logic to the solution of a particular problem.

'It's a bum rap. You got the wrong guy.' The cries came from a face now seen in close up as its owner was being hoisted up the wall of the alleyway. 'I ain't no Goddamn revolutionary. I'm a Republican.'

'I will count to three and if you do not disclose the whereabouts of the stolen billfold I will break open your head.'

'Listen, buddy, you're making me mad.'

'One,' said the voice.

Rex flipped back to the menu. He called up INSTRUCT and tapped in ABORT. Then back to AUDIO/VISUAL.

'Two,' said the voice.

'Shit,' said Rex.

The face on the screen said something. But nothing helpful.

Rex took to wildly tapping buttons. On screen he saw a big hand closing over the struggler's head.

'Three.'

Rex tapped OVERRIDE ALL PREVIOUS IMPERATIVES BILLFOLD RECOVERED AWAIT FURTHER INSTRUCTIONS.

He gaped at the screen. The big hand froze. The face relaxed and slid from view, the brick wall clouded and the screen blacked.

Rex breathed a very big sigh of relief. That was close. But close for who? Some innocent, he supposed, in the wrong place at the wrong time. Rex had evidently been viewing him through the eyes of a Repo Man. An LCP. Liquid Crystal Person. Some kind of robot? Had to be. But built by whom? And where? Find the central control and one might just find the Volvo. It seemed as likely as anything else around here.

'Goddamn. That was close. What happened to him?' The voice came from the terminal.

'Seems like he blew a fuse, chief. I reckon we'd best be away.'

'Chief?' Rex did big gasps. 'Barry! It's you. You're here.'

His words must have issued straight through the mouth of the now defunct Repo Man, because the next thing Rex heard was a small green cry of, 'We're rumbled, chief,' followed by much scrambling and scurrying and an increasingly distant voice going, 'Faster, chief. Get a move on.'

10

15. *And finally did the children of Elvis
get their bearings and dump Moses.*
16. *And they came unto Jericho, which
is just up from the Dead Sea.*
17. *But the people of Jericho did see
them coming and shut the gate, crying,
'Hippy convoy!'*
18. *For the people of Jericho were
unhip, favouring Trad Jazz and duffle
coats.*
19. *And so did Elvis have his road crew
set up a mighty speaker system outside
the walls. And thusly did he pump up
the volume.*

The Suburban Book of the Dead

Four men sit in a top-secret room. It looks very much the same as ever it did. But it isn't. This is a different room altogether. There is a long black table with chairs around it for thirteen. A big light shines down upon it, and the light isn't kind.

Three men huddle uncomfortably at one end of the table. The fourth, who was sitting at the other, is now standing. And he is also shouting.

'You useless bunch,' he shouts. 'You puny piss-poor pathetic pack of poltroons.'

There is no verbal response to this. Only the lowering of three heads accompanied by triple cowering.

'A thousand years of planning has gone into this. One thousand years. And you screw it all up in a single

121

day. Dee, Kelley, what did you do?'

Two mouths drop open. But that's about all they do. The lips quiver, but that's not a lot of help.

'I'll tell you what you did. You ballsed it up. I send you into the parallel continuum with orders to collect the final statue and do nothing more. But can you do that? No, you can't. You come back here with Rex Mundi on board, and if that isn't disaster enough, you stop off for lunch, he escapes and the Volvo gets stolen with the entire Presley hoard along with it. Everything. Gone.'

'And you.' A finger points at the man with the hangover. He is wearing a somewhat creased jumpsuit of the bell-bottomed persuasion. 'You, Bill. I have you pick up Mundi from the police station and deliver him to Heartbreak Hotel where he should have met with certain extinction. And what happens? He's away again. And not only that. Having arranged for you to be standing by when he surfaces today, you take him shopping. He damn near bankrupts me and all but gets me arrested. Then you get so drunk that he steals your cab and he's off on the loose once more.'

Bill chewed upon his knuckles. The speaker turned his glare once more to Dee and Kelley. 'And what do you do with Woodburn?'

'Wood*bine*,' said Dee. 'Lazlo Woodbine.'

'Shut up! You were to kill him in the alleyway and capture the Time Sprout. It's our escape route out of here. If we can't succeed with our plan in just two days all this goes up, and us along with it. If we can't lure Presley here and destroy him before then, we're history. History that never happened.'

The other Rex Mundi, because, of course, it could be no other, rent hair from his head and flung it to the floor where it exploded in small sulphurous puffs of smoke. 'A thousand years of running and hiding, and what has it come to? Speak someone. Bill, what are you going to do?'

'Me . . . I . . . ?' Bill made splutterings. 'I will . . . I will

122

. . . I will kill Mundi. Yes, that's what I'll do. I'll kill him, excellency. He doesn't suspect me. He'll be at Laura Lynch's. I'll wait for him there and kill him. That's what I'll do. Yes.'

'No! That's what you won't do.'

'No, excellency. That's what I won't do. No. Absolutely not. What will I do?'

'You will drive him around. That's what you'll do. He will be searching for the Volvo and with his kind of luck he will no doubt find it. When he does, then you will kill him and bring the Volvo to me. Do you think you can manage that?'

'Yes, excellency.' Bill nodded his hung-overed head.

Ed Kelley raised a shaky hand. 'What do you want us to do, excellency?'

'What do you think I want you to do?'

Ed scratched his head. 'Kill Woodbine, excellency?'

'No! Not kill Woodbine.'

'Not kill Woodbine. But you wanted us to . . .'

'Well I don't want you to now.'

'No, excellency. You don't.'

'So what do I want you to do?'

Ed gave his scalp further attention. Johnny Dee said, 'You want us to follow him.'

The other Rex nodded. 'Because?'

'Because he is also searching for the Presley hoard which is in the Volvo.'

'Exactly. And?'

'And when he finds it, then you want us to kill him and bring you the Volvo and the Time Sprout.'

'There you go. What could be more simple?'

'Well . . .' said Ed. 'I do foresee one or two slight difficulties . . .'

'Slight difficulties?' The other Rex put his hands to the long table-top, tore it from its legs and cast it away into the darkness. 'You will do it! This is my world and I'm keeping it. I can deal with the government, the loss adjusters, the bloody Repo Men and the accountants. They're nobody. Nothing. This is all mine and I'm taking it back.'

'Yes, excellency.'

'You, ASMODEUS.' The Anti-Rex glared at Bill.

'You, BALBERITH.' The glare turned upon Ed Kelley.

'You, SONNEILLON.' The glare finally came to rest upon Johnny Dee.

'You, the last remaining of my First Hierarchy of Hell. Stop fucking about, and get on with it. Kill anybody who stands in your way. I want it all, the past the present and the future. I want Presley dead and all memory of him driven from the Earth. I want him dead, dead, DEAD! What do I want?'

'Presley dead.'

'When do I want it?'

'Now.'

'Good. Then, gentlemen, you are dismissed.'

'Phew, chief. That was close.'

'You said it.' I straightened my belt buckle and tidied my trenchcoat. There was extensive second-degree smutting and several nasty blots of what appeared to be some kind of industrial lubricant. Normally this would have caused me considerable grief, but this time I was prepared to tough it out. I mean, there was no way I was going to come across as an anal retentive simply because I had pride in my appearance.

'That guy back there wasn't human,' I observed with more perspicacity than a panty-girdle pedlar at a Tupperware party. 'What do you make of that, Barry?'

'Can't say, chief. But that voice. At the end when he froze up. I know that voice, or knew it.'

'You keep bad company, little guy.' We were back in my office. The bolt was on the door and the top was off the bottle of Old Bedwetter that I generally reserve for moments such as these.

124

I took a deep slug. 'You feeling your old self yet, Barry?'

'You mean the time travelling? Well, no, as it happens.'

'Not good.' I took another slug. 'We got a real tight schedule if we're going to make it out of here before the Big Bang.'

'About the Big Bang, chief. Do you know why it happens?'

'Nope. History is schtum on the details, but pretty graphic about the scale. It took this city clean off the map.'

'So what are you going to do next, chief?'

'Well, the way I see it, Barry, we have two options. The first is that I sit here, hit this bottle of Old Bedwetter and fall into flashbacks of lost loves and hard times past.'

'Not too keen, chief. And the second?'

'The second is that we step out to the supermarket and pick up some supplies.'

'I quite like that one, chief. But I can't see exactly where it's leading to.'

'Then let me put you in the picture.' I leaned back in my chair and made the kind of smile that money just can't buy you these days. 'What are we searching for Barry?'

'The Presley hoard, chief.'

'And where is it now, Barry?'

'Search me, chief.'

'Well, it has to be somewhere.'

'Yes, chief.'

'And I reckon it's right—' I pulled a map from my pocket, spread it upon my desk and whacked my finger down on to it at a very particular spot '—here.'

Barry gave the map the once-over and went, 'Eh?'

'Come on, Barry. Think about it. Sir John Rimmer digs up the Presley hoard. And the location of where he dug it up is on every twenty-fifth-century map. So that's where we go. If it hasn't arrived yet we wait. And we take sandwiches. Enough to last us until you get your powers back and we can abscond with the hoard forward homeways. Pretty neat, eh? We know that the hoard survived the Big Bang, so if we stick with it, we survive, too.'

'Chief. I hate like damn to say this to you, but you are a genius.'

'Yeah, Barry. Ain't I just.'

'Rexy. You aren't leaving, are you?'

Rex was struggling into his leather trousers. 'I have to see a man about something. Or a something about something.'

'But we were just working up to the knees and you've still got $85,750 left on the meter.'

'Wait for me.' Rex managed his finest Arnie, 'I'll be back.'

'I'm coming with you.'

'No. I don't think that would be a good idea.'

'I do.' Laura produced a small intricate handweapon. As she was still naked, Rex had no idea where she had produced it from.

'Ah,' said he. 'I see.'

'No, I don't think you do. You're not the chap off the telly. I know that. You are the one we have been waiting for.'

'*We?*' Who is this *we* all of a sudden?'

'*We.* The Children of the Revolution.'

'Marc Bolan,' said Rex. 'One of my favourites. You don't happen to have a copy of "Pewter Suitor" in your collection by any chance? I've been after it for years.'

Laura shook her head. 'We, the Children of the Revolution, have been waiting for you to aid us. I know who you are.'

'You do?'

'I do. You are the Tomorrow Man.'

'I am?'

'You are. When you flashed the Repo Man card I

126

thought we'd been infiltrated. But I listened at the bedroom door when you found my terminal. You're one of us, aren't you?'

'I suppose I probably am. The Tomorrow Man. Yes,' said Rex. 'I certainly am.'

'So where are you going?'

'Back to the Tomorrowman Tavern, as it happens. The Repo Man who stole my car is frozen there, or at least one of his companions is. Perhaps the car might even be there also.'

'You're going to need my help.'

'I'm not altogether sure that we share all the same motives.'

'Then we can help each other. Trust me.'

'All right then. We shall go together.'

'That's fine.' Laura turned to take up her clothing. Rex spun around and kicked the gun from her hand. He plucked it from the carpet.

'I'll carry this, though,' he said.

We headed on up the alleyway, the map before us.

'Which way is north, chief?'

'Up thataways, Barry.' I have an uncanny sense of direction. Paid a fortune for it. In this business, a sense of direction can mean the difference between laughing like a drain or getting caught with your trousers around the ankles of a friend you never had. If you catch my drift. And I'm sure that you do. 'We go right at the top here. Or is it left?'

'Cab, sir? Well, cut off my legs and call me Shorty, it's you guvnor.'

'So it is,' said Rex. 'Something of a surprise. You being here. *And* in your cab.'

'No problems. I paid off the tab at the Tomorrowman and took a stroll over. I was a little over the limit. Thanks for looking after the cab for me. I appreciate the gesture.'

'Don't mention it. You had no difficulties back at the bar?'

'Nah. A slight misunderstanding. For some reason the barman got it into his head that I was the boss of your TV station. I soon straightened him out.'

'I'm so very glad to hear it because I'd like you to take us back there now.'

'Back there?' The cabby looked doubtful.

'Well, to the alleyway behind the bar. Could you manage that?'

'Anything for you, me old cock sparrow. The barman took my watch in payment by the way.'

'I'll get you another.'

'You are a scholar and a gentleman. Hop in then and we'll be off.'

Rex opened the rear door. 'Is this OK, Laura?'

'It's OK. Just let's go.'

'OK.'

'How are we doing, chief?'

'I think we just about ran out of alleyway, Barry. What is that up ahead, do you suppose?'

'Damnedest thing I ever saw, chief. Do you think that's it?'

'Has to be. X marks the spot. Let's put our faith in old Sir John.'

'OK. Let's do.'

'OK.'

Bill was whistling in a devil-may-care sort of way as they sped along. Rex said to Laura, 'Tell me all about it.'

'All of this is wrong, Rex. All of it. It's designed. It's not true.'

'Go on.'

'Presley City. The Department of Human Resources runs it all. Controls it. But you won't find the number in the phone book. The Department is everywhere and

128

nowhere, organizing everything. We just play our roles. There is no individual thought here.'

Rex gazed from the window. The streets seemed even more like theatrical backdrops. 'Actors on a film set.'

'Just like that, yes. It's all false, all of it.'

'I understand. But tell me, if you grew up in all this, how do you know that it's false? This society appears on the surface to function. There is law and order, well, sort of. How can you be so sure that it's not what it seems?'

'There are books, a book, that tells us the way it should have been. It's all very complicated. It would take time to explain.'

'On the contrary,' Rex put his arm around her shoulder, 'it's all a lot more simple than you think. I know what went wrong here and I think I know how to put it right.'

The cab driver went right on whistling. But he'd heard every word.

'If that's where we're going, Barry, there's one or two small things we have to do first.'

'Like get the sandwiches in, chief?'

'Like that. And also.' I ducked around the corner of the alleyway and flattened myself against the wall the way a flounder hugs the ocean floor. Only vertically. If you catch my on-shore drift. And I'm sure that you do. 'Dee and Kelley have been shadowing us ever since we left my office. I think it's time to settle those old scores.'

'Oh goody, goody chief. If I had hands to rub in glee, a rubbing of them I would be.'

'Nice couplet, Barry. You got real class.'

'More than can be said for you, you big girl's blouse.'

'What's that, Barry?'

'Nothing, chief.'

*   *   *

The cab came to a halt. The traffic tailed back. Sirens shrieked and coloured beacons went round and round the way some of them do.

'We'll walk from here,' said Rex.

'You want I should wait, bruv?'

'That would be just fine. Don't forget to keep the meter running.'

'Oh, I won't, never fear.'

Around the Tomorrowman Tavern there was all that pushing and shoving, toing and froing, shouting and swearing, flashbulb clicking and general mayhem that ever there was. Rex put on his sunglasses and elbowed his way into the crowd to gawp along with the rest.

Within the police cordon, ambulances stood, rear doors yawning. Body bags were being zipped and trolleys shuttled back and forth. Rex spied out Sam Maggott hollering at all and sundry and making good use of his over-sized red gingham handkerchief. He also spied out the Tomorrowman's barman. He had a strip of bandage tied around his head, a small dot of blood showing romantically above the right eye. He was sporting a Clark Gable moustache and being terribly brave about it all.

Laura tugged at Rex's arm. 'This way.'

They skirted the crowd and slipped away into the network of side alleys.

'Just along here, third turning on the left.'

'You know these alleyways well then, Laura?'

'Intimately. I once earned a thirty-six-inch George III mahogany tea table in the manner of Thomas Chippendale, behind those trash cans over there.'

'Thank you,' said Rex. 'I don't wish to know that.' They reached the third turning on the left.

'Sssh. There's someone there.' Rex pushed Laura against the wall and craned his neck to see what was what.

And *what* was most certainly *what*. The Repo Man stood, battle-scarred, speechless and stock still. But around it, the group of men was smartly clad, verbose and seriously agitated. Three wore the white coats of the back-room boffin, the fourth was diminutive, little more than a boy. But he was clearly giving the orders. He wore a natty black business suit and a pair of sunglasses just like Rex's.

'Oh no.' Rex turned his face away and covered it with his hands.

'It's him.'

'Him, who? Rex, look at me. Who is it?'

'A very bad memory. Does the name Jonathan Crawford mean anything to you?'

'Stick 'em up,' said I, spinning around the corner and thrusting the snout of the trusty Smith and Western Railway right up the unsuspecting hooter of Johnny Dee esquire.

'Shit,' said Johnny, doing a reasonable impression of a Dalek.

'I got you fellas banged to rights. You're nicked.'

'You're nicked?' Ed made the kind of face I usually keep for Tuesdays. 'Very New York private eye, that. You'll be taking our dabs and turning over our drums next.'

'Don't worry about the vernacularisms.' I waggled my piece in his crony's snoz. 'I got a big score to settle with you two.'

'Ah,' said Ed. 'You mean the matter of us costing you your wife, your job at the department, a dog named Blue and six months in intensive care?'

'Yeah, and that. I was thinking more about the unkind remarks you made about my trenchcoat.'

'We were just kidding around. It's a real nice trenchcoat. Although I notice extensive second-degree smutting and several blots of what appears to be some kind of industrial lubricant. You should dab those with lemon juice before they sink right in.'

131

'Don't try to smooth-talk me. You were going to saw my head off.'

'Ah,' said Ed once more. 'Then I suppose a formal apology, couched in ingratiating terms, wouldn't exactly fit the bill at this particular time.'

'Damn right. I'm taking the two of you in.'

'We can't do that right now, chief.'

'Who said that?' Ed looked hotter under the collar than a Tina Turner dress shield.

'Never you mind. OK. If I can't bring you in, then I'm just going to have to make a citizen's execution.' I withdrew the muzzle of the trusty Smith and Waistcoat from Johnny's nose and pointed it at his forehead.

'Hold hard,' said he, raising his hands and shaking his head. 'You can't shoot us. If you do you'll never recover the Presley hoard.'

'Don't bet on it. Offer your apologies to the deity, fellas. You and he are about to move mouth.'

'Is there nothing we can say to make you change your mind?'

'Nothing. Your time has come.' I had that flinty look in my eyes that told Ed all he needed to know.

'OK then.' Ed shrugged. 'That's the way of it, I suppose. We've had a good innings. I can accept my fate. How about you, Johnny?'

'Oh yes. I can accept it also. I have my regrets of course. But there you are. I only wish . . .'

'What do you wish, Johnny?'

'Oh nothing. A dying man's last request. Nothing to bother our flinty-eyed Nemesis with.'

'Come on now, Johnny. Certainly Mr Woodbine is a hard-boiled, tough as they come, lantern-jawed harbinger of our certain doom. But he is also an American and before he guns you down in cold blood, in the manner you so justly deserve I might add, I'm sure he will see his way clear to giving you a dying request.'

'Do you really think so?'

132

'Why not ask him yourself?'

'Oh, I couldn't. It's too embarrassing.'

'Go on,' said I, stroking my lantern jaw. 'It can't hurt to ask.'

'Well . . . it's just that I always wanted to die clutching something that was near to the earth. A flower perhaps.'

'Touching, Johnny.' Ed patted his chum. 'I can appreciate that. One should be near to the natural world when one meets with an unnatural death.'

'Well put, Ed. But where would we find a flower around here? Or even a vegetable if it comes to that?'

'Even a vegetable, yes. To touch a vegetable, clasp it in your hands when you met with what fate had to offer. What a joy. But it would take a pretty exceptional executioner to come up with a vegetable on the spur of the moment. Mr Woodbine's hardly going to be carrying around a vegetable in his pocket, now is he?'

'Oh yeah?' said I, plucking Barry from my top pocket. 'Well, check this out.'

'A miracle,' cried Johnny. 'The man is a saint.'

'Saint I may be but schmuck I ain't. What do you guys take me for? You really think I was going to fall for a line like that and hand Barry over to you?'

Johnny nodded his head. 'Yes,' said he, 'I did, as it happens.'

'So did I,' said Ed.

'Well OK then. I just wanted to be sure you weren't trying to pull a fast one on me.' I tossed Barry over to Johnny Dee. 'Ain't gonna do you the slightest good any which way. Barry's banjoed and you've got *An Appointment With Death**.'

'Chief. You're on a wrong'n. Take me back.'

'Let the man have his dying request, Barry. Don't be stingy. I'll catch you when he hits the dirt.'

'But chief . . .'

---

*A Lazlo Woodbine thriller.

'Bye, fellas.' I pointed my piece at Johnny and squeezed on the trigger. There was a pretty pathetic little click, it being out of bullets and everything. But suddenly there was something of a puff of smoke and I found myself standing all alone in the alleyway with what might well be metaphorical egg all over my kisser.

'Barry?' said I.

'You bloody fool, chief,' echoed a little green voice.

'What's that, Barry?'

'Nothing, chief.'

Rex took out Laura's pistol and peered along the barrel. 'What exactly does this do?' he asked. 'What is its range and what are its capabilities? Please be specific. An opportunity like this mightn't present itself again.'

'You are going to kill this Jonathan Crawford then?'

'I truly feel it would be for the best.'

'Have you ever killed anyone before?'

'No. Not as such.'

'Then let me do it.'

'Certainly not. What does this gun do?'

'It fires an explosive acid cap. Doesn't matter where you hit someone. Contact is always lethal.'

'Ideal for home defence, I have no doubt.' Rex took the gun in both hands. Both hands were trembling. 'He's evil.' Rex bit his lip. 'Very evil. About as evil as it is possible to get.'

'Then shoot him. Don't think about it. Do it quickly.'

Don't think about it. Rex took a deep breath, sprang out from hiding and drew down upon the boy in the business suit.

'Jonathan,' he shouted. 'Over here.'

The boy turned. 'Rex,' said he. 'Well, well, well.'

'I'm sorry, Jonathan.' Rex squeezed the trigger. Jonathan pulled one of the back-room boffin types into the line of fire. The bullet struck the white-clothed back. There was a muffled report, the man rose upon tiptoe but he didn't fall. His body seemed to swell and distort but he just stood there. Screaming and screaming. Rex turned his face away. Covered his ears. But the cries of agony went on and on.

'He's dead, Rex. He's dead.' Laura pulled his hands from his head and shouted into his face. 'Stop screaming.'

Rex tore himself away from her. 'Screaming?'

'He's dead. Look for yourself.'

Rex looked for himself. The body lay twisted at impossible angles. Jonathan had gone. The Repo Man had gone.

Rex turned away and was violently sick.

11

25. *And thus did the big tour continue.*
And Elvis spake unto his people
regarding such matters as crude oil,
gasoline and stretch Cadillacs.
26. *And the children of Elvis did hang*
on his every word. And when he had
spoken they did hasten unto Kuwait,
Saudi Arabia and Texas, saying, 'These
also are the promised lands.'

The Suburban Book of the Dead

This was just great. Dee and Kelley had done the now legendary vanishing act and they'd taken Barry along with them. I wasn't a little nonplussed.

I never had a fear of going it alone, don't get me wrong. I've gone it alone more times than a hermit with attitude. But it was going to be a real bummer not having the little guy around to chat with while I single-handedly solved my cases.

I refilled my piece. I had just about run myself dry of duff funnies regarding the trusty Smith and Whatsaname. Right now I had a job to do. Recover the Presley hoard and save civilization as we would know it. Because, as you may, or may not have realized, this is one big number. I wasn't being paid $500,000 a day to sit on my butt and watch *Blue Peter*. In fact, without Barry I wasn't going to get paid $500,000 at all. In fact without Barry I was possibly in the deep brown stuff up neckaways.

I looked up at the building. Biggest damn thing I ever saw. And somewhere inside it, was the Presley hoard, or was going to be real shortly. I straightened my shoulders, choked back a small ·tear for the loss of a good buddy and turned up the collar of my trenchcoat.

'OK,' said I with more determination than a sybarite in a sacristy. 'Now's the time to nail my colours to the mast, throw away the scabbard, buckle to, go the whole hog, cross the Rubicon, grab the bull by the horns, put my shoulder to the wheel and leave a note out for the milkman.'

I wasn't looking for trouble. But if trouble came looking for me I wasn't going to be hard to find. Only a dog dies in Brooklyn when Frank Sinatra's in the witness box. If you know what I mean. And I'm sure that you do-be-do-be-do.

'I don't know what to say, Rex.' Laura held Rex in her arms. They were back in her apartment. Bill had dropped them off and was lurking outside. 'You're feeling pretty bad, I can see that.'

'Bad? Laura, I shot a man in the back. I've never killed anyone. I don't do that kind of thing. I get into impossible scrapes but win through in the end. I can't live with this. A man's death on my conscience.' Rex covered his face and sobbed.

'He was one of the bad guys.'

'That doesn't matter. I don't even know his name. I killed him. One moment he was alive, then . . .'

'You did what you thought was right. It was an accident.'

'I took a man's life. Doesn't that mean anything to you?'

Laura shrugged. 'He was only a Repo Man. I can't see what you're making such a fuss about.'

'A Repo Man?' Rex was aghast.

'Sure. I saw all the sparks when he went down.'

'Saw the sparks? Laura, you let me throw up all over the alley, all over Bill's cab. Cry my eyes out, make an absolute wally of myself and now you tell me he was a Repo Man.'

'I thought you knew.'

'Laura,' said Rex, 'kindly take off all your clothes.'

'How did you do that? *I* didn't do that . . .' Barry was boggled. He had just materialized in a certain top-secret room in the bad company of Dee and Kelley.

'The transperambulation of pseudo-cosmic anti-matter,' John Dee explained. 'Surely you know all about the cross-polarization of negatively-charged beta particles.'

'Am I a sprout, or what?'

'You certainly are. And a very special one.'

'Well, thanks. But listen, chief. That was a pretty sneaky stroke you pulled on Laz back there. Him and me work as a team, you know, I don't do any freelance jobs, especially not with a pair of low-down—'

'Low-down?' Johnny Dee gave Barry a nasty tweak.

'Nothing, chief. So what's all this about, then?'

Dee smiled upon the sprout and patted him kindly.

'Turn me up the right way, chief. I hate having my bum patted.'

'My apologies. It's just that we have a little surprise for you and we didn't want Mr Woodentop spoiling it.'

'That's nice. I think.'

'There's someone we want you to meet,' said Ed. 'Close your eyes for a moment. You do have eyes, don't you?'

'I can't recall any mention of them, but I suppose I must have or I wouldn't be able to see anything, would I? Unless of course I have derma-optical perception. I do possess some pretty awesome powers, as you may well be aware.'

'Oh we are, we are. Now shut your eyes or whatever it is you do.'

'You won't do anything unpleasant to me, will you, chief?'

'Trust us.'

'Like shit.'

'What's that?'

'Nothing, chief. They're closed.'

'All right. Now keep them closed.' Barry heard a door open and footsteps coming in his direction. He was able to calculate that these were made by a man in his twenties, approximately six feet tall, weighing a little over eleven stone. Which was a little bit awesome, but not very.

'Open your eyes,' cried Johnny Dee.

Barry opened them up. Ed and Johnny were sporting foolish party hat and blowing those paper things that uncurl like a chameleon's tongue and go baarrrp. And standing between them was . . .

'Rex!' Barry boggled anew. 'Rex Mundi, as I live and osmose.'

'Barry,' the other Rex replied. 'I can't tell you how pleased this makes me.'

* * *

Rex lay on the bed smiling wistfully at the ceiling. 'That was wonderful,' he said.

Laura made a face. 'What a cop-out. I just knew the horny sex wouldn't get a mention. And if it didn't get a mention, then we didn't actually do it.'

Rex turned her a surprised stare. 'What do you mean? We've been humping away for a whole two and a half pages. Look at these saddle sores. And all the sandpaper I've used up.'

'So you say.'

Rex counted on his fingers. 'Half page 139 and pages 140 and 141.'

Laura flicked back. 'Blank. Tipp-Exed out! Typical!'

'Well,' said Rex. 'Well, I never did.'

'Evidently not. Shall I now wrap myself in the duvet and slip into the shower for a misty out-of-focus silhouette?'

'No.' Rex put his arm around her shoulder. 'Speak to me. There is a great deal I need to know if I'm going to do anything about it.'

'All right. Where do you want me to start?'

'Tell me about Elvis.'

'The Living God?'

'God? The King perhaps, but God? What is all this?'

'Elvis the Everliving.' Laura spat in a most unladylike fashion. 'That to him.'

'Quite.' Rex wiped his eye.

'Sorry, Rex.'

'Don't mention it. But tell me about Elvis.'

'You really don't know, do you? Where are you from, Rex? How did you get here? You're with us, aren't you?'

'One thing at a time. Just tell me about Elvis.'

'It's all in here.' Laura reached over to the bedside table, a Sheraton satinwood cabinet, with cross-banded doors flanked by pilasters inlaid with husk chains. She brought to light a slim black volume and tossed it to Rex.

Rex turned it to face him and read the title. 'THE SUBURBAN BOOK OF THE DEAD' it said in nice big letters. 'What?' Rex leafed through the pages. 'This isn't *my* book. The book I had all those years ago. This is . . .'

'It's a bible,' sneered Laura. 'The bible of the false messiah.'

'Oh dear, oh dear, oh dear.' Rex made a major sigh. 'I think I'd better give this a bit of a read. Would you mind terribly if I did this on my own?'

'Would you chaps mind terribly if Barry and I were left alone?' the other Rex asked. 'We have so very much to talk about.'

'No sweat, excellency – I mean, *Rex*.' Johnny Dee winked lewdly, and he and Kelley shuffled backwards through the doorway and were gone.

'You've fallen in with a right bad pair there, chief. They're wanted criminals, you know.'

'I know, Barry. I've tricked them into working for me. I'm trying to track down the Presley hoard. Those two stole it.'

'I know, chief. That's why Laz and I are here also.'

'Laz?' The other Rex asked casually. 'Who's Laz?'

'He's a detective from the twenty-fifth century. We work together now. I'm the straight man, he's my comic relief. Traditional set-up, you know the kind of thing.'

The other Rex nodded. 'A well-tried formula. But where is Elvis? I thought you and he . . .'

'Ah, chief. A sad business that.'

'Do you want to talk about it?' The other Rex placed Barry on the table and seated himself. 'I'm really keen to meet up with Elvis again.'

'Not much chance of that chief. He's . . .'

'Go on, Barry.'

'Nah, chief. It's better that you don't know.'

'Barry. You and I have known each other a long time. Elvis and me, we were, you know . . .'

'Sure, I know, chief. You were good buddies. OK, I'll tell it like it was. But it's a sad tale and it doesn't have a happy ending.'

Rex closed the book. It didn't have a happy ending.

So that was it. Elvis had travelled back to the dawn of mankind and persuaded God to let him do it his way. And God, in his infinite wisdom, or in a moment of severe brainstorm, had actually given him the go-ahead. Elvis had then travelled forwards in time, locating each potential mother of the Anti-Christ and wooed her away from the Satanic father to be. Something which, no doubt, he enjoyed a great deal. The result being that the Anti-Christ never got born. On the face of it a most ingenious scheme.

But along the way it had all got fouled up. Elvis's vanity had been given its full and well-quiffed head. He'd had himself painted and sculptured again and again, and he'd been there for all the world to see. Century after century. Elvis the Everliving. He had become God. But what of Jesus? Rex flicked back to the appropriate page and read aloud.

And Elvis said unto Pontius Pilate, 'Listen Pont, this is a bum rap. The guy's a first-time offender. All he did was shoot his mouth off a little. He's still prepared to render unto Caesar and stuff. How's about easing up on the sentence, it is Easter after all.'

And Pilate spake thusly, saying, 'Seeing as it's you and this is a fine case of Old Bedwetter you've brought me, I'll play the white man. But I'll have to give him a caution at least. What do you suggest?'

And Elvis in his wisdom replied, 'Let the kid off with a fine. Say thirty pieces of silver. I can get that off Judas, he's come into some cash lately.'

And Pilate said, 'So let it be.'

And let it be it was.

'Got him off with a fine.' Rex buried his face in his hands. 'Elvis, you steaming great buffoon. You cocked it all up. You caused all this.' A world that was nothing but image. A world where style was everything and the wearing of white shoes in a *blue suede shoe zone* was a capital offence.

'Brilliant,' sighed Rex. 'You really had the mother of all revelations this time, didn't you? But where?' Rex leafed through to the end of the book. 'Where are you now?'

'Where is he now?' the other Rex asked.

'Around somewhere, chief. You see, he and I had a bit of a falling out. It was all those statues and stuff. And the paintings. Everywhere, every time we were, he'd want to get his likeness done. He had this book, see, *A Complete History of the World's Art*. So every century we were in he'd say "We must drop in and say howdy to Michelangelo or Raphael or Donatello or Leonardo," and he'd get his picture painted.'

'The Teenage Mutant Ninja Turtles painted his picture?'

'Chief, that gag was done back on page 16 and it stank then.'

'Sorry. Please continue.'

'Thank you. So, like I said, we'd drop in on Van Gogh and Dali and Dave Carson . . .'

'Dave Carson?' the other Rex asked. 'Who he?'

'Only the greatest artist of the twentieth century, that's who. [All right for you, Davey?] He drew Elvis with all these tentacles coming out of his bonce. Not my cup of tea at all. Now don't keep interrupting.'

'Sorry, Barry. Go on.'

'Well, he got sculpted and frescoed and painted and even woven into the bloody Bayeux tapestry dressed as a Norman soldier. Century after century.'

'I see. And you didn't approve? You respected his motives but detested his vanity.'

'No, chief. That wasn't it at all.'

'Then what was it?'

'He never let *me* be in the sodding pictures.'

Laura returned from the shower. She was naked and she smelled like Heaven. 'You've read it then?'

'I've read it. But what I still don't understand is, if you were schooled on this stuff, how do you know it's wrong? What are you, an atheist?'

'An atheist?' Laura laughed. 'I'm one of the Children of the Revolution. I believe in the true God.'

'The true God. I see. That is most encouraging.'

'Then you believe also? But of course you do. He sent you to help us, didn't he?'

'I suppose he must've done.'

'Yes.' Laura seated herself on the bed and Rex gave her a good sniff. 'This crap,' Laura took the book from Rex's fingers and struck it with the back of her hand. 'None of this is the truth. Elvis was never, is never, the true God.'

'Bravo.' Rex moved in for a cuddle. 'I can dig that.'

Laura shifted out of range. 'Elvis was merely a vehicle.'

'Eh?'

'A vehicle for the true God. The true God spake unto him and controlled his every movement.'

'He did?'

'He did. The true God dwelt within Elvis. In here.' Laura tapped the back of her head. 'He dictated Elvis's every action, whilst remaining invisible and all knowing.'

'He did?' Rex went again. 'And who is *He*?'

'BAH-REAH.' Laura drew an invisible circle on her

forehead. 'BAH-REAH is the true God and we are the children of BAH-REAH. The Children of the Revolution. We will cast down the towers of the false god and raise the banner of the All-Knower. Hail BAH-REAH!'

'BAH-REAH?' The horrified expression on Rex's face wasn't as pretty as a picture. 'Could that be pronounced *Barry* by any chance?'

'So there you have it,' said the sprout that several hundred well-armed revolutionaries knew as BAH-REAH the All-Knower. 'We parted company and I took up with the bozo in the trenchcoat. I get a laugh out of it. Old Laz is a pretentious son of a gun, but he's got a heart of gold. He doesn't come cheap, but he gets the job done. With him you can expect a lot of gratuitous sex and violence, a trail of corpses and a thrilling roof-top—'

'Yes. I get the picture. But where is Elvis? Here, in the now?'

'I guess, chief. This was our last port of call. Elvis had this revelation, see? Said that the Anti-Christ was going to show up here. Said that as Mother Demdike had escaped at the end of *They Came And Ate Us*, there was a loose end. He was real concerned about it. But not too concerned that he couldn't find time to drop into Simon Butcher's to have his picture taken.'

'Simon Butcher, the society photographer?'

'That's the guy, chief. You know him?'

'We've never met. But they say he's the greatest photographer of all time.' [If it's another name drop then it gets cut. Ed]

'Couldn't say. I didn't stick around for the session. Utilizing some of the truly awesome powers at my disposal, I took, as Laz would say, a powder, and went on the lam. A sprout can take just so much and then no more. If you catch my drift. And I'm sure that you do.'

'I understand. But I'm puzzled. You came along with

147

Dee and Kelley without a fuss. Why was that?'

'Ah,' said Barry. 'Well I've run into a spot of bother. I find myself temporarily incapacitated in the time-travelling department. I can't seem to get it together at present. It will no doubt sort itself out in a few days.'

'A few days?' The horrified expression the other Rex now wore was exactly identical to the one the other other Rex had been wearing only moments before. Weird, eh? 'A few days? But in a couple of days the Big Bang goes up.'

'The Big Bang goes up. Yes, I know that.' Barry gazed upon the other Rex. 'But how come *you* know that, bucko?'

'What's that, Barry?'

'Nothing, chief.'

'He has to be here,' said the real Mr Mundi. 'Somewhere here, in the now.'

'Who has to be?'

'Elvis. He's here somewhere.'

'He's always here. That's what he does. That's why he is.'

Rex flicked through to the final page of *The Suburban Book of the Dead.* ' "And Elvis went unto the House of Light and was seen no more." What does that mean, do you suppose? The House of Light? That he died, would that be it?'

'Uh-uh.' Laura shook her head. 'The House of Light is right here in Presley City.'

'And built just like a jukebox, I'll bet.'

'You got it. But it's not in the phone book. I only discovered I was in it by sheer chance. The guy who owns it was shouting all kinds of stuff and he let it slip. I had this live eel and he liked to have me insert it . . .'

'Thank you, Laura. So who is this fish fancier?'

'His name is Simon Butcher and he's the most famous photographer of all time.'

'Famous photographer, it figures. And you know him well?'

'You gotta know a guy quite well before he trusts you to stick a live eel up his . . .'

'Quite so. Then I think we'd better pay this Mr Butcher a visit.'

I gazed up at the building. Biggest damn piece of architecture I've ever seen. And I've seen some. I only say this in passing, you understand. Just to set the scene and seeing as I haven't been in the plot too much lately. It costs nothing to say it was a big old building, not if you're standing in an alleyway. The way I was currently doing. I figured there were a whole lot of answers inside that building and I figured that like or not there had to be a back entrance to it somewhere. And I figured that it would be more than a racing cert that it was situated in another alleyway. So I struck out in search.

The sun was going down upon Presley City. It would do this twice more and then call it a day. As far as Presley City was concerned anyway.

Bill was leaning on his cab, spitting at the wing mirror and half-heartedly polishing it with his sleeve. He stiffened to belligerent attention as Rex and Laura approached.

'All better now, are we?' he enquired in a manner hardly calculated to endear. 'Got over our queezy tum?'

Rex opened the cab door for Laura.

'Ready to hit the night spots, eh?' the cabby continued. 'I've left the meter running by the way. Want to settle up now or later?'

'Later,' said Rex. 'Do you know Simon Butcher's studio?'

'Hardly miss it. Biggest damn building in town.'

'Then kindly take us there.'

'Your wish is my command, oh master.'

'Hmm.' Rex followed Laura into the cab which was becoming their second home and they were driven off into *A Night of Danger*.*

'We going shopping again tomorrow, squire?' Bill called over his shoulder. 'Only this jumpsuit's going through at the arse and the bellbottoms are getting well chewed up on the pedals.'

'I haven't decided yet. Do you have any music you could play?'

'I surely do.' Bill rooted amongst a rack of laser discs. 'I got the Cray Cherubs, the Lost Teeshirts of Atlantis, The Turbulent Priests, Sonic Energy Authority—'

'Got any Marc Bolan?' Rex asked.

'I got "Pewter Suitor".'

'Well bung it on and turn it up.'

Bill bunged it on and turned it up.

Rex nuzzled close to Laura's ear. 'I think we are going to have to lose the cabby,' he whispered.

Laura smiled back at him. 'Just say the word,' she replied, without moving her lips.

'In the meantime,' Rex whispered on. 'Tell me what you know about the chap off the telly. Make it look like you're singing along.'

'You don't ask much, do you? OK.' Laura sang along.

> 'He's a rel-ig-ious loon
> he's real loonie tune aha ha
> He tops the folk on his show
> and he loves the way they go aha ha
> The station says it ain't real
> but you can tell by how they squeal aha ha
> And that's all I know
> na na na nanana na
> na na na nanana na
> na na na nanana . . .'

*A Lazlo Woodbine thriller (although it shouldn't be on this page)

'Thanks,' said Rex. 'But that wasn't the tune of "Pewter Suitor", that was "Hot Love".'

'Oh, I'm *so* sorry.' Laura got a huff on. 'But all his later stuff sounds the same to me. And, seeing as it was only a cheap literary device anyway, and that not even the legendary Graham Gardner* owns a copy of "Pewter Suitor", who's ever going to know?'

'Point taken. Are we nearly there, Bill?'

'What say, guv? Hang on while I turn down "Telegram Sam", I can't hear what you're saying.'

'See what I mean?' Laura stuck her tongue out at Rex.

'I said,' Rex said when all was quiet, 'are we nearly there?'

'Yep. That's it up ahead. Pretty snazzy, eh? Some scam that photography game. Did you know that Cecil Beaton couldn't even load his own camera? I had that Robert Mapplethorpe in the back of my cab once.'

'No, you didn't.' Rex shook his head.

'Of course I didn't. Just trying to enliven the journey with a spot of cabby's banter. All part of the service.'

'Just drive the cab.'

'Just drive the cab.' Bill echoed Rex's words in a sarcastic sing song. 'No pleasing some people. So I said to Robert Mapplethorpe, I don't call that art, having your self portrait done with a whip stuck up your . . .'

'Bill, please just drive. You really must learn where to draw the line.'

'I'm easy, me. I never had a lot of time for good taste. I'm a take-me-as-you-find-me sort of guy, know what I mean? Give me a shellsuit, a pit-bull terrier and a wife to smack around after I've had a few, and I'm happy. I speak as I find. There's no side to me and I look after me old mum. The family's everything to me. I might abuse my kids, but where's the harm in that? Society's to blame

*The world's leading expert on the life and works of the metal guru. And author of *God Put the Tree There.*

151

when you come right down to it. If I'd had a proper education do you think I'd be driving this cab around?'

'I really couldn't say. But as you are, perhaps you might just do it in silence.'

'Blokes like you,' Bill continued, warming to his topic, 'you're privileged. You think you're better than me. But you're not. I can see right through you.'

'You can drop us off on the corner if you like, Bill.'

'Oh, *Bill*, is it? On first-name terms, are we? Just because you've run up $100,000 on the meter you think you own me. Well you don't.'

'I don't know what's brought this on all of a sudden . . .'

'You bastards get right up my bum. Bigfoot noses for lunch and a flashy whore on the end of your growler for tea.'

'Stop the cab!'

Bill accelerated and then rammed his foot on the brake pedal causing Rex and Laura to plummet floorward.

'Here do you, *chief*?' Bill smirked round at his struggling passengers. 'Give her one for me while you're down there.'

'Right, that does it.' Rex fought his way upright. 'Step outside.'

'Oh ho, step outside is it? Sure enough.' The cabby swung open his door and climbed out. 'Let me help you.' He opened the car door for Rex. 'Mind your head, *chief*.'

That's twice with the *chief*, thought Rex, who rather than have his head mashed by a slamming door, put his boot against it and offered a mighty kick.

The door shot open, knocking Bill from his feet and sending him sprawling across the sidewalk. A strangely-deserted sidewalk, Rex noted as he leapt out of the cab and stalked over to the fallen driver.

'What's got into you?' he demanded. 'Why are you behaving like this?'

Bill glared up at him. His face was a ghastly white and his eyes shone red as Cortina brake lights.

'I hate you.' The grounded cabby spoke the words in a low cold dead tone which left absolutely no margin for misinterpretation.

Rex took a precautionary step backwards. He was genuinely shocked. 'Why?' he asked. 'What have I done to you?'

Bill raised himself on his elbows and scowled fiercely. 'You don't know me, but I know you.'

Rex sought a speedy solution. He really was in something of a hurry and there was going to be nothing gained by engaging in either argument of fisticuffs with a cab driver.

'Look,' said he, 'I don't know what your problem is and in all candour, I don't actually care. Here, take this.' He pulled several wristwatches from his pocket and flung one down to Bill. 'I'm borrowing your cab.'

'I think not.' Bill's face took on an evil grin. He folded his arms across his chest and swung upright magically upon his heels.

'Hmm.' Rex didn't like the look of that one little bit.

Bill glared him eye to eye. 'I'm going to punish you,' he snarled. 'It will be a long painful lingering punishment terminating in a horrifying death.'

'I really don't have time for this' Rex was backing towards the cab. A voice inside him was saying 'drive like buggery if you know what's good for you'.

'Oh no you don't.' The cabby shot out an arm. He shot it straight out of his jumpsuit sleeve, through the skin and bones of his human hand and right at Rex's throat.

The hand, which missed the ducking Rex by inches, struck the cab, rocking it upon its wheels and leaving a fearsome five-knuckled intaglio above the driver's door. The hand was broad, black, scaled and terribly taloned.

Rex rolled across the sidewalk and came up with his

hand inside his leather jacket. Now where was Laura's gun? Rex patted himself frantically. Not upon his person, it so appeared.

'Oh dear, oh dear,' groaned Rex.

Bill turned upon him. 'Don't recognize me yet?'

Rex gaped at the cab driver in the soiled jumpsuit. The cab driver who now displayed a big black muscular right arm about four feet long, curtained by torn Lycra and ribbons of human flesh.

'Let's give you another clue. Tell me when you think you're getting warm.' Bill began to bulge in all directions. His shoulders spread to the accompaniment of sickening bone-cracking reports. His head expanded, the facial features flattening, but for the eyes which popped from their sockets. The crutch of the jumpsuit shot forwards as if under the impetus of some mighty erection. A tiger's head sprang out from it snorting and snarling.

Rex watched in horror as the black claw tore Bill's left arm from its socket and flung it far up the street. Another huge and hideous arm sprouted from the ruined shoulder. Rex felt that now really would be the time to make a getaway.

With a great heave the black claws ripped away Bill's scalp, his face split from top to bottom revealing the three demonic masks of Hades rising from within. One of a bull, one of a ram and the third a beast of terrible aspect.

'Asmodeus!' Rex did further backings away. 'But how? You're dead. Gone into the ether.'

'When you *killed* me back at the Miskatonic? You expelled me from that plane. Now I exist in this one. And I'm really hungry.'

The beast-face leered at Rex and then began to laugh. Now, it wasn't your average giggle, snigger, snicker, titter or tee hee. Nor, it must be said, a hoot, chuckle, chortle, crow or cackle. There wasn't even a hint of the belly wobbler or the throaty guffaw. What you had here was your one hundred per cent pure, full-scale Hell's-a-happening, deep-down Satanic bowel loosener. And it fair put the wind up Rex Mundi.

Asmodeus shook away the clinging remains of good old Bill. Gobbets of cabby flesh, splinters of fractured bone and jaded jumpsuit remnants sprayed over the sidewalk.

'That's better,' said he, flexing his titanic shoulders and thrusting out his great barrel of a chest. 'It was really cramped in there. I was just supposed to keep an eye on you and let you lead us to the enemy. But sod it, I'm really hungry. Those bigfoot noses don't hit the spot.'

'I could get you a takeaway.' Rex took another step backwards and found to his unhappiness that he had backed himself neatly into a well-barred shop doorway.

The monstrous tiger on which Asmodeus sat crept forwards, sulphurous plumes of smoke rising from its nostrils. Asmodeus dug his spurs in. 'Gee up, Tigger,' he cried.

For those who missed his performance in *They Came And Ate Us* it must be said that this wasn't a very nice demon at all. Heinrich Kramer, co-author of the merry *Malleus Maleficarum*, wrote of him thus:

'Et quosdam daemones, quos Dusios Galli nuncupant, adsidue hanc immunditiam et tentare et efficere, plures talesque adscurant, ut hoc negare impudentiae uideatur.'

And how true those words are, even today.

'Sweetmeats first,' crowed Asmodeus. 'I want this to last.'

He plunged at Rex, who had nowhere to run, scooped him up with a single movement and held him good and high.

'Yum, yum, yum.'

'No, wait. Let's talk about this.'

155

'Off with his goolies, nice and slow.' Asmodeus prepared to make a substantial, octave-raising munch. The lad in the leather kicked, struggled and called for mercy. But it really wasn't going to get him anywhere.

The beast-face pursed its lips and a set of those extendible animatronic teeth, which have become *de rigueur* for every good monster since *Alien* hit the screen, snuck out, dripping slime.

'Oh no. Don't do that.' Rex crossed his legs and thought 'retraction'.

The extendible teeth went 'snap snap snap'.

'Put Rex down!'

Rex turned his terrified eyes from the impending horrors below. Laura stood before the cab. She held the intricate hand weapon in both hands. 'Put him down.'

Asmodeus took his teeth back. 'What's all this?'

'Put him down or I shoot.'

The three faces turned and glared back over the demon's shoulders. 'Ah yes; you. I shall have uses for you once I've eaten.'

'Put him down. I mean it.'

'She means it,' said Rex.

'Don't be silly.'

'No, she really does. You'd best put me down if you know what's good for you.'

Asmodeus swung his faces back to Rex. 'What's good for me at about this time is a nice supper off the bone. Followed by a good cigar, a bottle or two of brandy and acts of gross depravity upon the whore.'

'Shoot him, Laura!'

Laura thumbed dials on her weapon and let off three rounds into the back of the demon's head.

'Oh ouch! Oh shit! Oh Hell!'

'Oh bah!' went the ram's face.

'Oh snort!' went the bull's.

Rex found himself crashing to the ground.

'That really smarts.' Asmodeus clawed at the back of his head.

'Shoot him some more.' Rex crawled away. Laura shot him some more.

'Oh bloody bleeding blimey.'

Rex was on his feet and running. 'Get back in the cab.'

Asmodeus shook his head and swung his mount around. 'Now I'm angry. Let's kill 'em and eat.'

'Get in the cab.' Rex thrust Laura into the back of the car and threw himself into the driver's seat. He scrabbled at the dashboard.

'Where are the keys?' he asked.

'I haven't got them, Bill must of taken them.'

'Aw shit!'

Asmodeus reined his devil steed around to the front of the cab. He climbed down and smiled thricely through the windscreen. 'You've upset me now,' he growled, 'and do you know what happens when I get upset?'

Rex considered that it probably wasn't anything good.

Asmodeus took hold of the front bumper and gave the cab an almighty shake.

'Rex, do something!'

'What can I do? Oh no!'

Asmodeus lifted the cab and held the front of it high above his head. 'Say good night people.'

'Good night, Rex.'

'Goodbye, Laura. It's been nice.'

'Yeah. It's been really nice, as it happens.'

'Goodbye!' screamed the three faces of Asmodeus the arch-demon.

12

Your really classic science-fiction movie usually begins with the big pan across deep space. It's a tradition or an old charter or something. The camera pans across all those stars and galaxies and lets the audience know that this is one big number. The audience, who have seen it all many times before, shift in their seats, chit chat and open bags of popcorn.

Then the panning is done. And something swells into view. It might be a dirty great slab of stone, the Starship Enterprise, a holiday craft with *Predator* on board, or even a free-falling sprout. On this particular occasion however, it is a nifty little flying saucer. One of those dome-topped affairs, circa 1958.

The saucer whizzes overhead, the camera follows it and the next thing you see is its destination. Good old Planet Earth.

The planet grows to fill the screen, the saucer glows as it passes into the atmosphere. Black becomes the blue of the sky. Seas and continents fall past. The saucer sweeps in lower.

Due to a now-realized continuity error, the blue sky turns to red, the sun goes down and the saucer flies on through the night.

Ahead the lights of a great city appear on the horizon. A wondrous city, its high towers resembling the *Jukeboxes of the Gods.**

The saucer drops between the towers, flies low over strangely deserted streets and comes suddenly to a grinding halt.

Rex stared through the up-turned windscreen.

'Cor,' said he. 'What's that?'

A blinding light filled the cab and a beam of raw blue energy pulsed down.

Asmodeus stiffened as the beam engulfed him, let out a roar of disapproval and was promptly atomized. The cab crashed down on to the street and there was a bit of a hush.

The head of Rex Mundi appeared above the dashboard of the cab. 'Golly. Laura, are you all right?'

Laura's face peeped from the back. 'What happened?'

'Something.' Rex craned his neck, but the saucer had gone. The cab's engine burst into life. 'I think we just had help from an unexpected quarter.'

'Then let's get out of here.'

'Yes. Let's do.'

The Butcher Building was, as has been mentioned, constructed after the style of a sixty-six-storey jukebox. For those lovers of the nickelodeon, anxious to know exactly which model it was based upon, tough titty. I've only got the one book on jukeboxes and I've used up all the good ones. And let's face it, as a running gag, it really wasn't up to much. Like all that psychology nonsense.

Dead pretentious.

*An Erich Von Daniken reject.

*   *   *

Bill's cab skidded to a halt.

'Is that it?'

Laura was fixing her hair and repairing her make-up. 'Are you sure this is wise? Shouldn't we go into hiding or something?'

Rex adjusted himself in the driving mirror. 'If I can find Elvis, then he and I can deal with this thing. We can put it right.'

Laura laughed. 'We get attacked by a monster, the monster gets zapped by a flying saucer and now you fancy a chat with God Almighty. Life's never dull around you, is it?'

Rex might have managed a smile. 'Elvis and I can handle it.'

'You talk like you're old friends.'

'We are.' Rex got a smile on the go. 'The very best. Come on.'

The doorman of the Butcher Building looked suitably imposing. Rex turned a blind eye to the fact that he was obviously Officer Cecil, poorly disguised in false moustache, tailcoat and spats.

'Just keep walking,' whispered Rex, as he and Laura marched up the marble steps which led to the plaza before the great building.

They were right at the top when doorman Cecil barred their way.

'Watcha want?' he asked.

'I'm Rex Mundi.' Rex explained. 'The chap off the telly. I've come here to have my portrait taken by Mr Butcher. If you'll be so kind as to tell him I've arrived.'

'Oh. All right then.' Doorman Cecil turned away. Laura passed Rex the gun and Rex bopped him on the head with it. Doorman Cecil made a slow and extremely unconvincing fall into unconsciousness. 'Oh,' he groaned from the deck. 'I've been knocked out cold.'

'Hmm,' sighed Rex. 'Let's get this over with.' He took

160

Laura by the arm and guided her through the revolving doors.

The reception area was about as broad as it was long. Which was very broad and equally long. The carpet was black. The walls were white. The pictures which adorned them were black and white. The celebrities, captured for posterity by the world's leading photographer, all seemed singularly lacking in clothes.

'He's keen on a buff shot, this Butcher,' Rex observed. 'Say, Laura, isn't that you over there?'

'Well . . .' Laura grew somewhat rosy about the perfect cheekbones. 'I don't remember him taking my picture when I was doing that.'

'A small price to pay for a 600 Wurlitzer.'

'Can I help you, sir?' The young woman behind the expansive chromium reception desk caught Rex's attention. She was slim, svelte and sophisticated. Rex was no stranger to reception desk psychology.

'Good evening Ms. My name is Rex Mundi. Chap off the telly. I have an informal invitation to see Mr Butcher. You won't find it in the appointments book. Could you just ring up to old Si and let him know I've arrived?'

'Mr Butcher's having a session at the moment.'

Rex shunned the obvious rejoinder. 'If you'll just tell him Rex is here. I'm expected.'

'Well, I'll see. But he's very busy.' She turned away to make the call. Rex handed Laura the gun. Laura bopped the receptionist on the head with it.

'Thanks,' Rex said. 'Striking women always goes against the grain with me.'

'That's funny,' Laura replied. 'I really get off on it.'

'Hmm,' went Rex once more. 'Which way do you think?'

'Floor sixty-six. Come on, I'll lead the way.'

I watched the lift as it rode up the side of the building. I didn't know who the guy riding it was, but through my police issue 200 x 6000 macroscopic laser-prism binoculars I could see he was the same guy who had just bopped the doorman in the head.

I didn't know what he was up to and I guess I didn't care. But you can imagine my surprise when I angled said state-of-the-art bins to the street, watched the long black car as it rolled up and saw the self-same guy step out of it.

Laz, I said to myself, Laz, something pretty weird's going on here, and if you don't get on to your agent and negotiate for the use of another couple of sets, you're gonna be standing in this Goddamn alleyway for the rest of the book.

The little light filled the number sixty-six and the little bell went ping. Rex dropped down from the ceiling.

'Fast lift,' said he.

'Bum gag,' said Laura. 'Come on this way.' The doors opened and she strode forth.

She made off along a long marble-floored corridor. Rex walked close behind, appreciating every swish of her stockings.

Laura sighed. 'Walk with me, or I'll charge for every swish.'

'Quite so. Where's the studio?'

'Right here.'

The door had one of those big printed signs which shout NO ENTRY at everybody. Rex didn't listen to it. He said, 'Give me the gun,' and Laura grudgingly parted with it.

'Now stand back.' Rex took the gun in one hand, turned the handle with the other, kicked open the door and leapt dramatically into the studio.

The scene revealed was not without its points of interest. The studio was large, low ceilinged and about as broad as it was long. It was very brightly lit. But there was no sign of any photographic equipment about.

A large portion of the large room was taken up with a large number of very large men. And these held very large weapons which were all trained upon Rex and Laura.

And beyond all these, seated behind a nice black-topped desk with chromium legs, was a diminutive, boyish figure in a smart grey business suit. He waved gaily.

'Hello Rex. I've been waiting for you. Do throw the weapon away, you are somewhat outgunned.'

'Jonathan.' Rex tossed Laura's pistol aside. 'How very unpleasant to see you again.'

The other Rex stepped over the fallen doorman. He spoke into a handset. 'Someone has bopped the doorman on the head. Immediate assistance required.'

'Jonathan, what are you doing here?'

'What is all this Jonathan crap?' Laura asked. 'This is Simon Butcher.'

'Oh great.' Rex turned his eyes to Heaven. 'You couldn't have mentioned this when I took a shot at him in the alleyway.'

'I didn't see him in the alleyway. You were being the big hero with the gun, if you remember.'

'Children, children.' Jonathan put up his hands and stepped from behind his desk. 'Let's have no acrimony here. We're all friends, after all.'

'Still the short-arsed little git that ever you were,' Rex commented.

'That's quite enough of that. How's the jukebox running, Laura?'

'It's buggered, as it happens. Only plays Richie Valens records.'

'Tell Laura I love her,' said Jonathan, painfully off-key.

'Are you going to have *me* shot?' Laura ran her fingers through her hair and raised her breasts.

163

Jonathan gazed up at them. 'No no, not you. I deplore needless waste. And I have a spiffing Regency mahogany Canterbury with fitted drawer and baluster supports, probably by Gillows. Look very handsome in your apartment.'

'Where does this leave me?' Rex asked.

'I have a little job for you.'

'Oh yes? Eel-handler's mate, is it?'

Jonathan's face fell. He gawped at Laura. 'You told him about . . .'

'Sorry. It just slipped out.'

'Just slipped out, that's a good'n . . . ah.' Rex suddenly sobered to the rifle butt which struck him between the shoulder blades.

'I won't be made mock of.' Jonathan waggled his finger at the fallen hero. 'You will speak to me politely or I will split my men here into two football teams with you as the ball. Do I make myself quite clear?'

Rex nodded bitterly and climbed to his feet.

'Good. As long as we understand each other. Now, about this little job—' A siren sounded and the room lights began to flash on and off. 'Oh dear. What is it now?' Jonathan returned to his desk and tinkered at a console. The siren ceased, the lighting stabilized and a large image sprang up on the wall behind him.

It showed the other Rex, who was standing on the plaza before the building waving his arms about. Lots of darkly-clad figures were moving around him. They looked equally as well armed as the large lads on floor sixty-six. And there were more of them.

'Well, well, well. This puts an entirely new complexion on things. I hadn't been expecting him quite so soon. What do you think we should do about him, Rex?'

'Why ask me?'

'Well, he is *you*, isn't he?'

'He's not me, he's . . .'

'Uh-uh.' Jonathan shook his little head. 'He's you, all

right. You in another reality. A parallel reality. This reality. He's the Rex you might have become. The big bad bogeyman himself. And there's not enough room for the two of you here. One has to go. Seems like he's made up his mind which one.'

'Are you sure it's me he's after? No-one knew I was coming here. If you ask me, you're the one he wants.'

Jonathan chewed upon a thumb nail. 'No, no, no. He doesn't know I'm here. No, no, no.'

'Well there's one way to find out. Let's ask him.'

'No. I don't think that would be a good idea at all. A confrontation now would ruin all my plans. I think I shall have to postpone our little chat about the job. In fact I don't think I will be requiring your services at all.'

Jonathan touched something on his wrist. A section of floor in the middle of the room slid aside and a nice bright-red Buick aircar rose into view. Jonathan did another couple of touchings and the large men with the large guns merged into a single figure. This figure opened the car door for Mr Crawford.

'Clever that, isn't it? A little innovation of my own. Shan't tell you how it's done of course. Would you care to ride with me, Laura?'

'No. I wouldn't.'

'Well, just do anyway.' Jonathan produced a weapon of mightier ilk than Laura's. 'Just get in.' Laura got in.

'So it's goodbye, Rex. There isn't a back door and I doubt whether even you with that charmed life of yours can come up with a way out of this one.'

'Don't you bet on it.'

'Game to the last, eh? Bye bye.' Ceiling panels swished aside and Jonathan's nice bright-red Buick aircar rose into the night sky.

Jonathan waved down at Rex. 'Bye bye,' he mouthed.

Rex glanced at the image on the wall. The plaza was

now deserted, but the corridor beyond the studio door sounded like it was pretty crowded. With the noises of all the marching feet and everything.

'Hmm,' went Rex Mundi. 'That's another fine mess I've gotten myself into. Mmm hmm.'

13

*The truth is flexible, white hot, but it
soon becomes brittle if tempered with
cold bullshit.*

Robert Williams

Stevie Wonder felt my face.

Louise Rennison

'There must be some kinda way outta here,'
sang Rex Mundi to no-one but himself. The
trouble was, for the life of him, he could not imagine
where or what it might be.

The big white room didn't have much to offer. It
boasted a desk and a chair to its account. But was
knowingly undersold in the window department. And it
only had the one door.

Rex stepped lively. He picked up Laura's gun and
considered his options. He could hide behind the door
and club them down one by one when they came in. Or
at a pinch he might be able to squeeze himself into the
desk drawer and hide. A heroic stand against impossible
odds was always a possibility. As was his stumbling
across the secret technique of effecting invisibility.

Rex numbered his options on to his fingers. 'I'll just
have to dip for it,' he said. 'Dip, dip, sky blue; who's it,
not you. There goes the desk drawer. Dip, dip, sky blue;
who's it, not—'

There was an almighty crash.

'And there goes the door.'

167

'Stick 'em up,' chorused the large men with large guns tumbling over each other through the doorway.

'Or I might just stick 'em up.' Rex threw down Laura's weapon for the second time and stuck 'em up. 'That's another option, I suppose.'

The latest crop of large men with large guns thundered into the studio and formed themselves into a chaotic firing squad.

'Ready,' cried one. They made themselves ready.

'Take aim.' They took aim.

'Fi—'

'Hold it right there!' Rex shouted. 'And that's an order.'

'Fi . . . oh . . . er . . . it's *you*, sir.'

'Yes.' Rex wondered how he had omitted this rather obvious option from his former list. 'It's me. How dare you point your weapons in my direction.'

'I'm sorry, sir. Just got a bit carried away with all the excitement of storming the building and everything. No offence meant.'

'Well, some taken, I can assure you. Atten*shun!*'

The squad came to attention. Rex reviewed his troops. 'This is a sorry business,' said he.

'Sir?' One of the ranks put his hand up. As they all looked very much the same it didn't matter which one.

'What is it, soldier?'

'Sir, how come you were behind us in the corridor and now you're in front of us here?'

'I'm glad you asked me that.' Rex paced up and down trying hard to look glad.

'And wearing different clothes, sir?'

'Yes indeed.' Rex turned upon the questioner. 'Do you know anything about the transperambulation of pseudo-cosmic anti-matter?'

'Er . . . no sir . . . not much.'

'Well then.'

'Well then, sir?'

'Well then, clear off. Carry on. Dismissed. Get moving.'

'Yes sir.' There was mass saluting, mass mumbling and mass pouring out of the door.

And Rex found himself once more alone in the big bright room. He picked up Laura's gun yet again and tucked it into his jacket.

'Rex Mundi, you genius. Time you left the building.'

He tip-toed across the studio floor and peeped up the corridor after the marching men. 'Up and away. Ahhh!' Rex felt the cold muzzle of the gun as it entered his left ear.

'My, my,' came the voice of the gun's owner. A voice that Rex knew almost as well as he knew his own. Even though he only heard it through his right ear. 'My, my. If it isn't the shopper.'

Rex turned slightly to view the owner of the voice. He knew that face almost as well as he knew his own. In fact equally well. It was his own face.

'Back inside,' ordered the other Rex. 'And you lot!' He bawled up the corridor. 'Here on the double!'

The gun left Rex's ear, nuzzled into his chest and pushed him back into the studio.

'Nice jacket.' The villain fingered Rex's lapels with his gun-free hand. 'What expensive taste you do have.'

Rex stared into the face of his mirror image. He'd known loathing and hatred before. But nothing on the scale of this. His body ached to leap upon this travesty and wring the life out of it.

'Oh yes. Love to, wouldn't you? It's funny, I don't feel nearly so badly towards you. *Even though you've nearly bankrupted me!* I suppose that's because I hold your life in my hands. That would be it, I expect. How does that feel by the way?'

'Not good.' Rex gritted his teeth.

The large men were flooding largely back into the room. They were looking largely confused. The other Rex turned to greet them. He kept his gun trained on Rex as he did so.

'Gentlemen, I would like you to meet my twin brother.'

'What?' went Rex.

'My twin brother, Max. Max the psychopathic killer. Recently escaped from the state mental institution. Placed there—' a plaintive tone entered the voice of the other Rex '—for the murder of our dear white-haired old mother, whom he killed and ate.'

'Oh shame, shame,' went the large men, who all had dear white-haired old mothers of their own. 'String him up. Shoot the bastard.'

'Quite so, gentlemen.' The teller of tall tales poked Rex in the chest with his pistol and steered him to the far end of the room.

'I could just let them lay into you now,' he whispered. His face was far too close for Rex's comfort and his breath smelt like dog shit. 'But there's still time for you to redeem yourself. Where is Simon Butcher?'

'You missed him. He had to fly.'

The other Rex hit him hard in the stomach. Rex doubled in pain.

'Our mutual friend Mr Presley. Is he here? In the building?'

'I don't know.' Rex gasped for breath.

'Pardon?' The fiend dragged Rex up by his hair. 'What did you say?'

'I haven't seen him. I don't know where he is.' Rex felt the knee as it made contact with his groin.

'Not much help, are you? Where is my Volvo?'

Rex gazed up at him. '*Your* Volvo. Ah, I begin to see.'

'You see nothing. And apparently you know nothing. It's all up for you then. But take comfort in this.' He dragged Rex up and spat the words into his face. 'When I'm all done here I'll be spending a lot of time in your world. I do so look forward to enjoying all the comforts of your juicy little wife.'

'Go to Hell.'

'I was there just this morning, as it happens. Getting

your room ready. And now I think it's time for you to move in.' The other Rex turned and strode back to his troops.

'Take careful aim for the head, men. I don't want the jacket spoiled. It's just my size and I paid for it. Ready.'

The troups made themselves ready. They were really going to enjoy this one. Dear white-haired old mother and everything.

'Take aim. Don't forget the head now.' No, they weren't going to forget the head.

Rex stared back at them. This was just about as bad as it could possibly get. He was really going to die this time. No trick endings. No ingenious escapes. No unlikely coincidences. This was it. He'd come all this way, been through everything, just to wind up here. To be murdered by his Satanic double who was looking forward to enjoying his wife. Rex began to shake. He tried to pull himself together, but it was impossible. It couldn't end like this could it? It was so unfair. So unjust. He didn't want to die.

'Oh Max,' his executioner called to him. 'Any famous last words you'd like recorded for posterity?'

'How about lay down your guns and back off asshole?' The voice didn't belong to Rex Mundi.

Rex looked up in no small surprise. Through the open ceiling panel, which he might easily have climbed out of, had he chosen to number pulling over the desk amongst his previous choice of options, the barrel of a trusty Smith and Wesson was visible, aiming down at the head of his other self.

His other self was staring right back up at it, and he wasn't smiling.

'Do it now,' said I, with more authority than a gymnosophist in a lesbian love-dungeon.

The guy looked kinda doubtful, so I let off two rounds.

Goons to either side of him took in the air through their foreheads.

'Drop the guns.' The guy said it like he was falling asleep, but his army took the hint. I let down the tow rope.

'Best climb up here, fella, if you're looking for another chapter.'

'Yes. Thank you.' The guy in the black leather took to scrambling.

'Don't you even think about it.' I cocked my piece towards the other guy, who was definitely thinking about it. 'We're out of here.'

I slammed into the driving seat. The guy slammed in beside me.

'Bill's cab,' said he. 'How did you get this up here?'

'It's a flying model.' I revved the engine. 'By the look of what's on the meter some sucker's been driven around at ground level. Did you steal it or what? Where's the cab jockey?'

'Don't ask.'

'OK. Then I shan't. The name's Woodbine, by the way. Lazlo Woodbine. Some call me Laz.'

'Thanks for saving my life, Liz.'

'*Laz*,' said I, letting out the clutch and hitting the air. 'Don't bite the hand that pulls you out of the shit.'

'Thanks, *Laz*,' said he.

The cab fades into the night sky over Presley. The camera pans to the full moon. There's a bit of a lap dissolve and the full moon becomes a paper cup viewed from above. Ice cubes clatter into the cup, followed by a large slug of Old Bedwetter.

I was pretty pleased with the effect. Cinema verity, film noir, that kind of thing.

And I'd come out of it looking sharper than a Connecticut Yankee at a 2 Live Crew concert. Four-set clause intact.

Because, let's face it, all you saw in the studio was the barrel of a gun, and on the roof-top, the interior of a cab. The cab could have been anywhere. Like in an alleyway, maybe. But I don't want to split hairs.

I passed the cup across my office desk, just to make my present location clear. The guy in the black leather took it in both hands. 'Cheers,' he said.

'Likewise.' I raised a cup of my own and took a belt. 'How are you feeling?'

'Still a bit shaky. And not a little confused. How come you pulled me out of there?'

'Seemed like the thing to do.'

'Well, my thanks. This is really appalling liquor by the way.'

'It's an acquired taste. Do you want to tell me all about it?'

'Well, it's the taste mostly, and the smell. Where do you buy this stuff?'

'Not the drink, buddy.' I leaned back in my chair and took a slug to go with the belt I'd just had. '*It*. Your *it*.'

'Oh, my *it*.' Rex hesitated. 'Sorry, is it you or me, but one of us appears to be working in the first person.'

'It's me. That's the way I do business.'

'Could get pretty confusing. Do you mind if I just go on in the way I'm used to?'

'You can give it a try,' said I. 'If it don't work out, I'm sure we can compromise. Or at least *you* can.'

'Sounds reasonable.' Rex settled into the client chair. 'Actually this isn't too bad. I've tasted a lot worse. Who are you exactly?'

'Woodbine. I told you. Lazlo Woodbine.'

'And some call you Laz?'

'Some do. You can.'

'Thanks, Laz. My name's Rex Mundi. Some call me, well, Rex, I suppose.'

'Good to know you, Rex.'

'I hope you don't mind me asking this. But what we

you doing on top of the Butcher Building, in Bill's cab, rescuing me?'

'I'm on a case. I'm a private detective, see. *The* private detective. Didn't you ever read *Blonde in a Body Bag*?'*

'I'm afraid not.' Rex finished his drink. 'Did you ever read *Armageddon: The Musical*?'†

'Can't say that I did. So, like I was telling you, I'm a detective and I'm here on a case. My lead takes me to the Butcher Building. I see you go in. Then I see you go in again, this time in real bad company. So I just follow a hunch. Did anyone ever tell you that you bear an uncanny resemblance to a young Harrison Ford?'

'Once in a while. Anyone tell you you look just like—'

'Hush up, guy. My face never gets a mention. The reader projects himself on to me. Hence the first-person. One of the secrets of my success.'

'Success?' Rex looked around at the jaded office. 'You're successful then?'

'I'm the hero of this novel. How much success do you want?'

'Hmm,' went Rex Mundi. 'So tell me about this case of yours.'

'I'm tracking down something called the Presley hoard.'

'Ah,' said he. 'Now there's a thing. Could I have a top-up over here?'

The other Rex shouted into his handset. 'Dee! Kelley! Where are you?'

After playing their parts in a fruitless search of the Butcher Building, Dee and Kelley were now dining out at the Drowning Handbag, an up-market eatery in the best part of town. The establishment's boast was that if it wasn't on the menu, then you could take your pick for

---

* A Lazlo Woodbine thriller.
† A Rex Mundi blockbuster.

free. This gourmet's challenge had been taken up successfully upon only one occasion, when a patron ordered elephant's testicles on toast and the chef was forced to admit that he didn't have a bit of bread in the house.*

Ed and Johnny were enjoying an unimaginative platter of boiled sprouts. But very much indeed.

'Where are you?'

'We're tailing Woodbine, excellency.' Dee spat sprout into his portable phone.

'That's a bleeding lie,' said the other Rex, slipping unexpectedly into his Michael Caine persona. 'Get out of that restaurant and get around to Woodbine's office. If he's there and Mundi's with him, kill them both. I'll be there as fast as I can.'

'Yes, excellency. Check please, waitress.'

Jonathan Crawford dumped ice into a tall Venetian baluster goblet and splashed pink liquor over it. 'I'm sorry I had to throw old Rex to the wolves back there,' he said, without a trace of conviction. 'I hope you two weren't an item.'

'No. Strictly business.' Laura accepted the goblet. She was draped across a glorious Queen Anne walnut-framed settee, upholstered in *gros point* floral needlework. A piece of furniture, she considered, which would look right at home in her apartment.

She ran her hand lovingly over the fabric, kicked off her shoes and exposed a length of leg.

Jonathan looked on appreciatively and filled his own glass with orange juice. 'Nice sofa, eh? Look right at home in your apartment.'

'Now that you mention it. Why have you brought me here, Simon, or Jonathan is it?'

'Strictly business. And it's Jonathan, by the way. Jonathan Crawford, boy genius and future Lord of

*The old ones are always the best.

Presley City. And everywhere else now that I come to mention it.'

'I like the sound of that.' Laura didn't like the sound of that one little bit.

'What do you think of my collection?'

'Very nice.' Laura had been mentally cataloguing it since the moment she entered the room. The room was of considerable size and contained more priceless antiques than an entire *Lovejoy* series.

'We have so very much in common, you and I.' Jonathan joined her on the sofa. His feet dangled three inches above the Marasali Shirvan rug. 'We appreciate the finer things of life. And we share a wish to change the system. To overthrow it, in fact.'

'Do we?'

'We do. I know all about your dreams of revolution. I took the liberty of planting a listening device in the jukebox you . . . earned. That's how I knew that you and Rex were on your way over.'

'You little shit.'

'Strictly business. I can give you everything you want. All this. All you have to do is throw in your lot with me. Join forces against the common foe.'

'And who is the common foe?'

'All in good time.' Jonathan tapped his nose. 'Tell me, do you know where you are now?'

Laura nodded. 'I watched the direction monitor on your pilot's console. We drove round in circles for an hour and now we're back in the Butcher Building. About the thirty-sixth floor, I think.'

'Clever girl. The thirty-seventh actually. Would you like to experience something truly wonderful?'

'It will cost you the sofa then.' Laura rose to undress.

'No, no, no. That's not it. Not yet, anyway. Come with me and I'll show you something you'll never forget.'

* * *

Rex and I exchanged expositions. He told me his and I told him mine. And when we'd both done I freshened our cups.

'Thanks,' said he. 'I'm gobsmacked. Fancy you working with Barry. Does he know where Elvis is?'

'He never even told me he knew Elvis. But listen. There's one thing I just have to ask.'

'Ask on.'

'This other you, with all the credit facilities. Does he have an account with a dry cleaners? I've got these real bad spots of industrial lubricant on the trenchcoat and I want to get them out before they sink right in.'

'You might try some lemon juice,' Rex suggested. 'Is the trenchcoat a running gag by the way? I like to know where I stand.'

The lift went down and it kept on doing it. It passed the ground floor and ran out of little numbers to flash. Jonathan looked up at Laura. 'Intrigued, eh?'

'Extremely.'

'Won't be much longer.' And it wasn't. The little pinger went ping and the lift doors opened.

'Go ahead, Laura.'

Laura took a step forward and then one back. 'BAH-REAH!' she gasped.

'Impressed?'

'I don't know what to say.'

'Then don't say a thing. Step out and have a good look around. There's a catalogue on the table there. Take it.'

Laura took it. The catalogue was large and glossily bound. Only three words were printed on it and these three were THE PRESLEY HOARD.

Laura wandered amongst the treasures. The gilded icons, the statuary, the great paintings, the bas reliefs. She flipped through the catalogue and drew breath time and again.

Jonathan sat upon a garish garden lounger which had once graced the poolside at Graceland. He wrung his hands in pleasure at her pleasure. And in the pleasurable contemplation of erotic scenarios to come.

'I may not approve of the theology,' Laura perused a Caravaggio, which pictured Elvis as one of the three kings offering gifts to the infant Jesus; Elvis was offering a tiny guitar, 'but the quality, the sheer magnificence. How did you come by it all?'

'I acquired it all as a job lot. A kind of cosmic car-boot sale. Except for the centrepiece. The real treasure. Would you like to see that?'

Laura nodded dumbly. Yes, she would like to see that very much.

'Follow me then.'

Jonathan led her through the vault. To either side of them the wonders spread, daunting in their opulent splendour.

They approached a blank stone wall and the lad touched certain buttons upon the contraption he wore on his wrist.

The wall dissolved to reveal a chamber, lit subtly by muted neon. In the centre stood a sarcophagus. It was fashioned into the likeness of a golden jukebox, inset with precious metals and gemstones.

'Take a look inside.'

'Inside?'

'Certainly. Have a peep through the viewing glass. I promised you something you'd never forget.'

Laura took a step into the chamber and then paused. A curious sensation overwhelmed her. One of unutterable sadness. Laura shook her head, cleared her thoughts, but to no avail. The very air was charged with a terrible heart-rending loneliness.

'No. I don't want to see.' Laura turned to leave.

'But I really must insist.' Jonathan displayed his pistol. 'Go on, look inside.'

Laura turned back to the chamber. The hairs rose upon her arms.

'Do it.'

She walked slowly over to the golden sarcophagus. The room had become impossibly cold. Her breath steamed before her face. She hugged her arms.

'Look inside, Laura.'

She leaned over the sarcophagus and peered through the viewing glass.

The head and shoulders of a middle-aged man were clearly visible. The face was gross and swollen, heavy jowls covered by thick black sideburns. A red silk scarf was tied around the bloated neck.

Laura stared back at Jonathan. 'Who is he?' she asked.

Jonathan began to laugh.

I left my office chair to pine for my speedy return and took myself over to the window. The neon light outside flashed on and off the way some of them do and brought my profile into full play.

'Would you say I had a lantern jaw?' I asked.

'What, and spoil it for all readers with weak chins?'

'Oh yeah, thanks.'

'So what do you propose to do next?'

'My plans haven't changed. Get to the Presley hoard, hole up there until after the Big Bang. Barry knows that's where I'll be, and if he's half the sprout I know he is, he'll meet up with me again.'

As Laz was now gazing at his reflection and feeling his chin, Rex finished the bottle of Old Bedwetter. 'I think I might join you there. But there are several things I have to do first.'

'Like move some mouth with Elvis, top your other self, wring the truth out of Crawford, get back your dame and generally put the world to rights. Right?'

'I think that covers most of it.'

'Well, I'll help you out as best I can. But we're working

179

on a tight schedule and if we're gonna keep to it, there's one thing we gotta do first.'

'Get to the dry cleaners?'

'Uh-uh. Get the Hell out of here. About half a dozen big black cars have just pulled up outside.'

'Kindly lead the way,' said Rex. 'I've had about all I can take for one day.'

'Elvis?' Laura stared at Jonathan in disbelief. 'That's not Elvis.'

'Elvis the Everliving. Except he's not any more. Died an unnatural death in 1977.'

'But he's so . . .'

'Fat?'

'Well, yes, and so . . .'

'Dead. That's the word I think you're looking for. Fat and dead.'

'A false messiah.'

'A false God. What do you think would happen to the fabric of this society if the truth were told?'

'There'd be a . . .'

'A revolution?'

'A revolution, yes.'

'Followed by a change in government and ideology. And theology.'

'With you in control?'

'And you beside me. If you want it.'

'Do you run the Repo Men?'

'Me? No. I designed them and I service them. I have one or two for my private use. But as for the rest, I have no control over them.'

'Then who does?'

'Our common foe.'

'The Rex Mundi on the telly?'

Jonathan laughed. 'No, not him. I know who he is. I've dealt with him before.'

'Then who?'

Jonathan tapped once more at his dear little nose. 'All in good time. Now I am going to ask you a simple question and you are going to give me a simple answer.'

'Go on then.'

'Are you with me or against me?'

Laura took in the boundless wealth surrounding her, the possibilities of power, she gazed back at the golden coffin of the false messiah and back at Jonathan. 'I'm with you,' she said.

Jonathan smiled. Complicated mechanisms networking his body buzzed and purred, as sensors woven into his scalp registered minuscule fluctuations of electrical resistance upon Laura's skin. Grafts beneath his fingernails monitored her brain activity and the modified ceramic film coating his contact lenses recorded changes in her body heat to five decimal places. The information fed directly into Jonathan's cerebral cortex.

The read-out between his ears said, 'She's lying in her teeth.'

'I'm so glad to have you with me,' smiled the lad.

Laura smiled too. You'll get yours, she thought.

Oh no I won't, thought Jonathan.

14

37. *And the children of Elvis did
multiply greatly. Even to the four
corners of the world.*
38. *And happy were they, what with
the oil revenues and all. And the natty
duds and the good rocking tonight.*
39. *And once in a while Elvis did dash
off on some divine business or other.
But verily he did return, smiling, if a
trifle shagged out, saying, 'That's done.'*

The Suburban Book of the Dead

The morning sun touched lightly on the eyes of Laura Lynch. In a white exclusive bedroom, halfway up the Butcher Building. Which somewhat spoiled the metre, but there you go.

Laura looked approvingly upon all the little 'sold' stickers dotting the finest furniture of the room. A good night's work. If a mite tiring. Jonathan was snoring loudly as she detached his hand from her breast and slid from the bed. The boy genius had been singularly unforthcoming and had told her no more regarding his revolutionary schemes. But Laura had made up her own mind as to her next move.

She crept across the bedroom, stepping carefully over the unlikely collection of 'marital aids' littering the floor.

She entered the kitchen and took herself over to the knife rack above the Aga. From this she selected a twelve-inch Sabatier filleting knife and ran her thumb

gently along the length of the blade. The bead of blood
gave her pleasure, she took it to her mouth and sucked
upon it.

Returning to the bedroom she crept back to the bed,
raised the knife and without a moment's thought drove
it down into the sleeper's chest.

Rex awoke with a start in the back seat of Bill's cab. It
was parked in an alleyway. There were a lot of trash-cans
about and one of those cast-iron fire escapes with the
really tedious retractable bottom sections. Rex clutched
at his chest. Blinked at his eyes. Focused at his vision and
wondered where Laz was.

'Breakfast, Rex.' The man in the trenchcoat opened the
driver's door and dropped into the cab. 'Coffee, two eggs
over easy, sausage, black pudding and a fried slice.' He
passed Rex a styrofoam carton labelled Old Shep Bar-B-Q.

'Thanks,' Rex made lip-smacking, yum-yum sounds,
and then, 'hang about – how could you afford breakfast?
I thought you were penniless.' Rex wasn't slow to notice
that Laz no longer sported the unfashionable open-
necked look. That he was wearing a spanking new
snap-brimmed fedora. And that stains of an industrial
lubricant nature no longer besmirched his immaculate
trenchcoat.

'I got up early and pawned your watch,' Laz explained.
'Just slipped it off your wrist. You were hunkered down
so cosy I didn't like to wake you.'

'How very considerate. So what time is it now, then?'

'About five in the afternoon. Your breakfast, my tea.
Eat up.'

'Five in the afternoon?' Rex was appalled. 'You let me
sleep all day?'

'I didn't mean to,' said I, slipping into the first-person
with more delicacy than a dog log in a dowager's duffle
bag. 'But I had to buy the hat and tie. And supervise th
dry cleaners. These things take time. You have to star

183

right over those cleaners if you want the job done properly. You can't skimp on good cleaning. I skimped once back in 'thirty-four. That skimp cost me a learned pig of prodigious memory, two weeks in Benidorm with a beautician called Tracey, a life peerage and my entire collection of Marc Bolan records.'

'Including "Pewter Suitor"?'

'Including.' I gave Rex the kind of nod you could tell your grandchildren about. 'So I don't take chances no more. The way I see it, only a plater's mate turns vegan when there's hair pie on the table.'

'Oh, I couldn't agree more. But tell me if you will, whilst you were attending to these sartorial niceties, the small, yet I feel not insignificant matter of our impending relegation to Sheol, didn't, perchance, wend its winged way into your mercurial consciousness?'

'Come again, fella?'

'Well, to paraphrase one of your own charmingly idiosyncratic bon mots. Only Beau Brummell powders his wig when his arse is on fire.'

'Ah, I got you. You're talking about the case.'

'I am.' Rex lifted a *Burnt Weenie Sandwich** from his breakfast pack and waggled it in my direction. 'What, if anything, have you found out?'

'Some, and then some more.' I tapped my hooter like I was shooting ducks in a cracker barrel. 'I've been sniffing around and nothing about this city smells kosher. For one thing, I walk into three hat shops and they ain't hat shops at all. Just store fronts. For another, what you got here is a city full of fops and only one dry-cleaners. And this don't even have a Gold Star Valet Service. What kind of deal is that?'

Rex shook his head. 'You tell me.'

'OK then,' says I, 'I will. This place ain't for real. I bet 'f you walked into any of those apartment houses or office

Frank Zappa LP.

blocks, you'd find zero. It's all a phoney. A big set-up.'

'A big *set*.' Rex tossed his sandwich out of the car window. 'It's a big set.'

'What? Like *film* set?'

'Something much more than that. This was all designed for a specific purpose. And it's not the work of Jonathan or the other me. They, I suspect, are both planning to tear it down.'

'Who then? Some higher power?' I get a real depth into my voice, but it doesn't come out too well in print. 'Some higher power?'

'Something like that, yes.'

'Then if it's a higher power you're looking for, you should go check out the shopping mall. There's a flying saucer in the car park.'

'There's a what?' went Rex, in the third person.

Eight hours earlier Laura considered her handiwork. Jonathan was well and truly dead. The Sabatier's hilt projected from his pigeon chest and the blade pinned him, without compromise, to the mattress. It said 'Gotcha' in the manner of the now legendary tabloid of old.

'Gotcha.' Laura was trembling from head to toe. 'It's done now.'

'Just about.'

Laura's stare left the corpse, travelled through several unfocused planes and came to rest upon the ceiling. There Jonathan stood, upsidedown, with no wires showing.

'I won't be a moment. Just have to close off this particular scenario.' He tinkered away at the mechanism upon his wrist.

'Jonathan.' Laura was shaking hard. 'But how?'

'Hold on. Ah. All finished. Not a very happy ending that. But one which had to be included.' The wrist-tinkerer strolled across the ceiling, down a wall and towards Laura.

'But you're dead,' she said, ever so softly.

'Dead? Me?' Jonathan gestured at the bed. The knife still impaled the mattress. But the body was no more. 'Insert another dollar and begin again. Strictly business, Laura. I won't explain because I don't have to. Oh look what I have here.' He produced the inevitable hand-weapon. 'You will kindly get on to the telephone and call up your revolutionary children. It's time they joined the game.'

'A flying saucer?' Rex asked.

'Yeah. I told you. Can't be having with spaceships myself. Ruins the detective genre for me. You get into too much whackiness when you suddenly start bringing spaceships into the plot. Especially this late. It reads like a device. Like a *deus ex machina* ending.'

'I had one of those in my first book,' said Rex brightly. 'Worked out very well for me. I got the girl and everything.'

'Well, it's not for this boy. It's the roof-top confrontation or nothing.'

'Perhaps the lord will provide.' Rex flung the rest of his revolting meal into the alleyway. 'For the loss of my watch I didn't exactly come up trumps in the breakfast lottery. Did I get any change?'

'Some. But I used it to pay off the barman at the Tomorrowman for the damage. We have to go back there in the next chapter and I didn't want any bad feeling.'

'Very big of you. Well, I'm going to have a look at this flying saucer. Would you care to join me?'

'No way. I don't work shopping malls. Meet you back here later?'

'I'd say half an hour. But I don't seem to have a watch any more.'

I considered the antique Rolex Oyster which now favoured my wrist with its collectability. 'I'd lend you mine but it looks too good on me.'

Rex made with the meaningful Hmm. 'I really have some severe doubts regarding this partnership,' said he, upping and awaying.

I didn't have anything to add. The way I see it, although *It takes a lot to laugh, it takes a train to cry.**

Jonathan gave Laura a good poking with his over-sized weapon. Which probably got a cheap laugh somewhere, although I can't imagine where. Laura picked up the bedside telephone and dialled the number. There was a short pause. Then a brr-brr brr-brr brr-brr. Then a voice which said, 'Who's making that noise?'

'It's Laura Lynch. Is Kevin there?'

'Who wants him?'

'I do. Is he there?'

'He's in bed.'

'Could you get him to the telephone? It's very important.'

'Who's that?' Jonathan asked.

Laura put her hand over the mouthpiece. 'Kevin's mum.'

'Kevin's mum?'

'Ssh. Leave this to me. Hello. Yes?'

'He needs his sleep,' said Kevin's mum. 'He was up late last night plotting the overthrow of the capitalist system. So I'm giving him a lie-in. Can you call back later?'

'No I can't. Get him to the phone now.'

'Don't you adopt that tone with me young woman.'

'Listen. This is really important.'

'You've called before. I recognize your voice.'

'Please let me speak to Kevin.'

'He's in bed. I'll give him a message when he wakes up. What did you say your name was?'

'Give me the phone.' Jonathan snatched the receiver. 'Who am I talking to?'

*A Bob Dylan classic.

'This is Kevin's mum. Who's this?'

'Police Chief Sam Maggott. Presley PD.'

'You don't sound like him. He was on TV last night talking about the alien kidnapping. His voice was much deeper than yours. Wasn't that terrible about Harpo/ Chico?'

'Really terrible.' Jonathan put on the deepest voice he could manage. 'I believe your son can help me with my enquiries.'

'My Kevin?'

'Please get him to the phone now.'

'He's in bed. I told that lady.'

'Madam, get your son to the telephone at once or I will have Officer Cecil give you a good poking with his over-sized weapon.'

'Kevin! Telephone! Get up you lazy little . . .'

Jonathan returned the receiver. 'If you want a job doing, then do it yourself. You speak to him. I will tell you what to say.'

It wasn't a bad-looking saucer and Rex was the first to appreciate that. It was a real George Adamski job, or a Dr Sir George King job, depending upon which contactee you happen to favour. It's a funny thing how so many contactees are called George, isn't it? No? Well please yourself then. Actually, a friend of mine who was once in the TA had a pal called George who claimed to have been spirited away to Venus in a UFO. He was kidnapped, apparently, while taking a pee in the pub bog at the Queen's Head in Brighton. My friend says that George was only gone for five minutes, but when he returned from the toilet he said that he had been captured, flown to Venus and then forced to have sex with several beautiful Venusian lasses, who required his 'superior seed for the creation of a cosmic super race'. Naturally my friend considered this a lot of malarky, but he was impressed that the previously clean-shaven

George now sported a five-day growth of beard. But I digress.

The saucer was about thirty feet in diameter, with a smart transparent dome on the top. It rested upon three extendible legs with big flat metal feet. These made enigmatic holes in the tarmac for scholars to puzzle and debate over later.

Rex approached the grounded UFO and waved cheerfully. 'Hello,' he called. 'Anyone at home?'

A ladder descended from the central portion of the lower disc area and a spaceman, suitably clad in inflatable atmospheric suit and weatherdome, did likewise. He turned towards Rex and approached in slow motion. Little lights flickered from the interior of his dome and a communication unit on his chest crackled with static.

' *2⸪☊℮ω⅟℀∿.* ' he said.

Which left Rex somewhat stuck for a reply.

'Hello. Kevin here.'

Jonathan nudged Laura with his you-know-what. 'You know what to say.'

'Kevin. It's Laura.'

'Laura. Mum says you're under arrest.'

'Kevin. I'm not under arrest.'

'But mum said Sam Maggott was with you. Do you want us to bust you out?'

'Sam Maggott is not with me.'

'Ah. You're on your own in the cell, eh? Shall we storm the station house?'

'Kevin. Listen to me—'

'You just say the word, Laura. I could come disguised as a priest with sticks of dynamite strapped to my chest and—'

'*Kevin! Shut up!*'

'Sorry?'

'Kevin. Do you have a piece of paper and a pencil?'

'Paper and pencil? Oh, I see. Blow dart, yes. Roll up

the paper, bit or curare on the pencil point. Good idea—'

'No, Kevin, it's not a good idea. I'm *not* under arrest. I'm *not* with Sam Maggott. I'm *not* in a police cell. Do you understand what I'm saying?'

'Gotcha.'

'Right, then—'

'You can't talk. I understand. Just say the word and we'll come in with all guns blazing.'

'Kevin. Everything is OK. *Do I make myself clear?*'

'A code word. That's what you want. How about "Pewter Suitor"?'

'Give me that phone!' Jonathan made a furious face.

'No. Let me deal with him.'

'Who's with you? It's Maggott, isn't it? I recognize his voice.'

'It's not Maggott. Forget Maggott. Just get a pencil and paper.'

'Pencil and paper? Is that the code word?'

'No, it's not the code word! There is no code word. Do you understand?'

'Yes. I mean, no. Why are you calling me?'

'Kevin. Do you have a pencil and paper?'

'Is that why you're calling me?'

'Yes.'

'To ask if I have a paper and pencil?'

'Yes.'

'Don't you have your own? I was in bed.'

'I want you to write something down. Something very important.'

'Ah. Well, why didn't you say so in the first place?'

'Kevin. Get a pencil and paper.'

'OK. Hold on.'

Laura put her hand over the mouthpiece. 'He's just getting a pencil and paper.'

'Hello. Laura?'

'Hello Kevin.'

'I haven't got a pencil. Is a biro all right?'

Laura looked to Jonathan. 'Is a biro all right?' she asked.

' *Ʊʞ⅃ᴙⱲ* ' said the spaceman.

'Come again?' said Rex.

The spaceman twiddled at his chest. 'Hello,' he continued. 'Are you Mr Mojo Nixon?'

'Possibly,' Rex replied. 'Who's asking?'

'My name is *ᴐ⋁ᴳⱱ⅃ᴙᴇⴲ⅄* ' said the spaceman. 'But you can call me Frank. Beta Reticuli Transportation Services plc.' He made a sweeping gesture. 'Whooosh. That's the kiddie.'

'Eh?' said Rex.

'There in a day,' the off-worlder went on. 'No distance too great. No package too small. No charge too large.'

'No gag too old.'

'Pardon?'

'Why are you here?'

'Why are any of us here?' Frank whipped out a clipboard. 'Do you want to sign for the return of your two-headed love-child?'

'The two-headed love-child on the newscast?'

'I never watch the telly, me. But surely you know your own two-headed love-child.'

'Naturally.'

'So, if you want him back you'd better sign here. I can't stand around all day chit-chatting. Space-time is money you know.'

Rex stepped forward. 'Where do I sign?'

'Just there.' Frank now produced a pen which worked upon an unlikely scientific principle, possibly to do with the transperambulation of pseudo-cosmic anti-matter. Or possibly not.

Rex signed Mojo Nixon.

'Cheers,' said Frank. 'Hey, Don,' he called up the ladder. 'Sling the kid down here, I've got a John Hancock on the body board.'

'Bloody good thing too,' came a voice from above. 'Smells like he's loaded his kecks again. Ugly little sucker.'

'You certainly provide a caring and consummate service.' The irony of Rex's remark was quite wasted upon Frank, who caught the tumbling tot more by luck than judgement.

'There you go, then.' He tossed the bundle of joy to Rex.

'Thank you.' Rex cradled the infant. 'Might I just ask one question before you go?'

'Will there be a tip?'

'Oh, certainly.'

'Then ask on.'

'Why was this baby kidnapped in the first place?'

'Well.' Frank couldn't reach his head, so he scratched his dome. 'The way I see it, it's probably part of some cosmic master-plan. We get a lot of this sort of business. Not as much as we'd like, you understand. And not nearly as much as we used to get back in the good old days, when alien abductions were all the rage. Generally, what happens is, subject gets kidnapped, taken off to a distant planet, clued up upon the celestial wisdom of the space folk, then dumped back here to fend for himself. It's just the way of things. Probably tradition or an old charter or something.'

Rex shook his head in wonder. 'But why kidnap a baby?'

Frank leaned forward and whispered through his translator. 'Cock up if you ask me. The name I've got on the manifest is for a Mr *George* Nixon. Typical isn't it.'

'It certainly is.'

'So, what about the tip then, Mr Nixon?'

Rex patted his pockets. 'You've caught me on a bad day, I'm afraid.'

'Bad day? Well next time you're in a taxi getting shaken about by a monster from Hell, don't expect us to come

192

to your rescue again. Bad day indeed.' Frank made an intricate gesture, which, although of alien origin, never the less conveyed its meaning with crystal clarity. 'Bloody skinflint.' He turned to take his leave.

'No wait, please, let me explain . . .'

' ♉⚡★*✱!! !' said Frank as he climbed back up his ladder.

'No. Please . . .'

The ladder retracted. The port closed. Lights around the saucer's rim winked cheerfully. And then, without a by your leave or kiss my elbow, the spacecraft rose silently into the sky and swept away. And Rex was left holding the baby.

'Well,' said he, 'I might have handled that a trifle better. So let's have a look at you then.' He turned down the cover and peeped at the baby's heads. 'Kootchie koo.'

Two small faces peered up at him. They were ugly little suckers.

'Harpo's shit in our nappy,' said Chico.

'Chico done it,' said Harpo. 'I want me mum. Take me home.'

'No. Take us to a TV station. I have an announcement that will alter the course of human history.'

'I want me mum.'

'Shut up you.'

'Bwaaaaaaaaaaah!'

'Hmm,' went Rex Mundi. 'And hmm again.'

'Thank you Kevin, and goodbye.' Laura replaced the receiver.

'I don't like this.' Jonathan paced up and down the bedroom. 'Are you sure you can trust these people?'

'I'd trust them with my life.'

'You just did. But are they sound? Will they do what I told you to tell them to do?'

'I shouldn't think so. Would you do it?'

'What are you saying?'

'I'm saying that not even a ten-year-old would fall for the line of crap you just had me feed Kevin.'

'*What?*'

'I'm saying, you're going about this all the wrong way. They might turn up on time and do all the right things, or they might not. But having read out your little list of instructions, I now know exactly what you're up to. And if you'll just let me handle it, I also know exactly how you can get everything you want. Including me.'

Jonathan's inbuilt circuitry went through its magical motions.

The read out between his ears said, 'She's actually telling the truth this time.'

And indeed she was. But for all the wrong reasons.

'Where did you get to last night, chief?' Barry enquired. 'A bit stiff leaving me in the lead bucket.'

'For your own protection, Barry.'

'You went to Simon Butcher's studio, didn't you?'

'I did as it happens.' The other Rex did a bit of pacing, up and down the top-secret room. 'I had the building searched, but I didn't find Elvis.'

'You won't find him, chief.'

'I have to find him. Find him and . . .' The other Rex held his words in check. 'How can you be so sure I won't find him?'

'Just a hunch, chief. You know you've changed. Can't quite put my finger, if I had one, on just how. But there's something.'

'I—' The door swung open and Johnny Dee stuck his head into the room. 'We've found them, excellency.'

'What's with all this excellency business, chief?'

'Nothing to worry your little green head about, Barry. Back in you go for now then. Recuperate, eh?' The other Rex tossed the Time Sprout back into the lead bucket and screwed down the lid. 'Where are they? Is Bill with them?'

'There's still no sign of Bill, excellency. It's like he just vanished off the face of the Earth.'

'I'll deal with him in my own time. So where are they?'

'They're parked in an alleyway off the Graceland Shopping Mall. And it looks like they've got a kid with them.'

I bounced the bambino on my knee. Kids bring out the natural father in me and I get a crinkly mouth every time I look at an ankle snapper. It's those little innocent faces, I guess. Looking up at you with all that trust. When I finally hang up the fedora and donate the trusty Smithsonian to the Smith and Wesson Institute, I'm gonna have a whole floor-covering of codlings.

Kids, yeah, I love 'em. They plum choke me up.

'Really ugly pair of suckers you got here, Rex,' says I. 'Smells like they've loaded their kecks.'

'You're a real New Man*, Laz.'

'Aw, Shiva's sheep! Look at this, will ya?' I hefted the bouncing bantling off my knee. There was a wet patch the size of the Bay of Pigs right across the lap of my trenchcoat. 'Take this dump shute back.'

'I demand to be taken to the plush offices of a disreputable publicity manager,' Chico demanded. 'I have a destiny to fulfil.'

'I want me mum,' cried Harpo.

'Get rid of this thing, Rex. I'll drive us to the rear door of a Doc Barnado's or something.'

'You can drive us to the front door of a pharmacy. And with what ever you have left of my watch money we will buy baby food, nappies, bum wipes . . .'

'You have got to be joking,' said I, slipping un-expectedly into my John McEnroe persona.

'Trust me. I know what I'm doing.' Rex went dandle dandle with the smelly brat.

*A mythical character very popular in the 1990s.

'I'm going no place until we get this sorted. Lazlo Woodbine doesn't work with animals or children.'

'I thought you had a dog named Blue, a fish called Wanda, a learned pig, a horse with no . . .'

'Only in passing references, buddy. Never on the job. Nothing and I do mean nothing is gonna make me move from here until you agree to dump the munchkin.'

The synchronized fire of two 7.62 M134 General Electric Mini-Gun machine-guns strafed the alleyway. Coming out of the sun, the long black ground-to-air limo dropped down between the buildings, shot up the trash cans and made a real mess of the cast-iron fire escape with the retractable bottom section.

'Let's get out of here,' said I, brrrming the engine and engaging drive.

'I still want me mum,' screamed Harpo.

'Don't mess about.' The Anti-Rex shook his fists. 'Shoot them up. Go around and come in again. And do it properly.'

'They're moving.' Johnny Dee was at the wheel. Ed Kelley manned the gun ports.

'Shall I start dropping the grenades?' Ed asked.

'Not yet. You have to build up the excitement first. Bring us in low for another assault, Johnny.'

'Will do.'

'Get us out of this alleyway,' Rex shouted. 'Get into the main street, we can try to lose ourselves amongst the other cabs.'

'I don't work main streets, Rex. You know that.'

The long black flying car came in low for another run along *An Alleyway called Death.** The machine-gun fire tore into the cab, narrowly missing all concerned.

*A Lazlo Woodbine thriller.

'You're carrying the future of the human race here,' cried Chico. 'Drive!'

'Mummy!' cried Harpo. 'Drive!'

'Drive!' cried Rex. 'Just drive!'

'I'm driving!' I cried. 'I'm driving already.'

The cab thrashed along the alleyway, mashing dumpsters and scattering bums from central casting. Big sparks sprayed off the brick walls and tyres screamed on the wet pavements. The big black car loomed overhead, its big guns spitting big big bullets.

'Hit the streets,' cried Rex. 'Or better still hit the sky.'

'Woodbine ain't licked yet.' I hung a right which cost us a fair amount of starboard body work and a couple of hub caps. 'We can lose them.'

'We can lose them? Ye Gods.' Rex cowered in the back seat shielding Harpo/Chico as best he could. 'We're sitting targets.'

'Never say die, buddy. I've been in worse scrapes than this. Back in 'sixty-two I was in a car chase with Gilles "de Rais" Gordon, the Bloomsbury Bluebeard. That chase cost me my twin sister Wilma, a night at the opera—'

'Clarence the cross-eyed lion and a weekend in a lift shaft with a sex-starved gorilla?'

'I told you about that, huh? Well, I won through. Stick with me kidder. Aw shit!'

There were further rattles of machine-gun fire and Rex found himself looking up at a troubled sky. 'We just lost the roof,' said he. 'Put your foot down or let's put our hands up.'

'Have a little faith in the hero.' I hung a left and wondered about the driver's door which parted company with us as we struck a portside wall. 'Getting a mite drafty in here.'

'All right Eddie.' The other Rex rubbed his hands together. 'I think we might employ the grenades now. Just lob one down through the open top of the cab, will you?'

'No problem, excellency.' Ed Kelley opened a case of evil-looking grenades. Took out the largest and pulled the pin. 'Take us in nice and low, please John.'

'Pleased to.' The big black car dropped down. Rex could make out all the fine detail of its undercarriage. He saw all the rivets and the little oily spots, the weld marks and the silencer mountings. All the things that you take a curious interest in when you are lying under a car after a road accident, waiting for the ambulance to arrive and thinking that you'd far rather be anywhere else but there.

Ed Kelley was a good shot. The grenade dropped right on to the cab floor in front of Rex.

'Oh my God!' Rex plucked it up and made to throw. He glimpsed the little digital readout on the lighted grey panel as it went 03.00 02.00 01.00 . . .

During the 01.00 and the 00.00 Rex gave a whole lot of things a whole lot of thought. He could have had his whole life flash before him. But he didn't. You don't really. I once cut my wrist on a guillotine machine at a picture-frame makers where I was working. The blood came pumping out and I was sure I was going to die. All I could see, that I now remember, was this fellow in blue overalls wandering down the street outside, drinking a can of Coca Cola. And all I thought was, I never liked Coca Cola and I suppose I'll never get to like it now.

Rex wasn't thinking about Coca Cola. He was thinking, what if this wally Woodbine really is the hero of this novel . . .

00.00
'Oh gO.Od gOd.'

The explosion ripped the cab apart. The black car soared away as mangled fragments spiralled into the sky. The tyres went and the petrol tank ignited. The alley walls absorbed the shock and a bloody mushroom cloud rose above the devastation now occurring behind the Tomorrowman Tavern.

'Gotcha!' The other Rex clapped his hands together. 'Mission accomplished. Let's go and have a drink.'

15

> 53. *And so great was the love of the*
> *people for Elvis that they made many*
> *laws. That all should honour him by*
> *being like unto him.*
> 54. *That all should dress as him and be*
> *as him in all ways of thought.*
> 55. *And they did cry aloud in one voice*
> *saying, 'There is no God but Elvis nor*
> *has there ever been.'*

The Suburban Book of the Dead

'Well, well, well.' The barman at the
Tomorrowman Tavern wiped his gloved
hands on his leather apron. 'If it isn't the chap off the
telly *again*. I never saw you come in.'

Rex blinked at him. 'What the . . . I mean . . . how . . .
I?'

The barman eyeballed Rex's bundle. 'What you got in
there? Money, I hope. I cashed in your driver's watch. It
was a bleeding Piaget copy. You still owe me bucks for
those bigfoot noses.'

'What am I doing here? Surely I'm . . .'

'Dead?' I tipped my hat, for I was there also.

'Yes, dead. Blown up.'

'Blown up?' The barman fixed Rex with another of his
one-eyed show-stoppers. 'Was that your racket in my
alley just now? If you've damaged any of my trashcans
you're in for it.'

Rex gave me the glance. 'What happened?'

'Search me.' I was more baffled than a pregnant postulant in a eunuch's prefab. 'We were there and now we're here.'

'Get the drinks in then,' says Chico. 'Mine's a Pernod and lemonade. The lemonade's for Harpo.'

'You what?' said I.

'Get the drinks in and I'll tell you how *I* did it.'

'How *you* did it?'

'What have you got in that bundle?' The barman craned his head across the counter. 'That a dwarf in there or what?'

'It's a ventriloquist's dummy,' said Rex hurriedly. 'For a new show I'm doing called *Rex Mundi's Big Night Out*. It's a quality act. Gottle a geer, gottle a geer.'

'You're wasting your time,' said the barman.

'Two bottles of Bud, a Pernod and a lemonade,' said I.

'Nice hat,' said the barman.

'Take it,' said I.

'I want me mum,' said Harpo.

'Very poor,' said the barman, taking my titfer and perching it on his head. 'If it's quality you're looking for, then I'm your man. I do them all. Songs from the shows. Oldies but goodies. Great literary figures past and present. Who's this then?' He pulled the hat down over his eye and made a peculiar face.

'I haven't the faintest. Give us the drinks, please.'

'Not until you've guessed.'

'Oh, all right then, Iris Murdoch.'

'Got it in one. Told you I was good.' The barman turned away to fetch the drinks.

'Iris Murdoch?' Rex asked.

'Sure, who did you think?'

'I thought it was Doris Lessing.'

'Doris Lessing?' I let a smile dwell upon my lips. 'Buddy, in my line of work, knowing your Iris Murdoch from your Doris Lessing can mean the difference between chewing on the curate's egg or sighing for the fleshpots of Egypt. If you catch my drift. And I'm sure that you do.'

'Absolutely.' Rex made a peculiar face of his own, but I couldn't put a name to it. 'You see to the drinks. I'll take Harpo/Chico over to a nice quiet corner.'

'Sounds about right to me.' I swapped a couple of impersonations with the barman. He nearly caught me out with his C. S. Lewis, but I had him sewn up like a kipper with my Hermann Hesse. He thought it was Sir Arthur Conan Doyle. Must have been the trench-coat.

I left him to muse on my brilliance and joined Rex in the quiet corner, where the brat was holding court.

'I bring greetings from a distant star,' said Chico Nixon. 'I have been made privy to the wisdom and knowledge of the Galactic Great Folk, and have returned here to solve all the world's problems.'

'That sounds most encouraging,' said Rex, who was changing the cosmic messenger's kecks. He had got himself a bar cloth and a bunch of paperclips and looked like he meant business. 'I haven't any talcum, I'm afraid, and you've got a bit of nappy rash here. When was the last time you were changed?'

'Time is a human concept. It has no universal existence.'

'Fair enough. I'll just clip you up, then.'

'Please spare yourself the trouble.' I don't know how the little sucker did it. But the next thing we knew he was all kitted out in a blue and white sailor suit, smelling sweetly of baby lotion and with not a wet patch to be seen. Real cute he looked. Except for the two ugly heads, of course.

'How did you do that?' Rex asked, which spared me the bother.

'The same way I got us out of the alleyway when the grenade blew up.'

'Does it have anything to do with the transperambulation of pseudo-cosmic anti-matter?'

'Nothing whatsoever. This is the power of The Word.'

Well, I've never had a lot of truck with the power of the word so I'm not into oral sects. 'How does that work exactly?' I enquired.

'Through forces beyond your wildest imaginings.'

I give the kid the kind of wink you could make a movie out of. 'My imaginings are pretty wild,' I told him.

'Oh, I don't know. Making jungle love to a lady wrestler across your office desk, while her twin sister rubs halibut oil into the epaulets of your trenchcoat isn't all that wild. Weird, but not wild.'

'How did you know I was imagining that? If I was. Which I wasn't.'

'He was,' said Chico.

'I'll bet he was,' said Rex. 'Do you want a straw with that Pernod?'

'No, I can manage thank you. You'd make a good father, Rex. You were very protective back there in the cab. I appreciate that.'

'And I appreciate you saving my life. Thank you very much indeed.'

'Now see here.' I took a wet from my bottle. 'This is all very cosy. And I thank you likewise. But what is all this about? What do you want?'

'I want me mum,' said Harpo. 'Pass my lemonade please.'

Rex passed it over. 'I could phone your mum if you like. Get her to come and collect you.'

'Very civil of you.' Both heads nodded, but Chico did all the talking. 'The number's in the book. Please inform the parents that my brother and I are in the best of health. But that we are being held in protective custody in a special private clinic. No visitors allowed. We have a serious mission to accomplish, we four and I don't want them getting in the way.'

'We *four?*' My Bud went down the wrong way and I had a fit of choking. 'What is this *we four* all of a sudden?'

'Talk it out amongst yourselves.' Rex dumped the two-headed sailor-boy back on my knee and took off for the phone.

'Here's looking at you, kids,' said I, raising my bottle.

'I'm thinking,' Johnny Dee raised his glass and took thinking sips, 'perhaps we acted just a tad rashly.'

He, Kelley and the other Rex were back in the top-secret room. Barry was still locked in the bucket. The bucket was locked in a cupboard.

'This thought has taken the occasional jaunt through my mind,' Ed agreed. 'Now that we have killed off Rex and Woodbum, we seem to have killed off our chances of having them lead us to the Presley hoard.'

The other Rex took a slug of Old Bedwetter and spat it in a flaming plume at the both of them. 'You craven dullards. Haven't you worked out where the hoard is yet?'

His cowering cronies raised their heads above the table-top.

'No, excellency,' they said.

'It's in the Butcher Building.'

'No sir, it's not.' Johnny shook his head, which was a trifle singed on the top. 'We searched that place from top to bottom. It's not there.'

'Oh yes it is.'

'Oh no it's not.'

The other Rex took another large swig. But this time he swallowed it. 'Reason it out for yourselves. Barry leaves Elvis there. We go there. Rex is there and Wood-bine is there. All roads lead to the Butcher Building. And this,' he pulled Lazlo's map from his pocket and flung it across the table, 'The great detective left this behind when he and Rex fled from his office last night. X marks the spot. You really should have known about this, shouldn't you?'

'But excellency, we searched the building.'

'All of the building?'

'All, yes.'

'Tell me, Ed, if you were in possession of the most valuable collection of artworks in mankind's history, where would you keep them?'

'In a bloody great . . . ah . . .' said Ed. 'A bloody great vault.'

'I knew you'd get there in the end.'

'But the lift buttons only went down to the ground floor,' Ed made little finger pointings.

'Really? You didn't happen to notice another big button with SECRET VAULT FULL OF STOLEN TREASURE printed in big letters above it then?'

'No, excellency. I'm sure I would have noticed.'

The other Rex rose from his chair, leaned across to Ed Kelley and bit off his right ear.

'Oooh and owww!' wailed Ed. 'Give it back.'

The other Rex spat the ear on to the table. Ed snatched it up and tried vainly to stick it back on.

'Let me put it simply for you.' The villain licked his lips. 'In a little over twenty-four hours Presley City vanishes from the face of the Earth. We know that it does, but we don't know why. No-one seems to know why. Do you know why, Johnny? Take your hands away from your ears, Johnny. Do you know why?'

No, Johnny didn't know why.

'Barry languishes in the bucket, bereft of his awesome time travelling powers. The Volvo is gone to who knows where. Do you know where?'

No, Johnny didn't know where.

'So where does that leave us?'

'Up shit creek,' Johnny suggested. The bottle of Old Bedwetter flew past his ducking head and smashed against a wall.

'It does, I agree, present certain difficulties regarding my intentions to destroy Presley, wipe out all memory of him, rewrite history and let chaos and evil reign supreme. But all is not yet lost, because *I* have a plan.'

Ed had got his ear back on. Upside down. 'I like a plan,' said he. 'Are we talking demonic stratagems here?'

'We are.'

'Fiendish plots of an unsurpassingly vile nature?'

'That's the fella.'

'A Satanic conspiracy aimed at the total destruction of all that is good, pure and true?'

The Anti-Rex smiled sweetly upon Ed Kelley, leaned forward as if to kiss his cheek and ripped off his other ear. 'I am talking no more Mr Nice Guy,' said he.

Rex returned with a tray of drinks, which I raised an eyebrow to.

'I've just given the barman his own show on the telly,' he explained, handing them around. 'I told Mrs Nixon her offspring were blooming. She said to say hello to Harpo for her.'

'Hello, mum,' said Harpo.

'What about me?' The head called Chico wore a wounded expression.

'I'm sure she loves you too,' Rex did an encouraging, but unconvincing, face.

'Chico's been telling me all kinds of interesting stuff.' I patted the brat. 'Seems he's been chosen to be the voice of Interplanetary Parliament here on Earth. And he's picked you out to help him Rex. That's why he had Frank and Don, the space guys, zap Asmodeus. And he can do all kinds of really neat magic. Show Rex the trick with the beer mats, Chico.'

'Are you sure mum didn't ask after me?'

'Would lying help?'

'No, I'd see right through it.'

'What is the trick with the beer mats?'

'Chico can change them into twenty-dollar bills.'

'But there aren't any beer mats on the table.'

'Not any more.' I patted my pockets.

Rex took a seat. I kept a firm hold of the lovable little rascal on my knee. 'Could you make diamonds out of pocket fluff?' I enquire, in an avuncular fashion.

'Laz, before you get your trusty Smith and Whatever platinum plated, don't you think we should be getting down to the business, which is your business. If you catch my drift. And I'm sure that you do.'

'My mum doesn't love me,' wailed Chico.

'Got outta town.' I gave the kid a chooky-chooky on the chin. 'I only met you a half hour ago and I love you like one of my own.'

'It's because I'm ugly, isn't it?'

'Ugly? Kid, you're beautiful. Now about this pocket fluff.'

'My mother hates me.' Chico made the kind of face that only a mother could love. But obviously not his.

'Kid,' I told him. 'You're lucky. I never had a mother.'

'Laz,' said Rex. 'Everybody had a mother.'

'Not me, buddy, I was conceived by a writer of detective fiction.'

'There is no answer to that.'

'I'll have myself decerebrated,' moaned Chico. 'Surgically removed.'

'I'll do it for you,' Harpo chipped in. 'It's no skin off my nose.'

'Oh, got a sense of humour all of a sudden, have we? Take that.'

Chico caught Harpo on the chin with a right uppercut. Harpo countered with a left hook.

'Children.' Rex waded in to hold the struggling arms apart. 'This is no way to behave.'

'Chico started it.'

'Yah to you, mummy's boy.'

'That's enough. Chico, you should know better. You're

207

supposed to be the voice of Interplanetary Parliament.'

'Yeah,' said I. 'You got more important things to do than fight with your brother. You should be using your magical powers for the good of mankind.'

'You're quite right.' Chico made with the nods. 'I have a destiny to fulfil. Tell you what, I'll say The Word and transfer Harpo's head on to your shoulder.'

'No, no. Hold hard there.' I bounced the bonny bicephalous back to Rex. 'Stick him on your pal here. He's the good father.'

'Oh no I'm not.'

'Oh yes you are.'

'That's enough!' Rex put on a fierce face. 'Quite enough. We don't have time for all this nonsense.'

'Nonsense?' If I'd had my hat I'd have taken it off to the guy. You need a certain kind of front to breeze in from an alternative reality in the back of a time-travelling Volvo and sit in a Presley City bar, with a two-headed nipper on your lap, complaining to a private dick from the twenty-fifth century that you don't have time for nonsense. Or perhaps you don't.

'OK,' said I. 'Let's talk turkey.'

'Harpo/Chico?' Rex asked.

'All right.' Chico shrugged his shoulder.

'Harpo?'

'Just tell Chico to stay off my back.'

'Our back.'

'Our back then.'

'All right. Sorry bruv.'

'Good.' Rex bobbed the babe. 'Now the way I see it, we all want something. Laz here wants the Presley hoard. Chico wants to solve all the world's problems. Harpo wants his mum. And I want—'

'Rex.' I interjected 'We don't have enough hours left to hear all the things you want.'

'Quite so. But I'm sure if we all pool our resources we might all be able to get exactly what we want.'

'I can dig that.' I could dig that. 'Speak on,' said I with more encouragement than a Brahman temple dancer at a Brown Shirt's bump supper.

'I shall. Now I don't pretend to have the answer. Because I don't know what the question is. But I know this. Crawford is here, the Devil himself is here, dressed up to look like me. I'm here, you're here. Everybody's here and something very big is about to happen.'

'Er, Rex?' Harpo put his hand up.

'Yes, Harpo?'

'Rex, did you have a lot of success in your other books? Excuse me for asking, but you seem a bit of a . . .' Harpo made wrist jerks at his nappy region.

'Oh thanks very much. I happen to be the hero, you know.'

'*I'm* the hero, Rex.' I gave the old trenchcoat a tap or two.

'*I'm* the hero. I mean, *we* are the hero.' Harpo/Chico did synchronized chest drumming.

A little green voice in a lead bucket said, 'I'm the hero actually, chief.' But none present heard it.

'All right.' Rex threw up his hands and nearly sent Superbrat tumbling. 'Everybody's the hero. I don't care. All I want to do is get out of this one alive. Go back to my wife and garden. Dig my septic tank and live happily ever after.'

'Then you'll really go for my plan,' said Chico.

'And that is *my* plan,' said Laura to Jonathan. 'What do you think?'

Jonathan stroked his pointy little chin. 'I like it,' said he. 'In fact, I love it. As long as your revolutionary chums do their bit, I can't see anything standing in our way.'

'And that's Laura's plan,' said Kevin. 'What do you think?'

'Is that all of it?' a Child of the Revolution enquired.

209

'It seems a bit short. The way it just sort of ends in the first sentence.'

'My biro ran out.' Kevin explained. 'I went off to get another one and when I got back to the phone she said "have you got it?" and I thought she meant the new biro, so I said yes and she said goodbye and hung up.'

'And that is *my* plan!' screamed the evil Anti-Rex. 'And I don't care what you think of it.'

'I love it to death.' Johnny Dee nodded enthusiastically. 'It's a real unholy stonker of a plan. With Rex and Woodchip out of the picture and the forces of darkness set loose upon the land, how can we fail? What do you think, Ed?'

Ed pulled his fingers from his newly-refitted ears. 'Pardon?' said he.

'And that's *my* plan.' Chico made smiles all round.

I looked at Rex and Rex looked at me.

'I like it,' said I. 'Especially the roof-top showdown. What about you, Rex?'

'I like the bit where I get to go home at the end. You are sure it will all actually work?'

'Trust me.' Chico finished up his drink. 'What could possibly go wrong?'

'Well . . .' said Rex Mundi.

16

Rex Mundi, Lazlo Woodbine and the two-headed offspring of a popular show-biz couple put up for the night in a room above the Tomorrowman Tavern. The barman had been most amenable, what with his new TV show coming up and everything. Laz had paid him handsomely with Chico's magic money and he was sporting once more his new fedora.

Rex pulled the bed covers in his direction and switched off the light.

'Do you know,' he whispered, as Harpo/Chico was sleeping. 'This is the first time I've ever shared a bed with a two-headed baby and a twenty-fifth-century detective.'

I pulled the covers back towards me. 'You've never lived, fella. I remember one time back in 'ninety-eight. I was on a case. I shared a sleeping bag with a male stripper from Delaware, a trained hound called Daniel and three members of the US Senate. That night cost me . . .'

'Zzzzzzzzzz,' went Rex Mundi.

'My virginity,' said I.

* * *

His Satanic Unpleasantness the Anti-Rex, Lord of the Flies, King of the Shadow Realm, fallen angel, father of lies, Supreme Spirit of Evil and locker of Barry in a bucket, paced the floor of his top-secret room. His shoes were off and his cloven hooves showered sparks across the concrete floor. At intervals he stopped, raised clenched fists, belched brimstone and roared things such as:

'This time I shall prevail!' and

'This time all will be mine!' and

'Today Earth, tomorrow the universe!'

But for the most part he shouted, 'How come if I'm the Devil Incarnate, I've spent half this book down here in this poxy little room?'

Johnny Dee lifted the manhole cover and peered without enthusiasm into the depths beneath. 'Down you go, then.' He nudged Ed Kelley in the ribs.

Ed leaned forwards and took a sniff. His ears might have been a bit wonky but his nose was working just fine.

'Smells a mite niffy down there. Are you sure this is a good idea?'

'Eddie, my pal. Have we not spent half the night listening to a plan of almost inconceivable fiendishness?'

'Well, *you* have.'

'And I told you all about it when his excellency had finished kicking you around.'

'You did, yes.'

'And, as Bill seems to have done a runner, is it not down to ourselves, as the very last of the First Hierarchy of Hell, to aid our evil master in his plan to unleash the forces of darkness upon this planet?'

'It certainly is.'

'Then down you go, then. I'll keep a look out here.'

Ed took another disdainful sniff. 'There's only one thing that puzzles me about all this.'

'And what is that?'

'How come, if he's the Devil Incarnate, does he spend half the book down there in that poxy little room? Aaaaaaaaaagh!'

'Sorry Ed, I accidentally pushed you. Are you all right down there?'

Other things were going bump in Presley City's final night.

Kevin and his revolutionaries carried out several daring raids upon government munition dumps, military vehicle compounds, hi-tech weapon factories and sweet shops.

The barman at the Tomorrowman polished up his impersonations and looked forward to the day after tomorrow, when Rex had promised him his own show. He counted the night's takings, swept the floor and then got really upset when he discovered that all his beer mats had been stolen.

Laura and Jonathan engaged in certain forbidden acts of love. These included such classics as, bow stringing, shouting at the wolf, doing the Rapids City roll, French whispering, taking tea with the person and grooving on the inner plane. Any one of which could get you either hospitalized or excommunicated. Except for the last one, which is a track on a Robyn Hitchcock LP.

Police Chief Sam Maggott was having a 'rough one'. At Police Headquarters alarm bells rang in from government munition dumps, military vehicle compounds, hi-tech weapon factories and sweet shops. Sam despatched all the men he could spare and paced the floor for several hours, the bells jangling around him. When he could stand it no longer he put out an 'all points' to demand progress reports.

The drunken voice of Officer Cecil informed him that he and his fellows were taking the calls one at a time.

And as soon as they'd finished questioning the To-morrowman's barman about the beer mat heist, they'd get around to the rest.

'You should see his impersonation of Ray Bradbury,' Cecil added.

In the bucket in the cupboard Barry the Time Sprout woke suddenly to find he was in the wrong chapter.

'And that is *my* plan,' he said.

I woke suddenly with my hand on my piece.

Rex and Harpo/Chico were all nuzzled up in the land of nod, so I took myself over to the window to watch the sun rise over Presley City.

> Now stirs the earth before the water's run.
> And watch our dust rise to the restoring sun.

A new sunrise always brings out the poet in me, even here in this Godawful town. I guess that if I hadn't taken up the trenchcoat and fedora to walk the alleyways of history as the greatest detective of them all, I might well have become a poet.

Or an estate agent.

Or a bank clerk.

It's all the same when you get right down to it. A job with a suit. Except for the poet, of course. Or the detective. Although you can wear a suit as a detective if you want to. Not that I ever wanted to. I figure that wearing a suit makes you look like an estate agent or a bank clerk. And the thing I don't like about poets is, they never wear really decent hats. Except for John Betjeman, that is. That guy had more hats than Gary Glitter's had come-back concerts.

So I guess I had no choice in the matter really. When fate marks you down for immortality you'd just better bite the bullet and lace your boots up tight. Because only a logomachist weaves a rope of sand when the saints go marching in. If you catch my drift. And I very much hope you do.

The sun had got his hat on, so I took time out from the deep and meaningful stuff and studied my reflection in the glass.

'Laz,' it said to me, 'you are one handsome sucker.' And on this we both agreed. 'But you ain't had a shave, changed your kecks, nor been to the bathroom since this whole fiasco began. Perhaps now might be the time.'

And perhaps it would. Because it was now precisely twelve hours from the big bang. And counting down.

11.59

High upon the roof of the Butcher Building the boy Jonathan was up and about. He was up and about and shouting at all and sundry. Above him vast silver dirigibles moved in the morning sky, great black crates strung beneath them. These were being lowered to the roof-top, where Repo Men guided them on to powered sleds and steered them into the lift.

'Careful, careful,' the lad ordered. 'This stuff is worth a fortune. Don't knock it about.'

High upon another roof-top, not so far distant, stood a tall dramatic-looking figure robed in black. He studied the dirigibles through a pair of those really amazing computerized binoculars that you see in movies. The ones with infra-red night-sights, little flashing digital displays, electric zooms and whatnots. The ones that you waste your time describing to the blank-faced school-leaver behind the counter in Tandys. The ones that a friend of mine who was once in the TA has been promising to get me for three years now.

'Just as I suspected.' The man in black lowered his binoculars to reveal that he was none other than the Anti-Rex himself.

'Big black crates arriving. If I'm not very much

215

mistaken, they would be for packing up the Presley hoard in.'

He was very much mistaken, of course. But at least he was out of his top-secret room and getting a bit of fresh air for a change.

High upon Old Bedwetter and barbiturates, Sam Maggott lazed back in his office chair and smiled placidly upon the bleary-eyed officer now lounging in his doorway.

'Anything to report?' he asked.

Officer Cecil grinned inanely. 'Not much, sir.'

'Not much, sir. I see. And would it be impolite of me to enquire exactly where you and the other officers have been for the last eight hours?'

'No sir. We have been following up leads.'

'Following up leads. Jolly good. And what leads might these be?'

'Well sir, we figured that the beer mats might have been stolen by some rival bar-owner. So we've been systematically checking out all the other bars in the city.'

'I see.' Sam popped several coloured capsules into his mouth and washed them down with another slug of firewater. 'And regarding the break-ins at the government munition dumps, military vehicle compounds and hi-tech weapon factories. Any thoughts on those?'

'Well . . .' Cecil gazed about the office as if in search of inspiration. His gaze fell upon the alarm board. 'I notice all the bells have stopped ringing,' he said brightly.

Sam rose shakily to his feet and pointed a fat finger at the grinning buffoon. 'They've stopped ringing because I pulled the bloody wires out of the wall. You useless, no good, drunken—'

But he never got to finish that particular line. His words were lost in the sudden explosion which took the front off Police Headquarters.

High upon life, I returned from the bathroom. Cleanly shaven, smelling good and feeling better than a basketeer at a codpiece competition. The room was just as I'd left it, except that it was different. Nothing major and it took me a minute or two before I could make out what it was. And what it was, was that Rex and Harpo/Chico had gone.

'Fellas?' I gave the place a twice-over. 'Fellas?'

The bed was made and I noticed a large handwritten note lying upon the pillow. A clue? I checked it out.

Dear Mr Woodbonn (it began)
There has been a last-minute change of
plan and your services are no longer
required.
All the very best.
Yours sincerely,

Harpo/Chico Nixon

'What?' said I.

P.S. I really hate to mention this,
but if you take a look around you,
I think you'll notice that you've
blown your four-set clause.

'What? What?' said I.

P.P.S. The magic with the beermats
will be wearing off around now.
I'd head for an alleyway if I were
you.

'What? What? What?' said I.

'Open up in there!' It's the voice of the barman and it's not a happy voice. 'Open up in there, you lousy crook, or I'll bust the door down.'

Not high upon anything much, Rex Mundi lifted Harpo/Chico up to the payphone across the street from the Tomorrowman Tavern.

'That was a bit mean on Laz.'

'The man is a complete prat.' Chico lifted the receiver.

'But he saved my life.'

'People are always saving your life. I saved your life.'

'But Laz and I were partners.'

'Well, *we're* partners now.'

'Yes, but . . .'

'Listen Rex, I'm sure this Woodworm is a very nice chap—'

'Wood*bine*. The name's Lazlo Woodbine. Some call him Laz.'

'Wood*bine* then. Nice chap, fine. But we have a lot to do. We really don't have time for all the trenchcoat humour, the meaningless catchphrases, the phoney reminiscences, the lame gags about the trusty Smith and Wee Wee, the—'

'The working in the "first person".' Rex put in. 'Got right up my nose, that. *And* he thought *he* was the hero.'

'There then. So what do you say?'

'The man's a complete prat,' said Rex Mundi.

'OK. Then put the coin in the slot, please Rex, and we'll get on with the new plan.'

'New plan? I don't remember actually being told the old plan.'

'Put the coin in, Rex.'

Rex put the coin in. Chico spoke into the receiver.

'Hello operator. Could you put me through to MTWTV? Thank you . . . MTWTV? Newsroom, please

. . . Newsroom? Ah, hello. This is Chico Nixon here . . . that's right, of Harpo/Chico fame. I'm in a spot of trouble so I can't talk for long. I am being held captive by Simon Butcher, the society photographer. He intends to perform unspeakable medical experiments on me . . . will I what? . . . World exclusive with MTWTV? Yes, of course. That's exactly what I had in mind. I'll have to go now, I think he's coming back. Get the cameras over here fast.' Chico replaced the receiver.

'There,' said he. 'That should start the ball rolling. Now if you'll just tuck me back into your jacket, I think we should go and have some breakfast.'

Sam Maggott's head rose from the debris of his office. 'We're under attack. Break out the weapons. The big ones. Cecil, fetch the assault cannon from the armoury. We're at war here.'

'Yes sir.' Cecil dusted down his uniform and sloped off.

'Attention Police Headquarters.' Kevin's amplified tones boomed from the public address system mounted on the roof of the recently-commandeered military vehicle. This vehicle was chock-a-block with government munitions, hi-tech weapon systems, bags of sweets and Children of the Revolution.

'Now hear this,' Kevin stuck a gobstopper into his mouth, 'grmmm mmmph mmmph mmm.' He spat out the gobstopper. 'Excuse me. Release all your prisoners and come out with your hands up. Or we will destroy the building.'

Sam crawled over to a shrapnel hole and peeped out.

'I feel a rough one coming on,' quoth he, digging in his pockets for further pharmaceuticals. 'Cecil!'

I could have lost my rudder, burnt my boats, turned turtle in a sea of heartbreak or gone down with all hands. But I didn't. A lesser detective might have. Or possibly a merchant seaman. But not me.

Sure, my partner had taken off with the two-headed bankroll.

Sure, I was standing here with a hole the size of an elephant's nose guard in my four-set clause.

Sure, there was a barman with a problem trying to bust down the door. Sure! But who are we dealing with? This is Woodbine. The doyen of dicks. That trench amongst trenchcoats. That man with the wherewithal and the know how to do. Come on now.

I took the fedora from the hat peg and perched it over my brow. Snapped my piece into my shoulder holster. Slipped into my coat and belted up. Then I took a walk past my chair, desk and watercooler and over to my office door.

'Good morning, sir,' said I, turning the handle. 'And how might I help you?'

The barman burst past me like salt in the suntan lotion.

'I got a cash drawer full of beer mats you lousy low-down no-good rotten—' He paused in mid rant, took a look around and made with the befuddlement. 'How did you do that?' said he.

'How did I do what?' asked I.

'This room, that watercooler, the desk, and that . . .' He points a finger at my unspeakable carpet, which had escaped mention for many chapters and would continue to do so for those remaining.

'And what have you done with my spare bed?'

'Spare bed?' I enquired, with more dignity than a bandy-legged clog dancer at a Star Trek convention. 'I never have a bed in my office, fella. I'm not that kind of detective.'

'Your office? What is all this? Where's my bed?'

I sniffed the air. Sniff, sniff, and then I said, 'Do I detect the twang of the brewer's craft about your laughing gear?'

'Do what?'

'You been drinking? You appear somewhat red of face and pink of eye. Perhaps you've got the DTs.'

'I . . . er . . .'

'What was it you were saying? Spare beds in my office and beer mats in your cash drawer? I'd ease up on the hard stuff if I were you. Or take a little water with it.'

'No I . . . I mean . . . how did you do that? How . . . er . . .'

'Sure like to chew the fat with you, fella, but I got a busy day on. Call back tomorrow, eh?' I steered the boggled barman right out through the door that bears my name etched into its glass and slam it shut upon him.

'Pull one over on Woodbine. Some chance.' I took myself to my desk. Parked my butt upon my chair. Pulled the bottle of Old Bedwetter from my drawer. Uncorked it, took a king-sized slug and stared up at my ceiling fan.

'How the bloody Hell *did* I do that?' I asked it.

'You didn't, chief,' said a small green voice coming from my top pocket. 'I did.'

11.15

Jonathan was hard at work. The top-floor studio of the Butcher Building was now crowded with electronic apparatus. Banks of TV monitors, mixing desks and technical wizardry of a high order. The lad tinkered happily with a multi-pronged screwdriver that couldn't possibly work in real life. He called to Laura, who was lolling in the kind of leather teddy, which I for one, would dearly like to see in real life. 'Open the case over there, would you?'

Laura studied her exquisite finger nails. Opening crates wasn't really her 'thing'.

'Jonathan,' Laura purred. 'This stuff. Did you invent it?'

'All my own work.' The lad adjusted the torque of three screws in the top of an inter-rositor of advanced design.

'So only *you* can assemble it correctly?'

'Only me. What are you on about?'

221

'Well, I was just thinking. There's so much of it and so little time. Couldn't you get one of your copies to help you?'

'Oh no, they're single-function only. I have to do all this myself.'

'I rather thought so.' Laura smiled to herself and leaned forwards to pry open the packing case. A keen observer, or possibly any male over the age of twelve, might well have noticed the small hand-gun nestling in her cleavage. Jonathan was a bit too busy, though.

'Attention Police Headquarters. We don't have all day. Release your prisoners now and make it easy on yourselves.'

Cecil crept up behind Sam and poked him with his over-sized weapon. 'All loaded up sir. Shall I blast the bastards?'

'Not just yet. Who do we have in the cells?'

'Usual complement from central casting. A drunk who takes his orders from a higher source. A pimp who's "gonna be walking" as soon as his solicitor gets here. A brace of homeboys in headbands and the Count of Monte Cristo. Same old crowd.'

'No terrorists?'

'None, sir.'

'Fetch me my bullhorn, officer.'

'Aw sir. You're not going to try and reason with them? Let me blast the bastards.'

'Fetch me my bullhorn!'

'Spoil sport.'

A convoy of five trucks moved out from MTWTV. The leading lorry was a large and swanky affair. A sort of luxury office suite on wheels. In it, seated around a grand-looking boardroom table in splendid high-backed chairs, were Mojo and Debbie Nixon, their agents, managers and solicitors. The head of MTWTV, his private secretary, right- and left-hand men, accountants, concubines and confidants. Intense conversation was on the go, centered around product placement.

'The way I see it,' the head of MTWTV drew upon his big fat cigar. 'We're talking major marketing strategies here. Tell me Mojo, when your kid got snatched by the aliens, was he wearing any brand-name designer-label clothing?'

'Barry.' I pulled the little guy from my pocket and set him down on my desk. 'It's you.'

'It's me, chief. Barry to the rescue. Back from my vacation at glorious unsunny Bucket World. Refreshed, revived and reinvigorated. And really cheesed off about being left out of the action for so long. My agent is going to have plenty to say about this, I can tell you.'

'Agent? I didn't know you had an agent.' And I didn't. But then Barry has more sides to him than the Sunday Football League.

'Agent? Did I say agent? I meant of course my . . . er . . . ageratum.'

'Your what?'

'Ageratum, chief. American tropical houseplant. Close personal friend.'

'If you say so.'

'I do. So how have you been making out without me, then? The going been getting pretty tough, I bet.'

'Not a bit of it. I've nearly got the whole case sewn up. Piece of cake.' I made a gesture that had more breeziness and gay abandon to it than a freezer full of fellators. The way I figured it; the little guy knew how much I'd missed him. And he knew I knew he knew. And he knew how much I needed him to wind up the case. And he knew I know he knew that too. But he also knew I have a hard bitten, tough as old boots, ice cool and unemotional image to keep up. He knew all this and he knew I knew it. Barry and me had an almost mystical rapport when it

223

came to stuff like this. So the one thing he didn't expect from me was a thank you.

'No chance of a thank you, then? You ungrateful palooka.'

'What's that, Barry?'

'Nothing, chief.'

'OK.' Rex wiped his mouth with a napkin. 'You're running the show. What do we do now?'

'Well, I'm for another round of toast,' said Chico.

'And I'd like some more milk,' said Harpo. 'But I'd like some of me mum's better.'

'All well and good. But I want to know exactly what's really going on here. I can piece some of it together, but you know the rest. I'll help you, but I have to know it all. Are you going to tell me?'

'I thought you'd never ask.' Chico sipped coffee. 'Of course I'll tell you. Lean over here and let me whisper.'

'Oh no,' Rex shook his head. 'This time I want to hear it out loud and see it in print.'

'Show me that map again.' Johnny Dee snatched the thing from Ed Kelley. 'We're lost, aren't we?'

'No, we're not. I know exactly where we are.'

'You lying git.'

'I'm not. See that manhole cover up there?'

'I see it.'

'That's just outside the Butcher Building.'

Johnny Dee studied the map of the Presley City sewerage system. 'You lying git,' he said again.

'This is Police Chief Sam Maggott.' Sam shouted through the bullhorn. 'Identify yourselves.'

'We are the Children of the Revolution. 42nd Street chapter.'

'What do you want from us?'

'We want you to release all your prisoners.'

'Let me blast the bastards, sir.'

'Shut up, Cecil.'

'Who are you telling to shut up? And my name's not Cecil, it's Kevin.'

'I didn't mean you. Do you have a specific prisoner you'd like released? We'd hate to lose all of them. Especially the Count of Monte Cristo.'

'Send out Laura Lynch.'

'Laura Lynch?' Sam switched off his bullhorn. 'Cecil, do we have a Laura Lynch here?'

'We did.' Cecil put on a lopsided smirk and giggled in his silly way. 'Her and me "took tea with the parson" in the men's locker-room a couple of days back.'

'You disgusting pervert. You can be excommunicated for that, you know.' Sam switched on his bullhorn again. 'Hello, Children of the Revolution. Laura Lynch has left the building. She is no longer here. Now lay down your weapons and come out with your hands up. You are all under arrest.'

'Fat chance.' Kevin pressed buttons and further sections of Police Headquarters fell into ruination.

Sam switched off his bullhorn. 'Blast the bastards!' he told Cecil.

11.00

The dirigibles had drifted away and the morning sky was clear and cloudless above the Butcher Building as the long black air-car dropped silently on to the roof. The driver's door hissed open and the Anti-Rex stepped out. He consulted his watch. 10.59 and counting down.

'Dee and Kelley will be in position by now,' he inaccurately informed himself. 'Everything is proceeding according to plan.'

Battle waged wildly around Police Headquarters. Kevin's commandeered military vehicle had some pretty awesome firepower. But Presley's finest were now coming into their own with big guns blazing. Shells burst in many directions other than those intended. There had, as yet, been no loss of life. But there was no shortage of gung ho machismo posturing.

Somewhere, right in the middle of no-man's land in fact, a manhole cover flipped aside.

'Bloody noisy up there,' Ed complained.

'Bit of thunder probably.' Johnny prodded Ed in the trouser seat. 'Go out and have a look around.'

'Well, I don't want to get wet. I'll just take a peep.' Ed took a peep. A ricocheting bullet took the top off his head.

'Which brings us to the matter of World Rights.' The head of MTWTV sucked upon his cigar. 'Naturally we shall expect to hold these. But I know you'll agree that the up-front payment and future percentage scales are most favourable to you both. Cigar, Mojo?'

'I don't mind if I do.'

'Excuse me.' The driver slid aside a little panel and addressed the assembled company. 'Sorry to interrupt, but there seems to be some kind of disturbance going on around Police HQ. Should I stop and check it out?'

'No.' The station head spoke through a plume of cigar smoke. 'We have important negotiations in progress here. Take a detour.'

'As you say.' The driver hung a left and left the combat zone.

'Look at my head.' Ed bobbed up and down in fury. 'I just get my ears straight and this has to happen. It just won't do.'

'You go up there and tell them,' Johnny urged. 'I'll back you up.'

'You lying git.'

'I will. Go on. Tell them.'

'I bloody well will, too.'

Ed climbed from the manhole. A bouncing grenade blew off his right arm.

Ed bitterly regarded the gory stump. 'You're making me mad,' he howled.

'You're telling me *what*?' Rex howled. 'This is all a *what*?'

'A game.' Chico offered Rex the kind of comforting smile Rex had offered him the night before. It was equally uncomforting. 'A game. *The* game in fact. The only game in town, and you're in it. Part of it.'

'Do you mean like "life's a funny old game"?'

'No, I mean like "life's a great big virtual-reality computer game being played with real people".'

'It's the Phnaargs.' Rex made a foul face. 'It's them behind it. Has to be.'

'No, Rex. More powerful than them.'

'More powerful than them?' Rex scratched at his chin. A look of enlightenment, the like of which we haven't seen in this entire book, appeared on his face. 'The Gods. It's the Gods.'

'More powerful.'

'*More* powerful? Who could be more powerful than the Gods?'

'Their accountants, that's who. Care for another coffee?'

'Who's that guy?' Sam Maggott peeped through his shrapnel hole. 'Where did he come from?'

'Came out of a manhole, sir.' Cecil hefted his over-sized weapon.

'Shall I blast him?'

'Looks like he just got blasted. Blast *them*.'

'Sure thing.' Cecil inserted another high-calibre short-range evil-doer into his assault cannon and pulled the trigger. The missile whistled past Ed Kelley, setting his clothes on fire.

'I'm losing my temper!' stormed the smoker.

'Did you see that?' Kevin gestured through a gun port. 'They fired on an unarmed one-armed civilian. Strafe the blighters.'

'Now just you all see here.' Ed waved a charred arm in the air. Rapid machine-gun fire from the military vehicle engulfed him.

'Right!' screamed the ventilated Ed. 'That's the last straw.'

The Anti-Rex climbed over the roof parapet of the Butcher Building and then proceeded down the wall, fly fashion. It wasn't a pleasing thing to behold. But then, he wasn't a particularly pleasing individual.

I stood in the alleyway and took a shufty through my police-issue 200 x 6000 macroscopic laser-prism binoculars. 'There's a guy crawling down the wall up there,' said I. 'You wanna take a look, Barry?'

'No, chief. I can make him out just fine, thanks. Now, as soon as the action switches to the next scene, let's make a run for the Butcher Building. Then I'll try and fix it for you to have your roof-top ending.'

'Gotcha.'

'Not that you deserve it.'

'What's that Barry?'

'I said *now*, chief.'

'AAARRRRRRRRRGGGGGGGGHHHHHHHH!!!!!' went Ed Kelley, who was, as they say, going through changes.

The arch-demon Balberith gets a mention in Joseph Glanvil's *Saducismus Triumphus*. A volume bound in human skin which had once passed through the hands of a certain Jack Doveston. In it old Joe writes:

... by eck as like lad I'll tell thee this. Yon Balberith is reet big orrid ruffy beast wi gurt black beard full o rats and green teeth gnashing and a grinding and flames coming out o bum that'd take wallpaper off front parlor. And if thee don't eat thy black pudding reet this minute he'll come doon chimney and out o feature coal-effect bar fire and gobble thee op. Or I'll go t' foot of our stairs. Put kettle on, mother.

It probably loses something in the translation from the original Latin.

The beast which now tore its way from Ed Kelley's shattered human form didn't look like a lot of laughs. It was abominable, atavistic and atrocious, big, black and brutal, cruel, cold and callous, and so on.

It rose, a good eight feet in height, a shimmering energy body pulsating with pure malignant evil.

'I don't like the look of that,' croaked Sam Maggott. 'Blast it, Cecil.'

'I'm getting a bit low on ammo, sir. Best let the guys in the military vehicle take a pop, eh.'

'What in BAH-REAH's name is that?' Kevin gaped through the gun-port.

'Don't ask me,' a Child of the Revolution replied. 'You're the one with the speaking part, you figure it out.'

'Eh?' said Kevin. 'What's all this?'

'We want proper parts,' another Child spoke up, 'or we're going home.'

'This is hardly the time. Come on gang.'

Silence reigned in the military vehicle. But not without.

'Listen gang. Be fair.' Kevin switched on the public address system and shouted into it. 'Send out Laura Lynch!'

'Eat my shit!' cried Balberith, raising long black talons to the sky.

'Er . . . um.' Kevin dithered, but not for long. 'She clearly isn't in there,' he told his nameless companions.

229

'I think we should try the Butcher Building now.' He brrrrm'd the engine and put the vehicle into reverse.

'Look at that!' Sam did a silly dance. 'They're getting away. Officer Cecil, get the cars out.'
   'We're going in pursuit, sir? You have to be kidding.'
   'The cars, officer.'
   'Yes sir.'

Balberith was up and running. His reptilian feet, with their three splayed claws, ripped chunks from the tarmac and left more enigmatic impressions for scholars to wonder over-later. His long black scaled body rose into the air and fell upon the now swerving military vehicle.

'Let's get gone,' cried Kevin.

'After them!' cried Sam Maggott.

'What's all the hubbub, bub?' asked Johnny Dee. 'Ed? Hello? Where are you?'
   He stuck his head out of the manhole and a police car drove over it.

17

67. *And* BAH-REAH *spake unto Elvis
saying wisely, 'I think we've screwed
up here, chief.'*
The Suburban Book of the Dead

The Anti-Rex crawled down the wall of the
Butcher Building and in through an open
window. He dusted down his dark and dapper duds,
drew out a really splendid hand-gun, which appeared to
have been borrowed from the *Robocop* props cupboard,
and released the safety catch.

One floor above, a light blinked from the implant on
Jonathan's left wrist, but he tinkered on with his impossible screwdriver. Information exchanged and fed into
his cranium. Without looking up from his work, he
flipped the top from his left thumb and spoke into the
minuscule microphone housed within.

'Intruder in room B, floor sixty-five. Seek and destroy.
The intruder is AAA category. Proceed as previously
informed. Also we have another, bumbling around in the
lobby. DDD category. Best put a stop to him as well.'

The armour-clad military vehicle was making considerable headway. Presley City's up-town morning traffic
was less than a match for it. The steel tracks ground along
at a steady rate, flattening glorious highly-finned autos,
scattering pedestrians and levelling lampposts.

Inside there was a whole lot of arguing going on. Up

on the roof Balberith drove his fists at the steel plate and howled obscenities, the way some of them do. Ahead, the MTWTV convoy was halted at a red light, and behind, Presley's finest followed the armoured car with its onboard demon, at a leisurely and unhurried pace.

'Get your foot down, Cecil,' Sam shouted.

Cecil wasn't keen. 'There's a speed limit in this city, sir, and as an officer of the law it's my duty to set a good example.'

Sam cuffed the dawdling example in the ear. 'You cringing coward. Get your foot down.'

'But sir, that's an armoured car, bristling with hi-tech weapons and there's that thing on its roof. It is my considered opinion that we should stay at a safe distance and await further developments.'

'Get your foot down and switch on the siren.'

'The siren?' Officer Cecil crossed himself.

'Now.' The MTWTV station head sucked at his cigar. 'We come to the matter of film rights. Obviously there is a TV movie in this. I suggest a three-parter, prime-time; how does *The Harpo/Chico Story* sound to you?' He didn't wait for a reply. 'So shall we discuss possible actors for the lead roles?'

'I'd rather like to play myself.' Debbie fluttered her eyelashes.

'And me me,' said Mojo. 'I've been taking acting lessons at the David Bowie Academy.'

The station head nodded in agreement. 'And what about Harpo/Chico?'

'Animated model!' said Mojo and Debbie.

'My feelings entirely. But it will have to look convincing. We'll need to hire a top animatronics team.'

The driver slid back his little hatch. 'Sorry to interrupt again, but the guys in the catering truck at the tail of our convoy are getting real excited. They say there's a big army tank with a monster on its roof bearing down on them.'

'Monster? What kind of monster?'

'I'll ask them, sir.' The driver spoke into his handset. A torrent of words came in ready reply. 'Golly, they say it's about eight feet tall, black as pitch, covered in scales, breathing brimstone and smashing in the top of the army tank.'

'I like the sound of that.' The station head made further puffings. 'We could write that in. Tell the catering guys to take some polaroids and fax them through to us. And ask them if they can find out who's doing the animatronics. We might well be on to something here.'

'Will do, sir.'

'Ed?' Johnny clutched his dented skull, climbed from the manhole and peered around. Police Headquarters was merrily ablaze, as were numerous other buildings in the vicinity. The earthly remains of Ed Kelley were liberally distributed about the street.

Johnny consulted the map. 'You had it upside down. His excellency isn't going to like this.'

His excellency crossed the floor of room B. It wasn't a particularly interesting room and it's doubtful whether it would have got a mention at all, had the Anti-Rex not chosen to enter it. So, the least said about it the better. He pressed his ear to the door.

Click clack click clack clock, came the sounds of weapons being cocked in the corridor beyond.

'Hmm,' went The Anti-Rex, withdrawing his ear.

'Hmm,' went the real Rex Mundi to Harpo/Chico. 'So where exactly do I fit into all this?'

Chico munched further toast. 'You're the spanner in the works, Rex. You're not supposed to be here.'

'You're preaching to the converted.' Rex gazed around

the café. It wasn't a particularly interesting café and it's doubtful whether it would have got a mention at all had . . . do you ever get that strange feeling of déjà vu?

'Listen, Rex, you're the only one who can put it right. That's your purpose.'

'So what do I have to do?'

'Win the game. Get your initials up for the ultimate high score.'

Rex made one of his most doubtful faces to date. 'But I don't know how to win this game. Even what this game is. Can't you be a bit more specific?'

'I'll tell you this, Rex. The game goes on and on, again and again until someone wins it. But it can be won, believe me, and when it is . . .'

'Then what? Tell me.'

'And spoil the trick ending? No way.'

'Trick ending?' Rex's doubtful face became a very sour face. 'There's going to be another one of those, is there?'

'Loads.' Chico finished his toast. Harpo drained the last of his milk. 'You'll sort it out, Rex, you'll win through. I shall be with you. Fear not and things of that nature. Now, shall we take a stroll over to the Butcher Building?'

'Sounds good to me. Check please, waitress.' Rex called over to the waitress, who was hovering near at hand hoping for a walk-on part. She wasn't a particularly interesting waitress and in truth it is doubtful whether she would have got a mention at all if . . .

Balberith tore a section of reinforced steel roof from the military vehicle and glared down through the hole. Five faceless individuals gaped up at him.

'Bloody Hell!' Kevin applied the brakes.

The lads in the catering truck, who had been happy-snapping through the rear windows, suddenly dropped both their jaws and their cameras. They saw the big armoured car shudder to a halt and the great black beast as it left the roof and plummeted towards them. 'Oooooooh!' they went, ducking variously.

Balberith smashed through the rear doors of the catering truck, careened along the spotlessly clean linoleum floor and came to rest in the fruit and salad bar.

'Ahoy there, intruder,' called one of Jonathan's Repo Men through the keyhole of room B, floor sixty-five. 'We are a heavily-armed militia, low on intellect but high on company loyalty and the work ethic. In precisely one minute we will come bursting in and shoot you. You may wish to give yourself up, or possibly make a getaway through the window. But quite frankly we'd prefer it if you put up a bit of a fight as we're a right sadistic bunch. Real nasty.'

'Real nasty?' The Anti-Rex cocked his *Robocop* special. 'You don't know the meaning of *real nasty*.'

'All done.' Jonathan straightened up and flipped a switch. Banks of electrical jiggery-pokery burst into life. Lights flashed, buzzers buzzed and multiple telescreens shone with 3D views of Presley City, interiors of the Butcher Building, close ups of Jonathan, graphs and charts, curious looping graphics and an old Marc Bolan video.

'Is he singing "Pewter Suitor"?' Laura enquired.

'Nah. That's "20th Century Boy". Not even *I* have got a copy of "Pewter Suitor".'

'Is the equipment complete then?'

'All set. This lot can override the World Casts, jam out all the competition, run the game scenarios side by side for the final showdown.' Jonathan looked upon all that he had made and found that it was very good. 'Not even my dad could have set this lot up.'

'Your dad? You've never talked about your family.'

'We weren't close.'

'What does your father do?'

'Not a lot, I shouldn't think. He was dead the last time I saw him.'

'Oh, I'm so sorry.' Laura wasn't of course, but you have to say that, don't you?

'I'm not.' Jonathan smiled grimly. 'Dad had this accident. He fell into a big flywheel. Very messy. Very final.'

'A big flywheel, where was that?'

'Nowhere you need trouble your pretty little head about.'

'My pretty-little-feather-brained-only-good-for-one-thing-bimbo-know-nothing-woman's-head, would that be?'

'What?' Jonathan asked.

'Nothing. Are you really sure that only *you* alone could have constructed all this?'

'Only me.' Jonathan did shoulder swaggers.

'I'm so glad.' Laura pulled the gun from between her breasts and pointed it at Jonathan. 'Then *you're dead*, sucker.'

Balberith rose shimmering from the fruit and salad bar.

'RRRAAAGGGH!' he went, wiping the residues of plum, pulse, pimento, pomegranate, pepper and passion fruit from his chest.

'AAAGHRRR!' he continued, stepping amidst the mess of pear, peach, pomelo, pineapple, papaya, parsnip and potato.

'GHAAMPRH!' he added, as he plucked a sprout from his left ear and crunched it to oblivion.

The catering personnel were taking the opportunity to depart via the fire exits. 'Run for your lives,' they went, and things similar.

Balberith swept his great arms wide, mangling the hostess trolley and spoiling the spice rack. One reckless fellow with an eye on the main chance (for there is always one) picked up a discarded camera and prepared to take another polaroid.

'Smile please,' said he.

Balberith ripped the remains of the fruit and salad bar from its mountings and flung it through the roof. Then he advanced on the reckless fellow.

'Just one more. Oh, ouch.' Balberith grasped him by the crisp, clean lapels of his waitering jacket and hoisted him aloft.

'What's your game?' growled the monster from Hell, gazing with sickly yellow eyes into the face of the far-from-happy snapper.

'A c-couple of p-pictures for the station head,' stammered the lost soul, wetting his pants.

'Pictures?' A long forked tongue darted from the scaly mouth and licked the tip of the stammerer's nose. Lick, lick, lick, it went.

'They're c-casting for a m-m-movie . . .'

'Movie?' The black tongue vanished from view.

'There'd be a p-p-part in it for you . . .'

Balberith lowered the damp-trousered main-chancer to the floor.

'A starring part?' he enquired.

Kevin stuck the open-topped battle wagon into gear and swerved into Lonely Street. On-coming cars skidded to either side, slamming into basement dwellings, ploughing along sidewalks, overturning and bursting into flames.

'We're well rid of that,' cried Kevin. 'Anyone got a jelly baby?'

There was silence all round.

'Aw, come on, gang.'

'Not until we get proper descriptions and solid characterizations,' said a short plump girl with a freckled face and a shock of ginger hair. Her name was Alison.

'Could I have a jelly baby, please, *Alison*?'

'*Plump*?' Alison screamed. 'I'm not *plump*!'

* * *

'Calling all cars. Calling all cars.' Sam Maggott did his finest Broderick Crawford (no relation of Jonathan). 'Heavily-armoured terrorist vehicle proceeding north along Lonely Street. Set up roadblocks on King Creole and Roustabout. Halt and detain.'

'Do what?' Drunken police voices filled the airways with talk of pressing beer mat investigations.

'We're coming in now,' called Jonathan's Repo Men. 'Time to die.'

'Yours, not mine.' The evil one stood his ground, raised his supergun and let off rapid and devastating fire through the door of room B, floor sixty-five.

Cries of distress poured through the bullet holes.

'Damned unsporting,' someone complained.

'Charge!' cried someone else. And charge they jolly well did. The punctured door was carried from its hinges and borne into the room. A mighty shield in the van of an avenging army.

The Anti-Rex emptied his pistol into it, but to little avail. He was outnumbered and outgunned. The mob poured at him, over him and then all around him. He flung aside the door he was suddenly lying beneath, stared up bitterly and ran a black shirt-cuff across his bloodied nose.

'You are going to pay for this,' he spat at the gun muzzles forming a circle of steel above him. 'You don't know who you're messing with.'

'Oh, but we do.' The circle of steel expanded and a Repo Man approached. He was rather a curious-looking Repo Man. Far from being the standard blank-faced, broad-shouldered six-foot-sixer, he was short, white-haired and portly. He was dressed in the garb of a Catholic priest and he bore an uncanny resemblance to the now legendary Spencer Tracy.

He was carrying a bible and a large silver crucifix.

'Big guns up,' he ordered. The big guns went up.

'Water-pistols out.'

'Water-pistols, what?' The stinker on the deck looked uneasy.

'Holy water capsules in.'

'Holy wa – oh no . . .'

'Inane childish chant.'

The Repo Men armed their holy water-pistols and angled them down at the devil-made-flesh.

'We know who you ar-are. We know who you ar-are,' they chanted in their silly way.

'I'd advise you to say your prayers.' The Spencer Tracy lookalike beamed down at the Anti-Rex. 'But who'd be listening, eh?'

'Barry, I can't see a goshdarn thing.' It was blacker than a coal heaver's codpiece in a Blitz blackout.

'Of course you can't see, chief. You've got your eyes shut.'

'Ah, sure, that would be it.' I cotton on pretty quick to this kind of stuff. 'Why do I have my eyes shut by the way?'

'So you can't see where you're going.'

'Which would explain why I keep bumping into things, I guess.'

'You got it, chief.'

'Barry, excuse me for asking this, but why wouldn't I want to see where I was going?' It seemed a reasonable question to me.

Barry made an agitated sighing noise which I didn't take to one bit. 'Because, chief, if you can't see where you are, then nobody else can. Pretty neat, eh? Remember that movie of yours, *Death Wears Patent Slingbacks*?'

'Yeah, sure. The one with the subjective camerawork, where the audience saw the whole film through my eyes. *The Camera is Woodbine*. Bombed out at the box office, I remember that.'

'The world wasn't ready, chief. So, do you want to

keep your eyes shut while I get you up to the roof, or open them now and get a nasty surprise when you and all your millions of fans see where you are?'

'I guess I'll keep 'em shut. But I don't like this one bit. Doing a whole scene in the dark ain't gonna look too good on the screen. Deaf people will think the film's over and take a hike before I get to do my roof-top ending.'

'Can't help that, chief. You got to stick to your four-set clause and I can't spare the energy to beam you up. Now take a step to the right here, there's a—'

THUD!

'Ouch!'

'Pillar, chief.'

The non-subjective reader saw Laz (in the third person) bump into the pillar and stumble blindly on across the lobby of the Butcher Building, clutching his skull. The same reader also saw the conga-line of Repo Men that followed him, tittering into their hands and nudging one another.

And as Laz reached the lift, this very same reader now observed the Repo Men form themselves into a firing line and cock their weapons noisily.

'Did you hear that, Barry?' I put my hand to my ear with more awareness of danger than an ashtray full of broken promises.

'Er, chief. Could you just lift me up above your shoulder and kind of swivel me round a bit?'

'Sure can.' I sure did. 'What's to see?'

'Nothing you'd probably want to hear about, chief.'

'Laura, no, don't do it!' Jonathan covered his face. 'You don't want to shoot *me*.'

Laura smiled and cocked the trigger. 'But I *do*, Jonathan. I really do.'

'No, you don't. Think about all I can give you.'

240

'I have. With you out of the way I can have it anyway.'

'Laura, please listen to me—'

'No, Jonathan. You are the enemy. You belong dead. I shall take all this. The Presley hoard, the dead messiah, the power. I shall make it right.'

'You don't know what you're saying. *You* can't stop what is going to happen. Only I can stop it. This time I know how—'

'Sorry.' Laura squeezed the trigger.

'You're making a terrible mistake—'

There was a bang and a thud. Jonathan gaped down at the neat little hole in his chest. 'You shot me.'

'This is true. You *are* shot.'

'But I'm not *dead*.'

Laura's latest wristwatch was an antique Patek Phillippe, emerald encrusted, very exclusive. She studied the tiny diamond-tipped second hand. 'Bet you can't count up to five.'

'One . . . two . . . three . . . four . . .' Jonathan laughed nervously.

Laura looked on expectantly. 'Five?' she asked.

'Four and a half . . .' Jonathan plunged forwards on to his face. Sparks flew from his wrist implants. His little feet twitched and kicked and then were still.

'Told you.' Laura strode over and booted him on to his back. The beady little eyes stared up at her reproachfully, but they didn't see anything.

'Nobody likes a smart-assed kid.' Laura grinned, placed her right foot upon the dead boy's face and ground down hard with her three-inch heel.

It was an act of needlessly gratuitous violence and one which ensured for good and all, that Meryl Streep would be declining to take the female lead in the film version of this one, just like she had with the last two.

Laura twisted her heel a second time. 'I never liked her anyway,' she sneered. 'I'd rather be played by Cher any day.'

'Go on then. If you're going to do it, do it!' The Anti-Rex glared defiance at the selection of water-pistols pointing down at him. 'What's the matter with you? Do it!'

But none of the gunmen looked like they were up to doing very much of anything.

'What's all this?' The evil one climbed warily to his feet, carefully avoiding the unmoving guns.

The Repo Men stood stock still. So many shop-window dummies, suddenly bereft of all life. Anti-Rex gave the nearest a violent shove. It toppled sideways and struck the floor, still frozen in its final pose.

'Perhaps I have a guardian angel,' mused the stinker. He retrieved his supergun, reloaded it and shot the head off the Spencer Tracy lookalike.

'Go on Barry. Tell me the worst.' I could take it and Barry knew that I knew that he knew I could take it.

'Seems like a false alarm, chief. I thought you were a gonna there, but it looks like you're not. Perhaps you have a guardian angel. Now, just reach out your hand and, *whisper, whisper, whisper* . . .'

'Press the lift button, did you say?'

'A complete no-hoper.'

'What's that, Barry?'

'Nothing, chief.'

'*I* never said you were plump, Alison,' Kevin complained.

'Well, someone did. I suggest we all do our own descriptions. All in favour say aye.'

'Aye,' said all in favour, including Kevin.

'Now, *that's* democracy.' Alison smiled. She was tall and tanned and young and lovely, with long golden hair and large passionate grey eyes.

'I can dig this,' said Kevin, the Tom Cruise lookalike.

'Which way do we go at the traffic lights?'

'Left,' said Reg, the Tom Cruise lookalike.

'No, I'm sure it's right,' said Jason, who also bore an uncanny resemblance to the Hollywood star.

'Now see here . . .' said Kevin.

'He is *what*? And he wants *what*?' The MTWTV station head spat out his cigar.

The driver spoke over his shoulder. 'The guys in the catering truck, well guy, the others split apparently. The guy says it's not an animatronics job. It's a real monster from Hell. And it wants a part in the movie or . . .' the driver paused.

'Or what?' The station head snatched up his smouldering cigar and patted furiously at his smouldering fly.

'Or he'll rip up our trucks and tear us all into little bite-sized chunks of meat, sir.'

'Does he have an agent?'

'I'll ask, sir.'

'Stupid pillock.' Johnny Dee, he of the flat-top skull and map-reading talents, wandered amongst the flaming buildings in search of a cab.

'Can't read a sodding map, gets his human body splattered all over the street, then takes off without a by your leave or kiss my elbow. You just can't get the help nowadays. Oi, taxi!'

The passing taxi crawled to a halt. And very strangely it did so too. It was literally carbonized, lacking a roof and rattling noisely upon four tyreless rims. On the bare and blackened springs of what once had been the driver's seat, sat the bare and blackened remains of what once had been something or other. It wasn't human and it wasn't nice. It was very angry though and in chapters past it had rejoiced in the name of Bill. (Some cheers from supporters of the away team.)

'Cab, sir?' barked barbecued Bill the driver, raising the charred relic of what once had been his cap. 'Hop in, Johnny, we've got work to do.'

Johnny Dee tried to open a rear door. It disintegrated in his hands. He climbed into the wreckage and sat where he could.

'Is there anything you'd like to tell me about, Bill?' he asked. 'You look a mite off-colour.'

'I haven't been in this for ages,' said Rex Mundi. 'What am I doing now?'

'Smuggling my brother and me into the Butcher Building.' Chico replied. 'Do try and pay attention.'

'Cor,' went Rex. 'Look at that lot. What aren't they doing?'

'They aren't shooting anyone, by the look of them. Let's go over and check them out.'

'Sure thing.' Rex carried the double-header across the lobby and inspected the row of frozen Repo Men. 'What happened here? Why are they just standing there like that?'

Harpo said, 'If you ask me, it's some kind of contemporary sculpture. Big enterprises like this always like this kind of stuff. It's probably got some pretentious name and cost a small fortune.'

'No, Harpo.' Chico shook his head. 'That isn't it at all.'

'Yeah, well you would say that, wouldn't you?'

'Because you're wrong. Kindly shut up.'

'Don't tell me to shut up. You shut up.'

'Come on now, you two.' Rex gave them a shake.

'Don't you shake my brother,' said Harpo.

'Nor mine,' said Chico.

'I looked like Tom Cruise first,' Kevin complained.

'So?' asked Reg.

'So?' asked Jason.

'So we can't all look like Tom Cruise.'

'You could be triplets.' Sharon suggested. She was tall and tanned and young and lovely, with a mane of golden hair and large passionate grey eyes. 'And it's straight on at the lights for the Butcher Building, by the way.'

'Put your foot down further and switch that siren back on,' demanded Sam Maggott.

'No agent, eh?' said the MTWTV station head. 'I think we can do business with this guy. Take his name and tell him he's got a deal.'

'I got zapped by a flying saucer,' Bill explained. 'It hasn't done much for my temper.'

'Simon Butcher!' The Anti-Rex waved his gun in the air. 'I'm coming to kill you!'

'My hair's blonder than yours,' said Alison to Sharon.
    'Oh no it's not.'
    'Oh yes it is.'

Laura seated herself before the controls. 'I think I can work all this out for myself.' She rubbed her hands together.
    'I bet you don't get the chance though.' The voice belonged to Jonathan Crawford.
    Laura looked up in horror. Jonathan's face grinned at her from the telescreens.
    Laura smiled. 'Still a little bit of you left in the machine, eh?' She touched buttons on the console and the faces of Jonathan blacked out. 'Soon have all your little tricks out of there.'
    'I doubt that.' The voice was Jonathan's once again.
    Laura studied the telescreens. 'Say that again.' Her hand hovered above the console.
    'I said, I doubt that.' A pistol butt caught her on the side of the head. Laura fell from her chair on to the dead boy on the floor.

'Not very nice of you, stomping on my face like that.'

Laura gazed up. Jonathan gazed down. 'I told you you were making a big mistake.'

Laura wiped blood from her eyes. 'But this was *you*. You said that only *you* could assemble the apparatus.'

'Yes, I did, didn't I?' Jonathan swung his foot at Laura's face. Before it struck home the chapter came to a hasty conclusion.

18

*Rock 'n' Roll is making love to the
Justice of the Peace's daughter in the
back of a stolen Chevy, drinking beer
you bought on a fake ID, at a drive-in
showing* Vanishing Point *or
something. That's what Rock 'n' Roll is.*
M. Nixon

*I'm only dancing cos I can't stop
shaking.*
John Spencer

Jonathan dragged Laura to her feet. He hadn't
really kicked her in the face; you've got to
draw the line somewhere, although I've never been
exactly sure where.

'You've worked out very well,' Jonathan told her. 'I
knew I couldn't trust you, although you checked out OK
on my instrumentation, I'll have to look into that. But,
you've been good value for money. Two different game
scenarios for the death of the boy genius. They will go
down a storm with my business partners. The big
question is now, what should I do with you? It wouldn't
come across as very credible if I trusted you a third time.
The second time was pushing it a bit.'

'You could let me escape,' Laura suggested hopefully.
'Not knowingly of course. I could just, well, escape when
you weren't looking.'

'You could. But I don't like it. Better if I just end your scenario right here and now.'

Laura looked down at the boy. He was clearly insane.

'Not very imaginative,' she heard herself saying. 'Not for the great Jonathan Crawford. The genius who turned life on Earth into a virtual-reality computer game for the Gods. That is what you've done, isn't it?'

Jonathan made a smug face. 'It's a bit more complicated than that as it happens. But you're close.'

'So you can hardly just kill me off now. I'm the female lead, the hero has to get me at the end. It's tradition or an old charter or something.'

Jonathan stroked his pointy little chin. 'Seems to me that just about everybody's had you already. But I take your point. Winner takes all, and as I intend to be the winner, shooting you would be a bit of a waste. Tell you what, I've got a far better idea. One that's always popular. Come on, this way.' Jonathan gestured towards the lift door.

'We're going up, aren't we, Barry?'

'Chief, press *that* button there. *That* one and be quick about it.'

'Barry, you're giving the game away now.'

'Chief, if you know what's good for you, press the damn button.'

'This one?'

'That one.'

Laura and Jonathan stood before the sixty-sixth floor lift door.

'Press the call button, Laura.'

'Where are we going?'

'Where do you think?'

'Down.' Laura's voice had that doomed quality about it.

'You got it. Where is that lift?'

Ping went the little bell, the way some of them do.
The lift doors opened.
The lift was empty.

'Barry, where are we?'
'Sixty-fifth floor, chief. And in the nick of time.'
'Is it all right for you to say sixty-fifth floor?'
'Do you see a sixty-fifth floor, chief?'
'Not with my eyes closed I don't.'
'There you go, then.'
'Barry, this is just plain stupid.'
'Should suit you fine, then.'
'What's that, Barry?'
'Nothing, chief.'
'You lying git, I heard you that time.'

The lift passed the ground-floor level and made for the vault.
'Down here,' whispered Laura.
Ping went the little bell. The lift doors opened.
'In you go then.'
Laura hesitated. Jonathan prodded her with his average-sized weapon. 'Get moving.'
'Jonathan, I don't think I—'
'Please shut up and go on. You know which way.'
'I don't want to go in there again.'
'But you must, my dear. You really must. Heroine trapped in the treasure cave, time ticking away until the Big Bang; can the hero reach her in time? If that's not a classic scenario, then I don't know what is.'
They moved amidst the massive paintings. The portraits of Presley, clad in the regal fineries of ancient times. The gilded icons, busts and figurines. The images of the false messiah. They approached the blank stone wall.
'No, Jonathan, please.'
The bad boy tinkered at his wrist. The wall dissolved

to reveal the chamber containing the juke-box sarcophagus.

'In.'

'No, please.'

'Get in.' Jonathan thrust her forwards. And then she
felt it again. That terrible loneliness. That fear. The
sorrow.

Jonathan's laughter rang in Laura's ears in the traditional manner as the wall closed upon her.

'We missed the lift,' said Rex. 'Never mind, we'll catch
it when it comes up again.'

'All right,' said Kevin. 'All right. There's five of us.
Three look like Tom Cruise and the other two like Julia
Roberts.'

'I look much more like her than Sharon does.'

'Oh no you don't.'

'Ladies, please. We are supposed to be revolutionaries,
fighting for a sacred cause. Followers of BAH-REAH the
All-Knower. We have to rescue our high priestess Laura
and overthrow the system. We can't carry on in this
bloody silly fashion.'

'I don't know about you lot,' said Jason. 'But I think
Kevin looks just like Danny De Vito.'

Officer Cecil finally switched on the siren. 'Happy now?'
he asked in a petulant manner.

'Overtake those trucks, then,' ordered Sam.

'With the greatest of pleasure.' Cecil swerved past the
MTWTV catering truck. Inside Balberith was on the car
phone.

'And I've always wanted to do a kiddies' series like
Sesame Street,' he was saying, 'but of course I'd want to
eat a couple of the little bastards afterwards, if that would
be OK with you.'

'Can't see any problem there, fella,' the MTWTV

station head put his hand over the mouthpiece; 'get your foot down,' he told the driver, 'lose this maniac.'

The Anti-Rex strode along a corridor of floor sixty-five. The *Robocop* super-gun swinging to left and right. He turned a corner and stopped in no small surprise. Coming in his direction was a man in a trenchcoat and fedora. A man who should surely have been blown to pieces in the alleyway behind the Tomorrowman Tavern. He was feeling his way along a wall with one hand and carrying a sprout in the other. A very familiar-looking sprout.

'Rex,' said Barry. 'Hi there.'

Ping went the lift bell at ground-floor level.

'Bother,' said Jonathan.

The lift doors opened.

Jonathan looked out.

Rex Mundi looked in.

'Oh!' said he.

'Oh indeed.' Jonathan aimed his gun at Rex. 'What the Hell is that ugly-looking sucker sticking out of your jacket?'

'Barry,' said the Anti-Rex. 'I thought you were still—'

'In the bucket, chief? Nah, I got fed up with that.'

'So you've got your awesome powers back then?' A cruel smile appeared on the stinker's lips.

'Can I open my eyes, Barry? It's Rex, isn't it?'

'Shut your rap, ass-wipe.'

'That's not very nice, chief. What's got into you? And where did you get that gun? That's the one out of *Robocop*, isn't it?'

'Toss Barry over to me, slimeball. And keep your eyes shut.'

'I don't know that I wish to be tossed anywhere as it happens. What's got into you Rex, you're not yourself at all.'

'I think you might just have something there, Barry.'

'You're a bit early, Rex.' Jonathan beckoned with his gun. 'I wasn't expecting you for another hour or so. But as you're here, you might as well stay where I can keep an eye on you. Come on, and quietly now.'

Rex came quietly.

'Floor sixty-six please, press the button please.'

Rex pressed the button. The doors closed and the lift rose.

'What's with the freak?' Jonathan waggled his gun at Harpo/Chico. 'Starting up your own circus?'

'I don't like this big boy,' blubbered Harpo. 'Turn him into a bunny rabbit.'

'Not yet, bruv.'

'How does it do that? It's too young to talk.'

'How's the big game going, Jonathan? Anyone getting close to winning it yet?' Rex leaned over to the lad in a chummy sort of fashion.

'Back off please,' Jonathan raised his gun. 'And what exactly do you know about *the game*?'

'Just about enough to win it.'

'Oh, I do hope so, Rex, I really really do.'

'Now!' shouted the Anti-Rex, cocking his great big pistol.

'Toss Barry over.'

'What should I do, Barry?'

'I think I shall have to check this out. I know I shouldn't, but I'm just going to pop forwards half an hour and see what's going to be going on. If you catch my drift, and I'm sure that you do.'

'No, Barry, wait. Take me with you.'

'Hold him or you're dead!'

'I'm trying.'

But it was all too late. Barry was gone. Laz had an empty hand and the Anti-Rex had a loaded pistol.

'Oh dear,' said he. 'Oh dear, oh dear. Seems like you're dead, then.'

'OK OK,' cried Kevin. 'We're freedom fighters and as such we're all free to look like whoever we want. Now, can we go and rescue Laura?'

The Tom Cruises and the Julia Roberts lookalikes nodded their beautiful heads. One of the twins (I think it was Alison) said 'There's an MTWTV truck belting up behind us and a load of police cars. Can't we go any faster?'

'Spin the gun turret around and take a pop at them, will you, Tom.'

Reg and Jason hastened to oblige.

In the lift Jonathan suddenly said, 'Oh golly. In all the excitement I've let the Repo Men go off-line.' He tapped furiously at his wrist. 'It's all the fault of that Laura.'

'How is Laura?' Rex did another chummy lean-forward job. Only this time he kneed Jonathan in the groin and tore the gun from his hand.

'Nice one,' said Harpo.

'Do you want to open your eyes before I shoot you?' the Anti-Rex asked.

'I'd prefer not, thank you. Barry might well be back any second to get me out of this.'

'Mr Woodbarf, nothing is going to get you out of this.' The evil one stuck the barrel of his super-gun into Laz's left ear.

'Any last words?'

'Pardon?'

'I said, *any last words*!'

'No need to shout.'

'Well?'

'BARRY, HELP!!!'

'Nice try.' Cock and click went the super-gun. Rumble

253

rumble, shout and holla, came the sudden commotion in the corridor.

So many big Repo Men and so many holy water-pistols all at once.

'Oh bollocks,' muttered the Anti-Rex, 'Dee and Kelley, *where are you?*'

'Talked all night,' said Johnny Dee to blackened Bill. 'Waffle waffle waffle. All kinds of plots and plans and evil schemes. All crap, if you ask me. Ed and I had to go along with it, of course. We were supposed to blow our way into the basement of the Butcher Building. The Presley hoard is in there, you see.'

'Oh, *that's* where it is. I was taking Rex there when I got blown up. Found my cab out back of the Tomorrowman. Frankly, I'm quite upset about the whole thing.'

'You look upset,' said Johnny.

'Where is Laura?' Rex inquired.

Jonathan clutched at himself. 'Where you'll never find her,' he mumbled.

'Jonathan, surely you've noticed. Half the plot of this book appears to revolve around people holding guns on other people. Now, at this moment, as you can see, I'm holding the gun on you. Tell me where Laura is, or I will have no hesitation in shooting you.'

'Floor sixty-five,' said Jonathan, with no hesitation of his own.

Rex pressed the button. 'You'd better not be lying.'

The youthful blackguard crossed his black heart. 'As if I'd dare.'

'Just sign here.' The MTWTV station head passed Mojo the fountain pen.

'The truck's swerving around a lot. What's going on out there?'

'Nothing to worry about. Steady yourself on the table. Here you go.'

Shell-fire suddenly tore into the roof of the mobile boardroom.

'Shit,' said Mojo.

'Sign,' said the station head.

'Well, I'm not too sure. What do you think, Debbie?'

'Hello!' shouted Balberith into the car phone. 'Anybody there?'

For those who like a time check once in a while, it was now 9.30 hours to go and still counting down.

Laura hugged her arms. The room was impossibly cold. The sarcophagus lay before her. Within it the body of Elvis. The false God. The reason behind it all. Behind everything she loathed and despised. But something more.

Laura was shaking. She found genuine fear in this tiny room. Beyond the walls life was unreal. It had been made to become unreal. But in here there was some kind of crazy reality. The reality of death perhaps? The inevitability of age and ruination? The very pointlessness of it all?

Laura placed her trembling hands upon the coffin's lid.

'Elvis,' she said. 'What are you?'

Ping went that little bell again. This time at floor sixty-five. The lift doors opened.

It was an interesting tableau. Lazlo Woodbine with his hands over his face. The Anti-Rex with his hands in the air. And a whole lot of Repo Men. Those who weren't training water pistols on the other Rex, swung other weapons in the direction of the real thing.

'I'll take my gun back now, if you don't mind.'

Rex handed it over.

'I've never liked you, Jonathan,' said Rex.

255

Jonathan smiled and then kicked Rex between the legs. 'Nor me, you, as it happens.'

'Drive us into the car park.' Jason rattled away at the gun turret.

'How many police cars can you see?' Kevin asked.

Jason counted as best he could. 'About a dozen. And some MTWTV trucks. We'll all be on television tonight. Must make sure we get home in time to watch it.'

'How much ammunition do we have left?'

'Not much. But we've got plenty of sweets.'

'And we have each other,' said Alison.

'Do what?'

'Kevin,' cooed Alison. 'Don't you think it's about time for a love scene? Something steamy, you know.'

'What, you and me? Not half.'

'No. I was thinking about me and Reg. No-one ever does a steamy love scene with Danny De Vito.'

'I don't look like Danny De Vito. Stop sniggering, Reg, or I'll give you a smack in the mouth.'

'Well, well, well, well, well,' crowed Jonathan. 'The gang's all here.'

'YOU!!!' The Anti-Rex threw up his hands. 'Crawford. You filthy stinking—' Several Repo Men took the opportunity to club him to his knees.

'Told you you were in for a nasty surprise,' Rex smirked awfully. The bruised genitals were almost worth it just to see the look on his enemy's face.

'And YOU! I thought you and this moron with the shut eyes were dead.'

'Hi, Rex,' said Lazlo, not opening up for one little peep. 'Guess we walked into some deep shit here, eh?'

'Hi, Laz. Say hello to Lazlo, Harpo/Chico.'

'The man is a prat,' said Chico.

'Language,' said Harpo. 'I'll tell mum if you talk dirty.'

'What an ugly little sucker,' said the Anti-Rex.

'I don't think there's room in the lift for all you old pals,' Jonathan smiled hideously, 'we'd best go up other ways.' He tinkered once more at his wrist. The ceiling spread. The sixty-fifth floor rose and soon they were all on the sixty-sixth.

'We're not on the roof, by any chance?' Laz asked.

Things were relatively quiet down in the car park. The big military vehicle was quiet. Two dozen police cars were quiet. Four of the MTWTV trucks, which were assembled, were quiet. The fifth was a bit noisy, though.

'Hello?' shouted Balberith. 'Someone answer me or I'm gonna lose my rag.'

Jonathan took a little peep at his watch. 'Nine hours and twenty minutes to detonation.'

'Rex,' Laz whispered through his fingers, 'are we on the roof yet?'

'Are you back in the first person?'

'I guess not. So where are we?'

Jonathan spoke. 'You are at the very centre of operations, Mr Woodbrain.'

'Wood*bine*, fella, the name's Lazlo Woodbine, some call me—'

'I don't really give a toss what they call you.' Jonathan swaggered to and fro before his private army. The Repo Men aimed their weapons at Rex, Laz, Harpo/Chico and Rex's dirty double. They had plenty of choice really.

'So,' said the swaggering one. 'What are we all going to do now?'

'My brother could turn you into a bunny,' Harpo suggested.

'Rex, kindly keep your pet quiet.'

'What is all this for?' The Anti-Rex indicated Jonathan's improbable electronic set-up.

'All this?' The lad's smile passed over his creation. 'You'd really like to know all about it, eh?'

257

'Before I tear your heart out of your chest and ram it down your throat, yes.'

'Don't you just wish! OK, why not. I can edit it out later.'

'Where is Laura?' Rex demanded. 'Where is Elvis?'

'One thing at a time, please. All that you behold is for the most part, simply broadcasting equipment. Although of a somewhat specialized nature, with certain modifications. But you'll find out all about them later. I propose to broadcast on a world-wide scale, a message to the good folk of this fair planet.'

Harpo looked at Chico. Chico looked at Harpo.

'Everybody wants to get into the act,' Chico said.

'What message?' the Anti-Rex asked.

'That Elvis is dead.'

'*Dead?*' The Anti-Rex sprang forward. Water-pistols rose up to meet him. Rifle butts clubbed him down.

'I love it when they do that,' said Rex Mundi.

'What do you mean, dead?' The Anti-Rex rose, none the worst for wear.

'I thought you'd be glad to hear it.'

'*You* killed him? *You?*'

'Not me.' The black heart was crossed once more. 'He killed himself.'

'He did what?' It was a bit of a chorus really, even some of the Repo Men joined in.

'He committed suicide, 16 August 1977. Not a lot of people know that,' he continued, dropping unexpectedly into his Michael Caine persona.

'You lying git,' said the Anti-Rex.

'Oh, but he did, you know. That is partly what all this is about. He came here to me. To the House of Light. You can read it in the scripture. *The Suburban Book of the Dead*. It tells you all the mistakes he made, before he finally saw the light. My light. I formulated the suicide pill for him. No-one back in 1977 suspected suicide.'

'But why?' Rex asked. 'Why would he want to kill himself?'

'You have to ask me *that*? You've read his little bible. Seen the Presley hoard. You know how he screwed up. It was guilt that made him do it. Guilt for how he'd screwed everything up. He changed history, he tried to make it right. It ended with all this, Presley City. Him being worshipped as a god. So he had no choice. The only way he could make amends was to go back and kill himself.'

'Ah,' said Rex thoughtfully. 'I see. What you're saying is that by committing suicide in 1977, none of this could occur.'

'Exactly.' Jonathan made a smug face.

'Er?' Puzzled head-scratching suddenly became all the rage.

'Is it just me?' Laz asked. 'Or is there a rather obvious flaw in the little punk's reasoning?'

'Bunny the big boy,' said Harpo.

'I think he just bunnied himself, bruv.'

'Shut up! The lot of you!' Jonathan had a bit of a rant. 'Elvis is dead. That's all you have to know. And in a little over nine hours you'll all be dead too. This city will be gone, nothing but blackened rubble. And do you know why?'

The puzzled head-scratching continued in some quarters, but helpless shrugging had now become the latest craze. That and head shaking. It was all a matter of taste, really.

'Interesting that, isn't it? We all know that it happens, but none of us know how or why. Rex, pardon me, but you don't seem to be shrugging helplessly or shaking your head. In fact, correct me if I'm wrong, but you're nodding, aren't you?'

'I certainly am.'

'And why might that be?'

'Because,' said Rex Mundi. 'I've just figured it all out.'

259

'Right,' said Kevin. 'Plan, anyone?'

'Uh uh uh uh uh uh uh uh uh,' went Reg and Alison steamily.

'You're proving a real disappointment to me, Reg.'

'Couldn't care less,' Reg drew breath. 'When did you ever get to give Julia Roberts one?'

Kevin bit his lip and shook his head. 'Jason, do you have a plan?'

'Uh uh uh uh uh uh uh uh uh,' went Jason and Sharon with much gusto.

'Aw, come on, gang. We've come all this way. We have to do something.'

'But *we* are, *Danny*,' said Jason, Sharon, Reg and Alison. '*We* are.'

Balberith munched upon the main chancer. 'Sorry,' said he, 'I lost my rag. That's showbiz!'

The MTWTV station head said. 'OK, the shooting's stopped and we're all parked up outside the Butcher Building. Mojo, have you signed the contract?'

'The pen's run out.' Mojo shook the thing fiercely, spraying ink over the station head.

'Sorry.'

'Just sign the contract. The cameras are ready to roll.'

'Er, if I might just interject,' Mojo's agent removed the pen from his client's hand and screwed back the top, 'I have certain reservations regarding several of the clauses.'

The bespattered station head rolled his eyes. 'Oh, you do, do you?'

'If we might just look at clauses 3–8, 17–19, 28–29, 56–58, 103–105, 130–134 . . .'

The station head lit another cigar.

* * *

'I'm going to tell him.' Bill drummed his charcoal stumps on the steering wheel.

'Tell who?' Johnny Dee shifted uncomfortably.

'His excellency. I'm going to tell him.'

'Tell him what?' The devastated cab rattled and groaned. Sparks flew from the wheel rims. Bits dropped off and clattered into the street.

'Tell him I quit.'

'You can't do that.'

'I can. I've been giving the matter a lot of thought. I really quite liked being a cabby. Got me out and about. Met interesting people. If you run your own cab, you're your own man, you can choose your own hours, plan your holidays. It's a smart job.'

'Bill, you're a demon from Hell. And a burnt-out one at that.'

'I had this revelation. Would you like me to tell you about it?'

'Not really.'

'You see,' Bill continued. 'It's like this . . .'

'Officer Cecil.'

'Yes, sir?'

'Officer Cecil. We now have what is called a "containment situation". The terrorists are surrounded. We have them "in the net".'

'In theory, sir.'

'In practice, officer.'

'Do you think *they* know that, sir?'

'Officer Cecil, I want you to immobilize their vehicle.'

Officer Cecil fell about in mirth. 'Yes, I bet you do.'

Sam ignored him. 'Get out of this car. Creep over to them and blow the tracks off their battle wagon with your over-sized weapon.'

Officer Cecil studied the face of Sam Maggott. It was a big fat sweaty face. The face of a police chief who was having a 'tough one'. It was unshaven. The mouth of the face had bad breath. The eyes were red-rimmed. There was a bogey up the left nostril.

'You want I should creep over to that great armoured tank of a thing, risking life and limb, and casually blow off its frigging tracks. Is that what you're saying, sir?'

'That's right.'

'OK then.' Officer Cecil saluted his superior. Climbed from the police car and marched away.

But not in the direction of the terrorist vehicle. In quite the opposite, in fact.

'Officer Cecil, come back or I'll put you on a charge.'

'Go stuff yourself.' Officer Cecil raised two departing fingers. 'I'm going for a beer.'

'Spit it out, Rex,' Jonathan advised. 'Tell us what you know.'

Rex smiled. 'Well, for a start, I know this. Presley City, all of it, is some kind of big computer game. And it doesn't take the brain of Einstein to figure out that you're behind it.'

'I never thought much of Einstein. He was a Phnaarg. But is that it, is that what you think you know?'

'I know you're stuck.'

'What do you mean?' The lad made a brave face. It didn't look all that brave. 'Stuck? Me?'

'The game ends in just over nine hours. What happens to you after that?'

'Well . . . I . . .'

'Go back and start again. Is that it? Is that what you have to do each time, if nobody wins? How long do you get, each time?'

'What is all this shit?' The Anti-Rex made furious fists. 'What game are you talking about?'

'Ask the boy-genius.'

'It's rubbish. All rubbish.'

'I don't think so. It all stems from here, from you. The Department of Human Resources, the Repo Men monitoring information, maintaining order in a city that isn't really a city. You're stuck here, Crawford. You can't get out until the game is won. And you don't know how to win it yourself. That's why we're here.'

'Rubbish.' Jonathan had a fair old sweat going.

'No, it ain't.' Lazlo Woodbine opened his eyes.

'Well, that's you out of it.' Jonathan sneered. 'You only had the four sets. You just lost.'

Rex turned to the man in the trenchcoat. 'What is all this?'

'I hate this stinking city,' Laz stared bitterly at Jonathan, 'but I never realized why until right this minute. It's a game all right. A big game and I've been here and played in it before. *The Tempus Fugitives*. My case. The only case I ever get. Time after time after time. I remember now. I've done this again and again.'

'And you always cock it up,' Jonathan managed another sneer. 'You never amounted to much anyway. A bit of nostalgia for the old folks.'

'And me?' Rex asked.

Jonathan shrugged. 'You're supposed to be the hero, aren't you? So you'd better do some heroing. You've got nine hours left to win the game. Because, if you don't . . .' the boy's eyes narrowed. 'You'll be in this again and again. Just like me. And I'll make sure you know it. I always wipe the detective's memory. But I won't wipe yours. Now you're in it, you'll stay in it. So you'd best win it *now*, eh?'

'Boo and hiss' said Harpo. 'This big boy is a rotter.'

'How is it won?'

'You've got to get the gold, Rex.' Jonathan danced a manic little dance. 'You have to get the treasure and neutralize the bomb. Then you win.'

'Where is the treasure?'

'It's in the vault under this building,' sighed the Anti-Rex. '*Hero?* You have to be joking.'

'So where's the bomb?' Rex turned back to the little blighter.

Jonathan threw up his hands. 'I don't know! If I knew where it was, do you think I'd get blown up time after time.'

Rex turned to his loathsome double. 'Where is the bomb?'

His other self glared back at him. 'Not *my* bomb,' he replied. 'I don't know.'

'So what are *you* planning to do?' Rex gave Jonathan another glance.

'To you, nothing. You want to live. So, find the treasure, stop the bomb and win the game.'

Rex laughed. 'But then you win, don't you? You are free. And you sell the game to—' he pointed skyward '—and go on running the show. In your own sweet fashion. Thinking up new scenarios, and in complete control.'

'Sounds OK to me,' said Jonathan, preening generally.

'But not to me!' The Anti-Rex made mighty fists. 'I'm going to run this planet, you little shit.'

'Don't be so silly.' Jonathan fluttered his hands in the air. 'You're no threat to me. But I do so like having you in the game. Comic relief, you know. But enough of all this chit-chat. Time is against us. And you must be getting on with your exciting adventures. So I shall say ta-ta for now.'

There was a grinding of gears and a meshing of cogs and a steel wall plunged down, effectively separating Rex, Harpo/Chico, Laz and the Anti-Rex from the boy in the control room and his private army.

'Best get to it,' came Jonathan's closing comments. 'Nine hours left. Every man for himself.'

19

Elvis is everywhere, man.

M. Nixon

☞ The Anti-Rex began to grow somewhat bulgy. Unsightly swellings pulsed on his face. His eyes rolled. Large lumps came and went on his forehead. Buttons popped from his shirt. It wasn't pretty, but it was pretty standard stuff. Harpo/Chico, for two, wasn't impressed.

'This is all crap!' roared the bulger. 'All of it. I've never been here before. I'm not in this "game".'

'I saw you last time, scumbag.' Laz straightened his belt. 'And the time before that. My memory's coming back clearer than a closet queen in a clergyman's cloister.'

'Did I kill you the last time?' the Anti-Rex asked. 'Because I'm sure as Hell gonna do it now.' He lunged toward the man in the trenchcoat.

And then . . .

'Aw shit!' A carpet of banana skins materialized beneath the feet of the Anti-Rex and sent him sprawling.

'About time too,' said Harpo. 'Nice one, Chico.'

'I suggest we make a break for it,' Chico said. 'We'd best take the lift.'

'You take yours and I'll take mine.' Lazlo Woodbine took to his heels.

'This is MTWTV broadcasting live on the air,' came a talking head on all available networks, wavebands and

265

whatnots. 'We are outside the Butcher Building in up-town Presley City, where today a most dramatic scene is unfolding. The building is now surrounded by police cars that have raced here because Harpo/Chico, two-headed love-child of popular showbiz couple Mojo and Debbie Nixon, recently kidnapped by aliens, is now known to be inside. Held hostage by Simon "Baby Slayer" Butcher, psychopathic maniac and photographer to the stars.'

'Do what?' went Sam Maggott, who was picking it up on the police band.

'Do what?' went Jonathan Crawford, alias Simon 'Baby Slayer' Butcher, who was picking it up on all kinds of sophisticated how's-your-fathers. 'Say again?'

'Earlier today Harpo/Chico managed to call us from his inhuman captivity to say that Butcher proposed to carry out obscene medical experiments upon the helpless infant. There have been no ransom demands and it appears that Butcher, described by a close friend as a "screaming shirtlifter and fish fetishist who should be strung up by the gonads", takes pleasure in acts of unrivalled barbarity against minors. We'll be right back after this station break.'

'*Osh Kosh By Golly.* Baby garments with that extra neck space. As worn by Harpo/Chico, the all-American boys. Doncha just love 'em?'

'Frig!' Crawford thumbed the channel into darkness. 'Or perhaps not frig. In fact, not frig at all.' He smiled his smug little smile and made free with the console tapping.

'This is just perfect,' he said.

'Did you hear that?' Kevin asked.

Jason, Sharon, Reg and Alison were all smoking cigarettes and looking a mite shagged out.

'Hear what?' asked one of the Julia Roberts.

'Up there in the Butcher Building. Simon Butcher's got

Harpo/Chico. He's a psycho. I'll bet he's holding Laura. Has to be. We've got to save her.'

'And how do we do that?' asked a Tom Cruise. 'We seem to be surrounded.'

'Storm the building.' Kevin prepared to do just that.

'Couldn't we hang on a while,' Reg asked. 'I fancy taking tea with the parson. How about it, Alison?'

'You filthy pig.' Alison hit him right in the mouth.

Reg rubbed his cheek. 'Sharon?'

'I'm game, Tom,' Sharon whispered. 'Which way up do you want me?'

'Aw, come on, gang . . .'

The lift went down.

'The vault,' said Rex. 'How do we get to the vault?'

'We go down, Rex. Right down.' Chico gestured to the row of floor buttons. 'Hold me over there and I'll use my X-ray vision.'

'X-ray vision.' Rex made a face. 'It figures.'

'Ah, yes.' Chico examined the button panel. 'Straight forward enough. Numerological sequence. Three-digit code. Cardinal numbers. Simple and obvious. 6 6 6.'

'Oh dear,' Rex made another face, 'not one of my favourites.'

'Had to be though, didn't it. After all, your other self's TV station is the next block down the street.'

'Down the street?'

'Sure. They're next-door neighbours. Crawford and the other you. Cosy, eh? Tap it out, Rex. Going down.'

Rex tapped six. Then six again. The lift shuddered.

Chico smiled. 'Sixty-six. Crawford's floor. He's set up defences to prevent anyone getting to him now. Best press the third six before we go off bang.'

Rex hesitated. 'We might well go off bang if I press the wrong button. Six six six is too easy.'

The lift began to heave violently from side to side.

267

'It's gonna drop,' howled Harpo. 'We're all gonna die. Save us, Rex.'

Rex's finger hovered before the six button. The lift rocked. Sparks began to fly.

'Press six.' Chico reached for the button. Rex held him back.

'It's wrong. It's a trap, I know it.'

The lights went on and off. The fear flasher flashed and the horror horn went Wooooooooooooooo!

'Press six like my brother says.'

'No.' Rex pressed eight.

The shaking stopped. The lighting sorted itself out and the lift proceeded down in an orderly fashion.

'How?' Chico asked. 'I missed it.'

'Crawford's not the Beast 666,' Rex explained. 'He lives right next door, though. You just told me. So six six eight . . . that's the code. The next-door neighbour of the beast. Smart thinking on my part, eh?'

'Dead smart. Except that the TV station is *down* the street. Which would make it six six four.'

'Hmm,' went Rex Mundi.

'This is MTWTV and this is Dick Adamski talking to you live. I have here with me Mojo and Debbie Nixon, distraught parents of America's favourite bicephalous. Who, if you missed us earlier, is being held captive by Simon "the Black Butcher" Butcher, necrophile, beastialist and high-society photographer. Mojo, how are you feeling right now?'

'I'm feeling pretty good right now, Dick, because I know that MTWTV, the station that cares, is right behind Debbie and me. And Presley City's finest are on the job.'

'And do you have a message for the black butcher himself?'

'I surely do, Dick. If you're watching, you son-of-a-suppository, I wanna tell you this, holding captives and conducting monstrous experiments can be a thirsty business. And if I were you, I'd be drinking Murdoch Brew, the beer that hits the spot any time. That's what I'm drinking right now. Cheers, Dick.'

'Cheers, Mojo.'

'The kid's a natural.' The MTWTV station head leaned back in his chair and smiled hugely.

'Clauses 689-692, 707-717 . . .' Mojo's agent continued.

'Goddamn . . . Oh and ouch . . .' The Anti-Rex skidded on another banana skin. He dragged a handset from his pocket. Pressed buttons, shouted into it. 'Dee, Kelley. Where are you?'

Johnny Dee tossed his howling handset out of the glassless cab window. 'He does go on, don't he?'

'It came to me in a flash,' Bill burbled on, 'a bolt from the blue, as it were. About the cabbying see. I could be like this sort of lone avenger with his own cab. You know the kind of stuff. Crime wave, society under attack, panic in the streets. The police chief is having a rough one. Everything is coming apart at the seams. Only one thing to do. Pick up the Bill Phone and call HELLCAB.'

Johnny cast his eyes towards heaven.

'When there's some deep shit in your neighbourhood,' sang Bill. 'Who you gonna call? Call HELLCAB!'

'Doesn't scan, Bill.'

'You could join me, Johnny. Remember *Randall and Hopkirk Deceased*? I could be the dead one. Even like this I'm better looking than he was.'

The Hellcab ground its way painfully through the late afternoon streets of Presley City.

'When something pongs and it don't pong good, who you gonna call? Call . . . HELLCAB . . .'

'Straight on at the lights,' said Johnny.

Balberith popped the main chancer's final foot into his mouth and swallowed. Then he stuck his head through the hole in the roof and took a bit of a look round. There were a good many cameras. But none of them were pointing in his direction. All were aimed up at the Butcher Building.

'So that's where the movie is,' Balberith dabbed his black lips with a table cloth, 'I'm on then.'

The lift doors opened.

'Ah,' said Rex. 'We're here.'

'Debbie.' Dick Adamski extended his mike. 'Would you be kind enough to share a word or two with us?'

'I'd love to, Dick.' Debbie thrust out a pair of breasts that really should have had considerable mention previously. 'I'd just like to say—'

The channel flickered. The screens of the viewing public became breastless. And then the face of Jonathan Crawford went world-wide.

'Hello, suckers,' Jonathan winked horribly, 'it's me, Simon "the bogeyman" Butcher. Maniac, destroyer and ruler of this fair land. Yeah, ruler. That's what I said. *I'm* in control here. I run it all, the Department of Human Resources, that keeps you little maggots working. The Repo Men who monitor you and keep you on the straight and narrow. The government. All of it. It's me. Never guessed that, did ya? Well now you do. So don't touch that dial because I'm gonna tell you all about it. You ready?'

The Anti-Rex pressed his fingers to the steel wall. They pulsed and throbbed. Lines of energy spread in red streaks. The steel began to melt.

'Ever had that feeling that your life wasn't your own? That someone was manipulating you? Well, you were right. It's me. You lot are nothing but pawns in my game. The ultimate game. Rubbish, that's all you are. And I've grown tired of you. So, guess what I'm going to do. I'm going to press my little button and wipe the lot of you out. The same way I wiped out Elvis—'

'Ooh, eek, and *what the Heck?*' went the viewing public. 'You done what?'

'Elvis is dead, suckers. What do you think of that?'

The millions of viewers really didn't know what to think. So they shook their heads, opened cans of beer and settled down to await further revelations.

They didn't have to wait long.

'You're all gonna get it in the neck,' crowed Jonathan.

He raised a finger and prepared it for the big plunge down.

'I shouldn't do that if I were you, sir.'

Jonathan's finger hovered in the air. The way some of them do. He turned to view the owner of the all-too-familiar voice.

'Oh no! Not you!' Jonathan's jaw hit his chest.

'Just back off is all.'

'But . . . it's . . . you . . .'

'It's me, fella.' The young man wore a gold lamé zootsuit and the very bluest of blue suede footware. He had a serious quiff on, cheekbones to stagger the senses of the gods and really killer side-burns. And he curled his lip. Just so.

'Move away from the console,' said Elvis Aaron Presley, for could it possibly have been anyone else?

'But you're dead . . . I . . .'

'Killed me? Killed me! Elvis the Everliving. Some hope, mister. Now step aside easy now and don't touch nothing.'

It was not to be noticed that the King held in his hand nothing more nor less than a trusty Smith and Wooden heart.

'And stick 'em up while you're about it.'

'No no no no no.' Jonathan took to shaking his head.

271

He also took to sticking his hands up, though. 'This is all wrong. This is not what's supposed to happen. And I think I've run out of lives. Go away, you're spoiling everything.'

'Uh-uh.' With the gun firmly trained upon Jonathan, Elvis addressed the cameras. 'People of the world,' said he, 'you all heard what the little guy here had to say to you and you all know who I am. So I guess you'll all approve of this.'

He cocked his pistol.

'No!' cried Jonathan, and it really must be said it was the real one this time. 'Stop, you don't know what you're doing.'

Elvis squeezed the trigger and without further words wasted, shot Jonathan's brains out. On prime time.

'Nice shot,' said Kevin. 'Do you think BAH-REAH told him to do it?'

'Goddammit!' croaked Sam Maggott. 'Storm that building!'

'Oh this is great.' The voice of the MTWTV station head called through a fog of cigar smoke. 'If Elvis liberates Harpo/Chico this is worth millions. Millions. Get Dick in there, try and arrange an interview.'

'789-807,' said Mojo's agent.

'Someone throw this bum outta here,' roared the smoker.

'Beer please.' Cecil placed himself upon a bar stool.

'In a minute,' the Tomorrowman's barman adjusted the TV set above the bar, 'I'm watching this. The last bit of the book's coming up and I want to see what happens.'

* * *

Rex wandered amongst the Presley hoard. 'OK,' he dandled Harpo/Chico, 'we've got this far. Where's the bomb?'

'I don't actually know that.' Chico scratched his little chin. 'I can't be expected to know everything, you know.'

'About this Cosmic Message of yours?' Rex asked.

'I'd rather not discuss that at the present moment, if you don't mind.'

The Anti-Rex's hands blazed upon the sheet steel. Molten metal dribbled away. The hole widened.

'People of the world.' Elvis straightened his hair. 'I'm back amongst you. Although I've never really been away. I've always been here to help and guide you. But other guys, bad guys, have been playing bad games with all of you. But that's all done now cos I'm here to deal with things in person. It's me, I'm here, I'm holy and I'm handsome. Elvis the Everliving. So, now listen up, there's something you gotta know. We got terrorists here in our midst.'

'Oh shit,' said Kevin.

'Terrorists unseen and unknown. And they plan to destroy this great city of ours. In less than eight hours a bomb will explode and kill you all. You, *my* people. So listen up and listen good. You gotta find this bomb. Locate it and then call in to me. That's what you gotta do if you love me. It's somewhere in the city. So find it and call it in. It's a test for my love. Do it for me.'

The screens blanked. Elvis was gone.

'Don't look at me,' Kevin shrugged, 'it's the first I've heard about any bomb.'

*   *   *

Presley City suddenly got very busy indeed. Folk issued from all quarters. Manhole covers came up, hoardings came down, shop windows caved in. There was a whole lotta searching going on. But it wasn't being done in the spirit of communal well-being, but in panic and hatred and the settling of old scores. Crowds poured into the streets. Buildings took fire. People began to die.

It was all wrong.

'It's all wrong.' Rex shook his head. 'How could he do it? How could he let this happen?' He wasn't talking about all that up there, but all he saw down there, all about him. 'I knew the man. He was honest. He cared.'

'He fouled up.' Chico shrugged his shoulder. 'Not his fault really. He did his best.'

'So now we've found the hoard, what should we do with it?'

'Burn it!' Harpo said. 'Burn it all.'

'What?' Chico asked.

'Destroy it,' Harpo continued. 'We have to erase it all.'

'What are you talking about, bruv?'

'Chico, the space-folk told you plenty, but they told me plenty also. Not that I'm really supposed to let on. Burn it, Rex, that's what you have to do.'

'Burn it?' Rex was very doubtful indeed. 'This is the work of masters, men of genius. You can't burn art, it's a sacrilege.'

'Rex, these paintings are blasphemy. Elvis isn't God. You know that. All of it must burn now. None of it can be allowed to leave this place again. No future archaeologist must ever dig up one fragment. The whole thing stops here, tonight. For ever.'

'He-a-vy,' said Chico.

'Then the game ends?' Rex thought he'd ask.

'The game ends when you defuse the bomb.'

'Hmm,' murmured Rex Mundi.

'Torch it, Rex, you know it makes sense.'

'OK.' Rex dithered. 'But I'm not happy.'

'Rex, I'm one half of a two-headed baby. Just how happy do you want to be in one lifetime?'

The face of Elvis was back on the screen. 'Find it for me my people.'

A hole appeared in the steel wall and the Anti-Rex stuck his head through it. And what he saw made him grin a very wicked grin.

Rex stood before Adoration of the Shepherds by Georges de la Tour (1593–1652). Elvis was right there in the middle, thinly disguised beneath a railwayman's cap and carrying a flute. [Check this one out if you're ever in the Louvre, I speak not one word of a lie.]

'You have to burn,' Rex told the canvas. 'Although I hate like damn to be the one to do it.'

'Torch it, Rex. Come on now.'

'OK Harpo.' Rex had about his person a Cartier slim-line computer-controlled cigarette lighter. It took flame the first time, the way all of them do.

Rex held it close to the priceless painting. The ancient paint blistered, the fire took hold.

Laura Lynch pressed her ear to the wall. Someone was out there. Someone.

Rex stepped back from the burning canvas and glanced around the vault. The da Vincis, the Michelangelos, the Van Goghs, the Caravaggios and Carsons gazed back at him. Dumb, it seemed, with disbelief at his act of unspeakable vandalism.

'Sorry chaps.' Rex backed towards the lift.

Laura began to beat at the wall. 'Help me!' she screamed.

'Well, it's burning.' Rex watched as the flames spread. 'So where is the bomb?'

'Rex, it's you, help me.'

'Let's get out, Rex, above it all, look down, try and reason it out.'

'Sounds good to me, Chico. Up it is.'

'*Rex!* Help me!'

'Who said that?'

'It wasn't me. Come on, into the lift, quick.'

'No, wait. I heard something.'

'Rex, help.'

'Rex, hurry, it's getting awfully hot in here.'

'Shush, Chico.'

'Don't you shush my brother.'

'Don't you start.'

'Help!'

'It's Laura. Laura!' Rex shouted. 'Where are you?'

'I'm here, Rex. Here.'

'She's here.'

'Oh shit, Rex, forget about her. She's not important.'

'Shut up!'

'Don't you tell my brother to shut up.'

'Laura, I'm coming.' Rex plunged forwards, taking Harpo/Chico.

'No, Rex, no.' The Presley hoard was fast becoming an inferno.

'We'll fry . . . ooh ouch . . . mum . . . do something, Chico!'

'Oh, all right.' Chico screwed up his face and hunched his shoulder. The flames parted before Rex and roared up harmlessly to either side.

'Neat trick,' said Rex.

All at once, because there's nothing to be gained by dragging it out, they were before the blank wall. Rex put a hand upon it. 'She's in here, but there's no door.'

'Let me,' said Harpo. 'Chico isn't very good with numbers.'

Chico hung his head.

Harpo rattled his share of fingers on the blank wall.

The wall dissolved and Laura Lynch fell into Rex's arms. Which would have been very romantic, if we felt we could trust Laura one inch.

'Oh Rex,' Laura kissed him passionately, 'you saved me.'

'I had a little help from my friends.'

Harpo/Chico smiled up at Laura. Laura didn't smile back.

'God,' she said, 'what an ugly little sucker.'

'Right,' said Chico, 'that does it.'

'No, wait,' Rex was staring over Laura's shoulder. 'What's that thing in there?'

'Oh, that's the coffin of Elvis Presley. He's dead, you know.'

'Well, actually I didn't.'

Rex looked down at the bunny rabbit. 'Turn her back,' he told Chico.

The truck began to rock and the MTWTV station head began to get a sweat on. 'What's going on out there?' he demanded to know.

'Trouble, sir.' The driver spoke through his little hatch. 'Lots of mob violence. But we're getting it all on tape, no worries. They've all gone mad since Elvis made his broadcast. They're tearing the city to pieces.'

'Here we go here we go here we go.' Kevin flung the big military vehicle into gear. It plunged forward, mashing police cars, scattering rioters, mounted the big front-steps and ploughed into the lobby of the Butcher Building. 'Let's kick ass.'

'I used to kick ass,' ex-officer Cecil swigged his beer, 'but, you know, you get fed up with it, type-cast, always the heavy. I want to get involved in something with a bit

277

more depth. Something to show my compassionate caring side. There's no future in this comedy stuff for me.'

The barman nodded thoughtfully. 'I know what you mean. I'm far too good for this nonsense. When this is finished I'm going to audition for something deep and hard to understand, something with Booker Prize potential. Would you like to see my previous reviews?'

'Yes, I'd like that very much. Could I have the same again, please?'

'On the house.' The barman spread his scrapbook on the bar-counter. 'Read what they said about my performance in *They Came And Ate Us*.'

The Anti-Rex opened a bigger hole. He could see what was going on in a big way now. Elvis stood before the cameras, throwing poses and making with the sound bites. The Anti-Rex slid his red-hot finger down the steel barrier. It parted before him.

'Search,' cried Elvis. 'Find the bomb. Kill all who stand in your way.' And the population were doing just that.

'You're a real bad boy carrying on like that,' said the Anti-Rex. 'Having some kind of a brainstorm are you?'

Elvis ignored him and continued with what was now becoming quite unbecoming. 'There are those who won't follow the light. The House of Light. My house. Kill them all. Find the bomb. Call me. Call me.'

'I'm calling you, asshole.'

Elvis carried on regardless.

'Ah, excuse me, I mean dear old friend. Elvis, it's me, Rex. I've come to help you.' The evil one approached the man in the gold lamé suit. 'Hello? Can you hear me?'

'Search,' cried the man of gold. 'Search.'

'Elvis, what is wrong with you?' The Anti-Rex stared him eye to eye.

'Search!'

'Search? It's me, shithead. Wake up.' The Anti-Rex

278

swung a fist at the head of Elvis Aaron Presley. It passed clean through into empty air.

'What the fuck?'

The screens went blank. Elvis wavered, faded and then was gone.

'What the . . .'

'You wouldn't let it lie.' The voice belonged to Jonathan Crawford (yet again!). He rose from the floor pulling prosthetic rubber brains from the side of his head. 'Do you know how much trouble I went to, faking up that hologram of Elvis shooting me, programming that speech, all at short notice? No, of course you don't. Because you never know what's going on. You really are such a stupid prat!'

Now, you really have to think about that remark. It takes someone with a rare amount of self-confidence to stand in front of Satan the Prince of Darkness, the Lord of Hell, and call him a prat to his face. I don't think I'd chance it.

'Well, I would.' Jonathan squared up to the now pulsating Anti-Rex. 'Prat, prat, prat!'

'You . . . you . . .' The beast seemed genuinely lost for words. Hardly surprising really.

'Come on then, spit it out.' Jonathan took a step backwards. 'Let's hear it.'

'You are going to die a death of such hideousness that the agonies of every death that has gone before will be as nothing. You will writhe in anguish for eternity.'

'No I won't.' Jonathan was tinkering with his wrist again, which old Beelzebub really should have recognized as a bad sign. 'You should be a bit more careful how you speak to me. Remember what happened to your last incarnation? Still in the dustbag of the Great Celestial Vacuum Cleaner, if I'm not very much mistaken. Do you know why you never win? Ever ask yourself that? How come you, with all the natural advantages, never win in the end? Generation after generation of aspiring sinners,

279

and how many ever end up worshipping you? A couple of dozen each century, and most of them stone bonkers. And do you know why?'

The Dark One's hair stood upon end, brimstone streamed from his ears, his black tongue wavered eighteen inches before his furious face. 'Tell me why,' he screamed.

'Because you're thick,' crowed Crawford. 'The Devil is a dullard. A dork. Evil, maybe. The very personification of evil. But that's the point and that's why you don't get it. You are the personification of evil, but evil is the manifestation of stupidity. Evil is brainless, heartless and soulless. It's negative and uncreative. See, there you go, then. Happy to have put you straight. Run along now and shape up.'

The Anti-Rex exploded. Became a tangle of twisting tentacles. A seething festering maggot-nest. A thing of such indescribable vileness as to be virtually indescribable. It flung itself at Jonathan Crawford. And splattered in a fashion, which probably came only as a surprise to itself, against an invisible wall.

'Missed me.' Jonathan did a little dance. 'Got to be quicker than that.'

The objectionable object thrashed violently and gave banshee hollerings. Jonathan put his finger to his lips.

'Don't go tiring yourself out. You can't get through. Little innovation of my own. Quite inspired, really. Based on the holy-water principle. Always fascinated me, the concept of holy water. What could the difference actually be between it and ordinary water? Are you paying attention?'

The thing was a-screaming and a-thrashing.

'Oh well, please yourself. As I was saying. What I wanted to know was what happend to the water on a sub-atomic level when it got blessed. What gave it its power. How was it done, how did it work, things of that nature. So I investigated. And do you know what I found? No, of course you don't. I discovered that the water became charged with energy. Magical energy. The blessing contained positively charged words of power. These triggered a chemical change on a sub-atomic level, making the water poisonous to the likes of you. It's polarities again, you see. Positive and negative. Energy. Matter is energy. The universe is composed of matter, there's hardly an empty space anywhere. What an interesting fellow I am, don't you think?'

The horrid nasty maggot-wriggling smelly evil thingy hurled itself again and again at the invisible wall and went, 'BLAAAAAAAGH!'

'Elvis Aaron Presley. Come out with your hands up.' Sam Maggott (no relative of any other maggot) stood on the rocking roof of his besieged police car hollering lamely through his bullhorn. Around him crowds surged and pushed and fought and struggled. Certain emboldened officers chose to draw down fire on the rear end of the big military vehicle which was now parked in the lobby of the Butcher Building. Others were doing their best to reverse their cars through the mayhem. These were those who had become aware of the monstrous black creature that was cutting the proverbial bloody swathe through the rioting thousands en route, apparently, for the leading truck of the MTWTV convoy.

'Let me stroke the nice bunny rabbit,' chirped Harpo.

'Chico, turn her back this minute.' Rex shook his spare fist.

'We'd best be going now,' Chico was unmoved, 'I can't keep the flames back forever.'

'Chico, we need her help.'

'You heartless sod. You'd deprive a poor little two-headed baby of its pet bunny.'

'*Chico!*'

'Oh, all right. I'll get you another bun, bruv.'

'I don't want another one. I want this one.'

'He wants this one, Rex.'

'Hurry up. It's getting very hot.' Rex stepped into the chamber to avoid the licking flames.

'No problem.' Harpo reached out twiddling fingers as Rex stepped forward. 'I'll close the wall. Don't want my bunny getting blistered.'

'No,' cried Rex. 'I don't think that's a good—' the wall closed, sealing Rex, Harpo/Chico and a lovable furry woodland creature into Elvis Presley's burial chamber '—idea,'

'So,' said Jonathan, 'I now enlarge the forcefield.' He tinkered at his wrist. 'Shape it and close it. With you inside, of course. Then once it has become a nice neat cylinder, like so,' another tap or two at the wrist, 'I programme the cylinder to contract into a long thin tube about one micron in diameter. You can just imagine what you'll look like by then, eh?'

The ex-Anti-Rex squirmed fearfully within the already shrinking cylinder of force. Jonathan smiled upon it.

'I hate to piss you off even further, you being so hard pressed and everything,' he tittered mirthlessly, 'but you'll really kick yourself when you hear this. If you hadn't muscled in when you did and interfered with the hologram all this would have been yours. At the end of Elvis's speech, once the bomb had been discovered and I had defused it, the hologram was programmed to self destruct. It would have confessed to the world that it wasn't really God and then proved it by committing suicide live on camera. And then *you*, as the last legitimate "god" left on the planet would have inherited the lot. I planned to take myself off to another quarter. So you'd have got it all. But now you don't. Ain't life a bitch sometimes?'

The furious thrashings within the contracting cylinder

confirmed the creature's agreement that life certainly could be a bitch at times.

'Well, must love you and leave you, as they say. I'm real fed up with getting blown up, so I intend to put a considerable distance between myself and Presley City before Big Bang time. So long, sucker.'

Downstairs in the lobby, Kevin's five-star revolutionary force was swapping gunfire with Jonathan's Repo Men. The going was being made somewhat difficult by the large volume of smoke issuing through the gaps in the lift doors.

Below all this, but by no means above it all, Rex was beating upon the blank wall in a foolish and futile manner.

'You might do something,' he told Chico. 'We're trapped in here.'

Harpo/Chico was perched on the jukebox sarcophagus. Harpo was stroking Laura rabbit. Laura rabbit looked anything but keen.

'It's really hot out there,' said Chico. 'We're far better tucked away in here for a couple of hours. Relax.'

'Relax?' Rex threw his arms in the air. 'The bomb is quietly ticking away somewhere and we're banged up here with *that*.' He pointed at the sarcophagus. 'We shouldn't be here, and *that* certainly shouldn't be here.'

'Hey, you're right.' Harpo stopped stroking. 'You'd best burn it too. Where's your lighter?'

'Now see here . . .' Rex made fists, but having nothing feasible to do with them he unmade them again. 'I was prepared to destroy priceless art treasures, but I draw the line at cremating the body of my closest friend. Especially in a room without a chimney. Here, shift over.' Rex lifted Harpo/Chico from the transparent panel and peered in at the defunct Presley. 'He doesn't look too good, does he?'

Chico's head peeped over Rex's shoulder. 'How good do you think you'll look after a hundred years in a coffin?'

Rex gave his head a thoughtful scratch. 'Not as good as this I shouldn't think.'

'Probably stuffed,' said Harpo. 'Bunny, don't scratch, or daddy will have to smack you.'

'What did you say?'

'I said I'll have to smack this naughty bunny.'

'No, not that, before.'

'I said, probably stuffed, with dollar bills more than likely. Take that, bad bunny.' Harpo clouted Laura rabbit across the ear.

Rex rubbed at the panel and leaned nearer to gaze into the passive face of the King. 'He does look a bit . . . odd, you know. It's funny, I really should feel something. He was the best friend I ever had. But . . . nothing . . . That's odd.'

And indeed it was odd, what with all that previous atmospheric stuff with Laura. But then, considering the constant shifts in emphasis, complications, characters coming and going, and general slipshod incoherence of the entire affair, it was about par for the course, really. And whatever happened to Barry?

'Let's have it open,' said Rex with unnerving suddenness.

'Oh no!' Chico was very sure about the 'oh no'. Harpo joined him in vigorous head shaking and Laura took the opportunity to make a run for it. She was shaking her head also.

'Yes.' Rex took Harpo/Chico and sat him on the floor. 'We should have it open. I have a hunch.'

'I don't care whether you have a club foot as well.' Chico waved frantically with his arm. 'Don't open it. The body will decay when the air hits it. There'll be terrible germs. We'll catch something chronic.'

'Imagine the pong,' Harpo added.

Rex made a passably tolerant face. 'You know all about the putrefaction of preserved corpses then? Possibly you hold a Master's degree in the subject?'

'No need to be sarcastic,' said Chico.

'Where's Mr Floppy Ears gone?' asked Harpo.

'It's *Mrs* Floppy Ears,' said his brother.

'It's my bunny and I'll say what sex it is.'

Rex sighed and shook his head.

Laura hid in a darkened corner twitching her dear little nose. Had she been able to speak, it is doubtful whether sufficient adjectives existed to express her opinion of the current turn of events.

'I'm opening the box,' said Rex.

'It will end in tears.' Chico put on a snooty expression and attempted without success to fold his arm.

'Where's my little Floppy Woppy?' went Harpo.

'What do you think?' asked the barman of the Tomorrow-man Tavern. 'I saved that book.'

Cecil held the barman's glowing reviews up to the light. 'I spy duplicity,' said he. 'I have copies of these very same reviews in a scrapbook of my own. They differ in only one significant respect. They bear my name upon them and not yours.'

'Rogue!' cried the barman, reaching for his knobkerry.

'Scoundrel!' cried Cecil, drawing himself up to his full and improbable height.

Rex struggled with the lid of the sarcophagus. He made all the appropriate groaning noises. There were close-ups of his gripping fingers, sweating brow, the coffin lid giving an inch or two and then falling back, Harpo/Chico's pained expressions, Laura's twitching nose.

The lid shifted and fell away with a resounding whack.

'Hold your hooters,' Harpo advised.

Chico did so. Rex didn't.

'Elvis,' he said. 'Do you know what you look like to me?'

Elvis had nothing to say on the matter.

'Dead pony.'

'Pony?' Chico asked.

'Pony.' Rex tweaked the nose of the dead man, took a grip and gave a mighty pull. The skin came away in his fingers. A sheath of latex rubber and nylon sideburns. Beneath the façade was a goodly amount of shining metal, blinking lights and complicated circuitry.

'Gotcha,' said Rex Mundi.

'I can't see from down here,' Chico craned his neck. 'But I assume it's the bomb.'

'Yep.' Rex spread apart the gold lamé jacket, exposing further wonderments, more burnished metal and an intricate-looking keyboard.

'Gosh,' went Chico unconvincingly. 'I wasn't expecting *that*!'

'Hmm.' Rex ran his fingers over the keys. 'Now all we have to do is crack the combination and disarm the bomb.'

'That would be the logical thing. How much time do we have?'

Rex looked at his watch. 'Do I still have my watch on?' he asked. 'I thought I lost it somewhere.'

Chico shrugged. 'Search me. Let's assume that you do.'

'Good idea.' Rex looked at his watch. 'Nearly seven hours. Time to spare. Brilliant. Harpo, would you care to check this keyboard out. You're the numbers man.'

'Why, thank you, Rex.' Harpo smiled his sweetest of smiles. 'I'd like my bunny back, though.'

'With pleasure.' Rex turned and scooped up Laura who was having a scratch at the wall. 'Shall I mind Mr Floppy Ears for you while you save the world?'

'Good idea.'

Rex lifted Harpo/Chico into the open sarcophagus. 'Do your thing,' he told Harpo.

'OK then.' Harpo flexed his fingers. 'Now, let's do this carefully. Assuming that there is a combination, what do we have? Well, all the letters of the alphabet for a start. Pity it's not just numbers. OK, if you were Elvis, Rex, what would you programme into it?'

Rex did some serious head scratching. 'My birthday, or perhaps the date of my death. This is whacky stuff after all.'

'Too obvious.' Harpo shook his head.

'His mum's, then,' Chico put in. 'What do you think, mummy's boy?'

Harpo ignored his brother. 'Could be his phone number, car licence plate, army service number . . .'

'I was thinking that perhaps rather than guess it, you might simply use your X-ray vision.' Rex made encouraging winks.

'Ah,' Harpo squinted. 'Apparently not,' he unsquinted.

'We're doomed, then,' said Rex. 'I shouldn't have expected anything else.'

'Never say die,' Harpo smiled cheerfully. 'Give us a cuddle of my bunny.'

Rex handed the struggling rabbit over. 'Of course we could just press keys at random, trusting to a power far greater than ourselves, a divine synchronicity, that would assure our salvation and that of the world generally.'

'Ooh,' said Chico. 'Hands up for Rex's inspired plan anyone.'

No hands went up.

'Prat,' said Harpo.

'Now just you see here . . .'

Harpo interrupted him. 'Rex, use your head, please. If we just press buttons at random we shall certainly die. This bomb has been placed here with the specific purpose of destroying Presley City, your *doppelgänger* and the beastly big boy who pointed his gun at us. It is bound to have all sorts of ingenious traps built into it. I'll bet we only get one go at this.'

'Hmm,' went Rex Mundi.

'Hmm,' went Rex Mundi again.

'Why did you go hmm twice?' Chico asked.

'Sorry, I thought they were going to cut to another scene there.'

'But they didn't, did they?'

'Seems not.'

'Then we'd better get on with it, hadn't we?'

'Certainly.' Rex rubbed his hands together. 'Harpo, do something.'

'Me? You're the hero, *you* do something. And try to make it something thrilling, eh?'

'All right. I will.' Rex squared up to the keyboard. 'I'm going for this.' He reached forwards and tapped out a series of figures.

'What was it?' Harpo asked.

'Elvis's birthdate.'

'Oh dead inspired. Bravo . . . ooooooh . . . ouch . . . blimey . . . what's happening?'

'Oooooooooooh ooooooooowww . . . what's going on?' Rex gawped at the keyboard, he gawped at his wristwatch. The hands were racing around the face.

Halfway up a stairway, Jonathan Crawford dropped his suitcase and clutched at his wrist. 'Oh horrors,' he groaned. 'Someone's touched the bloody bomb, time's leaping forwards. I've got no more lives left. Oh shit!'

'Hmm,' went Rex Mundi.

'I think we've done that bit.'

'This is another hmm altogether. Look at my watch.' He held it before the twin faces. 'I seem to have screwed up, just a little.' He smiled foolishly. The two little faces glared up at him.

'Seven hours!' shouted Harpo.

'Seven sodding hours!' shouted Chico.

Rex laughed foolishly. 'Where does all the time go to these days?' he asked.

'Seven hours.' Harpo said it again and again. 'He pressed the wrong combination and lost us seven hours, just like that.'

'Well, you did say do something thrilling.'

'Seven hours,' whispered Chico.

'Oh don't keep on. Anyone can make a mistake. How much time do we have left?'

Chico peeped at Rex's watch. 'Precisely one minute,' he said in a leaden tone.

'Hmm,' went Rex Mundi. 'That long, eh?'

Time.

What can you say about time, huh?

It's always a great healer, I guess. And it can be your bestest buddy or your worstest woman. Some say it's the father of truth, that it waits for no man, devours all things, tames the strongest force, breaks youth and undermines us all.

The way I see it, time is the continuous passage of existence, in which events pass from a state of potentiality in the future, through the present, to a state of finality in the past. But that's me all over, sharp as the day is long. I guess a physicist would tell you that time is a quantity measuring duration, usually with reference to a periodic process, such as the rotation of the earth, or say, the vibration of electromagnetic radiation emitted from certain atoms. Then he'd like as not go on to tell you that in classical mechanics, time is absolute, in the sense that the time of an event is independent of the observer. Because, according to the theory of relativity, it all depends on the observer's frame of reference. So time is considered as the fourth co-ordinate, required, along with three spatial co-ordinates, to specify an event. Or at least fly when you're having a good time.

Yeah, there's a whole lot you can say about time. If

you have the time, that is. Which I don't at present. Because I'm here on business, and in my business, time is money.

From where I was standing alone on this roof-top, silhouetted dramatically against the full moon, I could see the greater part of *A City in Terror*.* Flames were rising like Old Glory at a witchfinder's weenie roast. There was a chill wind blowing from the east and it was bringing me the sounds of running footsteps. So I hiked up the collar of my trenchcoat, hiked down the snappy brim of my snap-brimmed fedora and hiked off into the shadows *nil desperandum, per vas nefandum*, as the French say.

A short sputum hawk away a Caddy air-car hugged the roof-top with more splayed black rubber than a bondage queen's laundry list. On the polished hood that old devil moon cocked a cyclopean at the racing heavens. And mirrored in the polished chrome of the bulbous bumperwork, was the image of a small running figure, all swells and distorts. Atmospheric stuff. We're talking a pretty classy finish here.

The kid threw open the driver's door and threw himself into the driver's seat. I counted slowly to three. Because I knew what was coming next.

'Shit shit shit shit shit.' The door flew open again and the kid came flying out.

'You sound like shit, kid. Looking for these?' I held out his car keys. Just the one hand, see, stark and white in moonlight, coming out of the shadows. I gave the keys a little jiggle jiggle. They sparkled better than Crawford's conversation.

'Shit!' The kid had a big sweat on which didn't go too well with his suit. His mean little mouth twitched and his beady little eyes bulged in their beady little sockets. He fingered his shirt collar and looked kinda edgy. 'Give

*A Lazlo Woodbine thriller (although not one of his best).

me those keys, you bloody bastard,' he said with hardly the hint of a social grace.

I flipped his keys back into my pocket and showed him the muzzle of the trusty Smith and Well-I-never-did. 'Stick 'em up,' I told him.

'Stick 'em up? Stick 'em up? Have you gone stark raving mad?' He came on like St Vitus with Saturday Night Fever. 'Look at your watch. Look at the time. Someone's tampered with the bomb. There's less than a minute left. There's no more time left. No more time!'

'Time?' said I. 'What can you say about time, huh? It's a great healer, I guess. And it can be your bestest friend or your worstest . . .'

'Shut up!' The kid was getting real foamy about the jaws. 'Give me the keys. I have to leave *now*. No more time. No more lives.'

'Kid,' said I with more perlocution than a pox doctor's zany on a five-day furlough. 'You got time to listen to me. This is Lazlo Woodbine you're soiling your underlinen to. Lazlo Woodbine, the greatest private eye that ever trod those mean streets along which a man must go. Now I don't know what happened to all the gratuitous sex and violence and the trail of corpses that traditionally permeate the peerless prose of my prepossessing publications, perhaps it's a more caring nineties kind of an image, I don't know. But there's two things I do know. Firstly, I'm here. And secondly you're here. That's firstly, this is the end of the book. And secondly, this is the final roof-top showdown. Get the picture?'

'Have you quite finished?' Johnny boy was running on the spot. But frankly I'd seen better leg-work on a foldaway beach lounger. 'Have you finished you . . . you . . .'

'Finished? Kid, we've hardly started. Now, I'm gonna read you your rights and you can take it from there. You may feel like trying to make a break for it. That's OK, I can put a couple of slugs in your leg. Or you might feel up to wrestling the gun from me, in which case we can tumble about on the edge of the roof-top until it's time for you to plunge over the edge. I'm easy.'

'Listen,' Crawford came a-creeping in my direction, 'I can get you out of all this. You won't have to come back here and ever get involved in it again. I'll fix it so Dee and Kelley steal the hoard next time two hundred years before you're even born. You can go back to being a regular detective.'

I raised an eyebrow of admonishment. 'A what?'

'A *great* detective, I mean.'

I raised the former eyebrow's suave companion. 'What?'

'*The* great detective. Come on. Hurry. What do you say?'

'I say. Jonathan Alberich Carver Doone Bluebeard Foghorn Lecter Claude Frollo Crawford, I arrest you for the murder of your dear little white-haired old father . . .'

'What?' The kid looked like he'd ordered *Chateau Rothschild* and had been served a time-share apartment in Benidorm. 'You can't—'

'I quit the Presley Hoard Case kid. No future in it for me. I went back to my office and what did I find on my desk?' I displayed a paper. 'Warrant for your arrest. Dead or alive, naturally. It says here that five days ago you pushed said dear little white-haired old father into the Big Flywheel which powers this planet through space [As explained fully in *They Came And Ate Us* and far too complicated to go into again here]. The body of the previously mentioned dear little white-haired old father caused irreparable damage to the Big Flywheel resulting in a continuous loop whereby you go through the five days leading up to the Big Bang again and again and again. Although there seems to be some technical details about lives getting lost which I can't get to grips with. But never the less. You're here, I'm here, and that's about the strength of it. Shall we tango?'

'This is ridiculous. There's only seconds left.'

'Seconds? Sure, check your watch.'

He checked his watch. 'It's stopped,' said he, shaking it furiously.

'No it's not. Just slowed down a bit. I always get extended seconds in my roof-top showdown scene. It's written into my contract. So there's time for all the necessary exposition to tie up all the loose ends satisfactorily. I always think that's so important, don't you? Twenty seconds can be strung out to include the criminal's confession, an unexpected surprise or two, a nail-biting barn-stormer of a punch-up. And of course the inevitable doom plunge. That would be your doom plunge, of course.'

Crawford bit his lip. 'Give me my car keys, please,' he said.

'Sure kid.' I tossed him the keys. 'Move one inch and I shoot you dead.'

'All right, all right. You want a confession, yes?'

I nodded my head. I do it just the once and I do it real subtle. Nothing fancy. I never go over the top or make a big thing out of nodding, I figure a slight cranial inclination of, say, five or six degrees, is sufficient to signify the affirmative, more than that and you're looking like a 'yes man' or some damn felt pooch in a Cortina window. So I keep it concise and to the point. That's the kind of guy I am.

'Was that a yes or a no?' Jonathan asked.

'A yes.'

'OK.' The kid stroked his pointy little chin. I bet he wished like Hell he had a lantern jaw like mine to call his own. 'OK, you want a confession you can have one. But please put away your gun. I'm getting really fed up with being shot.'

'OK, what harm can it do?' I figured, OK, what harm can it do. So I pocketed my piece. 'There you go.'

'Yeah. And now stick up your hands.' I didn't know

where he got the gun from; guess I never will. But there it was winking at me in the moonlight like a one-eyed whore on a blind date. I stuck up my hands, the way one does.

'You got me, kid,' I declared.

'Yeah, I certainly do.' Crawford was backing to the Caddy. 'Sure I killed my old man. But I had to. The auditors were in. The books didn't balance.'

'Books? What books?'

'The accounts. The planetary accounts. Planet Earth is a business. Always was, always will be. It has to run at a profit or the accountants, the *big* accountants (he points skyward) sell it off for scrap. Time is money, you know?'

'I did "time is money" earlier on, kid. I don't think I did "time and tide wait for no man", if you want to use that.'

'Shut up! I mean time *is* money. Literally. Time costs money. The universe is a big business run by the Corps of the Celestial Accountants. Populated planets pay for their orbits. For their *time* in space. The local gods usually work it out. But due to my father's incompetence and Elvis buggering up the status quo "god-wise", this planet was behind on the mortgage and in danger of being repossessed. Luckily I was here to come up with a brilliant financial package to save the world.' He's right by the Caddy now and looking ready for the off.

'This financial package of yours.' I tried to keep him talking. You never know, something might happen. 'This involved turning the entire world into a virtual reality computer-game for the gods to play?'

'Well, not all of it. The bit I was stuck in mostly. Presley stinking City.'

'And these accountants, they went for it?'

'Sure, they're playing it now. Can't you feel them?' He was getting in the Caddy. His gun was still on me and time was ticking away.

'Just one more thing kid. About the "lives getting lost" bit. I don't understand that.'

'It's simple enough.' He was in the car. 'I may be stuck in a five-day time loop, but I'm not immortal. As with any game you only get so many lives. I've used all of mine but one this time trying to make it real exciting. So I've got to get away from here before the Big Bang. And that means now. I'll see you again *last week*. If you catch my drift, and I don't give a shit if you do.'

'Hold it right there, scumbag.' Now, I never said that, it's not my style. And this voice had more decibels to it than a dancing dog at a Blue Cheer gig. I turned and Crawford turned. But as Crawford turned he also turned the ignition key.

'This is *my* game, *my* business and *my* planet!' The owner of the megaton voice rose up from a kind of melted hole in the roof-top and he looked real pissed off.

He came out real thin. About one micron in diameter would be my guess. Then he swelled out in all directions. And it was tentacles here tantacles there, Goddarn tentacles everywhere. I dragged out the trusty Smith and Whatever-I-haven't-got-around-to-calling-it-yet and squared up the way that only I can do.

'Up with your . . . things,' I told it. 'I'm taking you in.'

Out of the squirming worming mass came a twisted face that looked like it used to belong to Rex. It hung in the air before me, drooling and wobbling and generally being unpleasing to the eye. It opened its mouth and uttered thusly, 'You got bullets in that gun, soldier?'

'Of course I've got bullets. You were expecting perhaps, water?' I had to laugh at that one. But it seems 'it' didn't.

'Then I'll get back to you when I've dealt with this piece of sh—' Crawford had the Caddy in gear. The wheels were spinning. But before you could say 'What a handsome fellow that Lazlo Woodbine is', the whole car looked like chow-time in the octopus tank.

'I run this planet!' The big big voice came out of the big big face, and I don't know how you feel about brimstone breath but it brings *me* out in hives.

'Hey guy.' I figured I'd better get my twopenny worth in now as ever. 'You're the Devil. Am I right or am I right?'

'The god of this world!' roared he, spreading halitosis to the four winds.

'And you're saying that *you* are responsible for, how shall I put it . . . all this crap?'

Broooom broooom and Roar went the Caddy. The wheels were burning more rubber than a non-rubber-burning entity at an unrelated event, but the car wasn't going no place.

'Get off my car!' Crawford howled. 'Let me go!'

'Well guy,' said I. 'Seems like I'm gonna have to shoot you.'

'Shoot me?' Now we were talking the big Satanic ho-ho-hos.

'Afraid so. This roof-top ain't big enough for the three of us. I have to tangle with the mad kid, so I'd best shoot *you* now. It's nothing personal. Hope you understand.'

'Oh, I do. I do.'

'Good, then . . .' I raised my piece, but that's about as far as I got with it. Suddenly I was heavily tentacled and was feeling a proper Charlie, I can tell you.

'This little dog plop.' Certain tentacles shook the Caddy all about. 'Works for me. Although he doesn't know it. Before Elvis went back in time and screwed everything up, things were ticking over just fine for me and mine. The Big G ran up there. And I ran down here. He got his jollies and I got mine. But there's always some little entrepreneur with delusions of grandeur hoping to cop the pot of gold. Well, not this time and not at any other time. You die here, Crawford. Right here and right now.'

'Is that it?' I asked.

'Is that what?'

'Is that all you have to say? I was just wondering if there were to be any more explanations or confessions or whatnot, or whether we were going to go straight into the exciting climax now.'

The beast from the bottomless pit scratched his bonce with a wiggly thing. 'I can't think of anything else off-hand,' he rumbled. 'All the loose ends generally get tied up on the last page. After a fashion, anyway. What about you, Johnny?'

Crawford shook his head. 'I did my bit before you arrived. It's mostly just the shouting and screaming left for me now.'

'Nope.' The swellyhead bobbed again in my direction. 'All said. I'm going to wring the life out of Crawford now.'

'OK.' I tipped him the wink. 'Could you loosen up on the vice-like gripping? I have a hernia.'

'Sorry.' A goodly number of black and eely things left my person and set about the Caddy with a thing called vengeance.

I raised my piece and let two go into the back of the big bad head.

'Ho ho ho ho . . . ooooh bloody Hell!!!' Mr Nasty swung his ugly-looking mug around.

'Didn't like that eh?' I gave him one right between the baby blues. 'Take that also.'

'Aaaaaaaaaaaaagh!!' The scream rocked the roof-top and I was tentacle free. 'Care for another?'

'You shot me. What have you got in that fucking gun?'

'Bullets pal. Silver bullets. Never leave home without them. Blessed by the current pope, these boys. Care to taste another?'

'No I wouldn't.'

'I remember one time back in 'fifty-seven. I was on the trail of Carmel Shane, the Vampire of Vermont. I came out packing ordinary ammo. That case cost me ninety per cent of my bodily functions, most of my chestnut chest hair, a Welsh mountain rescue team called Philip, twelve lords a-leaping, four months topping the bill at Bognor Regis (summer season with Russ Abbot), and all the salad you want at an inclusive price of £4.99 per person. I couldn't look at a theodolite for a year after that without dreading the smell of boiled cabbage. Hey guy, are you listening to me?'

But it seemed like he wasn't. He was all wrapped around the Caddy. The Caddy's wheels were screaming and the whole kith and caboodle of them were coming in my direction pretty damn lively in the acceleration department.

'You're gonna get yours, Woodbine!' screamed Crawford.

'And you yours!' The phantom hitch-hiker took up the hue and cry, and thrashed all about the place.

The car tore at me and I took to my tapered toes. The Caddy's headlights threw my fleeing, yet stylish shadow across an expanse of roofscape that held about as much hope for me as for Bobby McGee. I kept right on running but it looked like I had very little more roof to pursue this particular past-time upon. It didn't seem like I had a lot of options.

Not that I've ever really been an 'option' man, don't get me wrong. I'm more your intuition and impulse kind of guy. I don't stand on ceremony weighing things up. I go for broke.'

It's the only way I know.

The Caddy was hard on my heels. There was nothing for it.

I jumped off the roof-top in the nick of time.

'Time.' Rex leaned over the keyboard of the big bad bomb. 'How much time do we have?'

'Forty seconds,' Chico replied. 'No, make that thirty-nine, no, thirty-eight, no thirt—'

'I get the picture. Not much then.'

'Not much.'

'Do you think that if I pressed Elvis's birthday in reverse, we might get our seven hours back?'

'Do you think you'd fancy spending your last thirty seconds wearing big floppy ears and a powder puff tail?'

Rex considered Laura. 'Well,' said he, 'now that you mention it . . .'

'This is Dick Adamski reporting live from the combat zone in the lobby of the Butcher Building. I'm holed up behind the reception desk where I'm talking to a pair of beautiful twins who tell me they represent the Children of the Revolution, is that right?'

'It certainly is, Dick.' Sharon fluttered her eyelashes. Alison primed a stun grenade and lobbed it across the lobby.

'Now, you know the question everyone will be wanting me to ask. Do you actually have a copy of "Pewter Suitor"?'

Kevin leaped over the reception desk and dropped down amongst them.

'The lifts are jammed. The fire's spreading. This place is going down. We have to split.'

'Hold it right there,' Dick raised his mike, 'ladies and gentlemen, I've just been joined by none other than Danny De Vito . . .'

Kevin drew out a pistol and shot Dick Adamski.

'Mojo.' The MTWTV station head made a grave face and switched off the TV monitor. 'They got Dick. The lousy rotten no-good sons of . . .' His face brightened. 'So this is your chance, Mojo. You have to go into that building and get to Elvis. What d'ya say, boy?'

'*I* say, who's in charge around here?' Balberith tore the side off the truck and climbed aboard.

'*He is!*' Mojo, Debbie, the driver, the accountants, yes men, contract specialists and camp followers all pointed with unwavering fingers towards the man with the big cigar.

Crawford's creature-carrying Caddy passed above me. It screamed over my ducking head. I was clinging to the parapet by my fingernails praying for my fedora not to blow away.

The car shot forwards into the night sky like a great black shiny bug and I counted up to three beneath my breath. Because, believe it, or believe it not, I knew what was coming next.

I heard the sounds of gears being grornched, stops being pulled out, engines failing and then a brief, ever so brief moment of silence.

'Shit shit shit shit shit!' Crawford's voice came loud and clear and not a little tearful.

The Caddy hovered a moment in the air, the way some of them do, and then took that *Long Plunge to Oblivion*.*

I dragged my aching body back on to the roof. It took sheer granite guts, true gritty grit, nerves of steel, an iron constitution, whipcord muscles and a genuine dislike of falling sixty-six floors to my certain death. I was back on that roof before you could say 'Woodbine triumphs again' – *Crime Fiction Monthly*.

I straightened my tie, cocked my hat at a rakish angle, shook a ruffle or two from my trenchcoat hem and dug from my pocket a plastic bag containing some complicated mechanical gubbins. *The air-car's vertical drive system!* I'd taken the liberty of liberating it when I removed the ignition keys.

Pretty smart move, huh?

I mean. If I hadn't sealed it in the plastic bag like that I might easily have got engine oil on my pocket lining. And that can be a real blighter to get out. If you can get it out, which you can't always. Sometimes the whole

*An Inspectre Hovis whodunnit.

pocket has to be replaced and that can mean your trenchcoat being off at the menders for up to a week.

But not this time.

This time I'd won through. Pulled off the exciting roof-top ending. Disposed of not one, but two super-villains and come out of it all with only minor trenchcoat smutting and absolutely no interior pocket besmirchment whatsoever.

Pretty *damn* smart, if you ask me.

I checked my watch. All this and I still had fifteen seconds left.

Fifteen seconds to locate the Presley hoard, take shelter from the Big Bang and wait for Barry. Fifteen seconds. No, make that fourteen seconds . . . no, thirteen . . . oh shit . . .

'Have you seen Laz, chief? I was supposed to meet him here.'

'Barry! Do something!'

'What did you have in mind?'

'The bomb! *The Bomb!*' Rex pointed desperately. 'Dis-arm it.'

'And get a move on,' Chico suggested.

'I want me mum!' wailed Harpo.

'What an ugly little sucker,' Barry observed.

'No!' Rex waved his arms about. 'Don't say *that*. Too late . . .'

Barry the bunny looked up with a puzzled expression.

'Nice one, Chico.' Rex sank on to his bum and buried his face in his hands. 'That would be our last hope gone then.'

The explosion was devastating. A mushroom cloud, all boiling flame and very bad news, rose above Presley City.

'Cor, that was loud.' Harpo shook his head. 'I wonder what it was.'

'Crawford's air-car hitting the car park, I shouldn't wonder.' Chico winked. 'Very messy. Very final.'

Rex smiled up from the floor. 'Oh good, that's pleased me no end. I shall spend my final few seconds gloating, if you have no objections.'

'You might at least push a few more buttons,' Chico suggested. 'It's now or never.'

'It's now or *ever*, actually,' said Barry the bunny. 'I programmed it in for Elvis myself. Pretty clever, we thought.'

IT'S NOW OR EVER

Rex's fingers flew over the keyboard. But the seconds were going

3

2

1

Z

I stood on the roof-top. Tall, erect and precisely detailed.

I'd played my part. Done my bit. I'd come out of it all bathed in glory. Head held high. If now was the time for me to meet my maker, so be it. I could look the big guy square in the eye and say. Mister, the name's Woodbine, Lazlo Woodbine, but you can call me Laz.

E

Sam Maggott staggered around in the big smoking crater, which had, shortly before, been the car park of the Butcher Building. His face was blackened and his clothes were all in tatters. But he was otherwise unhurt. The incidental music went WAB-WAAAH.

Sam was having the mother of all rough ones.

'Officer Cecil!' he shouted.

302

R

Officer Cecil sat in the Tomorrowman Tavern. A pint at his elbow, an unconscious barman at his feet and a typewriter on his lap. He typed:

What was otherwise a complete no-hoper, carelessly constructed, lacking in direction, run of the mill, uninspired, derivative and above all, unfunny, relying on cheap gags, gross obscenity, sexual perversion and mindless violence, was saved for me by the touching and deeply felt portrayal of Cecil. It is to be hoped that some publisher of merit will seize the opportunity and commission a writer of talent to develop this wonderfully charismatic young star . . .

0

'Uh uh uh uh uh uh uh,' went Barry the bunny.

'Yes, yes, yes!' went Laura. 'Give it to me, big fella. Oh yes, oh yes . . .'

0
0.1
0.2
0.3

The lad in the foetal position opened his eyes.

'It's stopped.

'It's stopped!

'IT'S STOPPED! We did it! Barry, we did it! We stopped the bomb. We stopped the bomb, Barry. Barry? Barry, you dirty little sod. Stop that at once.'

0.4

The towers of Presley City glowed with an inner light.

Within their mighty jukebox domes, huge records, the size of Wiltshire crop circles began to turn and great needle-bearing arms descended upon them.

The music began to play. And Elvis said, 'Let there be Rock 'n' Roll.'

And Rock 'n' Roll there was.

20

Hari BAH-REAH
Hari BAH-REAH
BAH-REAH BAH-REAH
Hari Hari

The surviving members of the cast were gathered in the Tomorrowman Tavern, swigging cheap champagne.

On the counter-top stood two tall temple candles burning brightly. Between these was a comfy velvet cushion. And lording it there upon sat Barry the Wonder Sprout.

Laura Lynch stood to the right of him wearing a very satisfied expression. Kevin, Jason, Reg, Alison and Sharon knelt with their heads bowed to the floor.

Barry was explaining things to Rex.

'And so you see, Elvis never wanted to get involved in any of this. He was never a fictional character, he was the King of Rock 'n' Roll. So when he found he'd got lumbered with appearing in a third book he had this revelation. He decided to go right back to *Genesis* and change everything. Prevent the Anti-Christ ever being born. And it almost worked. Trouble was, we knew Old Demdike had escaped at the end of *They Came And Ate Us*, so there was bound to be one Anti-Christ that had slipped through the net. So Elvis set out to destroy him by luring him to this time and blowing him up. You see, when Elvis and I got here and discovered Crawford stuck in his time-loop, it was the ideal set-up. The Anti-Christ got stuck in Crawford's game and he couldn't get any further. Elvis primed the bomb. I returned him to the twentieth century and he died his unnatural death. He never committed suicide. Or perhaps he did. We'll never know for sure.

'But it's all finished now. Crawford is dead. The Devil is defeated. The Presley hoard is gone forever. Elvis is memory. And when you return to your own continuum we can all live happily ever after.'

'Hmm.' Rex scratched his head. 'If you'll pardon me, I don't think all this ties up. Why exactly did the Anti-Christ, or Anti-Elvis, or whatever, take my form?'

'Simple, chief. To fool me. He wanted me to get him away from here before the Big Bang. How else could he escape?'

'He could have used the Volvo. It brought Dee and Kelley here from the future.'

'You mean the Volvo that said, "We thank you for travelling in the cause of Ultimate Truth"?'

'It was *you*. You powered the Volvo.'

'Of course it was me, chief. Cars can't travel through time. Who ever heard of such an absurd idea?'

'All right then. What about the statue? If this is a separate continuum, caused by Elvis changing history, how could a statue of him, carved by Michelangelo, be buried in *my* back garden?'

'Ah,' said Barry. 'I'm afraid Elvis and I put it there.'

'*You?*'

'Well, be fair, chief. We didn't have a lot of choice. If we hadn't buried the statue and I hadn't guided Dee and Kelley to it, and you hadn't jumped into the back of the car . . . you wouldn't have been in the plot at all. Apart from digging a septic tank, that is.'

Rex was speechless. When he found his voice it said, 'I've been had!'

'Come off it, chief. You saved the world, well, part of it.'

'And what about this world? What about Laura and Laz and all this lot?'

'We go on,' said Chico. 'I relay these cosmic truths to the world. Fictitious or not. We build the New Tomorrow.'

'And we go back to mum,' said Harpo. 'We do, don't we Chico?'

Chico put on a worried expression. He felt quite certain that Mojo and Debbie had been blown up in the car park. Unless, of course, they had made a very lucky escape before Crawford's car hit the MTWTV truck. 'Well . . .' said Chico.

The door flew open and in flew Mojo and Debbie.

'My baby,' cried Debbie.

Chico glanced over to Barry. 'Nice one,' he said.

'Don't mention it, Chico. We could hardly leave you without a happy ending, could we?'

'So, is that it?' Rex asked.

'Pretty much so. You want I should drop you home?'

'Very much indeed. Might I just say goodbye to Laura first? In private?'

'Sure thing, chief.'

Rex took Laura in his arms. 'I suppose it's goodbye,' he said in a soft and romantic tone.

'I suppose so.' Laura wriggled free. 'No need to get so physical.'

'Laura, please. You meant, well, how can I say this? You meant so much to me.'

'Did I?' Laura straightened her hair.

'Well, no, not really. You were great in bed, though.'

'You weren't.'

'Hmm.' Rex put on a brave face. 'So what are you going to do now?'

Laura had a glazed expression. 'BAH-REAH came unto me. He planted his sacred seed within my womb. I'm to be the mother of the New Mankind. The Bride of BAH-REAH.'

'Ah.' Rex felt that now was definitely the time for the off.

He rejoined Barry at the bar. 'Right,' said he. 'No point in hanging about.'

'Don't you want to say goodbye to Laz, chief?'

'Nah,' Rex shook his head. 'The man's a prat. Imagine him thinking he was the hero of this book.'

'Yeah, chief. Imagine that.'

'Bye lads.' Rex called out to Harpo/Chico, who was being seriously cuddled by his (or *their*, it's anyone's guess) mum.

'Goodbye Rex. Good luck.'

'Goodbye all.' Rex waved to the crowd.

Grunt grunt grunt, they went, not giving a monkey's.

I returned from the bog. All spruced up and looking pretty chipper. Spruced and chipper. That was about the strength of it. And some strength.

'Hey, guys' I hailed Harpo/Chico. 'Where's Rex?'

'Had to go.' Chico called over his mum's left shoulder.

'He sent his regards.' Harpo called over the left. 'He said to tell you thanks. He'll be forever in your debt.'

'Well, how about that. And I thought the guy was a prat.'

I knew the kid was lying of course. Just trying to give me a happy-ever-after. But that was OK. In my line of business you don't expect too much gratitude. You do the job because it's there to be done. It's a dirty game but someone has to play it. I stepped over to the bar.

'Old Bedwetter,' said I. 'Make it a double and on the rocks.'

'We're closed.' The barman gave me the kind of smirk you could dip a sheep in. 'Piss off, Woodbran.'

I pulled out the trusty Smith and We'll-meet-again and show him the end with the hole in it. 'Bring the bottle,' said I with more finality than a fan dancer in a fuse-box factory.

'And barman.'

'Yes, sir?'

'The name's Wood*bine*. Lazo Woodbine. Some call me Laz.'

Rex and Barry flew through time.

'Could I ask a small favour, Barry?'

'Ask on, chief.'

'Could we go back and say goodbye to Elvis?'

'Chief, we can't do that. He won't know who we are. He went back to his world. We don't exist for him. Never did. Never will.'

'Aw, come on, Barry. You owe me this at least. What harm can it do?'

'He won't know you, chief. It's a bad idea. Bad.'

It was the King's final performance. He'd run through his repertoire, given the crowd what they wanted to hear, forgotten his words and retired from the stage to thunderous applause. The fans didn't know that it was all finished.

But he did.

In the six-star changing suite Elvis raised a fat hand and dismissed the hoards of hangers-on, security men, hopeful nymphets and good-time Charlies. He wanted to be alone.

The quilted door closed and the suite was silent. Elvis gazed at his reflection in the long make-up mirror. His thoughts were all his own.

There came a sudden rustling behind the ten-foot rack of diamanté-studded jumpsuits. A face poked out. 'Elvis,' it said.

The fat man turned. 'Who the Hell are you? How did you get past security?'

'Elvis. It's me, Rex. I just wanted to say . . . thanks.'

'He don't know you, chief.'

'Who said that? Who else is there?'

'It's Barry.'

'I don't know no Barry. Listen buddy, if you're a fan, then OK, hi, good to know you, get lost. If you're some kind of crazy, watch out, I know karate.'

'It's me . . . Rex.' Rex waved foolishly. 'And Barry, look.' He held out the sprout.

'Shit. A grenade. I'm reaching for the house phone, buddy.'

'I told you, chief. He doesn't know us, let's get.'

'You'd better,' said Elvis.

'OK. Goodbye Elvis. And thanks again. For everything.'

'Yeah, goodbye, chief. Good luck.'

The jumpsuits twitched. The apparition faded and was gone. Elvis was once more alone.

He shook his head, wiped sweat from his ample brow and turned once more to the mirror.

A tear rose in his left eye and trickled down his bloated cheek. 'Goodbye, green buddy,' he said.

'Home,' said Rex. 'Take me back.'

'Back it is, chief.' There was a crash, a bang and a wallop, and Rex was right back where he started out. In his ghastly apartment in the north-west corner of Odeon Towers. Right back at the beginning of *Armageddon: The Musical*.

Rex sat in his homemade armchair facing the flickering TV screen. A tiny doodad, concealed in the chair's back, sang happy awakenings into his cerebral cortex. Rex awoke with a start. He took in his surroundings.

'Oh no NO NO!' cried Rex. 'This isn't a happy-ever-after. Barry, where are you? Barry, HELP!'

'Only kidding, chief. Just my little joke.'

Rex was suddenly back in his cottage garden. The sun shone, bees buzzed. Fido snoozed. Rex laid his spade aside and mopped his brow. The last finishing touches

310

to the new septic tank were last and finished. Rex tossed his spade over the hedge. 'A job well done,' he said.

Christeen called to him from the bathroom window. 'It's working,' she called. 'It flushes and everything. Come inside and take a shower and I'll say thank you properly.'

'Hmm.' Rex looked around suspiciously. If there was a trick ending coming. Now would about be the time.

The bees continued to buzz and the sun to shine. Rex scratched his head. 'Blimey,' said he. 'It really is a happy ending.'

And it was.

The Hellcab ground its way through the endless void of Time and Space.

'On to adventure.' Barbecued Bill raised his carbonized cap.

'And where exactly would that be?' asked Johnny Dee.

'The past, chief.' Barry bobbed up and down on the decomposed dashboard. 'And let's step on it. I have a pressing appointment in Presley City. I'm fathering a new order of mankind. Half man, half sprout. I did this deal with the Great Accountant.

'But first, 1959. I want to persuade Buddy Holly to take the bus instead of the plane . . .'

'Weeeeeeeeelll, that'll be the day,' sang Barbecued Bill the cabby.

'Fade out and roll the end captions, chief.'

Cast

Rex Mundi	HARRISON FORD
Christeen	MADONNA
Ed Kelley	BRUCE WILLIS
Johnny Dee	JACK NICHOLSON
News Vendor	ROGER MOORE
Lazlo Woodbine	RUTGER HAUER
Dame	KIM BASINGER
Fangio	ORSON WELLES
Tomorrowman Barman	KENNETH BRANAGH
Garth	SYLVESTER STALLONE
Laura Lynch	CHER
Bill the cabby	ROBERT DE NIRO
Cecil	KEVIN COSTNER
Sam Maggott	ROBBIE COLTRANE
Murphy	EDDIE MURPHY
Bell Hop	WOODY ALLEN
Desk Clerk	MICKEY ROURKE
Jonathan Crawford	MICHAEL J. FOX
Thaddeus Meek	SEAN CONNERY
Kevin	ARNOLD SCHWARZENEGGER
Reg/Jason	TOM CRUISE
Alison/Sharon	JULIA ROBERTS
Mojo	SEAN PENN
Debbie	WHOOPI GOLDBERG
MTWTV Station Head	MIKE McSHANE
Driver	RONDO HATTON
Harpo/Chico	BROS
Set Dresser	SIR HARRY CORDWELL
Production Buyer	MIKE PETTY

Weapons	LORD JIM CAMPBELL
Motor cars	SKODA
Continuity	JENNY PARROTT

SPECIAL VISUAL EFFECTS BY BIRO

Produced by	JOHN VINCENT OMALLY
Written and directed by	JIM POOLEY

ELVIS PRESLEY IS A FICTITIOUS CHARACTER AND NOT TO BE CONFUSED WITH ANY OTHER ELVIS PRESLEY, PAST, PRESENT OR FUTURE.

BARRY THE TIME SPROUT © APPEARS THROUGH KIND PERMISSION OF BLOKE DOWN THE PUB WORLD MARKETING INC ©.

A FLASH IN THE PAN
PRODUCTION

ARMAGEDDON: THE MUSICAL
by Robert Rankin

From the point of view of 2050, you're history.

Theological warfare. Elvis on an epic time-travel journey – the Presliad. Buddhavision – a network bigger than God (and more powerful, too). Nasty nuclear leftovers. Naughty sex habits. Dalai Dan (the 153rd reincarnation of the Lama of that ilk) and Barry, the talkative Time Sprout. Even with all this excitement, you wouldn't think a backwater planet like Earth makes much of a splash in the galactic pond.

But the soap opera called *The Earthers* is making big video bucks in the intergalactic ratings race. And alien TV execs know exactly what the old earth drama needs to make the off-world audience sit up and stare: a spectacular Armageddon-type finale. With a cast of millions – including you! Don't touch that dial. It's gonna be a helluva show!

'To the top-selling ranks of humorists such as Douglas Adams and Terry Pratchett, let us welcome Mr Rankin'
Tom Hutchinson, *The Times*

'He crams enough gags into *Armageddon: The Musical* to last anyone else for a trilogy. And nothing's sacred. So buy this quick, before he ends up sleeping in Salman Rushdie's spare bedroom'
Terry Pratchett

0 552 13681 6

THE CAME AND ATE US
ARMAGEDDON II: THE B-MOVIE
by Robert Rankin

'Mr Rankin levitates even more amazingly than in his first novel, and is a flotation not to be missed . . . *Hellzapoppin* with hallucinatory knobs on and a talent to bemuse which is hugely welcome in this grey-suited time'
The Times

QUIVER AT! horrible demonic stuff oozing out of computer screens!

SHOCK HORROR! Elvis Presley pulling his face off!

GASP AT! a talking brussels sprout!

SEE! Cannibal on the rampage!

HEAR! Fido the Dog do Frankie Howerd impressions!

SEE! Rex Mundi, Rambo Bloodaxe, Deathblade Eric, Hugo Rune and a cast of millions caught up in Events Beyond Their Control!

THRILL TO! all the loose ends from ARMAGEDDON: THE MUSICAL magically tied up!

WATCH! A comic genius doing the business!

SEE?

0 552 13832 0

THE ANTIPOPE
by Robert Rankin

'Wonderful . . . a ready mix of Flann O'Brien, Douglas
Adams, Tom Sharpe, and Ken Campbell, but with an
inbuilt irreverence and indelicacy that is unique – and
makes it the long-awaited, heavy smoker's answer to *The
Lord of the Rings*'
Time Out

*'Outside the sun shines. Buses rumble towards Ealing Broad-
way and I'm expected to do battle with the powers of darkness.
It all seems a little unfair . . .'*

You could say it all started with the red-eyed tramp with
the slimy fingers who put the wind up Neville the
part-time barman something rotten. Or when Archroy's
wife swapped his trusty Morris Minor for five magic
beans while he was out at the rubber factory.

On the other hand, you could say it all started a lot earlier.
Like 450 years ago, when Borgias walked the earth.

Pooley and Omally, stars of the Brentford Labour Exchange and the Flying Swan, want nothing to do with it,
especially if there's a Yankee and a pint of Large in the
offing. Pope Alexander VI, last of the Borgias, has other
ideas . . .

'Wonderfully entertaining . . . Reads like a Flann O'Brien
rewrite of *Close Encounters*'
City Limits

The first book in the now legendary *Brentford Trilogy*

0 552 13841 X

THE BRENTFORD TRIANGLE
by Robert Rankin

'A born writer . . . Robert Rankin is to Brentford what William Faulkner was to Yoknapatawpha County'
Time Out

'*Omally groaned. "It is the end of mankind as we know it. I should never have got up so early today" and all over Brentford electrical appliances were beginning to fail . . .*'

Could it be that Pooley and Omally, whilst engaged on a round of allotment golf, mistook laser-operated gravitational landing beams for the malignant work of Brentford Council?

Does the Captain Laser Alien Attack machine in the bar of the Swan possess more sinister force than its magnetic appeal for youths with green hair?

Is Brentford the first base in an alien onslaught on planet Earth?

The second novel in the now legendary *Brentford Trilogy*

0 552 13842 8

EAST OF EALING
by Robert Rankin

'Robert Rankin is a deep-down humorist, one of the rare guys who can always make me laugh'
Terry Pratchett

'Ahead, where once had been only bombsite land, the Lateinos & Romiith building rose above Brentford. Within its cruel and jagged shadow, magnolias wilted in their window boxes and synthetic Gold Top became doorstep cheese . . .'

Something is happening east of Ealing. Lateinos & Romiith, an important organization, has changed all the rules. A personal account enumeration scheme using laser-readable implantations on the right hand of every living punter instead of old-fashioned money. A scheme to end civilization as we know it, even to change the drinking habits of regulars in the Swan . . .

Can Armageddon, Apocalypse and other symptoms of progress be stopped by the humble likes of Pooley and Omally, even with the help of the Professor and a time-warped incarnation of Sherlock Holmes of Baker Street . . . ?

The third novel in the now legendary *Brentford Trilogy*

0 552 13843 6

A SELECTION OF HUMOROUS TITLES
AVAILABLE FROM CORGI BOOKS

☐	99527 4	**A YEAR NEAR PROXIMA CENTAURI**	*Michael Martin*	£4.99
☐	13760 X	**THAT RUBENS GUY**	*John McGill*	£3.99
☐	13893 2	**THE COLOUR OF MAGIC**	*Terry Pratchett*	£3.99
☐	12848 1	**THE LIGHT FANTASTIC**	*Terry Pratchett*	£3.99
☐	13105 9	**EQUAL RITES**	*Terry Pratchett*	£3.99
☐	13106 7	**MORT**	*Terry Pratchett*	£4.99
☐	13107 5	**SOURCERY**	*Terry Pratchett*	£3.99
☐	13460 0	**WYRD SISTERS**	*Terry Pratchett*	£3.99
☐	13461 9	**PYRAMIDS**	*Terry Pratchett*	£3.99
☐	13462 7	**GUARDS! GUARDS!**	*Terry Pratchett*	£4.99
☐	13463 5	**MOVING PICTURES**	*Terry Pratchett*	£3.99
☐	13464 3	**REAPER MAN**	*Terry Pratchett*	£3.99
☐	13465 1	**WITCHES ABROAD**	*Terry Pratchett*	£3.99
☐	13325 6	**STRATA**	*Terry Pratchett*	£3.99
☐	13326 4	**THE DARK SIDE OF THE SUN**	*Terry Pratchett*	£3.99
☐	13703 0	**GOOD OMENS**	*Terry Pratchett & Neil Gaiman*	£4.99
☐	13945 9	**THE COLOUR OF MAGIC – GRAPHIC NOVEL**	*Terry Pratchett*	£6.99
☐	13681 6	**ARMAGEDDON: THE MUSICAL**	*Robert Rankin*	£3.99
☐	13832 0	**ARMAGEDDON II: THE B MOVIE**	*Robert Rankin*	£3.99
☐	13841 X	**THE ANTIPOPE**	*Robert Rankin*	£3.99
☐	13842 8	**THE BRENTFORD TRIANGLE**	*Robert Rankin*	£3.99
☐	13843 6	**EAST OF EALING**	*Robert Rankin*	£3.99

NAME (Block Letters)..

ADDRESS...

....